HIDDEN PASSIONS

JANE ARCHER

ZEBRA BOOKS
KENSINGTON PUBLISHING CORP.

ZEBRA BOOKS

are published by

Kensington Publishing Corp.
475 Park Avenue South
New York, NY 10016

First printing: September 1987

Printed in the United States of America

*For Speedy
and the Critter Corps*

Part One
Hot Prairie Nights

Chapter One

"Pardon me, ma'am, but I'd like to buy you for the night."

Raven Cunningham whirled around and recognized the tall man looming over her. For some reason he'd been turning up at the same saloons and gambling houses she'd been frequenting all evening. Probably just coincidence. Most likely she would never have noticed him if not for his height.

She didn't think she'd ever seen a taller man. Tall and lean and maybe mean. He had the kind of quiet menace she'd come to expect of men in the West and she didn't like it, or him. He had no right to be so intimidating. And she was much too near a dark alley for comfort.

He stepped closer. He had to be several inches over six feet, and it made her five-foot-two-inch height seem like she was standing in a hole. She disliked him even more with each passing moment.

"Name your price, ma'am. I'll pay it."

For some reason his low, smooth, accented voice caused a vibration to start at the base of her spine and end in chills at her nape. This man was dangerous, and she had to get rid of him without causing a scene. But how without drawing attention to herself? "I'm afraid I'm not interested."

"I'm just off the trail from Texas and I've got money to burn. I want a soft, sweet-smelling woman."

"I'm sure there are a number of women who would be happy to oblige you, but I have other plans this evening." Maybe now he would go away.

"You're the filly I want to brand tonight."

She couldn't stop the blush that quickly spread over her face. A cowboy! Just her luck. He wouldn't have any information she could use either, not if he were just in from Texas. That explained his accent and his uncouth words.

While she waited for her face to cool, she glanced around. There was absolutely no need to get concerned about his forcing himself on her. They were standing in the middle of a street in Topeka, Kansas, on a Saturday night, and there were plenty of people around.

In 1883, Topeka was always busy, and its dance halls, saloons, brothels, and silver exchanges spilled light and noise into the streets. Lots of people were inside the establishments, and all Raven had to do was get inside one of them to feel relatively safe. Besides, if necessary, she could take care of herself, but she didn't want anyone to know that. She was playing the role of a lady of the evening and she had to be convincing.

"I'll even take you to a fancy hotel," the cowboy added, running a strong, long-fingered hand down her bare arm.

She shivered, suddenly fascinated by the size of his hand, the long, tapered fingers and gentle touch. Then she shook her head, quickly pushing his hand away. "Sorry, but I'm not available. I'm looking for someone."

"Make that me and we'll both be happy."

"No," she said firmly. She had a snub-nosed Colt .45 in her reticule, but his reach had to be very long and she wasn't at all sure he would be intimidated by the pistol. Also, her father had always warned her not to draw a weapon unless she planned to use it. She didn't even want to consider shooting this man.

"I told you I'd pay your price. I've been bird-dogging you all evening. You're mighty choosy, aren't you?"

"I beg your pardon?"

"Think you're too good for cowboys?"

"For your information, Mr. — "

"Slate. Slate Slayton."

"Mr. *Slayton,* my service, at least that type of service, is not for sale."

Suddenly hard fingers bit into her arm and pulled her away from the alley and under a streetlamp. The soft light illuminated her small, slim form in the red satin gown which showed to perfection her high full breasts, tiny waist, long graceful neck, and the smooth skin that was exposed by the décolletage of her expensive gown.

Her soft, ash-blond hair was arranged high on her head, with a few curls allowed to dangle and brush her bare shoulders. Her eyes were black, like a raven's wing, and at the moment were narrowed. Her nose was straight with a thin bridge, her cheekbones high, her eyebrows delicately arched, her eyelashes long, but her lips caught the man's attention most for they were full and a deep crimson.

"I guess you can afford to be choosy. Nobody'd pay your price?"

"I told you. Tonight I'm busy. I don't have a price."

11

"Which means you're damned expensive. Okay. I've got an itch only you can scratch. Name it."

"You're right," she finally said in exasperation, realizing he wasn't going to give up easily. "My services do not come cheap. I'm sure yours don't either."

"Are you interested in buying me for the night? I won't complain, and I'm cheap."

She stiffened, determinedly ignoring the humor in his voice, and said, "I referred to the fact that whatever job you do, I'm sure you're paid well."

"You're right. I'm a damn good Texas cowboy, and I just got paid. Now, if you're not buying, I am. What do you say?"

Surprising herself, Raven hesitated. The man's body looked whipcord strong, the long muscular legs encased in denim, the broad shoulders and muscular chest covered by a dark blue shirt. A wide leather belt, darkened with use, rode low on his hips, a heavy silver buckle emphasizing his hard flat stomach. She quickly averted her eyes from the bulge below.

"Like what you see?" he asked in an amused voice.

A light blush warmed her face, but she determinedly returned his stare, noticing that his black hair was thick, and cut long. Intense eyes, either blue or gray or both, watched her hungrily. He was clean-shaven and tanned, his nose prominent in a face of all planes and angles, but his lips were full and sensual. Her perusal hesitated there and she wondered how it would feel to have the heat of his mouth against hers. Shocked at her thoughts, she looked away, but not before he'd seen the change in her dark eyes.

He put a strong hand under her chin, lifting her

face so she would look into his eyes again, but now her eyes were guarded. He nodded thoughtfully and dropped his hand. "I'll pay your price. Any price."

"Mr. Slayton, I am *not* for sale."

"Why are you on the street then?"

"I . . . I'm looking for someone."

"Maybe I can help."

"No, I don't think so. I must be going."

"The night's still young. After you've finished your business, why don't you meet me at the Blue Bird Saloon? I'll still be ready to pay your price."

"I told you, I—"

"Look, I don't know why you're pretending you're something you're not. Any man can tell what you are with one look. You must be making a fortune, and I'm willing to add my money to your cache. Any time, any place while I'm in Topeka."

Raven gave up. She'd be better off playing along with him so he'd give up. No other man had been this persistent and it was disconcerting. "Look, cowboy, I'll—"

"Slate. You ought to use the first name of a man you're going to get to know real well."

"Slate, I have some unfinished business, but if you insist I'll try to stop by the Blue Bird later." Of course, she had no intention of meeting him anywhere.

"Don't just try. Be there. By the way, what's your name?"

"Raven."

"Nice. Real nice." He leaned close, tilted her chin up, and slowly lowered his face until his lips were close to hers, his breath warm on her face. "Just to make sure you meet me later, Raven," he said, then set his firm lips to hers.

Raven was shocked at the intense heat that enveloped her, the sudden craving that ran through her, and knew he felt the same, for his body tensed. He raised his head, his eyes filled with blue fire. He searched her face a long moment, then lightly touched her lips again.

"The Blue Bird," he said before turning and quickly striding away.

Raven watched his retreating form, then curiously touched a fingertip to her lips. Whatever had come over her? He was just a cowboy who had wanted what other men who had approached her wanted. And yet? She shook her head, disgusted with herself. She had better things to think about than an overly tall . . . no, as they would say in the West, a "too tall" Texas cowboy.

Forcing her mind back to business, she hurried into the next silver exchange. The lavishly decorated combination dance hall, gambling house, and saloon was in full swing. A huge mirror glimmered behind the long bar, glass chandeliers hung from the high ceiling, and red-flocked paper covered the walls. Round wooden tables with green cloths occupied most of the floor space, but there was a small dance area in back. A tinny piano vied with the sounds of gambling, clinking glass, and laughter.

Raven looked around eagerly. Perhaps she'd finally get the information she needed here. Steeling herself once more for the leers, pinches, and comments she got whenever she entered a silver exchange, she walked up to the mahogany bar and ordered a whiskey.

Raising an eyebrow, the bartender served her, obviously noting that she wasn't a regular.

Raven leaned casually against the bar, grasping the small glass of cheap whiskey, and said, "I'm looking for someone."

The bartender nodded.

"A one-handed man. In place of his left hand he has a hook."

"Hard to miss a man like that."

"Have you seen him?"

"Might have."

"When?"

"Can't rightly remember."

Raven placed her reticule on the smooth surface of the bar, then slid a silver coin toward the bartender.

He took it, bit it, then smiled. "There was a one-handed man in here about two weeks back. He met with several other men, they had a few drinks, then left together."

"That's all?"

"It don't pay to be nosy around here."

"What did the men look like? Where did they go?"

"You ask a lot of questions, lady. That ain't healthy."

"Can you describe them?"

"Just regular cowboy types. Nothing special except the guy with the hook."

"Did you hear them say where they were going?"

"Nope. None of my business."

"I see." She wasn't going to get any more out of him. That was obvious. "Thanks."

Maintaining her role, she took a sip of whiskey and felt it burn down her throat. She choked back the cough that threatened to follow, felt her eyes sting, and held her breath. When the onslaught of the whiskey had passed, she silently damned the favorite drink of the West, nodded casually to the bartender, and walked out, ignoring the men who caught at her, wanting her to stay and drink with

15

them.

Once outside, she hurried down the street. Should she try to confirm the bartender's information by finding someone else who had seen the one-handed man? Would that be possible? It certainly hadn't been up to now. This was the fifth consecutive night that she had gone from one silver exchange to another, plus as many saloons, dance halls, and gambling houses as she could fit into an evening. Tonight was her first clue, if the bartender had been telling the truth.

But she suddenly felt overwhelmingly tired. She hadn't had much sleep in a long time. First there had been the long train ride from Chicago, then the nights searching Topeka. And, of course, she hadn't been sleeping well for months. And she wouldn't until she got justice for her father and fiancé.

She walked on, hearing the laughter and music coming from the silver exchanges. She hadn't laughed in several months. There was no reason to laugh anymore. There wasn't much reason for anything now, except seeing that justice was done.

Giving in to her fatigue, she headed toward her hotel room. She'd gotten her information and now she deserved an early night. When she found the one-handed man, she had to be prepared, and that meant getting enough rest so that her reflexes were good.

The snub-nosed .45 in her reticule bumped against her thigh. She gently cradled the revolver to her breast. It was all she had of her father now, of her fiancé, and she would use the pistol to exact their justice.

She entered the hotel and climbed the steps to her room, oblivious to the appreciative and questioning

16

stares of the men who followed her with their eyes. Stepping inside her door she surveyed the small, neat, comfortable but not luxurious, room. She didn't have the money for an expensive place, and anyway, under the circumstances it was better for her anonymity if she kept a low profile by staying in this nondescript hotel.

She sat down on the soft feather mattress of her narrow bed and slid the .45 from her reticule. In the soft light of the lamp, the initials engraved on the pearl handle gleamed as she stroked the letters. *R.C.* Robert Cunningham. Her father had never been without the revolver while he lived, and after his death, it had been returned to her. Now she was never without it.

Her father had made sure she could take care of herself, not only by training her to handle a variety of weapons but in self-defense methods as well. It was a good thing he had because now she had to carry on alone.

The Cunningham National Detective Agency was her legacy after her father and fiancé were killed on an important case in Kansas. When the law made no arrests and turned up few clues, she knew it was up to her to find the criminal who had killed the two men she loved.

So Raven Cunningham had become R. Cunningham, and had boarded a train for Kansas, leaving Chicago far behind. Now she was on her own, in a land where the rules were made by outlaws just as frequently as by the law. She had to live by the code of the West, not by what she had come to expect in Chicago.

She straightened her right arm, sighted down the short barrel of the .45, then lowered her hand and thought about the case.

The Atchison, Topeka and Santa Fe was an important train line from eastern Kansas to El Paso, Texas, where it joined the Southern Pacific. Both lines had been plagued with robberies for months before they contacted the Cunningham Agency. The train companies wanted the robberies stopped without publicity, without alarming their passengers and freight customers.

It was the biggest account the Cunningham Agency had ever acquired, and her father, Sam Fairfield, and she had only briefly questioned why two railroad lines which could afford any detective agency, even the famous Pinkerton's, would hire their small one. They concluded it was because the railroads wanted as little publicity as possible and very personal service. The train lines got both because the Cunningham Agency worked primarily in the Chicago area and had only three employees, her father, herself, and Sam.

Thinking about Sam brought a brief smile to her lips.

Not long after he had come to work at the agency, she and Sam had discovered how much they shared. Theirs was a sweet, tender love, and when they became engaged Raven felt completely fulfilled because Sam understood her desire to continue working at the agency.

Raven had practically grown up in the Cunningham Agency office. Her mother had been a Kiowa maiden her father had met on one of his early jobs in the West, but when she died, her father had moved back with Raven to Chicago.

Not wanting to be parted from the one link to his wife, her father had brought Raven frequently to his office and she had naturally learned the detective business, gradually helping him more and more until in her late teens she began running the office. But she had never done any field work until Sam's death and her father's leaving to track down his killer.

She thought back to how much Sam hated leaving her. Sam had known how much the railroad job meant to their agency. Certain Sam could handle himself in any situation, they had been shocked when the telegram had arrived stating that he had been killed in a small dusty town in Kansas. The only information the local sheriff could give them was that a one-handed man, the left hand replaced with a hook, had been seen leaving the scene of the crime, but no arrests had been made.

Raven had been heartbroken, but her father had been furious. He had left immediately to find the murderer and to complete the railroad job. Raven had been afraid for him, but could not dissuade him from going.

Raven remembered how after her father left for Kansas, she continued to work in the office. Soon she began accepting new jobs because they needed the money and she wanted something to take her mind off her father and fiancé. She let the clients believe that R. Cunningham was her brother who did all the field work while she handled the office. Her subterfuge worked, and soon she was effectively handling all aspects of the cases.

Anxious to share her newly discovered success with her father when he returned, she took on more cases. She received only occasional letters and telegrams from him, indicating that he suspected the two special representatives of the railroad lines were involved in the robberies, but it was obvious he was having problems proving his suspicions, running into one dead end after another. She became concerned, not wanting to lose him, too. She sent a telegram asking him to come home.

But her telegram had barely been sent when one arrived for her, brief and to the point. Robert Cunningham had been shot in Topeka, Kansas. There were no clues and no arrests. When she inquired if a one-handed man, the left hand replaced with a hook, might have been involved, a report was sent that such a man had been seen in town that day but could not be connected with the murder.

That had been enough connection to both murders for her, and her only clue. She had decided to go after the one-handed man. To combat the pain of her loss, Raven had thrown herself into making plans. She could not let the deaths of her father and fiancé go unavenged. She had to apprehend their killer, bring him to justice, and complete the railroad investigation to keep the Cunningham National Detective Agency alive, for it was all she had left. Fury had replaced mourning, and she had set out for Topeka, Kansas.

But she had trusted no one. Two men had died trying to solve the case, and she was not going to be the third person killed. Inexperienced, she would have to use anything she could to succeed and come out alive.

She had already sent telegrams to T.R. Simpson, special representative for the Atchison, Topeka and Santa Fe, and his counterpart, Jeremy Luis Centrano, special representative for the Southern Pacific, the two men who had hired the Cunningham Detective Agency. She had told them both that the Cunningham Agency was still on the job and would be sending R. Cunningham to continue the work.

She had known the two railroad men would assume R. Cunningham was Robert Cunningham's son and that was the way she wanted it. Perhaps a woman could succeed where two men had failed because no one would be expecting a young lady on the case. Even so she could not afford to trust anyone, especially not Simpson or Centrano. Both men had ample information which they could have given to the robbers, and she would treat them as suspiciously as she did everyone else.

At least tonight she had gotten her first clue. The one-handed man had accomplices, which did not surprise her. She had also confirmed that he had been seen in Topeka recently. She felt sure he was connected with the railroad robbers, and that was why he had killed both her father and fiancé.

If she could find the one-handed man, she would probably also find the person behind the outlaws. Someone, or several people, was masterminding the robberies from Kansas to Texas, and that mastermind must have several outlaw gangs working for him. It was the only way to have successfully robbed so many trains in so many areas and gotten away with so much loot. At least, that was what her father had decided, and she agreed with him.

Now it was up to her to stop the mastermind and make her father and fiancé proud, plus bringing their killer to justice. She clutched her father's pistol and tears glistened in her eyes. He and Sam had been all the family she had, and now she was alone, so very alone. But she would not allow herself to be weak, to cry again, or feel sorry for herself. She had a job to do, and she would do it.

She placed the .45 under her pillow, then began to undress. It was late and she needed her sleep. As she slipped the red satin gown down her body, she suddenly remembered a cowboy named Slate Slay-

Chapter Two

A late breakfast or an early lunch was Raven's
primary concern when she stepped from her hotel
the next morning. She felt more energetic and confident than she had in months, and knew it was due
to finding her first clue the night before. Only now
did she realize how tense and worried she'd been
about coming West all alone and tying to solve the
case that had killed both her father and fiancé.

But finding the clue made her feel like she could
win, if her luck held and she was very, very careful.
Of course, one piece of information didn't make the
danger any less or make her any more experienced,
but it did mean that with her training and persist-
ence she could actually make progress.

As she walked briskly down the boardwalk, she
began to appreciate the fact that spring had arrived,
bringing warmth and greenness to the land. Topeka
was humming with activity. Freight wagons lum-
bered noisily down the street, horses were tied in
front of businesses, idly flipping their tails at flies,
and men and women hurried past her as they did
their errands.

As she passed a dry goods store, she abruptly
stopped, causing the tide of people to flow around
her. If the one-handed man had been in town, he
and his friends would have needed supplies when
they left, especially if they were hiding out or had

an outlaw camp somewhere in the area. Perhaps a merchant would remember the man with a hook, or even the members of the gang.

Excitedly she entered the store. The clerk, a woman with gray hair neatly pulled back in a chignon, glanced up over the top of metal-rimmed glasses, smiled, and beckoned Raven closer. "What can I do for you, dear?"

Raven looked around, then focused on the long counter where several tall glass jars of candy sat tantalizingly on top. "I'd like two peppermint sticks, please."

The clerk smiled pleasantly, extracted the peppermint, and expertly twisted paper around one end.

"During the last few months, have you had a customer, perhaps a cowboy, who had a hook in place of a left hand?"

The clerk hesitated, looked more closely at Raven, then shook her head. "No, can't say that I have, but I'm surprised a nice young lady like you would be looking for somebody of that description."

"He is . . . someone who knew my father. I thought I might find him in town."

"In that case I understand, but I must warn you that a young lady has to be very careful in Topeka. Her reputation can be easily ruined. I wouldn't say that to just anyone, but I have a daughter and—"

"Thank you. I'll remember," Raven replied, taking the candy and hurriedly leaving the store.

She couldn't be concerned about her reputation, not now, not after all that had happened. Anyway, she'd never really been a proper lady and had not been considered proper marriage material because she had grown up in her father's office, and she was much too independent and outspoken at twenty-five. Sam hadn't minded, of course. He had liked her just the way she was. A man like Slate Slayton wouldn't mind, either, but that was because he didn't think she was a lady.

Raven sighed and began to suck on one of the long red and white sticks of candy as she continued down the boardwalk. She sometimes wondered what her life would have been like if she had grown up a proper young lady in Chicago.

She knew she was supposed to be more refined, more delicate, but there had just never been a place in her life for that. And if she were a proper lady, would she now be in Topeka, alone, working as an undercover private investigator to catch a killer and the mastermind of train robberies? No. And if she had to make a choice between being a proper young lady or a detective, then she would choose the latter. Justice had to be done.

Raven continued down the street, her stomach now complaining for food. She crunched down on the peppermint stick, and the minty flavor exploded in her mouth. She smiled. For some reason, it felt good to be alive again and she suddenly felt sure she could handle the case.

Several blocks later she started to cross the street, then stopped in surprise. She thought she had seen Slate Slayton's tall form entering the same silver exchange where she had obtained her information the night before. Of course, there was nothing unusual in that except it wasn't noon yet.

She had learned in her first few days in Topeka that the cowboys who came in off the range spent their money all night and slept all day. The saloons did a slow business during the day, especially in the morning. She started to walk on, then hesitated when he came back out. He obviously hadn't gone into the saloon to drink. So why had he gone in there? Then she laughed at herself, realizing she had a tendency to analyze everything. What Slate Slayton did was his own business. She had more important matters to consider.

She continued down the boardwalk, then started the hazardous trip across the street. Dust billowed up around her. She had to dodge several wagons, carriages, and horses. In the confusion, she dropped her candy in the dirt. She stopped and looked down at it, wondering if it was worth trying to save. Suddenly she was picked up by strong arms, held tightly to a hard chest, and carried cross the street.

Shocked, she glanced into a pair of blue-gray eyes. Slate Slayton. She began struggling to get free, vividly aware of the warmth and strength of his body as he held her, and of the answering warmth that had begun to spread through her. When her efforts made no difference, she stopped and glared at him.

"Put me down."

"You almost got yourself killed. What were you doing standing still in the middle of the street, and what are you doing up and around this early?"

"I'm hungry, and I dropped my peppermint sticks in the street."

He smiled. "I'll buy you some more. They're certainly not worth getting killed over." Then the tone of his voice changed. "Work hard last night?"

"Yes."

"Why didn't you come to me? I waited a long time."

"I had an early night. Put me down." She pushed at his shoulder and felt the hard muscles tense beneath the soft cotton shirt. "Slate, take your hands off me. *Now.*"

"Glad you remembered my name. Come on, I'll

get you some food, then we can talk about what else I can do for you."

Slate gently set her down, took her hand, and started to walk away. She pulled back, determined to stop him from making decisions for her. He stopped, and glanced at her mutinous face.

"I'm hungry, too, Raven. It won't hurt you to eat with me, and I'll pay. I'll even take you to a fancy place. Now, a woman like you would never turn down an offer like that, would she?"

Probably not, Raven thought. "All right," she agreed, determined to stay in character for the sake of her investigation.

She pulled her hand free, and noticed again how large his hands were, with long strong fingers. She would have expected more roughness, more calluses on a cowboy's hand, but what did she know about cowboys?

Pushing thoughts of his hands from her mind, she joined him. As they walked, she realized he was shortening his long stride so she could easily keep up with him. She didn't know whether to blame his long legs for making her feel short, or to appreciate his thoughtfulness.

Slate took her to one of the better hotels in town, explaining that he had a room there, then got them a table in the small cozy restaurant on the main floor. Not long after he ordered, crispy fried chicken with mashed potatoes, gravy, and corn were placed on their table. Slate ordered a whiskey and Raven gratefully got tea.

They ate in companionable silence until they had taken the edge off their hunger, then Slate leaned back in his chair and regarded her thoughtfully.

"I'd never have recognized you if it hadn't been for the way you affect me, even across a street."

Raven blushed a soft rosy hue, then tried to cover her reaction by taking a quick sip of tea.

But Slate had noticed and was looking at her even more intently. "I've never seen a woman of the night, not even a real fancy one, wear a pale gray cotton dress all buttoned up the front with little black buttons. You're completely covered up, Raven, from the tips of your little black boots to your pretty chin. And you blush, too. I wonder why."

"How I dress, or . . . blush is none of your concern."

"Everything about you is my business, at least until I leave Topeka."

"You're mistaken," Raven said firmly, losing her appetite. "Anyway, it's easier to get waited on in stores if I'm more conservatively dressed."

"I suppose so. Ladies of the evening aren't real popular in all parts of town, are they?"

"I wouldn't know. I mean, you're probably right. Anyway, I can change my line of work any time I want."

"What else would pay a beautiful woman like you as much? Or maybe you're just planning to make enough, then get out. That's common, isn't it? Or find some sucker to marry you."

"Do you think it would take a 'sucker' to marry me, Mr. Slayton?"

"No," he said slowly, taking a long hard look at her. "You could probably get about any man to marry you if he didn't mind a coldhearted woman who measured everything in gold."

Insulted, even if it was only a role she was playing, Raven said coldly, "Is that what you think of me?"

"That's what I think of women in your profession."

"Then you can, of course, understand why I turned down your offer last night."

"No, I can't. I told you then I was willing to pay top dollar. I still am. Right now. Let's spend the afternoon upstairs in my bed. I may not be able to warm your cold heart, but I can guarantee I'll warm your body."

Raven took a deep breath, willing the blush not to come, but she couldn't stop the rosy tint that slowly spread over her face. No one in her life had ever spoken to her like this, and she couldn't just get up and leave. She had to play the scene through to preserve her cover. But, hereafter, she would do her best to avoid Slate Slayton.

"That little blush is nice. It would almost make a man think you were innocent."

"Thank you. Despite what you may think, Mr. Slayton, I *am* innocent, and I'm turning down your offer. Again."

"A man might almost think you were a lady, too. You're good, no doubt about it. Come upstairs with me, Raven. I don't care about your past. I want you like I've never wanted a woman before. I can make it good for you." His eyes had turned a deep blue and he pressed a knee against hers.

Raven jerked her leg away and stood up, but not before a flame had seared up her thigh, shocking her. What was this man doing to her? He insulted her and still her body responded to him. She had to stay away from him. "Good-bye, Mr. Slayton."

She turned and started away, but Slate grabbed her arm and forced her into the shadowed alcove under the stairs.

"I'm tired of hearing you say no, Raven," he hissed, then pulled her into the circle of his arms

29

and pressed his lips to hers.

She struggled, but even as she tried to get away her body began to melt against him, craving the kiss he was giving her, craving the feel of his body against her, craving his ruthless determination to make her succumb.

"Open your mouth to me, Raven," he said huskily, stroking a hot hand down her back to her bustle. "Damn! I want to get you upstairs and out of these clothes." He kissed her again, intensely, demandingly, his hands now cradling her face, his body promising her untold delights if she would give in to his desires.

Suddenly Raven was reveling in the feel of his long, sensitive hands on her face, the way his body curled down to fit her to him. She responded to his demand and opened her lips. He quickly pushed inside, foraging deep with his hot tongue, exploring, demanding, exciting.

His hands slid to her shoulders, then down her arms to her sides where they slowly, expertly slipped up under her breasts. Startled, she tried to pull away, but he held her, bound her to him with his hands and his kisses. She moaned, feeling her body ignite, craving more, much more.

Then the sound of a group of people entering the restaurant broke their solitude, and Raven jerked back, suddenly aware of where she was, whom she was with. "No! How dare you touch me like that?"

Slate groaned, threw a murderous look at the intruders, then said quietly, "It's not like it was the first time for you, Raven. No woman kisses like that with her first man. You want me, and I'm willing to meet your price. What else is there to it? Let's go upstairs. Now."

"No!" she groaned, pushed away from him, and

ran. She bumped into a group of men entering the hotel, apologized, then darted around them. At the door, she glanced back. Slate was coming after her, but he was detained by the men. She had to get away while she could. She wasn't sure she could trust herself with him anymore. For some reason he affected her much too strongly and she couldn't allow that.

She hurried outside, turned a corner, crossed the street, turned another corner, then practically ran into a dry goods store, panting. She hesitated in the shadow of the doorway for a long moment, but didn't see Slate. Sighing in relief, she turned to look around.

She obviously wasn't in the best part of town. The store was dusty, dark, and the merchandise was strewn about in disorder, but it was open for business.

"Can I help you, miss?" a small wiry man asked, then spat tobacco at a spitoon nearby. The floor was stained around the spitoon where he obviously missed as often as he hit. "Need some pretty material? I've got some nice cotton prints here somewhere. Or how about some candy?"

"I . . . I need bullets," she said distractedly, then realized she'd ordered them out of a need to feel protected from Slate.

"Bullets?"

"Yes."

"Got a little derringer to protect you?"

"A .45."

"You carry a .45? Mighty big gun for a little lady."

"The bullets, please."

"Sure. Sure. Right back here."

As the clerk looked for the bullets, Raven reminded herself that she was a private investigator in Topeka on business. There was no reason to let a man like Slate Slayton bother her. She could take care of herself. Slate was simply a too tall Texas cowboy looking for a good time.

Recovering her confidence, she asked, "By the way, a friend of mine recommended your place. He has a hook in place of a left hand." Raven glibly let her cover story roll off her tongue as if she'd been doing it all her life.

"Comanche Jack's a friend of yours?" the clerk asked, raising his head above the counter to examine her more closely.

"Well, you might say we have mutual friends. When's the last time you saw Jack?"

The clerk eyed her suspiciously, then set the package of bullets down on top of the counter. "Don't rightly remember. Few weeks back."

"His friends with him?"

"You ask a lot of questions, lady."

"I've got a little job I need done, and I'm hoping Jack and his friends can help me," she said, planting her next lie.

"So that's it, then. Now that I know your line of work, I believe you *can* handle a .45. A pretty little thing like you must do well."

She smiled, nodded conspiratorially, then continued. "Wouldn't know where I could find Comanche Jack, would you?"

"No, ma'am. He keeps news about him scarcer than hens' teeth."

"Smart man."

"One of the best in the business. I hear he lived with the Comanche. That's where he got his cunning. You know Comanches could steal everything in my store right out from under my nose. Damn

32

clever redskins."

"But didn't they roam farther south?"

"Texas, but they went anywhere they wanted before the bluecoats killed most of them off. The ones left are mostly in Indian Territory now."

"What about the Kiowa? Are they in Indian Territory, too?"

"Sure. Get along real well with the Comanche, I hear. Good thing, too. Comanche'll tear the heart out of anything that moves, if they want. All the tribes know it."

"I see, and Comanche Jack lived with them."

"If what I hear is true, he lived with some Comanche renegades down in Texas. Mean hombre. You want a job done right, hire him."

"Thanks. You sure you don't know how to reach him?"

"Not me. But if I can I'll pass a message on to him and tell him a pretty lady named . . ."

"Raven."

"Raven is looking for him."

"Thanks"

"Oh, you might try the Silver Slipper. Margarita's entertaining there and from what I hear he liked her shows."

"Thanks." Raven paid him for the bullets, then left.

She could hardly believe her good luck. She had just stumbled into a store where someone knew about the one-handed man. She was a little amazed she was doing such a good job of undercover work. People actually believed her when she was pretending to be someone who fit into their world. They even believed her story about having a job for Comanche Jack and opened up to her and gave her valuable information. Her father and Sam would have been proud of her. Imagine, already finding out the name of the one-handed man. Comanche Jack. It would be easier to track him down now. Much easier.

Raven started down the street, then remembered the package of bullets in her hand. She glanced around, hoping no one had noticed, for it would ruin her cover, then hastily stuffed the bullets into her reticule.

It had been a good day so far, even if Slate Slayton had been a problem. But she was learning that when people believed the role she was playing, the consequences could go a lot farther than just the information she needed. She'd also have to be careful not to get so involved in her undercover role again. It obviously could make her actually want to act out the part. That had to be the explanation for her strong reaction to Slate's kisses. She had simply identified with her role too strongly. She'd be more careful about that in the future, too.

Suddenly she realized she was in a part of town she didn't recognize. The buildings were shabby. Tough-looking men sat in chairs leaned back against storefronts. They smoked and watched her with eyes showing a growing hunger for her.

She hurried, but came to even more dilapidated buildings and heard the clink of glasses and the rattle of dice. The saloons and gambling halls here were very active in the afternoon, and Raven didn't want to be anywhere near them. She felt vulnerable, even with the pistol in her reticule.

A train whistle pierced the air, and Raven looked in the direction of the sound. The whistle blew again. Good. She would follow the sound of the whistle to the train station. Once there, she would be able to regain her bearings and go back to her hotel. She moved quickly down the street, ignoring the calls and whistles that followed her.

Finally she arrived at the Atchison, Topeka and Santa Fe Railway station. The impressive, two-story wooden building sported many windows and chimneys, and several train tracks ran along one side. A crowd of Topeka citizens stood around the building while some waited in buggies pulled up near the tracks for the train due in from the West.

Raven was back in a part of town she knew. She had debarked here from Chicago. As she walked by the station, she saw a sign advertising the Harvey House restaurant. She thought of Sadie Perkins whom she had met on the train from Chicago and had become friends with during the long trip.

Sadie, an orphan from New Jersey, had made the journey West to become a Harvey Girl, one of the waitresses in the Harvey House restaurants. After responding to an advertisement in a young woman's magazine back East, Sadie had been selected from many applicants to begin a rigorous training program.

Sadie had told Raven that being chosen to become a Harvey Girl was a wonderful opportunity. Not only did it allow Sadie the opportunity to travel West with her expenses paid, but she considered herself a railroader at heart and was excited at the opportunity to work with railroad people.

Also, she had added, the job paid very well at the starting salary of $17.50 per week plus tips, room, and board. It was an elite job, for wherever there were Harvey Houses, the Harvey Girls soon set the standards for courtesy, cleanliness, and comfort.

Sadie had gone on to explain that the Harvey Girls presented a sharp contrast to the painted ladies of the saloons and bordellos in the wild Western towns, for they lived in dormitories under the strict supervision of a matron who maintained a ten o'clock curfew and a strict moral code of conduct. Dressed in clean, neat uniforms, the Harvey Girls were noticed by local merchants, cowboys, miners, and railroad crewmen, and the young ladies were much sought after as brides.

Sadie had given Raven a brief account of the restaurant chain's history, saying that Fred Harvey had opened the first Harvey House in Topeka, Kansas in 1876 because he was tired of eating the bad food served along the train lines. His restaurant was quickly a success because delicious food was served in clean, elegant surroundings by attractive, efficient waitresses. Soon he expanded to include restaurants along the entire Atchison, Topeka and Santa Fe line. Harvey Houses and Harvey Girls quickly became world famous and set the standards for food and service in the West.

Looking up at the building, Raven felt a twinge of guilt. She knew she should have visited her friend sooner, but she had simply been too busy. Besides, she didn't have much hope that she and Sadie could continue their friendship very long now that they were in Topeka. Raven would be moving on, following clues, and after Sadie was trained, she would be assigned to a Harvey House somewhere along the Santa Fe train line.

Whatever the case, Raven wanted to see Sadie as much as possible before they were separated. Smiling with anticipation, Raven walked past the people waiting outside for the next train, and entered the depot.

Chapter Three

The Harvey House met all of Raven's expectations, and more. The restaurant was elegantly decorated, yet retained a homey atmosphere. Round wooden tables with four chairs and long tables seating six were placed comfortably around the room. Each table was covered with a white linen tablecloth, and white lace drapes hung over each window, allowing only diffused sunlight and soft breezes to enter the room. Original oil paintings in gilt frames hung on walls covered with dark green flocked paper, and the hardwood floors gleamed brightly.

Several young women in uniform were serving a few late-lunch customers. Raven looked around for Sadie, but didn't see her.

As one of the Harvey Girls came to greet her, Raven looked over the uniform. It was a simple black dress with an "Elsie collar" and black bow, long sleeves, and a full skirt. Over this was a heavily starched, long white apron which fitted snugly around the neck, then fastened with a wide band around the waist. The uniform was completed with black shoes and stockings, and the Harvey Girl's hair was pulled neatly back in a chignon.

"Good afternoon, ma'am. May I help you?" the Harvey Girl asked pleasantly.

"Yes, thank you. I'm looking for Sadie Perkins. Can you tell me where she is?"

"Sadie is in training and very busy right now. She has a great deal to learn before becoming a Harvey Girl."

"Yes, I understand, but Sadie is a friend of mine and I promised I'd look her up after she got settled here."

"Let me ask in the kitchen. Would you like a seat while you wait, or perhaps a cup of tea? Have you had lunch?"

"Yes, thank you, but I'd like tea."

"Very good. I have a nice table by a window."

"Thank you."

Raven followed the Harvey Girl, who pulled out the chair, seated her, then left. Raven was impressed with the service, especially since it had been rare before Harvey Houses.

As Raven was gazing out the window at a tree just turning green with new leaves, a steaming cup of tea was set in front of her. Surprised at the fast service, she glanced around.

"Sadie!" Raven exclaimed, and stood up.

Sadie Perkins smiled, her soft, dark-blond hair pulled neatly back from her cherublike face. Her round blue eyes sparkled, and her grin revealed even white teeth. She was shorter than Raven, a little plump, with dainty hands and feet. She was also the best sight Raven had seen in several days.

Raven hugged Sadie, and as they sat down, asked, "How have you been?"

"Fine. Wonderful. The Harvey Girls are so friendly. I felt right at home immediately. It's just perfect, Raven."

"I'm so happy to hear that. You look good, and the uniform becomes you."

"Thank you. I think it's attractive, too. But how have you been? Have you had news of your uncle?"

"No . . . not yet," Raven responded uneasily. She still felt guilty about having lied to Sadie with her story of looking for a lost uncle. But she had done it to protect them both. With two men already dead, she didn't want to endanger anyone else. The truth could put Sadie in a vulnerable position, and she didn't want to do that to her friend.

"I'm sorry. I know how important your family must be to you."

"Don't worry. I'm sure to get a lead soon."

"Raven, I can't stay long. I really shouldn't be here now, but they told me to take a break since you're my friend."

"I understand."

"Have you been safe? I know it's wild here, and you have no chaperon, no guardian, no one. I worry about you."

"That's sweet of you, but I'm all right."

"What about your money? Do you still have enough to stay in a fairly decent place? You told me you had limited funds so I worry about that, too."

"You're such a good friend, but I'm fine so far although my money won't last forever. I must find some clues soon." Raven looked at her friend fondly. Sadie treated her like a long-lost sister, and she felt the same way about Sadie. They were both orphans and their friendship had helped take some of the fear out of the long trip from Chicago.

"Raven, the Harvey Girls are wonderful, just like family, and we're well chaperoned. I'm learning quickly, and soon they'll assign me to a house along the train line. So I've been thinking. Why don't you become a Harvey Girl? I'm sure you could handle the job if they'd accept you, then maybe we could work together somewhere. Wouldn't that be wonderful?"

Raven hesitated. "I don't know, Sadie. It might be too confining. How would I look for my uncle that way?"

"Well, you could question the people who came through, and I understand they're thinking of trying out a few experimental diners on the trains. Maybe we could request working on a train. What about that?"

"A train?" Raven suddenly looked at her friend with great interest. What better way to infiltrate the railroad line than as a Harvey Girl? No one would ever suspect a Harvey Girl was R. Cunningham, the tough Chicago detective. She could easily question customers, railroad employees, plus people everywhere they stopped. "Sadie, that's a brilliant idea."

"Really? Would you actually become a Harvey Girl?"

"Yes. I think it's a wonderful idea, if they'll have me. I just hope we can get on a diner."

"You can ask them about the diners. And don't worry about being accepted. Who wouldn't want you? I'll speak to someone in charge as soon as possible."

"Good. I'll stop by again tomorrow."

"I'm so excited I can hardly wait. As if everything weren't already wonderful enough, now I'll have my very best friend with me as a Harvey Girl."

"Sadie, I can't thank you enough for thinking of this. It's really perfect, and this way I won't have to worry about money while I look for my . . . my uncle."

"That'll be a relief for both of us, and you won't

need to worry about your reputation so much, either. Now we just must get you accepted." Sadie hesitated, looked down, and asked, "By the way, how do you like your tea?"

Raven had forgotten it in all the excitement, but she quickly took a sip. "It's delicious, and the cup and saucer are lovely."

"Everything about the Harvey House is so special. When I lived at the orphanage I always dreamed of having nice things of my own, but this is almost as good. Well, I've got to go now. The trains will soon be stopping for dinner. Let's talk more tomorrow." Sadie squeezed Raven's hand as she stood up and said, "Now, don't worry about a thing. Leave it all to me. And don't pay for the tea. I already told them to take it out of my wages."

"No, Sadie, please."

"I want to, and that's that."

"Thank you, for everything."

"I wouldn't do any less for a sister." And with a wink, Sadie slipped away from the table.

Raven watched until her friend disappeared into the kitchen. Sadie really was the closest she'd ever come to having a sister, and she couldn't have had a better one.

Raven sipped the tea, thinking of Sadie's scheme. She felt guilty for not being able to tell her friend the truth, but it just wasn't safe. Now, if everything worked out, she'd be with Sadie, have an income, and track down Comanche Jack and the mastermind. She just wished her father and fiancé had lived to meet Sadie, but then she might never have met her new friend if she hadn't been forced to come West.

She shook her head at how complicated life could be, then finished her tea and left the Harvey House.

As the sun slowly made its way toward the western horizon, Raven questioned one dry goods proprietor after another, but learned nothing more about Comanche Jack. Tired but not disheartened, she walked back toward her hotel. She had learned a lot in the past two days, and she kept that in mind so that discovering nothing new on the case that afternoon would not discourage her. Finding clues was not fast or easy, and she had to remember that.

Dusk was settling over Topeka as she took the last few steps down the boardwalk to her hotel door. Suddenly a tall dark shape standing in the shadow of the hotel stepped out and grabbed her arm. Surprised, Raven jerked back, ready to defend herself.

"Raven, Slate said, "I've been looking for you all afternoon. Where've you been?"

"Oh, Slate. You startled me."

"Sorry. I bought you some more peppermint." He thrust a dozen sticks, the paper around them damp and crushed, into her hand.

"Peppermint? Slate, I shouldn't accept anything else from you."

"Sure you should."

"How long have you been carrying these around?"

"All afternoon," Slate said with disgust. "There was no reason to run out on me, Raven. I'm not going to force you into anything. I just don't see why you're being so stubborn. After all, it's your business."

Raven sighed. "Thanks for the candy. It was thoughtful of you. But don't give me anything else."

"You know what I want to give you."

"Please. I'm tired. All I want to do is go upstairs to my room." Then she hesitated. "How did you find my hotel? You don't even know my last name."

42

And neither did anyone else, except for the hotel clerk who had registered her under her assumed last name.

"West. Raven West. I tracked you down. Did you think I wouldn't?"

"No, I didn't." Raven suddenly remembered she had told him her first name and she had seen Slate leave the silver exchange where she had gotten her first information on Comanche Jack. He had obviously tracked her to her hotel and asked the clerk who she was. Could he be a professional like her? No, of course not. He was just a lonely cowboy.

Yet her mind wouldn't stop. He thought she was a lady of the evening. Could they both be playing roles to get information in Topeka? But what would he be after? She looked at him more closely. Could he be part of an outlaw gang? Had he gone to the silver exchange for information, or to leave information about a job? Ridiculous. Her mind was really running away with her. He was a cowboy, nothing more. He just wanted a good time in Topeka.

"Well, now that we're together," Slate said. "Let's go have dinner. I'll buy again, then maybe I can finally persuade you that I *will* pay your price for the night."

"No, I really can't, Slate. I'm tired, and—"

"I'm not taking no for an answer. How about I take you to the Harvey House? I understand they have the best mesquite-grilled steaks in town. You can't pass up that offer. It's the best you'll get."

"No! I mean, I can't tonight."

"Business? Forget it. *I'm* your business for the evening."

"I have to go upstairs and change."

"I'll come with you."

"No."

"It's not like a man's never seen your body before, Raven, and I want to see yours real bad. Let's go upstairs now, then we'll be ravenous later."

"No. Let's just go on to the Harvey House," Raven said in exasperation. She wanted to get rid of him, but didn't know how to without giving up her undercover persona. And she couldn't afford to do that. At least she should be safe with him in a public place and she'd get a free dinner at the Harvey House.

"All right. I'd rather go to your room first, but if you're tired and hungry, we might have a better time after you've relaxed."

"I'm going to have dinner with you, Slate, but nothing more."

"We'll see," he said as he took her arm and began leading her toward the Harvey House.

Raven bit into a peppermint stick, crunched it with satisfaction, then offered one to Slate. He grinned, took a stick, then bit down hard. As they walked, alternately nibbling and sucking the peppermint, Raven began to relax.

There was simply no rational reason to worry about Slate. She would just keep in mind he was attracted to her because he thought she was a woman of the night and it was that role which made her susceptible to his charm.

However, as she watched him sucking the peppermint stick, she began to feel a warmth invade her body. What if Slate were to do to her body what he was doing to that candy? It was a tantalizing and shocking idea. She immediately forced herself to look away, then took several deep breaths. Maybe there were some things she couldn't control, and if there were she'd better learn about them now to avoid them later.

Suddenly, she desperately wished she hadn't agreed to have dinner with Slate at the Harvey House. But it was too late.

"Here we are," Slate said quietly, putting a warm hand against Raven's back. "I've been looking forward to eating here, but with you along the pleasure'll be double."

The restaurant was very crowded, but they were given a table in a back corner. Raven was glad the location was inconspicuous, and glanced anxiously around for Sadie. Since her friend was still in training, she didn't expect to see her, but there was always the chance Sadie might be there and she didn't know how she would explain being with Slate.

The service was excellent, and the Harvey Girl waiting on them was pleasant and polite. Slate was obviously impressed and ordered the biggest steaks in the house, with potatoes and corn. Smelling the delicious food being served around them, she felt ravenous.

"Those Harvey Girls are something, aren't they?" Slate said, leaning back in his chair.

"Yes. Why don't you try one of them instead of me?" Her eyes were a mysterious black as she regarded him, and her hair gleamed silvery gold in the soft light.

"Don't you know? Those young ladies are for marrying only. A cowboy wouldn't even get to hold one of their hands without proposing first."

"So you're strictly interested in brief—"

"It wouldn't be brief between us, Raven. I want you bad, and you know it." Then he grinned, showing strong white teeth. "I could eat you up, instead of the steak I ordered. You'd be mighty tasty, I bet."

Raven glanced away, not knowing how to deal

45

with Slate. She was startled to see Sadie. Her friend looked up, saw her, and smiled before going back to helping one of the Harvey Girls. Raven immediately wanted to drop through the floor. How could she ever explain to Sadie why she was here, alone, with a strange man.

She was momentarily distracted from dealing with that problem when the food arrived. Huge, hot, simmering cuts of choice beef were placed before them, then a platter heaped high with fried potatoes and a bowl of steaming, buttered yellow corn were set on the table. Hot crusty bread with pale creamy butter was added last.

"Enjoy your meal," the Harvey Girl said, then disappeared back into the crowded room.

"Dig in," Slate said, tackling his steak with a sharp knife.

Raven followed suit, mumbling, "I'll never be able to eat all this."

"Don't worry. What you can't handle, pass to me. This is going to be the best meal I've had in months."

Silence reigned at their table for a long time as they both eagerly ate the delicious food. When Raven was finally full, she pushed her plate toward Slate. "Think you can handle that?"

His blue-gray eyes gleamed as he eyed what was left of her large portion of steak. He sunk a fork into the tender meat and slipped it onto his own plate. "Just watch me."

As he sliced into the meat, Raven smiled, realizing that, despite everything, she had been enjoying the evening with Slate. She also suddenly realized that his table manners and demeanor were not those of an ordinary cowboy, or what she had assumed would be common for cowboys. Who was this man?

She was beginning to find him an enigma, and that worried her almost as much as his determination to seduce her. In her line of work anything that didn't fit into its proper place could be very dangerous, even fatal.

"We have apple pie, vanilla custard, and blueberry tarts for dessert," a Harvey Girl informed them. "Which would you like?"

"All of it," Slate replied, finishing off the last of the potatoes.

"All?" Raven questioned.

"*All,*" Slate insisted. "You want the same?"

Raven chuckled. "I'm so full now I don't know how I can manage any more, but I'll take a piece of apple pie and coffee."

"Coffee for me, too," Slate added, then smiled at the Harvey Girl.

She returned the smile, then motioned for someone to remove their empty plates.

"I don't know how you can eat so much," Raven said in amazement.

"On the trail you croon to the cattle and think of hot food and warm women. Tonight I've got both."

Raven blushed and glanced away. "Slate, I—"

"Here's your dessert," Sadie said, smiling as she expertly set several plates on the table, then returned with coffee. As she poured, she said, "Raven, I didn't know you knew anyone else in Topeka."

Raven inhaled sharply, then glanced at Slate, who was looking at Sadie with interest. "Sadie, this is Slate Slayton. Slate, this is Sadie Perkins."

"Good to meet you, Miss Perkins. As pretty as all the Harvey Girls, I see."

Sadie dimpled in pleasure. "Nice to meet you too, Mr. Slayton. Any friend of Raven's is a friend of mine."

47

"Mr. Slayton and I aren't exactly friends," Raven added firmly.

Sadie looked at her in confusion, then smiled knowingly and nodded, obviously thinking that Raven was getting clues about her uncle. "Then don't let me interrupt your meal and conversation," Sadie said. "Enjoy your dessert."

"Thank you. I plan to," Slate replied.

"Nice to have met you, Mr. Slayton," Sadie said, then started away.

"Always glad to meet a friend of Raven's," Slate answered, then glanced at Raven. "You've got some interesting friends. Surprising a woman like you would know a Harvey Girl. Real surprising."

"Perhaps I've decided to change my occupation."

"Won't pay as well."

"Maybe being a Harvey Girl has other bonuses."

"Like snaring a man."

"You've already said I wouldn't have trouble doing that."

"Be easier as a Harvey Girl. Good way to meet a lot of eligible men. Don't know if I like your change of heart, though. But as long as I can still pay for your old skills, I don't care."

"I didn't say I *was* going to become a Harvey Girl. Anyway, it's none of your business."

"They'd never know what you really are, would they?" he mused, watching her with eyes that were more blue than gray as he bit into a blueberry tart. "In that gray gown you could pass for a genteel lady. Only I know the difference."

"I don't care what you know, or —"

"That's why you won't accept my money, isn't it? You've been wheedling into that innocent young lady's confidence, and easing out of your old business at the same time. Got to hand it to you, you're

48

clever. Everybody knows how strict they are when choosing Harvey Girls. You'd make a good one, no doubt, but I prefer you as a lady of the evening."

"Really! I've taken just about enough from you. I agreed to have dinner with you to be polite. Now I wish I hadn't. What I do is no concern of yours." She resolutely tackled her apple pie, the crust flaky and the filling sticky and sweet. The pie was as delicious as the rest of the meal had been.

"It's my concern now, Raven. I know your deep dark secret, and if you aren't nice to me I might tell."

"You know what?" Raven asked, suddenly terrified he'd somehow found out that she was R. Cunningham, not the Raven West she'd signed in the hotel registry.

"I know you're a lady of the evening who plans to become a Harvey Girl. If they knew about your past, they'd never accept you and all your plans would come to nothing."

"Oh," she said in relief, then remembered she was supposed to be concerned about what he had learned. It was all getting terribly complicated. Slate was surprisingly quick at putting things together, then trying to use what he'd learned to his advantage. Could he really be an outlaw? He certainly seemed to think like one. "You've just made this all up, Slate. It has nothing to do with either of us. Besides, you'll soon be leaving Topeka, won't you?"

"Maybe I won't be leaving as soon as you'd like."

"I've had enough of this. Thank you for the dinner. Good night." She stood up, and threaded her way through the tables and other diners. She heard Slate curse behind her, but she didn't stop until she was outside in the cool clean air.

Slate was infuriating, and much too smart for her

to spend time around. Besides, she didn't think she could ever find a way to control him. She quickly started walking down the boardwalk. It would take him time to pay the bill, and she planned to be hidden in a new hotel under a new name before he could find her again.

Suddenly she heard footsteps running to catch up with her. She stepped back into the shadows of a building, but wasn't quick enough.

"You forgot your peppermint, Raven, and I've had it with you," Slate said as he handed her the candy, then pulled her into his arms. He pressed fiery lips to hers, sending chills throughout her body. His warm hands roamed over her back, pulling her tightly against his body. His lips wove a spell that threatened to make her forget everything except the excitement he created.

Finally, he raised his head, and looked down at her with passion. "Let's go back to your hotel room now and stop all this nonsense. I want you and I know you want me. Forget everything but the two of us."

Before she could reply, he took her hand and began determinedly leading her toward the hotel.

Chapter Four

"No," Raven said, wrenching away from Slate. "You don't seem to understand. I have business to take care of here."

"I understand, all right. *I'm* your business."

"No, you're not."

"It's that Harvey Girl situation, isn't it?"

"What makes you think that?"

"I'm getting tired of bird-dogging you all over Topeka."

"Then let's settle this now. You go your way and I'll go mine."

"You think it's that easy?"

"Of course."

"For a smart lady, Raven, I don't think you understand what's going on here."

"Of course I do. You want a lady of the evening to cater to you while you're in Topeka."

"Sure I want that, but *you* make it different. I think you feel the same way about me."

"I have no idea what you're talking about."

"Need some proof?"

Raven stepped back. She didn't need any more proof that Slate Slayton did something dangerous to her, something that she couldn't seem to control.

What she needed was to get far away from him, and stay there. She couldn't let anyone or anything distract her from her job. She took a deep breath, and said, "You're an attractive man, Slate. I'm sure you know it. Another time, another place, well it might be different between us, but now I've—"

"—got other business."

"That's right. But, look, I'm going over to the Silver Slipper later. Why don't you meet me there?"

"Isn't that a little dangerous for your new persona?"

Raven hesitated. He obviously wasn't going to give up on his idea that she planned to change her vocation and become a Harvey Girl. Well, maybe she should play along with his game and work it to her benefit. If she became a Harvey Girl, he'd have to back off. "All right, I'll level with you. I do want to become a Harvey Girl. I think I'd like the work and the people."

He nodded. "And it's a good way to catch a husband who'd never know about your old background. But I do, and I'm not letting you forget."

Raven shrugged with pretended indifference, but noticed that the peppermint sticks she clutched were getting hotter and stickier the longer they talked. "What's the word of one lone cowboy from Texas against mine?"

"Maybe not much, but it'd make them wonder, especially if I showed up with several other men swearing to your former occupation."

"That's not nice, Slate. I don't guess you're planning on us being friends."

"Hadn't counted on it."

"Just as well. I've decided to have one last fling tonight, say good-bye to some friends, then meet my Harvey Girl connection tomorrow. So like I said, why don't you join me later at the Silver Slipper? I want to see Margarita."

"You and everybody else in town. Margarita's got the best song and dance act around."

"Then you'll meet me?"

"Not a chance. I'm not letting you out of my sight."

"Slate, I want to change."

"Better yet."

"Oh, all right, you can wait in the lobby of my hotel."

"I told you I'm not letting you out of my sight."

"Outside my door."

"In the room."

Raven took a deep breath, holding her temper in check. The man was infuriating. She looked up the entire length of him, and frowned. What was she going to do? She simply couldn't let him see through to her true identity. She'd just have to play along with him a little longer. Surely he'd have to go home soon, then she'd be free of him and his disturbing influence.

"It'll cost you," she finally said.

"What? Just to see you change?"

"Yes. If you don't want to pay, then you can stand outside the door."

"You couldn't stop me if I decided not to play your games anymore."

"You may be tall and strong, Slate Slayton, but don't think for a minute I can't take care of myself. If I were you, I wouldn't push me too far."

"So you've got a temper, too, and the gall to threaten me."

"That was not a threat. That was fact."

"I like you better all the time. Okay, I'll pay. How much?"

"A gold piece."

"What!"

"Well, you knew I was expensive from the first."

"Cowboys aren't paid *that* well."

"Then you can wait outside the door."

He took hold of her elbow and began drawing her down the boardwalk. "We'll negotiate this on the way to the hotel. I don't want to wait any longer than necessary to see you."

"I don't think you'll get your money's worth."

"Matter of opinion. Now about that price."

"I told you what it'd cost. No negotiation."

"Heart of steel, that's what you've got."

"Not at all. Heart of gold."

"That, too, probably. You must have made a fortune to treat cowboys with ready cash like me the way you do."

"If you think I'm usually worth so much, you won't mind paying that gold piece, will you?"

Raven knew she sounded much cooler than she felt. She would go through with the game if she had to, but she was hoping the enormous price she was asking would make Slate stay outside her door. But, she consoled herself, if she did have to change clothes in front of him, with her corset, camisole, and petticoats on, he wouldn't see much.

They walked down the boardwalk silently for a while, then Slate pulled her close. "All right, but you drive a hard bargain."

Raven dropped her peppermint sticks in surprise, then cried, "Oh, Slate, look what you've done."

"Never mind the candy. I'll buy you more tomorrow. Let the stray dogs have it. Come on, I can't wait to get to your room."

She started to protest, but Slate was already pulling her down the boardwalk. She was more nervous than she had realized she'd be once he agreed. Being an undercover detective was dangerous in a lot of ways she'd never imagined. What if Slate couldn't be controlled once he was in her room? What if he decided to overpower her? She had her pistol. She'd keep it close by, but somehow she couldn't conceive of shooting him.

"Give me the coin now," Raven insisted as she stopped outside the hotel, determined to stay in character.

"And then slam the door in my face? Oh no, I'm not that green."

"All right, then let me see the coin now."

"I've got it all right," Slate said, pulling a shiny gold cartwheel out of his pocket. He flashed it before her, then pocketed it in his leather vest. "Ready now?"

"I suppose so."

With as much dignity as she could muster, Raven entered the hotel's lobby, well aware of the curious stares that followed her and Slate as they walked upstairs. She just hoped none of this would get back to the Harvey people. She didn't need that kind of problem at this point. If Slate Slayton would just go away, she could relax and get on with her job.

But he didn't. He followed her closely up the stairs to her small room on the second floor. When she took out the key, he took out the gold piece. She looked at the coin, then inserted the key into the lock. He held out the gold, keeping a firm grip on it, and watched the key turn in the lock. As she turned the knob, he pushed the door open and handed her the coin at the same time. His body was warm against hers as he pushed her inside.

Raven clinched the gold piece in her fist, not

wanting it, not knowing what to do with it.

"Go ahead. Bite the cartwheel. It's good."

She did as he bid, determined to stay in character no matter what. She nodded, then slid the gold into her reticule. She heard it clink softly against the snub-nosed .45. Relief flooded her. She had to remember the important part of what she was doing. She was on the trail of justice for her father and fiancé. She was finally getting some good leads, and Slate Slayton was simply part of the job.

"You know, Raven, I could have had several women tonight for the price I just paid you, and all I'm supposed to get is a peek at your underclothes. Doesn't seem fair, does it?"

"No, it doesn't. Why don't you take back the coin and leave?"

"Wouldn't think of disappointing a lovely lady like you."

"Don't worry about that," Raven replied, and waited.

But Slate made no move toward the door. Instead, he looked at her expectantly.

There was only one way to make a bad situation better, her father had always told her, and that was to get it over with as quickly as possible.

"Why don't you sit down while I change?" she suggested, trying to sound in control, then immediately regretted her words, for there was only one place to sit in the room. The bed.

"Don't mind if I do."

Raven was momentarily disconcerted as she watched Slate plump up the pillows, set them against the headboard, then stretch out, crossing his booted feet in midair. Suddenly she couldn't help but laugh. "You're too tall for that bed, Slate."

"No. It's too short for me. But don't worry, you'll

get used to sleeping slanted across a bed. I promise."

"I don't have to get used to it. I'm not too tall."

"Maybe not, but you're sure too tough, too stubborn, and too beautiful for your own good. You're losing out on cold hard cash, and if I didn't know better I'd think you needed it," he added, glancing around at the small, clean but very plain room. "Just move here recently to impress the Harvey Girls people?"

Raven didn't reply. The man was working out an entire scenario about her, much as she might have done about him. She hesitated a moment, realized what she'd thought, and glanced at him more closely. Could he really be undercover, like her? Once more she decided against it. That would be too much of a coincidence.

Besides, after a lifetime of living and working with detectives, she was naturally suspicious and on this dangerous case she had to be more cautious than usual. Her mind was imagining problems where there were none. Slate Slayton was just a Texas cowboy on the prowl.

"Need some help changing, Raven?"

"No thank you," she replied, setting out the red satin gown that was her lady of the evening costume.

"I'm surprised a woman like you wouldn't have a whole room full of fancy gowns. Sell them already?"

"That's right," Raven agreed, then took a deep breath and began unbuttoning the tiny black buttons down the front of her gray cotton dress.

"Turn around, Raven. No fair otherwise, and I'll have to take back my gold."

Reluctantly she turned to face him, her chin high

as her fingers clumsily continued their job.

"Sure looks like you could use some help. That's an awful lot of buttons."

"No. I don't need any help. I got dressed alone this morning just fine."

"But I'm anxious, Raven. You're moving much too slow for me."

"I'm trying to give you your money's worth."

"Oh, I plan to get it all right," Slate replied, dropping his feet to the floor.

He was quick, and before she could react he was pushing her hands away and carefully unbuttoning the tiny black buttons to expose her bare flesh. "Beautiful skin, Raven. So smooth, so pale. I've wanted to touch it since the first moment I saw you."

Her breath caught. His nearness was making her senses reel. She felt slightly dizzy, a weakness beginning to move through her. He hadn't really touched her yet, just his fingertips on the black buttons, but his breath was warm on her face and his body heat was reaching out to her. He smelled of leather and that unique scent that was his alone. She suddenly thought she could recognize him by his scent anywhere, even in a dark crowded room. But she didn't want to be with him in a crowded room. She wanted to be with him here, now, alone.

"You're making me feverish, Raven, and I'm not even touching you. You do that to all your men?"

Raven couldn't speak. She swallowed, taking a deep breath and her breasts moved naturally outward, touching his hands. She caught her breath in horror.

Slate didn't move, then said, "You do that too many times, and I'm not going to bother with the buttons. I'm going to rip this dress right off you."

"Sorry. I didn't think."

"Don't breathe, or better yet take a deep breath."

"I said I don't need your help, Slate."

"Sure you do, and I'm almost done. I don't have to go all the way to the bottom, do I?"

"No. Just a little farther and it'll slip down."

As if to prove her correct, Slate suddenly pulled the shoulders of the dress down, slipping it to her wrists where it clung, imprisoning her. He followed the movement of his hands with his eyes, feasting on her bare flesh, the swell of her breasts above the décolletage of her cotton lace camisole. Then his blue-gray gaze feasted on her face a long moment before he said, "It'd take a lot to get tired of you, Raven."

"You can let go now," she said, her voice husky. His hands were heavy around her wrists, where the fabric of her gown clung, covering her hands.

But Slate didn't let go. Instead, he pulled her hands behind her back, pushing her breasts toward him. Then he crushed her to him, groaning as his lips covered hers and his tongue pushed deep into her mouth. One long hand was all he needed to hold her hands behind her, the other he used to caress her bare shoulders, her straight back, and down to her rounded hips. He held her hips still as he pushed against her, driving his growing hardness against her.

She moaned deep in her throat, caught, trapped, and yet craving the feel of him, his sure touch, his need. Chills ran through her, then heat, and finally she succumbed to what had been building in her from the first moment she had seen him. Passion.

"Raven," he groaned, leaving her mouth to place small kisses down the side of her neck to her shoulder where he nipped the flesh, felt her shudder, then bit harder.

"Slate," she breathed, and felt him jerk the dress over her hands. Free, she reached out to him, needing to feel him closer still. She ran hard nails under his leather vest, testing the muscles of his back, feeling them tense, tighten, and respond to her. "Oh," she sighed, planting a small kiss on the black-haired triangle of flesh exposed by his open shirt. He tasted of salt and man and she wanted him more intensely than she could ever have imagined.

"Damn, Raven, what're you trying to do?"

"Slate," she murmured, pulling his head down so she could capture his lips.

He responded by pushing deep into her mouth again, toying with her tongue, teasing it back into his mouth. They tasted each other, reveling in the intimacy, feeling their passion rise to ever greater heights.

Until finally Slate jerked her away from him. His eyes were the color of molten metal as he stared at her. "Now, Raven? You'll share your bed with me now?"

Without his warmth, Raven suddenly felt cold, and with that cold came a degree of clarity. No, she couldn't go to bed with a man she hardly knew. She was a virgin. She had been engaged and she had loved Sam. How could she suddenly be untrue to her former fiancé with this man? It was unthinkable.

"No. That wasn't part of the bargain." It took all her will to say the words and step away from him.

"No?" There was a stunned, then angry look on his face. "Is this a joke?"

He was mad now, and it scared her, for she suddenly realized that his anger could fly as high as his passion. "No. It's no joke, Slate. The situation just got out of hand."

Trying to appear casual, she pulled the red satin gown over her head, trying to cover herself as quickly as possible. But her hands were clumsy and she felt a terrible chill inside.

"You've just been taunting me all along, haven't you? Well, I'm warning you, Raven, I'm not a man to cross."

"I'm not crossing you. We had a bargain. Are you going to stick to it or not? What is your word worth?"

Slate scowled, ran a hand through his thick dark hair, and said, "If you were a man, I'd punch you for questioning my word. As it is, I'm going to ask you again what sort of game you're playing?"

She gave up on the gown, and said, "No game, Slate. I don't know what you do to me."

Something in her voice or eyes must have gotten through to him, for he suddenly, gently pulled her against him, held her there for a long moment, then slipped the gown into place. "I guess a woman of the night has a right to feelings, too, but I warn you if this is all a game to you, you'll regret it."

"Business, Slate. I'm here on business, and you're just making it all harder."

"I'm here on business, too, and you're not making my life any easier, either. I can't take much more of this and you know it. Neither can you. Why don't we just try to get it out of our systems before you join the Harvey Girls, then we can go our separate ways?"

"I don't think that'll work."

"Why not?"

Raven didn't have an answer. She was playing a role and she couldn't let him know that.

"You don't have an answer to that. I think you're

61

afraid, Raven West. You're afraid of me, aren't you? Afraid of what it'll be like when we finally do come together in your bed or mine. You're afraid of being on the other end of the little games you've played with men all your life."

"Games?"

"Sure. Lead them on, get what you want, maybe given them a little happiness, then move on. But they're still left wanting you. Now you're afraid of that happening to you, aren't you?"

"No. I hadn't thought that."

"Of course not. It's too new for you. Well, I know passion, Raven, and you've got it for me. Not just some act to make me happy. Listen to a man of experience. The best way to get over this thing between us is to get in bed and work it out."

"In bed?"

"Absolutely. I don't want thoughts of you left hanging around to fire my blood when we've gone our separate ways. Like I said, I've got business to concentrate on. And you're going to try to be a Harvey Girl, which means you want a good husband, not a man like me. You'll want a home and babies and family. I'm a roving cowboy."

Anger began to filter through Raven's bemusement. Who was this Texas cowboy to plan out her entire future, what she would want and what she wouldn't want, who her lover should be, and who she should marry. He had his nerve!

"Now see here, Slate Slayton. You don't know anything about me. You just think you do. I'll make the decisions about my life, and I'll decide what I want. And right now I'm going to the Silver Slipper, with or without you. What you do is your business and what I do is mine."

"You're just mad because I don't want to marry

you."

"Of all the nerve! I *don't* want to marry you. It'd take a lot more man than you to get me to the altar."

"I'm plenty of man for you, if you'd just let me show you."

"I've had enough of your showing me," she said, checking to make sure the red satin gown was in place, then grabbed her reticule. "I'm going out, and I don't care what you do. I'm not afraid of you, or any man. You may be big, but you're not big enough to scare me."

Raven finished by giving him a hard stare, then slammed the door shut behind her.

Chapter Five

Slate caught up with Raven outside the hotel and fell into step beside her. "I'm not trying to run your life for you, or tell you what to do. I'm just offering to pay for what you're selling. It seems simple enough."

"But it isn't simple," she protested, even as her anger began to cool. His words made sense. He was caught up in something with her that he didn't know anything about, but it affected everything. If he hadn't been so persistent they wouldn't be in this mess now. But he was right. There was this strange power between them that wouldn't go away. It was nothing like the warm gentle love she and Sam had known. This was like wildfire that could consume all in its path.

But there was no point in taking out her frustrations on Slate. In effect, he was an innocent bystander in the dangerous game she was playing. If she didn't encourage him, maybe he would give up and seek out another woman. But that idea brought an unusual tightness to her chest. She didn't want to think about Slate in another woman's arms.

But that was stupid. He had his own life. She had hers. They were going their separate ways, and that was that.

She finally broke their silence as they neared the Silver Slipper. "Look, Slate, let's just have a good time tonight. Everything else is in the past. I'm starting a new life tomorrow, I hope, and I can't let the old one continue to influence me."

Slate stopped, and looked down at Raven. Her hair shimmered silvery blond in the moonlight. It was obvious by the intensity of his eyes that he still wanted to take her to bed, but he simply said, "All right. We'll have a good time. I'll even introduce you to Margarita."

"You know her?"

"Sure. She's from San Antonio, and has been driving Texas cowboys wild for years."

"Does that include you?"

"Could be," he evaded and pushed open the swinging doors to the silver exchange.

The Silver Slipper was much like other combination gambling houses, bars, and dance halls, except that it also included a stage and brought in singing, dancing, and acting talent to lure business away from its competitors. The Silver Slipper's entertainment was popular in Topeka, and the establishment was crowded and noisy as usual.

Raven was impressed with the rich furnishings, the imported crystal chandeliers, oil paintings, and heavy oak furniture. The bar was huge by any standards and sported a massive oil painting of a nearly nude woman reclined on red velvet. The rest of the wall behind the bar was covered with shimmering mirror and glasses.

Slate bought them each a whiskey, and as they looked around for a table near the stage, the curtains parted and an announcer ran out, wearing an orange plaid suit and mopping his face with a white handkerchief.

"All right, all right, all right. Everybody listen," he boomed into the room. "It's time for Margarita, the lovely Spanish rose from Texas—where they've got the ugliest bulls on God's green earth but the most beautiful women in the world. Margarita. She'll make you forget your troubles. Come closer, men. It's time for Margarita."

As the announcer exited, Slate and Raven found a table and sat down near the stage. Soon cowboys were crowded around them, standing up in all the available space and calling for Margarita. Their voices grew louder and louder until they were rewarded with the appearance of a small woman with dark hair piled high on her head, her large almond-shaped eyes outlined with dark kohl, her high-boned cheeks pink with rouge, and her body encased in purple satin.

The deep purple gown was an exotic creation that hugged the young woman's lush curves and was split up the front to expose her black mesh-encased legs. A large ruffle covered by sheer black lace ran around the hem of the gown, and was matched by a similar ruffle at the neckline which plunged low to reveal deep cleavage. Margarita also wore black high heels, and carried castinets. A black mantilla topped her crown of hair and hung down her back.

As the piano player opened with a fiery Spanish ballad, Margarita began to move sensuously around the stage, keeping time with the music as it increased in tempo. Soon she was stamping her small feet, clicking the castanets, and tossing her lace mantilla. The cowboys were fascinated, and begged for more when the number was over.

The announcer returned, bringing a stool and a guitar. Margarita gave him the castanets, and as he left propped herself on the stool, letting a long length of leg show as she began strumming the guitar.

Margarita sang in Spanish, sometimes throwing in a few English phrases, and the ballad was obviously about love and desire, about loneliness, loss, and isolation. All the things dear to a cowboy's heart.

Once more the audience was delighted, and Raven was very impressed. Margarita was good, and Raven understood how the entertainer could easily steal a man's heart.

She glanced sideways at Slate, who was totally concentrating on Margarita's song, then looked back at the singer. She was surprised to realize Margarita was singing to Slate, and found she didn't like it at all. Did Slate understand Spanish? What was Margarita singing to him? But most important, she suddenly realized, had the fascinating Spanish woman already stolen Slate's heart?

But Raven immediately chided herself. She had no interest in Slate and Margarita's relationship, past or present. Slate had his own life to live; so did Margarita. What they felt for each other was none of her business. But they obviously knew each other well, and that fact bothered Raven more than she cared to admit.

Margarita sang two more songs, then danced again before leaving her audience wanting more.

Slate glanced at Raven. "Well, what did you think?"

"She's as good as I'd heard."

"Better. You ought to see her down in San Antonio. That's when she really shines."

"I enjoyed her performance a lot."

"Thought you would. Come on backstage. I'll introduce you."

"Do you think she'd mind?"

"Not Margarita. We're friends from way back."

Which was not what Raven wanted to hear and which made her reluctant to meet this women who meant so much to Slate. But Slate didn't notice her hesitation, and swept her backstage, where he'd obviously been before.

He knocked and called out to Margarita. The entertainer opened the door and pulled Slate into her arms. She was almost half his size, diminutive enough to make Raven feel almost large. When Slate introduced Raven, Margarita embraced her warmly, then motioned for them to sit in the two wooden chairs that took up much of the room.

Margarita sat down in front of a large mirror, wearing a lavender silk dressing gown over her costume, then turned back to face her guests. "I'm so glad to see you, *mi amigo*. The work goes well."

Slate stiffened beside Raven, and she looked at him in surprise. But he immediately relaxed and she glanced at Margarita who was even more beautiful this close but older than Raven had expected, perhaps around thirty.

"I'm glad to hear your work goes well, Margarita," Slate replied. "Raven was very impressed with your performance."

"That's right," Raven quickly agreed. "You were wonderful on stage. I was completely captivated."

"Thank you. I enjoy what I do, although I miss my beautiful Texas."

"Do you travel on tour frequently?" Raven asked.

"No. Not as often as I should since I hate so to leave home. But this time—"

"This time Margarita couldn't refuse the offer,"

Slate finished for her.

"That's right," Margarita agreed, raising a finely arched brow at Slate. "This time I was compelled to leave home."

"Well, I'm glad you did. It was certainly a pleasure to see you perform," Raven replied, feeling strangely like she was not hearing all of the conversation, or that there were undercurrents between Slate and Margarita that she was missing. But before she could ponder this more, Margarita suddenly began speaking rapidly and intently to Slate in Spanish.

Raven was shocked. It was so unexpected. She was even more surprised when Slate replied in the same language, obviously as comfortable with Spanish as he was with English. Slate was, indeed, a man of mystery, but she supposed it was not uncommon for people raised in Texas to speak both languages. But why did Slate and Margarita feel compelled to use it around her? What were they trying to conceal?

Then she took a deep breath and relaxed. There was no need to be a detective all the time. Margarita was probably more comfortable speaking Spanish and Slate was merely being polite, although speaking another language in front of her could certainly be considered rude.

She waited, watching them more intently, then noticed Margarita make chopping motions at her left wrist. Slate leaned toward her intently, then sat back, a pleased look on his face. Raven suddenly remembered that she had originally decided to visit the Silver Slipper and question a woman named Margarita about Comanche Jack because of a tip. The dry goods proprietor had suggested the one-handed man frequented the Silver Slipper and Raven thought the entertainer might know something about him.

Could Margarita be telling Slate about Comanche Jack, unconsciously indicating the loss of a left hand by using a chopping movement? A shiver ran up Raven's spine. She had pushed back all her instincts about Slate long enough. There *was* something suspicious about him.

Could he be working for Comanche Jack or the mastermind and already know she was R. Cunningham? Could that be why he was so persistent? Could all his passion have been an act? Margarita was a talented actress. Could she also be part of the gang, part of the plot?

Raven slowly pulled her reticule into a position so she could get to the pistol more easily. She opened it, took out a small white handkerchief, rubbed her nose, and left the reticule open, her hand near it. She was in a dangerous situation if her speculations were even half right, and until she could be sure of what was going on, she would have to be even more careful.

Margarita finally stopped talking to Slate, looked at Raven, shrugged her shoulders, and apologized. "I'm so sorry to speak when you can't understand, but Spanish is so much easier for me and I wanted to catch Slate up on all my news. He's such a dear friend."

I'll bet, Raven thought furiously. She couldn't trust anything this woman said and she certainly wasn't going to ask her about Comanche Jack. "That's perfectly all right," Raven said sweetly. "I understand perfectly."

"Wonderful. Why don't you two let me buy you a drink, or perhaps dinner after my last performance?"

Raven was getting ready to refuse when Slate surprised her by saying, "Thanks, Margarita, but Raven has promised herself an early night."

Margarita nodded, and smiled wistfully. "Slate's a good man. Take care of him for me, yes?"

Raven swallowed her anger. Margarita must be very sure of her relationship with Slate if she could send him off with another woman for the night, and it was obvious by Raven's clothes that she was a lady of the evening. The nerve. But she held her temper and replied, "You can rely on me."

"*Bueno*. I can see you are good for him. Thank you for coming by."

"Our pleasure," Slate said as he opened the door and ushered Raven outside.

"Please come again," Margarita said, then added, "*Buenos noches.*"

Slate nodded, then led Raven away.

Nothing about the Silver Slipper seemed quite as exciting to Raven now. She wanted nothing more than to be gone from it and Slate Slayton. If he knew she was R. Cunningham, could he be planning to kill her? Take her to the one-handed man who would kill her? Or use her in some other devious plot?

Well, he wouldn't get the chance. She was not her father's daughter for nothing. She had training, experience, and she was not about to let some outlaw take advantage of her. She could play this game as well as Slate or Margarita, and she'd prove it.

But first she had to have some facts. After all, she didn't know for sure that Slate and Margarita were in league with Comanche Jack or the mastermind. It just seemed a pretty good guess. After all, she'd seen Slate coming out of the silver exchange where she'd gotten her first information about the one-handed man and he hadn't gone in there to drink since he'd stayed such a brief time.

The overriding question was whether he knew or suspected that she was R. Cunningham. Or did he actually believe she was a woman of the night who'd decided to better her marriage chances by becoming a Harvey Girl?

She needed to know, badly. She didn't want to believe that everything Slate had told her and made her feel had been a lie because what she had felt in his arms had been unmistakable passion. But what to do now?

"Let's get a drink at the bar, Raven," Slate interrupted her thoughts, "then we can plan the rest of our night. You know what I want to do."

As Slate ordered two whiskeys, Raven glanced around the room, trying to get her emotions under control. She must not let Slate suspect by word or expression what she was really feeling and thinking. She must continue their game as if nothing had happened.

When she tilted the whiskey glass to her lips, she did her best not to grimace, but no amount of contact with the stuff seemed to make it more palatable to her. She felt it hit her stomach with a burst of fire, then settle into a low burn.

Slate had already downed his whiskey and ordered another when she casually set her drink, half finished, down on the bar.

"Want another?"

"No thanks. I have to think of tomorrow."

Slate downed the second drink and ordered another.

That's when she noticed something different about him. It was as if he were suppressing a deep excitement. What had Margarita told him? Raven just hoped it wasn't about her.

Raven took another sip of whiskey and wondered how she was going to find out what Slate knew.

"I'll be leaving town in a few days, Raven. I got a new job."

"Margarita have anything to do with it?"

He glanced at her in surprise, looked suspicious a moment, then said, "No. But she'll be moving on soon, too. She's got engagements in New Mexico."

And, she thought, that's where the Atchison, Topeka and Santa Fe ran, all the way to El Paso. But maybe Slate and Margarita were just outlaws, and had no connection with Comanche Jack or the mastermind. Perhaps she was jumping to too many conclusions, including their knowing who she really was. When she stopped and thought about it, there was really no way anyone out here could know she was R. Cunningham. No one had ever seen her before, she'd been careful with her questions, and no one would expect a woman to be an experienced Chicago detective.

She downed the last of the whiskey with a sigh of relief. She felt better. Her true identity was surely safe, but that didn't mean having anything else to do with Slate and Margarita was a good idea. The best thing to do was part company with them immediately. Make it quick and clean.

Turning toward Slate, she said, "Well, maybe I'll see you or Margarita in a Harvey House somewhere. If they accept me, I could be placed anywhere along the line or on a train."

"I'd like that, but right now neither one of us is going anywhere. There's too much unsettled between us. Once you join the Harvey Girls, there won't be the chance and it won't be the same."

"No, it won't. Maybe they won't accept me."

"They'd be crazy not to."

"Well, I'm glad I got to meet Margarita. Thanks for introducing us. I can see you're close friends."

"I've known her a long time."

"Yes, I realize that. I think I'll just go on back to my room now. You could wait here for Margarita."

"Why? She won't expect me."

"I know, but it'd be better. I should get an early night."

"Just what I had in mind . . . together."

"No, Slate. You're going your way, and I'm going mine. I think it's best if we part now, here."

"What are you talking about? If I didn't know better, I'd think you were some kind of prim little lady or something. What's going on in your mind, Raven?"

"Plenty. Now, good-bye."

"Not so fast." He grabbed her shoulder, preventing her from leaving, downed the last of his drink, then propelled her outside.

"Don't make this difficult, Slate. You've lost. That's all. You can't afford my price."

"I don't think I ever found out your price, unless it's marriage. If that's the case, you're damned right I can't afford it. I've got business, just like I told you, and there's no place for marriage in my life right now."

"Then let's say good-bye."

He pulled her roughly into the shadows, his hands hot and heavy on her bare shoulders. His grip was so hard it hurt. "Raven, don't do this to us. We have a few nights left. Let's use them. Get this out of our system. I want you so bad I'm hurting. You must be, too. And all for some misguided sense of loyalty to some outfit you don't even work for yet. Don't turn away from me now."

Slate was right. It did hurt. She didn't quite know why, but she seemed to ache all over. She needed this man, wanted him in a way she could scarcely believe. And he wanted her. She didn't believe he was playing a game about needing her, too. But it didn't matter. None of it mattered. Not their pain. Not their desire. They were not their own people. He, somehow, belonged to Margarita and some outlaw gang, and she belonged to her father and fiancé until their killer was caught, as well as the two railroad companies who'd hired the Cunningham Agency.

She had to say no, and she didn't want to, didn't want to sever what little they had between them. And it was stupid to feel the way she did. He was just some outlaw Texan on his way to a hanging tree.

That thought made her pause and tremble. The sight of his long legs swinging from the wrong end of a noose made her hurt even more. She didn't want him hurt, or lost, or alone. And that was stupid, too. He didn't mean anything to her, couldn't. It was all just some strange body hunger that had tried to take over their better senses. That's all it was, and she would deal with it, just like she'd dealt with losing her father and fiancé. Pain was not new to her. She could handle it.

Taking a deep breath, she slowly put her small hands on top of the ones gripping her shoulders. As she pushed his hands away, she said, her voice oddly hollow, "It's too late or too early for us, Slate. There's just no place for us together now. I'm going home, alone."

"You mean it, don't you?"

"Yes."

Chapter Six

Three nights later, Raven was having tea with Sadie in the parlor of Chadwick House, where the Harvey Girls of Topeka lived. The dormitory, actually a boardinghouse, was a quiet, clean, comfortable place with few luxuries but an impeccable reputation. It was owned and operated by Nan Chadwick, a Harvey matron who treated each of her Harvey Girls like a daughter.

Raven was still musing over her incredibly good luck with the Harvey Girls. True to her word, Sadie had spoken to her superior and, fortunately, there had been an opening. Raven was accepted for an interview and hired the same day.

After that, it had been a whirlwind of fittings for uniforms, learning how to walk, talk, dress, and act like a Harvey Girl, as well as learning to deal properly with chefs, patrons, and how to serve meals. She still wasn't as smooth as she'd like to be, or as good as the experienced Harvey Girls, but she'd been assured that it was only a matter of time before she would become a full-fledged Harvey Girl.

She hoped that was soon, for she needed to get on with the railroad investigation. To that end, she worked long hard hours and was exhausted by the end of the day. Having tea with her friend Sadie in the peaceful surroundings of Chadwick House was a relaxing and pleasant way to end a hectic workday.

Everything she was doing took her mind off Slate Slayton and she was glad of that. Yet, she still wondered about him. Had he left? Was Margarita with him? Would she ever see him again? Did she want to? That was a question she didn't answer, didn't trust herself even to consider, for there was a tight hard knot deep within her when she thought of Slate. She didn't want to explore that knot, didn't want to admit it was there. Slate Slayton was part of her past, and that was the way it had to be.

She was a professional investigator. She had no one to depend on but herself. There was no room in her life for a man, and certainly not a man like Slate Slayton, a possible criminal in love with another woman, who was able to stir her senses dangerously. All rational thought told her to stay as far away from him as she could get, and that was what she was doing.

"You sure are quiet," Sadie said. "You seem far away."

"I'm just tired, I guess."

"You have a right to be. You're working harder than two other Harvey Girl trainees put together."

"I'm just trying to catch up so we can be assigned posts together."

"It'd be wonderful if we got to work together, Raven, but we mustn't count on it. We can ask, but that's all."

"I know, but I'm sure going to try for it."

"Me, too."

Silence filled the room again, and Raven's thoughts returned to Slate. He was so tall and well built. His fingers were long and gentle when they touched her face, tracing her features. And his eyes. Were they blue or gray? She'd never really decided.

"You know, Raven," Sadie said, breaking the silence again, "if I didn't know better, I'd say you were mooning over a man."

Raven snapped back, embarrassed and furious with herself. Sadie was right. She was, indeed, *mooning* over a man, an outlaw even, and it was despicable. She couldn't allow herself to do it anymore. "Sorry. I was just . . . just thinking, I guess."

There was a sharp rap on the front door.

"I'll get it," Sadie murmured as she got up. "You need your rest."

"Thanks," Raven replied, leaning her head back against her chair and shutting her eyes. She was so tired, and it was wonderfully peaceful in the parlor. She felt sleepy. No need to worry about anything. Sadie was taking care of it all. She yawned, and began to doze.

Sadie opened the front door and looked way up before meeting the eyes of the man standing there. She recognized him immediately as the cowboy who had been with Raven at the Harvey House. "Hello. Can I help you?"

"I hope so. I'm looking for Raven West."

"She lives here, but Chadwick House doesn't allow male visitors downstairs without prior approval by the matron."

"It's important I speak with Raven now. I have some—"

"Information for her?"

"That's right."

"About her uncle?"

79

"Her uncle?"

"I know about her lost uncle, and I understand how urgent it is for her to have any news of him at all. However, there are strict rules here."

"I understand. Would you give her a message and perhaps she could meet me somewhere?"

"The matron would have to approve of her going out, and since it's so late that would be difficult."

"Could you accompany her?"

"The matron would still have to approve, and it's very late."

"I need to get the information to her tonight."

"Perhaps I could give Raven your message."

"It's private."

"Maybe she could come to the door then."

"The message might take awhile."

"Perhaps you should return tomorrow night at an earlier hour. You could meet the matron then, and—"

"I'm leaving at dawn. I've got to see Raven tonight. If you'd call her downstairs, maybe into a parlor, we'd be very quiet. No one needs to know."

"But it's against regulations."

"You're in the West now, ma'am, and sometimes you have to bend the rules. Believe me, Raven needs this information and I need to give it to her. If you're her friend . . ."

"I understand. Well, if you're quick I guess I could stand outside the door while you talk to her."

"Thanks. Will you get her now?"

"No need. The first door to your right."

"Thanks. I'll see you don't regret this."

Raven awoke to long fingers trailing down the side of her face, sending shivers throughout her body. She should have been frightened, or angry, or both, but she recognized Slate's touch, his scent, and couldn't stop the quickened beat of her heart.

He shouldn't be here. Why had Sadie let him in? Now she would have to deal with him, and she hadn't wanted to do that again, hadn't even know if she'd have the strength to reject him once more.

"So, you've a long-lost uncle you're trying to find?" Slate asked quietly, amusement in his voice. "Did that explain why you were with me in the Harvey House?"

So that's how he'd gotten Sadie to let him inside. Sadie must have believed he had important news for her. One more mess to untangle someday, but not now. Now she had to stay calm, cool, and far from Slate's roving fingers, for they had strayed to her hair and were playing in its softness.

"I missed you, Raven. But I see you've achieved your goal. You're now well on your way to becoming a Harvey Girl and catching a rich, successful husband. Congratulations."

"Thanks," she responded, and shivered as his hand made feathery movements down her neck.

"I'm riding out at dawn.

That opened her eyes. This was the last time she'd see him, and she didn't know what color his eyes were. But that was a silly thing to think. What did it matter? There were so many things that mattered more. Nevertheless, she looked deep into the blue-gray depths of his eyes, and wished nothing else existed except the two of them.

"Wanted to see you again before I left."

She nodded, trying to think of something light to say, but couldn't. All she could think of were his eyes, and how she could almost drown in their depths. "What color," she finally asked, "are your eyes?"

"My eyes?"

"Yes. I can't quite tell."

Slate picked her up, sat down in her chair, and cradled her in his lap. "This close enough to tell?"

She should have struggled, but didn't. "I should charge you."

"Can't. Not anymore."

"Then you're taking unheard of liberties with a lady."

"If you insist I'll give you an extra large tip someday."

Raven didn't want to think about that. There'd never be another day for them. Now was all they had. It made her feel soft and vulnerable inside. "Forget the tip," she murmured. "Let me see your eyes."

He pulled her closer, gazing into her dark eyes. His warmth and scent surrounded her. Slate. So much to want, so wrong to want it.

"They look blue now," she finally said, "but I've seen them look gray."

"Changeable, like you."

"I'm not changeable."

"Most changeable woman in the world. I think you could keep me fascinated forever."

She took a deep breath, trying to still her racing heart. How could he say such things? It just made their parting all the harder, but she couldn't let him know that. She shook her head in denial. "You'd tire of me soon, Slate. Remember, that's what we were supposed to do."

"I remember. Get it out of our system and go on with our lives. Maybe I was wrong."

"Doesn't matter now, does it?"

"If I didn't have this business hanging over my head, I'd stay and find out. But as it is . . ."

"You're moving on."

"Got to. But when I'm done I'll be back."

"No, Slate. I've got a new life. Who knows what may have happened by then, or where I'll be."

"Doesn't matter. We'll still have something to settle between us, no matter where or when. I'll stake my life on that. Now, stand up and say good-bye the way I want it."

Raven stood up and took a few steps toward the door. "Good-bye, Slate. And be careful."

"Careful? Now that I've met you that word means more than just a mother's constant wish. I'll have to be careful to get back to you, won't I?"

"Just be careful for your own sake, and that of your mother's."

She was surprised to see him frown, then quickly hide a look of pain. Now his eyes were gray, not blue.

He grabbed her roughly, pulled her against him. "You don't know how short life can be sometimes, Raven, when a good-bye could be forever."

But she did know, and her own eyes filled with pain, remembering her recent loss. Then all the pain and loss and sorrow was pushed from her mind as Slate's lips touched hers and wildfire burned through her, leaving nothing in its path but the desperate need to be joined with Slate forever.

He dug urgent fingers in her hair, freeing it to fall in a silvery blond mass down her back. Then he buried his face in the fragrant locks, murmuring endearments in Spanish. But one hand he kept free to bind Raven to him, feeling her curves against the hard heat of his body.

"Damn, Raven, I want you so much," he finally said, trailing burning small kisses down her face to her neck where he reached the stiff fabric of her dress. "And damn these clothes. He jerked on the neckline, and buttons popped free. She gasped in shock, and he nuzzled the warm smooth skin now exposed to him.

"Slate, stop," she moaned. "Remember where we are."

"I don't care. Not anymore. You've damned me to hell anyway." He jerked her bodice open, tracing kisses down to the top of her chemise. Then he stopped and glanced into her flushed face. "You going to stop me?"

"Of course," she said weakly. "All I have to do is call out."

He put a palm over her mouth. "Now?"

She glared indignantly at him, even as she felt her heart begin to race with excitement and mounting desire.

He tore at the lace of her bodice with his teeth, exposing more and more of her breasts, until only the tips remained covered.

She groaned, struggled against him, then felt his hand push away her bodice and his tongue caress a nipple. She was instantly stung with fire, her body melted against him, and as he continued his assault on the sensitive tip of her breast, she moaned and clutched at his shoulders, no longer trying to push him away, for her hidden passion was suddenly overwhelming her. He sucked and teased, making her taut with desire, and then he began again, tormenting the other nipple until she was weak with pleasure.

Finally he raised his head, taking his hand from her mouth. "I've never seen such beautiful breasts, Raven, nor been with a more passionate woman. Let me make love to you."

She moaned, felt her body cry out in need for what only he could give her, felt the tension and heat beg to be cooled by his touch. But still she shook her head, denying them both. He pulled her closer, scratching her sensitive breasts against the fabric of his cotton shirt.

Long fingers dug into her hips, forcing her into his hardness, proving to her how much he wanted her, how much he had to give. But still she denied them. She had to even when she caught his earlobe with her teeth and bit him, feeling savage inside with pain and desire. She blamed him and bit him harder, following his neck down to his shoulder, where she pushed aside the fabric and worried his flesh with her teeth.

"Damn, Raven, you're driving me crazy. You say no while your body says yes. It's a wonder I can control myself at all. If I don't leave now I'm going to say yes for both of us."

She bit him harder in reply.

He jerked her away, gazed for a long moment into her dark, desire-clouded eyes, then said huskily, "You've got more willpower per inch than any man or woman I've ever met." The his eyes swept to her exposed breasts, the tips reddened and hard. "But your willpower's no match for us. We've got to do it, and do it now, Raven, or so help me, I'll never get out of Topeka a sane man."

As he began to gently lower her to the floor, she protested. "Slate, not here. Not now."

"We can't wait. It's too late."

Suddenly there was a sharp rap on the door, and Sadie hissed, "Someone's coming."

Slate hesitated.

"Go," Raven insisted, pushing at him. "Go, before everything's ruined."

Slate jerked her against him, his eyes blazing blue fire, hugged her tightly, then set her aside and took long strides across the room.

At the door he looked back, and said, "It's not done yet, Raven. I've got your scent and I'm bird dog enough to keep it."

When the door shut behind him, Raven collapsed into a chair, feeling more distraught than she would have thought possible. How she'd had the will to send him away she didn't know, but she'd done it and now felt the loss acutely.

Then she heard the outer door shut and voices in the hall. She jerked her clothes back into place, covering her breasts, but knew that if someone besides Sadie found her here, looking like this, that her days as a Harvey Girl would be over.

Raven waited, not knowing who would come through the door, and felt her desire and rage with Slate slowly sink into a dull ache. There was nothing she could do about him. There had never been a future for them. Never. It was better to end it here and now before it got any worse. She had been stupid and foolish, naive enough to think she could control a man like Slate Slayton and what he did to her.

But he was gone now, forever, and that was for the best. She could truly get on with her life and the investigation. But first she must confront whomever came through the door. The voices ceased, then the door slowly opened.

Raven took a deep breath.

Sadie stepped inside, shutting the door behind her. "It was close, but I sent Mrs. Chadwick on her way."

"Thanks, Sadie," Raven replied with a sigh of relief.

"Raven! What happened to you? What did that man do? Are you hurt? Oh, it's my fault. I'm so sorry."

"No, Sadie. Please. Everything's all right. It just got . . . out of hand."

Sadie hurried to her friend's side and took her hand. "So you *were* mooning over a man."

"Not exactly. Or maybe I was. Anyway, he makes me feel things I've never felt before, and . . ."

"True love. Then it's all right, but you must be more careful."

"No, it isn't all right."

"You mean he hasn't asked you to marry him?"

"No."

"Oh, that *is* terrible."

"Worse yet, I think he's an outlaw."

"An outlaw! Raven, you lead the most exciting life, but we mustn't let anyone know. You know what everyone would think . . . especially if he hasn't asked you to marry him."

"I know. It's all wrong. You think I'd marry him if he asked me? No. I couldn't live with an outlaw."

"No, I guess not. But he's awfully handsome, and intriguing."

"Are you going to see him anymore?"

"No. He's leaving town in the morning, and I wouldn't see him again anyway."

"Then there's nothing to worry about. We won't say anything to anyone. We'll make you presentable, then hurry you to your room. I'll watch the hall. Then you can just go on as before."

"I guess you're right. It's not like anything happened between us."

"Certainly not. And look, Raven, you came out here alone, innocent, and an experienced outlaw took advantage of you. But you can get over your first love. Everyone says so."

"Love?"

"Yes. That's obviously the trouble, although I admit I'm a romantic and that man was enough to make any woman's heart flutter. But he's gone now, and you'll get over it. I'll help you, and you'll be so busy with the Harvey Girls you won't have time to think about him anyway. Though it is kind of a shame he's an outlaw and didn't ask you to marry him. You made a handsome couple. But you'll be all right. I'll see to that."

"Thank you, Sadie. You're a true friend."

But it wasn't as easy or as simple as Sadie made it sound. Still, Raven knew her friend was right. She couldn't give up now, and nothing really *had* happened. Perhaps it was just as Sadie had suggested. She'd been overwhelmed by a handsome, experienced man. It wouldn't be the first time that had happened to a woman.

But there was one thing Sadie had been wrong about. There hadn't been love between them. She knew that for a fact. She had loved Sam and that had been gentle, caring, tender, and nothing like the wildfire that had burned through her when Slate touched her. That was not love. It was some sort of primitive emotion that he released in her, and him. It was best not to feel something like that. It was too overwhelming.

This time she *would* put Slate Slayton out of her mind. She would concentrate on her job with the Harvey Girls, her friendship with Sadie, and her job for the railroads. There was plenty to keep her busy.

Raven began to gather the pins that had flown from her hair when Slate had pulled it free. For a moment there was a tightness in her chest as she relived that instant with him, then she pushed the image away and began to pin up her hair. There was no place in her life for thoughts of Slate and what they had shared.

When Raven was fairly presentable, Sadie checked to make sure no one was in the hall, then motioned to her friend. Raven hurried to their room, shutting the door soundlessly behind her.

were attendants to the passengers, and owners of
prestigious eating establishments around the
world. They run smoothly with even and to have
all provided, were required to be friendly, while
maintaining discipline.

Chapter Seven

A month later, Raven returned a book to the shelf
in the library car of the Atchison, Topeka and Santa
Fe train, then glanced out the window. The flat
prairies of Kansas rolled by, tall dry buffalo grass
glinting golden in the afternoon sun.

Time had flown since she'd been accepted as a
Harvey Girl. Two weeks of training in Topeka, then
two weeks of work at the Clifton House, a Harvey
hotel and restaurant in Florence, Kansas. Then back
to Topeka when she and Sadie had been selected to
serve on the Montezuma Special, a new train running from Topeka to Montezuma, New Mexico.

Raven had been told when she was assigned to the
train that Fred Harvey had built the Montezuma,
an elaborate luxury hotel, for the Atchison, Topeka and Santa Fe Railway on the side of a beautiful valley in the mountains of northern New
Mexico.

The spa resort was the railway's first venture to
entice tourists to stay at a Harvey hotel longer than
one night. Prior to this, as Raven knew, the Harvey
hotels and restaurant/lunchrooms were primarily
utilitarian. They were there to provide overnight
lodgings and serve quick good meals in clean attrac-

tive surroundings to the passengers and crew of Santa Fe trains that stopped for twenty minutes at breakfast, lunch, and dinner. But according to Raven's trainer, the food was so good that locals soon began frequenting the Harvey Houses, too.

Raven also learned that the Montezuma was opened with great fanfare on April 17, 1882, and that the railway was anxious to see if its customers would exercise "stopover" privileges, and they did. Soon Montezuma was a major health and pleasure resort with four trains carrying passengers to it daily, for the hotel's furnishings, food, and service rivaled the hostelries at Saratoga Springs in New York.

Almost a year later with this success solidly behind them, the Atchison, Topeka and Santa Fe decided to try running a luxury train from Topeka to Montezuma. Not only would the train offer the latest in Pullman Palace Cars, but it would also add a dining car, advertising "Meals by Fred Harvey." The train would be fast, and its accommodations would rival anything on the East Coast.

Raven and Sadie were on the Montezuma Special's first run, and they couldn't help being excited and awed by the prestigious Pullman coaches. But Raven hugged a secret excitement to her, too, one she couldn't share with Sadie.

When the train had pulled out of Topeka that morning, Raven had learned that a private business car had been coupled to the end of the train. That coach belonged to T.R. Simpson, special representative for the Atchison, Topeka and Santa Fe and one of the two men who had hired the Cunningham Agency. Simpson would be traveling all the way with them to Montezuma, checking the efficiency of the train and the comfort of the passengers.

Now Raven was truly back on the case. This was the man she had needed to get close to, and now they would be working together. The situation was perfect. She could observe him, talk to him, and perhaps break the case soon, if he turned out to be the mastermind.

In any event, she was sure now that her decision to become a Harvey Girl had paid off. Even though she hadn't obtained any new information on the case during the past month, she had learned a lot about living in the West which could help her now.

As the library attendant until the dinner hour when she would help Sadie serve, Raven was responsible for keeping the books shelved in their proper order. She glanced around the library car, still amazed that so much area on a busy train was set aside for reading. Mahogany cases, with glass doors and brass trimmings, were kept locked by the library attendant who would help a passenger select a book from one of the one hundred and forty leather-bound volumes. Several chairs of green velvet, with tassels and hassocks, plus reclining chairs of gold velvet were placed about the area, and light streamed in through open windows. A brocade curtain in a green and gold floral pattern was pulled back to allow entry or exit to the barber shop and shower bath which shared the library car. One of the sleeping car stewards also worked as the barber and was frequently on duty until he made up the beds for the night.

Sadie was in the observation car, making sure the passengers had cards or magazines or drinks to keep them occupied when they weren't watching the scenery rush past. It was a beautiful car, too, with swivel chairs of bright brocade, tassels along the bottoms and arms, high backs, and deep cushions. Velvet drapes were at every window, and the ceiling and walls were of inlaid wood. Ornate chandeliers hung from the ceiling.

Raven had seen the Pullman sleeping cars and they were also luxurious. During the day there were high-backed seats of plush velvet to recline in and at night beds were pulled down from overhead and the seats turned into beds so that there were two berths. A linen closet provided fresh linens and washrooms completed the comfort of traveling overnight.

Like many of the passengers, Raven felt she was suddenly experiencing how the rich must live. And, in fact, the trains were bringing a style in living quarters and food quality that many people had never experienced until they had traveled on a train, this luxury train in particular.

But enjoying the luxuries of the train was not Raven's primary concern now, especially since she was on duty. Beyond her work as a Harvey Girl, she was anxious to meet T.R. Simpson and get on with the investigation. Later she might have time to relax and enjoy traveling by train, but not now.

She stroked the back of a velvet chair and suddenly thought of Slate. She tried to imagine him sitting there, asking for a book. A smile touched her lips. If he were there, he would certainly not ask for a book. He would draw her into his lap and pull her close and . . .

She stopped her thoughts, knowing they led to dangerous territory. Slate would probably not like the luxurious accommodations at all. He was more used to the rough-and-tumble life of horseback and campfires. He was an outlaw, not a gentleman.

Since their last encounter in Topeka, she had managed to keep him out of her mind most of the time with hard work and early nights, but at idle times like this he would suddenly appear in her mind, feeding her thoughts and senses with his presence. Then she would feel the loneliness of her loss and wish for him, but she knew there could never have been a future for them.

Instead, she thought of Sam. He had been the perfect fiancé. They had shared so much, had had so much in common, and their gentle tender love had been perfect. Whatever she had felt for Slate Slayton could not have been love, as Sadie had thought. No, not love but a strange, overwhelming passion. Now that Slate was gone, that was gone, too, and she was glad.

Still, a small part of her refused to forget Slate or what they had shared, and she found it harder to remember Sam's face and easier to recollect Slate's strong, taunting features. The only rational explanation for her continued thoughts of Slate was the fact that she must have been more vulnerable, more lonely then she had realized in Topeka. With her father and fiancé gone, she had been open to another man's advances. But that was over now, over and done, and she might as well forget him, if she could.

She glanced at the small timepiece on her bodice which her father had given to her on her sixteenth birthday. The gold pin was a valuable memento as well as an important tool in her new job, for everything about the train was run on a strict schedule and she had to be punctual. She didn't want to be late to the dining room, although she wasn't exactly anxious to get there, since she had to change cars.

One thing her trainers had carefully explained and given her practice in performing was getting from one coach to the next. On a moving train, with strong wind currents, a passenger had to be very careful when crossing from one car to another. She knew many of the ladies would not cross without a male escort. She could understand their trepidation, but at the same time there was an exhilarating thrill about it, too.

As Raven stepped from the library car onto the platform outside, a gust of wind caught her, whipping her skirts around her ankles. She held on to the railing and sniffed the air, inhaling the rich scent of grass and earth. As the train curved up ahead she could see the shiny new Baldwin locomotive, one of the best made. Smoke billowed from its stack and the sound of its engine and wheels on the track filled her ears.

It was a fine moment, and Raven wished once more that her father and fiancé were there, sharing each new experience with her. But they weren't, would never be again, and it was left to her to bring their killer to justice. She had no time for enjoying the luxury of special trains, or special food, or enjoying the excitement of being on her own. She was on the trail of a murderer. Danger lurked all around her, no matter how bright and beautiful the day.

She carefully crossed over, opened the door to the observation coach, and stepped inside. Patting her hair back into place, she placed a subdued, professional smile on her face and walked toward Sadie.

Her friend looked up, saw her, and smiled, setting aside some magazines.

"Ready for the dinner hour?" Raven asked.

"Well, it can't be as hectic to serve here as it was at Florence. Imagine serving fifty people in twenty minutes, and then repeating that as each train came in."

"We had to be efficient, didn't we?"

Sadie laughed softly as they stepped on to the platform outside the observation car. "Or four-handed."

Raven joined her laughter and they both watched the beautiful sunset a moment.

"You know, Raven, this is the most exciting time of my life. If I'd been a man, I'd have come West sooner and worked at anything I could get on a train, but since I was a woman there were few, if any, openings."

"But you came anyway and now you're working on a train."

"Yes. Working at Clifton House in Florence was fun, getting to meet all the railroaders and all, but actually being on the train, living on it, is my dream come true. I couldn't be happier, except . . ."

"Except for what?"

"Well, you know what a romantic I am."

"A man?"

"Yes. Although I don't see how it could possibly work out now. I mean, he'd have a job somewhere, or be on a train. And I'd be working here. How could we ever get together?"

"I don't know, Sadie, but if I know you it'll all work out fine. And in the meantime—"

"I should just enjoy what I've got."

"Well, something like that."

"You're right, of course, but I can't help remembering how it was for you in Topeka. I don't want to be attracted to a man like that, someone I could never live with. I don't mean he was awful, or anything. He was gorgeous, after all, and exciting in a dangerous sort of way. I guess I just want a perfect man."

"And neither of us wants an outlaw."

"I'm afraid I couldn't live with that."

"No. I couldn't, either."

"But I'm happy, Raven. I guess I just dream about love making my life perfect."

"Maybe we all do. I'm sure the perfect man's out there for you. Just give him a chance to find you."

"You really think he'll come along?"

"Yes. You'll find your man, just wait and see."

"Thanks. And you'll find somebody right for you, too, Raven."

"Maybe, but I'm not very interested right now."

"I know. You want to find your uncle first."

"I like being a Harvey Girl, too."

"So do I. And speaking of that, we'd better get to the dining car quick."

When they entered the diner, Raven was not surprised to find it was as luxurious as the rest of the train, with a long row of tables down each side of the coach. Irish linen tablecloths covered the tables, which were set with English crystal, china, and silver. Thick carpets in a rose pattern covered the floors, the walls and ceiling were of inlaid wood, and elaborate chandeliers illuminated the car's interior.

For a dollar, the diner received a six-course meal, offering such delicacies as prairie chicken, buffalo, veal pie, elk, antelope, grouse, and beefsteak accompanied by seven different vegetables, four salads, and a wide variety of pies, cakes, and custards, followed by cheese and coffee. Several good wines were also available. All of this was produced in a small but efficient kitchen ruled over by a skilled chef and his helper.

As Raven and Sadie took their places, diners began to arrive and soon they were busy taking orders and serving customers. The aroma of delicious food filled the dining car, and soft laughter and low conversation soon joined the sounds of eating.

Several hours later, when the last passenger had left the dining car, Raven and Sadie sank into chairs and looked at each other with amusement.

"What did you say about it being easier to serve on a train since you had so much more time?" Raven asked.

"I did say that, didn't I?" Sadie replied. "Well, I hadn't counted on so many courses, or so much food, or so much lingering."

"Me neither, but didn't that food look and smell delicious?"

"Yes. I'm starved. I hope the chef saved us some of it all."

"Whatever he's got, I can eat it."

But at that moment another diner walked into the dining room. "Good evening, ladies. I'm T.R. Simpson."

Raven was surprised. The man didn't look in the least like he might be a criminal, let alone the mastermind of the train robberies. He was short, just an inch or so above Raven's own height, and plump, as if he really enjoyed good food and wine. He had luxurious red hair and an elaborate red mustache. His blue eyes twinkled as he walked toward them, looking intently at Sadie.

"It is a pleasure to meet more Harvey Girls. There's no need to be formal since we have a long trip ahead of us so please call me Ted. No one could possibly endure Theodore Randolph, especially not me, and I do hate the formality of Mr. Simpson. And your names are?"

When Sadie didn't respond, Raven replied, "This is Sadie Perkins and I'm Raven West."

"Lovely names. This is a first time for Harvey Girls to be serving on a train. How do you like it?"

"It's wonderful," Sadie replied breathlessly. "I've always dreamed of working on a train."

"Have you?"

"Yes. You see, I'm a railroader at heart."

"So am I. I've never lost my fascination with the rails, and this experiment with the Montezuma Special is of great interest to me."

"I feel the same way."

"Did you come for dinner?" Raven asked, watching the railroad man suspiciously.

"Yes, if you don't mind serving me this late."

"It'll be our pleasure," Sadie replied quickly.

"Thank you," T.R. Simpson said, then took a seat.

Sadie handed him a menu, poured water for him, and waited for his order while Raven hurried to warn the chef that the railroad representative was getting ready to judge them. Raven wasn't worried that there would be a problem. They were trained to serve all their customers equally and the chef was famous for his food. It was just that serving someone who could cost them their jobs made the situation more tense.

When Sadie came back with the order, Raven went to stand in the dining area, on call should Simpson need anything. It also gave her a chance to watch him. He was certainly smooth, trying to lull them into a false sense of security by putting them on a first name basis. He had also been friendly and polite, as if he really were glad to have them on board. No matter how smooth he was, she wasn't going to be taken in by clever tactics. Maybe he was sincere, or maybe he was a good actor. Either way, she'd learn the truth about him, and if he were the mastermind she'd take him in, no matter how nice he was.

He was an easy man to serve, exclaiming in delight over the food and wine. When he was finally finished, he smiled at them. "That was one of the best meals I've had in some time. Harvey has really outdone himself for the Montezuma Special, but you Harvey Girls made it even better. I appreciate your excellent service."

"It was our pleasure," Sadie replied.

"Actually," he said, standing, "it was *my* pleasure. Please give my compliments to the chef. I'll see all of you tomorrow." Then he nodded politely and left.

Sadie collapsed weak-kneed in the nearest chair.

"What's wrong?" Raven asked in concern.

"Raven, would you clean up and get us something to eat?"

"Certainly, but are you all right?"

"I don't know."

"What?"

"Please, I think I need to eat."

Raven hurried away, removing the last remaining dishes on Simpson's table. Sadie was never sick, was always sunny and happy. What could be wrong?

Raven hurried back with several plates of food, but she almost lost her appetite at the sight of Sadie's white face. Still, she didn't stop until she had a full meal set out on the table. When she sat down, she said, "Eat, Sadie, then tell me what's wrong with you."

Sadie made several attempts to eat, then set down her fork and looked at Raven morosely. "I think I'm in love."

Raven just looked at her a long moment, then laughed and began eating the delicious food.

"It's not funny, Raven."

"You're teasing me, aren't you, trying to make me laugh about that Topeka business."

"I'm very serious."

"Sadie, you haven't met anyone. Or is it some passenger?"

"Yes, in a way."

"You're joking, aren't you?"

"No. I wish I were."

"Oh, dear. Have some wine. It'll put some color back in your face."

Sadie took several sips, looked a little better, then asked, "Did it make you hurt inside? I mean being with that outlaw?"

"His name was Slate Slayton, and I don't actually know that he was an outlaw. He just acted like one."

"And looked like one, too."

"I suppose so. No, it didn't hurt all the time. Only at the end, I guess. And it wasn't love anyway."

"My heart hurts."

"Sadie, that's ridiculous."

"It feels big and full and hurts when I breathe."

"Your stomach's just upset."

"I've never felt like this before."

"Maybe you're train sick, too much motion."

"He looked at me and I just melted inside. Just one look and I knew I was his forever."

"You're making me lose my appetite, Sadie."

"Such beautiful blue eyes. So intelligent. So warm. So strong. Yet gentle."

"I was right. You're getting sick. You've been working too hard."

"And such full, sensual lips. I couldn't help but wonder what it would feel like to have those lips touch mine. Am I bad to think that, Raven?"

"I don't know. Are you sure you haven't caught something?"

"And his hands, such beautiful, tapered fingers, such well-groomed nails, so sensitive, so smooth."

"We know he's not a cowboy, anyway."

"Certainly not. Don't you know who I'm talking about, Raven? Didn't you feel the magnetism, too?"

"You mean, I've met this perfect man?"

"Don't make fun of me. This isn't funny. I told you it hurts."

"Why does it hurt?"

"Because, like you and that outlaw, it can never be."

Raven finished eating, leaned back in her chair, and took a long sip of wine. "You really are serious, aren't you?"

"Of course I am. Stop being cruel. My heart is breaking."

"All right. Who is he then?"

"Theodore Randolph Simpson. Ted."

Raven choked on her wine. "You mean that little—"

"The man of my dreams."

There was obviously no accounting for passion. Although, now that Sadie mentioned it, she could see the two of them together. They were sort of similar. But the worst of it was, somehow she and Sadie both had developed passion for possible criminals. It was terrible and sad and ridiculous.

"Are you sure, Sadie?"

"Yes. I knew it the minute he walked in. Just like that, after all these of years of wondering if the right man would ever come along."

"Then why are you so unhappy?"

"Raven! He couldn't possibly be interested in me. I'm just a Harvey Girl, an orphan from New Jersey.

He's an important railroad man and probably married."

"But he might still be interested."

"Do you mean love without marriage?"

"Well, if you really wanted him . . ."

"I couldn't. Not without marriage. It wouldn't be right."

"Then what are you going to do?"

"Nothing. And that's why my heart is breaking. I've found the man of my dreams and marriage is impossible."

"Wait a minute. First, we find out if he's married. If he isn't, then there's nothing to worry about."

"I wouldn't be good enough for him. He probably has important family."

"Nonsense! Don't give up yet. Maybe he was smitten, too."

Sadie smiled wanly at her. "Thanks for trying to cheer me up, but it's not going to help."

"Well, eat something. This is ridiculous."

"I may never eat again."

"Sadie, you're being melodramatic."

"I feel that way."

"If you aren't going to eat, then let's go to sleep. Maybe you'll see it all differently in the morning."

"I don't think so."

"Then we might as well get some sleep anyway. I'l clean up the table while you pull yourself together."

Just as they were ready to leave, the door opened and T.R. Simpson walked into the dining car.

Sadie sank into the nearest chair.

"Ladies, I'm glad I caught you. Would you like to have a cup of coffee with me? I found I was rather lonely after I left you."

"I'll get some," Raven said, knowing they couldn't refuse a man of his importance. Also, she was more than glad to get to know him better. He was making her investigation easy. Plus, Sadie would want to spend as much time as possible with her new love.

When she returned, setting a tray with cups of coffee on it on the table, she heard Simpson say, "So, although I enjoy railroading, I do get lonely for others of like mind."

"Your family doesn't travel with you?" Raven asked, sitting down beside Sadie.

"Most of the men in my position have their wives and children travel with them in their private cars, but that's impossible for me."

"Why is that?" Sadie asked.

"I'm not married."

"But surely a man like you . . ." Raven started.

"I've never found the right woman before."

Raven was beginning to realize that Sadie wasn't the only person at their table who'd been affected that evening. T.R. Simpson obviously couldn't keep his eyes off Sadie, and both seemed to have forgotten the coffee.

Raven set a cup in front of each of them and they absentmindedly picked it up. By now it was obvious that her companions were interested in nothing but each other.

However, T.R. Simpson's interest in Sadie didn't mean they could trust him. Quite the contrary. It could be a ruse to throw anyone watching off guard. But for Sadie's sake, she hoped it was real. In any case, she would find out the truth about T.R. Simpson, as much for Sadie as for her father and fiancé.

Raven took a large gulp of hot coffee and asked, "If the Montezuma Special is popular, are they going to run more like it?"

"We're looking at the future with this train," Ted

replied, never taking his eyes off Sadie. "We plan to extend our line to California."

"Really?" Sadie asked.

"That's right. All the way to the Pacific. And then specials like this, running fast with few stops, are going to be important. We plan to take them right into Chicago."

"That sounds like a lot of expansion," Raven said, watching him closely.

"Expand or die. We've already built south through New Mexico to El Paso, but we'll lay tracks through Texas, too. It's clear that we'll need fast trains, specials like this one to run the long routes, especially the Santa Fe route. We're trying it out with the Montezuma Special, but it'll probably be years before we have the specials running from the West Coast. Nevertheless, we'll get there."

"I'm so excited to be part of it all, Mr. Simpson," Sadie said. "I love trains."

"I'm glad," he replied, his eyes saying much more. "But I insist you both call me Ted."

"I don't know if that would be proper," Sadie said softly.

"I insist."

"Well, all right, Ted," Sadie relented.

He smiled. "But I've kept you both up long enough tonight. I appreciate your hospitality."

"It's been our pleasure," Sadie responded.

Ted nodded once, then left.

Sadie took several deep breaths. "I don't know if I'll be able to move."

"We've got to get some sleep," Raven insisted. "While I get these dishes to the kitchen, you get yourself up."

Sadie groaned. "He's not married, Raven."

"That's what he said."

"I think he might be just a little bit interested in me."

"I think he might be a *lot* interested in you."

"Really?"

"Yes. But let's go to bed. We've got a long day tomorrow, and there'll be plenty of time to talk about T.R. Simpson."

"Ted."

"Yes, Ted."

"Until tomorrow then," Sadie said wistfully, and followed Raven down the coach.

Chapter Eight

As the Montezuma Special continued across Kansas, slowing at the important railway stations of Newton, Hutchinson, and Dodge City, Raven watched the romance between Ted and Sadie blossom and flower. Raven was thrilled for her friend, but worried, too. She had so far been unable to prove Ted innocent of the railroad robberies and, worse yet, she was beginning to genuinely like the man, which was especially dangerous if he were the mastermind.

She had gained no other information on the case, for Ted had not confided in them, and it was impossible for her to bring up the robberies because they hadn't been publicized and were not common knowledge. However, she had asked Ted about robberies in general and had noticed the pained expression that had crossed his face. But he had not discussed any of the railroad's problems with her or Sadie.

Raven had come to enjoy the luxury of the train, even beginning to take for granted the special food and accommodations. She had to keep reminding herself that she and Sadie simply worked on the train. They were not paying passengers and by no means owners. It could all be gone in an instant. In fact, in her case, it would last only as long as the train helped her solve the case.

It was not that she hadn't lived in a nice comfortable home in Chicago, but their house had not been filled with the type of modern luxury that was so much a part of this train. She also hadn't been accustomed to the unusual and wide variety of food available to them at every meal. She had come to like all the luxury, yet knew that her safety depended on not getting too comfortable or too soft.

Sometimes it was hard to remember that her real job was as an undercover private investigator, not as a Harvey Girl on a new experimental train going to an exotic resort called the Montezuma. Ted had assured them that they would have time to enjoy the hotel and all it had to offer, but she wondered if it would be possible to take time away from the case to enjoy the Montezuma. Yet, how could she pass up such a wonderful opportunity?

In fact, it had crossed her mind a time or two that she could simply forget the Cunningham National Detective Agency existed. She could forget that there had been no justice for her father and fiancé. She could just go on being a Harvey Girl for as long as she wanted. She liked the West, and was making friends. Was there any need to cling to the past?

But she knew she couldn't live that way, knew she had been brought up to see that justice was done, knew that she could never rest easy until the killer had been found. Besides, even though she liked being a Harvey Girl, she was at heart a detective, had been all her life, and she was not going to see all her father had worked for during his lifetime disappear. The Cunningham Agency would stay alive, and she would see that it did.

She knew it wouldn't be easy, but her father had repeatedly told her that the easy way was not always the best way. She believed him, and no matter how hard it got she would complete the railroad job and see that the killer answered to the law.

But in the meantime she could allow herself to enjoy the pleasures of the special train, watch her friend happily in love, and try to force thoughts of a man named Slate Slayton to a far place in her mind. That wasn't always easy, for she couldn't seem to forget his muscled body or the way he'd touched her, wanting her with an intensity she'd never have thought possible and awakening that same intensity in her.

Still, he was just a Texas cowboy, probably an outlaw, who had no place in her life.

The train whistle blew as they raced through another small Kansas town, drawing near the Colorado border. From the library car window she could see the winding Arkansas River, which they'd been paralleling since Dodge City. The land was flat and empty out here, buffeted by strong winds and blowing soil, but it had a haunting, stark beauty all its own.

That night they went through the large railroad station at La Junta, Colorado, then turned south toward New Mexico, leaving the Arkansas River behind. Early the next morning the train slowed as it passed the Trinidad railway station, and not much later they were through Raton Pass and in New Mexico, with mountains rising high in the distance and with hills and valleys nearby.

Late that afternoon the Montezuma Special pulled into the train station at Las Vegas, a small but important town on the Atchison, Topeka and

Santa Fe line south. From there, Montezuma was just six miles west over the tracks of a branch line, deep in the foothills of the Sangre de Cristo Mountain Range and on a tributary of the Pecos River.

It was beautiful country, and Raven could hardly wait to get to Montezuma. Everything she'd heard about the luxury hotel made her want to see more. She had finally decided there was no reason she couldn't enjoy herself and investigate at the same time.

There were only six more miles to go, and they would all dine in the plush surroundings of the Montezuma. Ted had promised to take them to the dining room himself. It would be nice to be served by someone else for a change, and Ted was such a delightful companion that she knew the evening would be fun. Of course, she would leave Sadie and Ted alone after dinner. She knew how much the two wanted to be together, and the Montezuma must surely be the perfect place for lovers.

Which made her think of Slate Slayton. She touched the gold piece he had given her in Topeka. It was a ridiculous thing to do, but she had wrapped it in a handkerchief and always wore it tucked in her clothes above her heart. Somehow she felt she would be safe so long as the gold coin was with her. Naturally she didn't carry it because it reminded her of Slate, although it did, but rather because it had become a good luck charm. That was all it represented, simply good luck and nothing more.

As the train picked up speed out of Las Vegas, Raven checked to make sure all the books were back in place, then locked all the cabinets and made her way to the observation car. It was full of passengers eager to see the breathtaking scenery on the way to Montezuma.

Sadie was standing near the entrance and smiled at Raven. "Isn't it gorgeous? It's everything Ted said it would be, and more."

"I agree. It's beautiful country."

"And the Montezuma. I could never have imagined staying anywhere so fine when I was at the orphanage."

"You've got to remember that everything's changed, Sadie, and now you've got Ted."

"I wish," Sadie said with a sigh. "He's wonderful, but he's still an important man with Santa Fe and I'm still just a Harvey Girl."

"Do you really think that makes a difference to Ted? Besides, the Harvey Girls are very important to Santa Fe."

"I know our work is important, but Ted still has his reputation to think of."

"Nonsense. That man's crazy about you. I think he'll ask you to marry him at Montezuma."

Sadie's eyes widened. "Do you really think so?"

"I don't think he can wait. But perhaps you should be cautious. I mean, you don't know much about him."

"I know I'm in love with him and that's all I need to know."

"You're probably right, but still—"

"I'd marry him in a minute if I didn't think it'd hurt him some way."

"Hurt him!"

"Well, I mean with his job or family. Those are important things, Raven. You know that. Look how much trouble you're going to for a lost uncle. I have no relatives and I would never cause trouble between Ted and his family."

"Has he mentioned them, suggested they might not like you?"

"No, but he might be too polite to mention it."

"Sadie! He's crazy in love with you. That's all that matters."

"It's that way for me, too, but still . . ."

"Just be sure he's what you want and what you think he is."

"What do you mean? Of course he's what I want. I love him. And as for as who he is, well, he's Ted. That's all I need to know."

Raven nodded, but didn't say more. How could she warn Sadie about Ted without giving away her true identity and placing Sadie in even more danger? She couldn't. She would just have to watch over her friend and try to keep Ted from hurting Sadie if he turned out to be the mastermind.

Suddenly the train started to slow. Everyone in the car looked around, puzzled. The train shouldn't have begun slowing until Montezuma, and it was too soon for that. It was breaking hard now, about to stop.

"Do you think there's been a rock slide or something?" Sadie asked.

"I don't know," Raven replied, trying to see up ahead, but found it impossible. The track was straight and their view was limited to either side of the train.

But the passengers were growing restless.

Raven looked around in concern, then stepped forward and announced, "There is obviously a short delay, but please don't be concerned. I'm sure the engineer has everything under control." Then she whispered to Sadie, "I'm going forward and see what's wrong. You stay here and keep the passengers calm."

"All right, but be careful."

Raven pushed open the door to the platform, and

found a Colt .45 leveled at her head.

"Back it up nice and easy, lady, if you don't want to be splattered all over the inside of the car," said a tall man with a bandanna over the lower half of his face and a gunbelt slung low on his hips. Behind him, several more masked men were coming out of the library car.

Raven carefully stepped back into the coach, and kept backing up as the robber gestured with his gun. Her mind raced as she remained outwardly calm. Her pistol was in her reticule in the sleeping car. No good to her there. Anyway, she didn't want to give herself away by using it or her self-defense methods. She could only know what a Harvey Girl knew, unless their lives depended on her other skills.

She could almost hear her father say, "Wait it out. See what their next move will be. There are six armed men to deal with. If it's just robbery, let them take what they want and leave. Try to keep everyone safe. Go after them later."

Her father had always given good advice, and she followed it now. She remained still and composed.

"Good evening, ladies and gentlemen," the outlaw holding the pistol on Raven said. "My friends are going to relieve you of any valuables you don't need."

The passengers were obviously frightened, but they remained in their seats, with only a few protesting as the five robbers began going from one person to the next, collecting jewelry and money.

Meanwhile, the leader glanced at Raven. "You may be able to help us, lady. Your friend, too. You're Harvey Girls, aren't you?"

Raven nodded.

"We have a problem. The express man has locked himself in with the Montezuma's payroll. We want the money."

"How could we help?" Raven asked, thinking of Ted Simpson. Where was he? His absence was very suspicious, especially since he had to have known about the payroll being carried on this train.

"I figure that express man knows you two pretty Harvey Girls, and I figure he won't want you hurt."

"You could blow the door," Raven suggested.

"Clever girl. We might also blow the express man, his key, and the safe at the same time. We want this nice and neat. Come on." He gestured forward with his gun.

Raven hesitated. "There's no need to take both of us. I'll go with you."

"Friends, are you? Good. You men done?"

The other bandits took a few more pieces of jewelry, then looked satisfied as they walked back to their leader with bags full of loot.

Fortunately, none of the passengers had been physically hurt, but Raven didn't know what the outlaws might do after the express car door was opened.

"You passengers don't get any smart ideas. Don't move till dark and maybe you'll live," the leader commanded. "Okay, men, get that Harvey Girl and I'll take this one."

"Please," Raven protested. "I'll be enough."

The leader didn't respond to Raven. He simply grabbed her arm and pulled her with him. He rushed her through the library car, the others following. He kicked in the door of the baggage car and pushed her through. It was chaos in there. The outlaws had ripped through the trunks, taking whatever struck their fancy. He hurried Raven through the coach and onto the platform of the express car.

He hammered on the door. There was no sound

inside. The other outlaws joined them, and Sadie pushed close to Raven. She was trembling and Raven squeezed her hand in encouragement.

"Hey, express man," the leader called. "We got friends of yours out here. Not the old engineer. We had to shoot him. Not the fireman. Had to kill him, too. We've got two pretty Harvey Girls here, and we know what to do with them, that is if you don't open up."

"Roy, don't do it," Raven cried out.

"Shut up, woman!" the leader hissed, slapping her face.

Raven clenched her fists, feeling her face go numb from the slap. She wanted to fight back, but couldn't. It would endanger them all. There were too many outlaws and they were all on a hair trigger.

"Raven, that you?" came from inside the express car.

"Answer him, Harvey Girl."

Raven still refused to reply.

In response, one of the outlaws drew a hunting knife and grabbed Sadie's hand.

"She don't need all those fingers, now does she?" the leader asked.

"You wouldn't," Raven challenged.

"Try me, lady."

Raven didn't dare call his bluff. "Roy, it's me. Do what you must, but don't endanger yourself."

"Open up, express man, or we push these fine ladies down on the ground and teach them what they're made for."

There was a long pause, then came the sound of locks clicking, but before the door could be opened from inside, the leader forced it open and strode into the express car firing. Another outlaw followed him.

Raven heard only one short sound from Roy, then nothing. Sadie whimpered behind her. She had hoped they'd let Roy live, but there was no chance of that now. Three more people to add to the list of the mastermind's victims.

But where was Ted? He had to know the train was stopped. Why hadn't he marshaled some of the railroad crew and come forward? But did they have any guns? Worse, maybe Ted had planned it all and was carefully staying hidden. There was no way to know, and right now it didn't really matter. She had to deal with the outlaws here, now. Ted would come later.

Soon the outlaws returned, carrying four heavy payroll bags.

"Okay, men, we got what we came for. Let's go."

The leader glanced at Raven, then Sadie, "Ever have a Harvey Girl, men? Think I'd like the taste. How about you?"

The outlaws quickly agreed.

"Then let's have some fun in the mountains. With hostages like these, those railroad men'll keep their distance."

The outlaws didn't hesitate, but lifted Sadie in the air and carried her down the steps to the ground. The leader dragged Raven, protesting and fighting, after them. By the tracks, the outlaws fired several shots into the air to scare the passengers, then headed for the hills nearby. Soon they disappeared, into the dense brush.

It was dusk and shadowy in the woods, and Raven found it hard to see. Soon she was panting from trying to stay on her feet as the leader pulled and pushed her along. She was wearing a corset and could hardly catch her breath. The Harvey Girl uniform was not made for running. Her black stockings caught and snagged in the brush, and her ankle turned when the heel of her black shoe caught in a hole, making her stumble.

Cursing, the leader jerked her up and threw her forward. She caught herself against a tree, scratching her palms and ripping her dress. She had only a moment to catch her breath before the leader was upon her again, forcing her forward.

Sadie was ahead, floundering, falling, and being pushed and pulled just as Raven was. Her hair had come down, and was a long, dark-blond tangle down her back. Soft sobs drifted back to Raven and she bit her lower lip, furious that she was unable to help either Sadie or herself.

The horses were tied in a hidden arroyo. The outlaws quickly mounted, and Sadie was pulled onto the lap of one of the men. The leader forced Raven onto his horse, then mounted behind her.

In a short time, they had left the train far behind and darkness was closing in on them. Raven's thighs ached and burned, for her dress had been pulled up high when she straddled the horse and now her legs, covered only with torn black stockings, were rubbing against the hard leather of the saddle. She could scarcely breathe for the stench of the man behind her, and she constantly fought his roving hands.

"You can hold me off only so long, Harvey Girl," he muttered into her ear. "Tonight we celebrate. Me, you, the other pretty, and my friends. Going to be a fine party, lots of liquor, song, and women. Just the way I like it."

"You are going to be very sorry," Raven said firmly.

"Only thing I'm going to be sorry about is not

117

getting a Harvey Girl sooner, but they keep them locked up tighter than gold in a bank."

"It's a bad idea to kidnap us."

"Don't rile me, Harvey Girl. I want your body, not your smart tongue. Keep it up and I'll cut it out."

"You should leave us behind now while you have the chance. We can make our way to Montezuma. No one knows who you are. We won't say anything."

"Think you're smart 'cause you're a Harvey Girl, don't you? Well, I got news for you. My men and me do what we want in these parts. You stay real sweet and we'll buzz around you for a while. Turn vinegary on us, and we'll cut your life short."

"Please let us go. It'll go easier on you if you—"

"You ain't near as smart as you think. Go easier on us? We just killed three men. There ain't no harder way to go. Taking a couple of Harvey Girls is just like taking a couple more bags of gold. Don't matter much one way or another on our record."

"It *will* matter. The Sante Fe won't stop until you're caught and punished. They have to. No one will ride the train if outlaws start taking hostages."

"I'm getting tired of your chatter, woman. Like I said, you stay sweet and you get to live. Turn sour and you're good to nobody. Now, stop pushing my hand away. I like the feel of you, all soft and womanly."

Raven took a deep breath and let the man grope at her breasts for as long as she could stand it, then twisted out of his grasp.

He laughed, his hot, putrid breath rushing over her. "Like to fight, do you? All right. I like a woman who scratches."

"I do *not* want your hands on me."

He nuzzled against her neck, then bit her hard.

She tried to wrench away from him, almost fell, but he pulled her back. "Got to stop playing with you, Harvey Girl, or we'll never get back to camp. And I'm real anxious to get there."

"Please, let us go."

"No. Now shut up. No more games."

Raven finally accepted that he was not going to let them go. The situation was worse than she could ever have imagined, but she wouldn't give up. There had to be some way to get free.

Darkness settled over them as they rode on, silent now as the outlaws concentrated on the trail home. After a time, they began transferring the women from one horse to another, saving the animals for a long trip. With each exchange, Raven and Sadie had to fight off a new set of hands groping at them, teasing them, and low voices whispering obscenities in their ears.

Finally, as the sun began to rise behind the mountains to the west, the outlaws turned down a dry canyon bed, followed it awhile, then turned again, letting the tired horses make their way up a steep cliff, then down again and into what looked like a sheer rock face. But there was a break in the cliff and the horses picked their way into a hidden arroyo.

The deep gully was home for the outlaws, and Raven knew it was a hiding place that would be almost impossible to find, and because of the darkness and winding trail, she had no idea of the way out. No wonder the outlaws had been so confident. She didn't know how anyone could track them there, or how she and Sadie could escape. But escape they must, or die.

As the outlaws made their way toward a campfire,

three men walked out from recesses in the rock walls of the arroyo. Two were bandaged, and one was tall. Very tall. Too tall.

Raven started, her eyes straining to see the tall outlaw better in the early morning light. He walked toward them, a puzzled frown on his face.

The leader behind Raven shouted, "We met the train, men, and look what we got. Gold. And Harvey Girls."

For a moment silence reigned in the arroyo, then the sun rose over the mountains and a clear golden light illuminated the face of the tallest outlaw.

"Slate," Raven gasped.

Chapter Nine

"Raven," Slate said in amazement, then walked over to her and pulled her from the horse.

She stood trembling against him.

"You know this Harvey Girl?" the leader asked.

"Met her in Topeka."

"She's mine now. Took her and the gold off the train."

"That was damn stupid," an outlaw with a bandaged arm said, coming forward.

"Now, Arn, what harm's it going to do? Me and the men are getting all fired tired of these mountains."

"Those were not our instructions," Arn said. "You know we always follow the plan, or there'll be trouble."

"We're doing all the work. We ought to get some fun now and then."

"We're getting gold, Hank, and you buy pleasure with that."

"But this is free. Besides, only way to get a Harvey Girl is to take one. Ain't that right, men?"

The other outlaws quickly agreed.

Raven had begun to realize that the outlaw leader on the train robbery was not the final leader, just a lieutenant of sorts. This Arn wasn't the ultimate leader, either. Could Arn have been referring to the mastermind, or Comanche Jack? Maybe she could learn something, then escape with the knowledge. But what was Slate doing here?

She knew the answer to that question, and didn't want to admit it. He was exactly the outlaw she had feared he was. He had been in Topeka to gather information, probably for the mastermind or Comanche Jack, then he'd brought that information here and the robbery had occurred. It was the only rational explanation she could think of, and she wished it wasn't true. But she had to face facts.

And one of those facts was that her body still wanted him. For in that instant when the sun had illuminated his face, a fierce exaltation had shot through her, denying everything she had fought so hard to convince herself of on the trip from Kansas. She still wanted him, no matter that he was an outlaw, no matter that he was all wrong for her, no matter that she shouldn't be thinking of anything but escape.

"Sometimes you can be damn stupid, Hank."

"Wait a minute. I ain't going to take—"

"Gold's one thing. Killing men is one thing. But kidnapping women—damn Harvey Girls at that—will get us caught and strung up faster than a greased pig."

"You're turning yellow, Arn, old and yellow. If you can't lead this outfit no more, I can. Right, men?"

Hank swung down from his horse and faced Arn, hand near his gun.

Slate pulled Raven closer, and said, "Arn's wounded, Hank. He can't draw on you. Wouldn't be a fair fight."

Hank spit on the ground. "Who're you to talk? You just rode in a few weeks back."

"He's right, Hank," another of the outlaws said. "Wouldn't be a fair fight. Besides, Arn's led us right so far."

"Never got you no women, did he?"

"No, but I bought plenty."

"No Harvey Girls, did he?"

"No."

"All right. *I* got us Harvey Girls."

"And you got us trouble, Hank," Arn added.

"Okay, so you can't fight, Arn. I'll let you off now, but when your arm's healed we're going to have this out."

"Suits me, but we'll have to give the Harvey Girls back first so we'll be alive to do it."

"No!" Hank exclaimed. "They're ours. Nobody'll ever find us here."

"I'm still boss of this outfit," Arn replied.

"Can't take them back. Harm's done," another outlaw said. "Besides, we want them."

"That's right, and I'm taking my Harvey Girl right now," Hank added. "No more talk." He took several steps toward Raven.

"That's far enough, Hank. This one's mine," Slate warned him.

"Hell if she is. I stole her. Give her here."

"She's been mine since back in Topeka."

"A Harvey Girl?" Hank laughed. "Nobody's going to believe that, Texas. Now just give her back like a good boy."

"The rest of us want a turn at her, too," another outlaw said, pushing Sadie forward. "We want them both."

"I don't care what you do with that one," Hank said, "but this black-eyed beauty is mine."

"Nobody's touching her," Slate repeated.

"See the trouble we're getting 'cause you brought

123

those Harvey Girls in here?" Arn said. "We haven't argued before, but just sure as the sun rises you bring in women and men'll start to fight. The way I see it is—"

"We don't care what you see," Hank interrupted. "We want the women and we're going to get them. Now, you turn her over real nice like, Texas, or—"

"You're going to have to fight me to get her, Hank."

"You may be a tall Texan, but you ain't half as mean as me."

"Try me."

Raven couldn't believe what was happening. Two outlaws wanted to fight over her? What if Slate were hurt? What if he lost? What if he won? She couldn't believe what she was seeing or hearing. And what of Sadie?

She looked hard at Hank. He was a big man, heavily muscled, although not as tall as Slate. He had long brown hair pulled back and tied with a leather thong at his nape. His brows were heavy and he was missing two teeth in front. He looked like a fighter, mean and formidable. Raven didn't want to be anywhere near him and she didn't want Slate to fight him, either.

"Gentlemen, please listen to reason," Raven interrupted, pushing away from Slate as she gathered her strength. "Your leader is correct. The Santa Fe will hunt you down no matter where you go if you keep and abuse two Harvey Girls. Take us back to the tracks and we can find our way to Montezuma. We won't tell anyone what we saw. Please, let us go."

"Don't she beg pretty?" Hank said, his eyes bright with lust. "Been begging me all night. Soon as she gets to like what I've got, she'll beg to stay. Wait and see."

"That will never happen," Raven responded. "My friend and I want to leave. Now. If someone will simply guide us out of here, we will say nothing. Isn't that right, Sadie?"

Sadie nodded, and tried to move closer to Raven, but the outlaw holding her wouldn't let her go. She tried to jerk free, but he pulled her closer and began rubbing rough dirty hands over her torn dusty uniform.

"Stop him," Raven hissed, furious.

"Leave off, Tim," Arn said. "What the woman says makes sense. I don't know what the boss'll say about this."

"Chicken. Be sprouting wings any time," Hank replied. "You want them, same as us. Look at you. You're just scared."

"You haven't met Comanche Jack, or you'd know what I mean," Arn said quietly.

Raven's pulse leaped. She was right. This was one of the mastermind's outlaw camps. She was glad of the information, but wished she and Sadie were in a less vulnerable position so she could use it.

"I've heard of Jack, and no Indian-lover is going to scare me. Now give me the girl, Texas," Hank demanded.

"No," Slate repeated.

"Then we fight."

"Winner gets her for himself," Slate insisted.

"All right by me."

"Wait a minute," an outlaw protested. "We want *both* Harvey Girls."

"Take the one and be satisfied," Hank said. "This one's going to be mine. All mine."

Slate stripped off his shirt and handed it to Raven. Hank did the same. Then they took off their gunbelts and set them carefully aside. Even in her present situation, Raven couldn't help but notice the way Slate's muscles rippled, or the way he moved, like an animal on the hunt.

"Please don't do this. Either of you," Raven protested once more. "Just let us go."

"Stay out of it, Raven," Slate insisted.

"You might as well," Arn agreed. "You've fired their blood and there's no going back now. Nobody can stop them. Come over here. I'll protect you till we get a winner."

"No —" Raven started.

But Slate pushed her toward Arn, then turned his full concentration on Hank.

The outlaws formed a circle around Slate and Hank. Arn kept a tight grip on Raven's arm, while another outlaw clutched Sadie. Raven held the sweaty, grimy shirts without hardly realizing they were in her arms. She didn't want Slate hurt, especially not over her, but she didn't know what to do. She could never have imagined men fighting over her like wild dogs over a hunk of meat.

It was disgusting, and yet deep inside her excitement was creeping upward, beginning to overcome her rational thoughts. Slate must truly want her, or he would never have insisted on fighting for her.

As the two men circled each other, it was immediately apparent that Slate had longer arms and therefore more reach, but Hank was more heavily built and obviously an experienced brawler. They grabbed each other, rolled, and came up with Hank on top, his hands around Slate's throat. Raven tensed, for the first time realizing it was no game. Hank might well try to kill Slate. She stepped forward to prevent the fight, but Arn stopped her.

Slate broke the grip, flipped Hank off him, then jumped up, grabbing Hank as he got to his feet and spinning him backward into the dirt. Hank hit hard, coughed, and came slowly to his feet, a mean look in his eyes. He ploughed into Slate's ankles, grabbing hold, and threw Slate with a resounding thud to the earth.

While Slate was recovering, Hank threw his entire body weight on top of Slate, and Raven winced at the sound of the impact. How could Slate sustain those kinds of blows? But he did, reaching for Hank and pulling him back before slugging him hard in the face. Hank kicked out at Slate and both men ended up in the dirt.

Hank got to his feet slowly, shaking his head, blood running from his nose. He wiped at it with the back of his hand, then rubbed it against his dusty denim trousers. Both men were getting winded and Slate was slow getting to his feet. It gave Hank time to get a running start and he plowed into Slate with his head. Slate staggered, tried to stay on his feet, then went down hard.

Once more Raven started forward, but Arn restrained her. It was horrible. They were beating each other mercilessly and it didn't make sense to do it over a woman, *any* woman. But perhaps it had become something more than a fight over a woman now, something to do with a deep male instinct to win over all opponents at all costs.

Slate struggled to his feet, but Hank was ready for him and hit him in the face. Slate didn't go down, but moved in closer, blood running from a cut lip, and began to pound Hank with his fists, his long reach finally beginning to make a difference. Slate was total concentration, determined to win, and Hank was tiring fast, unable to reach Slate and taking the brunt of one blow after another.

Finally Hank tried one last move, a hard punch

with his right fist, but Slate was waiting for him, taking him down with one powerful blow. Hank collapsed unconscious to the ground.

Without stopping to think, Raven jerked away from Arn and threw herself at Slate, terrified that he had been hurt. She was not reassured until she could feel his heart pounding strong in his chest. He held her tight, sweat glistening on his body.

"Are you all right?" she asked.

"I've been better, but I'll live," Slate responded. "And so will Hank."

"Okay, Slate gets that Harvey Girl," Arn said, "and I suppose the rest of us'll take the other. But I still think we're going to get bad trouble from this."

"We'll worry about it then," the outlaw holding Sadie said. "Now all I want is some warm woman flesh."

Raven suddenly realized that the battle wasn't nearly over. She couldn't go off with Slate and she certainly couldn't leave Sadie to the mercy of these men.

"I think you'd better reconsider this decision," Raven said, turning to Arn. "This is Sadie Perkins, and she is under the protection of T.R. Simpson, a very important man with the Santa Fe Railway."

Arn looked surprised, then interested. Raven could tell he'd heard of Simpson. If Ted were the mastermind, these men would think twice about hurting his woman. And if he weren't the mastermind, it would still hopefully make a difference.

"That so?" Arn asked.

"Yes. They met on the Montezuma Special."

Arn looked thoughtfully at Sadie. "She's a pretty little slip of a girl, all right. So Simpson's sweet on her. Is that right, little lady?"

Sadie blushed, then lifted her chin and said, "Ted

and I are simply friends."

"Ted, is it?" Arn chuckled. "I hate to tell you this, men, but the little lady could do us more good tied up than with her legs spread."

The outlaws began to protest.

"Shut up! Let me think. This could make us look really good. I'm going to get a telegram off to Jack."

The men groaned, and the one holding Sadie pushed her behind him. "I'm going to have her no matter what."

"You'll take the message to the telegraph station, and now." Arn drew his Colt .45 with his left hand, clumsy but effective. "I'll buy you all the women you want. Later. But now this is important. Do as I say."

The outlaw reluctantly released Sadie.

"But you can tie her up," Arn added.

The outlaw brightened, and went to his horse for a rope.

Arn turned back toward Raven. "No reason you can't have what you won, Slate, but take her away where we can't see or hear you. It's going to be bad enough watching this one and doing nothing. We don't need you to remind us what we're missing."

"Wait a minute," Raven protested. "I'm a friend of Ted's, too."

"But he ain't sweet on you," Arn replied. "Besides, I want you broken in by Slate here. It'll make you more cooperative later once you know what can happen to you."

"I'll cooperate," Raven said. "Please, this isn't necessary."

"That's right," Sadie agreed. "I want my friend here. Ted'll be upset if she's been harmed."

"Slate's not going to harm her, little lady. He's

going to make her feel real good. Now, get her out of here, Slate, before we all change our minds and join you."

Slate took Raven's hand, noticed she still clung to the shirts, and flung Hank's shirt on top of his still form. "Somebody pour some water on Hank. Otherwise, he'll be out till dark."

Slate picked up his gunbelt, buckled it on, and began pulling Raven away from the camp. They heard the splash of water and Hank bellow. But when Sadie began crying out in protest, Raven dug in her heels and turned back. Her friend was being professionally tied by what must have been a former cowboy and she shuddered at Sadie's discomfort.

But Slate forced her forward again, down the arroyo and away from the others. When no one else could hear them, he said, "Trust me, Raven. Sadie will be all right, and I'm not going to hurt you. I simply couldn't let Hank have you."

"I can't see that there's much difference between the two of you," she countered.

"You know there's a hell of a difference," he muttered, then took longer strides, hurrying them away from the camp.

The gully narrowed and Slate headed for a break in the arroyo's steep walls. He climbed up broken rock, helping Raven to keep up with him. Outside the gully, they were in thick forest again. He turned west, following a narrow overgrown trail through fragrant evergreen trees.

A quiet peacefulness surrounded them as they left the outlaw camp, as if they were completely alone in the world, and, despite herself, Raven began to relax, feeling the terrible tension that had gripped her since the outlaws had entered the observation car drain away. Her thoughts then turned to Ted.

130

What had he done? Had he sent men searching for them, or was he waiting for his outlaw gang to report? Would there be help from him, or would he leave them to the outlaws? No, he would never leave Sadie to the mercy of these desperate men. He genuinely cared for her, whether he was the mastermind or not. But they couldn't wait for rescue. They had to find some way to escape before then. She had to get away from Slate, but he was taking her deeper and deeper into unknown territory.

"Slate, please. I can't go on. I'm too tired."

"Not much farther now. We'll be safe from the others. I've got a little food stored up here. There are a couple of blankets. You can eat, relax, tell me what happened."

"Tell you what happened?"

"Yes."

"That's ridiculous. You were in on the plans. You know."

There was a long silence, then Slate said, "Did he hurt you, Raven? I'll kill him if he did."

He meant it. Raven was shocked. "No. I mean, I'm scratched and sore, but he didn't really hurt me."

"Did he touch you?"

"He groped at . . . at my breasts."

"Damn!"

"But I kept fighting him off all night."

"I never dreamed something like this would happen. Didn't even know you'd be on the train."

"Would it have mattered? If it hadn't been us, it'd have been some other Harvey Girls."

"Believe me, I had no idea they'd kidnap anybody. Although I can't blame Hank for wanting to. I wanted to kidnap you in Topeka and carry you right out of that boarding house. Hardest thing I ever did

131

was leave you there."

Raven was having trouble remembering he was an outlaw and that she was furious with him. For some reason she kept thinking of him as she had in Topeka. "It was hard to send you away," she finally said.

"I'm glad." He squeezed her hand. "Here we are."

He pushed apart several bushes, and indicated for her to squeeze between them. She bent down, started through, then felt a tree limb catch her hair. She stopped, and Slate moved closer to help her. She could feel his body heat, and suddenly trembled. What was she doing out here, completely alone with a man who could make her react so wildly to him? But what choice did she have? Slate carefully freed her hair, then they both slipped inside.

She was surprised. They were in a beautiful mountain glade. Evergreen trees rose majestically all around them and the scent of pine was strong in the air. They stood on soft pine needles which had collected over the years to make a thick bed around a small sunlit pond in the center. It was spring fed, and when Raven sent a ripple across its smooth surface she discovered it was warm. She looked up at Slate in amazement.

"Beautiful here, isn't it?"

"But the water's warm, like it's been heated."

"Natural mineral spring, probably connected to those at Montezuma. Long before Harvey built the hotel, the Indians used to bathe in the healing springs around here."

"It's lovely, Slate."

"And safe. And private."

"But you're here."

"With me, you'e safe and private, Raven."

"I don't think so."

"You'll see. But you must be tired and hungry."

"And dirty. I would love a bath."

"So would I."

"In private."

"Like I said, you can be private as much as you want as long as it's with me. I was going to see you nude some time, Raven. Why not now?"

"It's daylight."

"Better yet." He sat down and pulled off a dusty boot.

"You're not going to undress, are you?"

"I don't usually bathe with my clothes on."

"Then I'll have to leave."

"Where're you going?"

"I could wait outside."

"You're in the mountains. Lots of bear. Mountain lions. Wolves."

Raven hesitated. "I'll take your gun with me."

"No. You'll stay right here. Take your clothes off, Raven. I've been wanting to see you for a long time. I just won you in a fair fight. You're mine."

"I am *not* yours. You can't win someone."

"I'm not even going to pay." He let the other boot drop.

"I don't want you to pay. I don't want you at all."

"You don't mean that." He stood up, unbuttoned his denims, and let them fall to the ground.

Chapter Ten

Raven gasped, and whirled around so she could no longer see him. But imprinted on her mind was the long tawny strength of him and the long hard shaft that was so ready for her.

"Raven?" Strong fingers bit into her shoulders. She tried to shrug him away.

"What's wrong? Don't you like the way I look?"

"No. I mean, yes. Of course I like the way you look. It's just that . . ."

"You're the damnedest woman I've ever known. It's not like you'd never seen a man's body before. Anyway, I thought we were through playing games."

Raven took a deep, ragged breath. "Go ahead and take your bath. I think I'd like something to eat."

"No. We're going to do everything together. Now turn around and I'll undress you. Damn, they really dragged you through the woods, didn't they?"

"Yes. I can undress myself, Slate, but —"

"I know you can. This reminds me of another time. I wanted you so bad then it hurt. We aren't going to wait this time, Raven." His breath was warm on the back of her neck.

What was she going to do? Just being near him made her all hot and cold at the same time. And the

134

sight of his nude body made her want to caress him, and yet she couldn't. She was a virgin and she'd been engaged to a wonderful man. Slate *wasn't* a wonderful man. He was a criminal, and yet . . .

He turned her around to face him, and she trembled.

"If I didn't know better, I'd think you'd never been with a man. I'll be gentle with you. I know you've been scared and hurt. I'm sorry. But I'll make it all better for you now."

He'd been hurt, too. She'd seen the bruises and old scars on his body, and his lip was swelling where Hank had cut it.

He tilted her face up so he could look into her eyes. His were a deep warm blue, hers midnight black. "I could drown in your eyes, Raven. I could take you right now, but I want it to be good for you, too. We're going to bathe first, eat, and then I'm going to make love to you like I've wanted to since I first saw you in that red satin gown in Topeka."

"Slate, I don't think—"

"Don't say anything. You don't have to think or worry or talk right now. Let me take care of you."

She shuddered as he began to remove the white apron, now sadly wrinkled, soiled, and ripped. She should run away, or scream, or hit him, or grab his gun. Instead, she couldn't seem to move, didn't want to think anymore. She just wanted to feel all he had to offer. It was wrong, and she didn't care.

He threw the apron aside. "You don't need that anymore anyway. This black dress is enough, more than enough." His hands were quick and sure until he reached her camisole and petticoats. Those he dealt with quickly, too. Soon she stood in just her corset and drawers, her black stockings tattered rags barely clinging to her legs.

She could hardly believe she stood before him in so few clothes, but she was glad her gold piece had been hidden in a pocket of her dress, for she wouldn't have wanted him to know she carried it with her all the time.

"Damn, you've got bruises and you're raw where that damn saddle rubbed you. Hank should have been more careful with you."

Slate knelt and gently removed her shoes, then pulled her stockings away, softly kissing her wounds.

His touch sent a wave of weakness through her, and she put a hand on his back to steady herself. How could he affect her so strongly?

"You've got beautiful legs, but I suppose you've been told that before."

"I think I'm undressed far enough, Slate."

"Worried that bunch will bust in here? Forget it. I'm the only one who knows about this place. It's all ours, for now and always."

"No. It's not that. I'm just . . ."

But his hands were on her corset and Raven's breath caught in her throat. When the corset came free, he tossed it aside, saying, "You don't need one of those. Ever. You're perfect. Most beautiful breasts I've ever seen. You've kept me awake a lot of nights. Never had a woman affect me like you do. *Never.*"

Raven tried to take a deep breath, but could hardly move she felt so weak, so pliable, so hot deep inside. His body, his words, his presence were already entering her, making her a part of him, making her want to complete their union.

Then he slipped her drawers down, exposing the last of her, and caught his breath, hesitated a long moment, as if unable to breathe or move or act himself, then hugged her to him. She felt his long hard shaft slide between her legs, and moaned, unable to stop the sound.

"I know, Raven. I know. Let's get in the water before I can't stop myself."

Raven only began to come back to herself when the warm clear waters of the pond lapped around her breasts. Slate was vigorously rubbing himself with sand and she watched as his body reddened, the skin smooth and sleek except for the dark hairs everywhere. He was a handsome man, no doubt about it, and she wanted him.

It was wrong to want him, wrong even to consider merging her body with his. But in a short time he'd be gone, out of her life forever. She didn't want to lose him before she'd known fully what her body demanded. It was wrong, but she wanted him and he wanted her.

He began to rub sand against her body. She eased out of the warm, mineral-scented water, letting him do whatever he wanted. It all felt good. She shut her eyes against the light, against the truth, and let only her inner feelings surface. He was very gentle when he came to the bruises, scratches, and scrapes, and she felt the tension and fear and worry drain out of her.

He eased her back into the water. "Do you believe in fate, Raven?"

She shook her head, too relaxed to speak.

"I hadn't thought much about it until I met you. I think we were fated, no matter our pasts, to be together."

She smiled softly, opening her eyes. He was regarding her very intently and his eyes had turned slightly gray. "Does it matter? We're here now, together."

"The feelings are so intense, so unexpected. That's why I think of fate when I think of you."

"Am I fated to go hungry?"

He laughed. "No. Will dried beef and hard bread do? I hid some up here earlier when I found the place." He brought out the food and offered it to her.

"After the fare I've been serving and eating on the Montezuma Special, this hardly seems like food at all."

"But it is, and better than nothing."

They ate slowly, contemplating each other. Raven felt almost safe concealed beneath the warm spring water and almost content, as if she and Slate had known each other a long time, had done this before. Maybe he was right about fate. Maybe from the first they were destined to end this way, far from home and in each other's arms. Whatever the case, she could fight him no longer, could fight herself no longer. She needed him, wanted him, no matter how wrong it was because it was right for now, for her, for him.

"I can keep you away all day, Raven, but we'll have to go back tonight."

"I don't ever want to go back to that outlaw camp, but I'm worried about Sadie."

"Sadie'll be all right. You were smart to mention Simpson. No one would dare hurt her now. She's their ace in the hole".

And yours, too, Raven wanted to say but said instead, "I had to do something."

"You did the right thing. I wish we didn't have to go back, either. I know we've both got unfinished business. But I don't want to think about anything except you."

He slipped through the water to her, then let his body trail the length of hers. She could feel his hardness probing, ready for her, and she was just as ready for him. Her nipples hardened. She leaned her head back against the bank, unconsciously arching herself up against him.

Slate groaned, and spread soft kisses up her throat to her lips. There he nibbled, teasing, until she bit him, then he pushed inside, probing, searching, taking. She responded in kind, hungrily meeting every thrust of his tongue, until he broke away, muttering, "I don't know if I can wait any longer."

"Love me Slate. I need you so."

He pulled her up on the soft green moss that lined the mountain pool, then stretched out beside her, running long sensitive fingers down her body, pausing to circle each nipple, then explore the depth of her navel before disappearing between her legs.

She moaned and moved restlessly, deep fires beginning to stir, and pulled him down to her, wanting to feel the heat of his flesh against hers. He was burning up, on fire for her. She bit his shoulder, tasted his flesh with her tongue, then nibbled at him until she reached his neck, moving up to his ear, where she toyed with the sensitive skin as her fingers dug deeply into his thick black hair.

He couldn't remain still under her touch. He moved lower, kissing, licking, tasting, to her breasts where he cupped the soft mounds with his hands. He touched their hard tips with his tongue, then teased them with his teeth before sucking until Raven arched up against him with desire. He moved lower, stroking with his tongue down her hot flesh, his hands going before him, tormenting her satiny skin until he reached her ankles.

He tickled her feet, the high insteps sensitive to

his every touch. She giggled, kicked out at him, and he teased her more before suddenly becoming serious. He quickly stretched over her, easing his long length down on top of her, then spread her legs and raised them. As he prodded at the entrance to her very core, Raven suddenly became afraid, for at that moment she could see a very clear picture of Sam in her mind. How could she do this to Sam, her dead fiancé?

She began struggling, pushing at Slate, trying to wrench away from him, furious with herself, with him, with the situation.

"Damn, Raven! What're you doing?"

"No! Please, no."

"Did I hurt you? What's wrong?"

"No. No. It's all wrong."

"You're upset, that's all. Quiet down."

He pressed soft kisses to her face, but she didn't want that, didn't want to be stroked gently, or caressed into compliance. She was hot, felt tortured inside, and bit him. Hard.

Slate jerked back, his eyes growing dark. "Raven, why are you angry?"

"It's wrong." She bit him again, scratching his back, trying to push him away, and yet at the same time pulling him closer.

She seemed to ignite something in him. His gentleness faded, replaced by a hunger that she had not seen before, had not realized lay just under the surface of his desire. But it matched her own urgent need, her own dark desire to have him.

He kissed her hard, and she tasted blood. She had forgotten that he had fought for her, that he was just this side of unleashing that violence again, but she didn't care. She cared only about the hot passion and fury that were burning through her and the pain that was part of it all. This should have been Sam with her on their wedding night, a sweet, tender, thoughtful love. But it wasn't. This was dark forbidden desire, hidden passions, haunted by everything that had gone before. She could deny it no longer. She dug her fingers into his hair, pulled his face to hers, and kissed him hard with a pulsing need that surprised them both.

His fingers bruised her as they dug into her every curve and valley, determined to reach into her and devour every part of her. But she was devouring him, too, biting him, licking him, sucking at him, unable to taste him, or feel him, or be with him enough.

It was the same for him until he finally could stand no more and jerked her hips upward and plunged into her fiery heat. Then he stopped. Brought up short.

"Raven?"

She tossed her head back and forth, caught up in the frenzy of the passion they had created. "Please, Slate. Please . . ."

"Raven, are you sure?"

"Yes. Yes, please."

Then he forced past her last defense and she cried out at the sudden pain, then forgot everything in the intensity of feeling that came with every stroke that he struck deep within her.

"Slate," she cried out, raising her head to look at him. Sweat beaded his forehead. There seemed to be as much pain as pleasure in his eyes, then he moved hard and fast and she flung back her head as she went swimming through eddies of passion and pleasure, fire and ice, before falling at last into a cool mountain glade of release.

Slate followed her, crying out with his own fulfillment as he clasped her to him, rocking deep within her as if he would never let her go. Then he fell beside her, sweating. "Damn you, Raven, you were a virgin."

She took several deep breaths, trying to still her racing heart. He was angry. But why?

"What game are you playing? You had me convinced you were an experienced woman. Then you turn out to be a virgin. You'd better have a good explanation."

"In some areas of the country virginity is considered valuable."

"To catch a husband."

Raven hesitated. "Do you think this was some ruse to get you to marry me?"

When he didn't reply, she continued. "Of all the big-headed, egocentric, stupid things to think. If you'll recall, you pursued me in Topeka. If you'll recall, you fought for me a little while ago. And if you'll *also* recall, I was against this from the first."

"But you weren't against it a little while ago."

"It was wrong. I knew it was wrong, but . . ."

"But what?"

"I don't know." She stood up, tears burning her eyes. It was all a stupid mess, a mistake. "I'm going to get dressed. Take me back. I'm going to get out of all this somehow."

"Sit down."

"No."

"Sit."

She got in the water. She'd never felt such a need to be clean.

He followed her, but stayed across the pool, watching her intently. "Why didn't you tell me? I wouldn't have forced a virgin . . . but I didn't force you anyway . . ."

142

He didn't sound as angry now, more confused than anything.

"I forgot."

"You *forgot* you were a virgin?"

"Well, in the heat of the moment . . ."

"This doesn't mean I'm going to marry you, Raven."

"I *wouldn't* marry you. Do you think I'd commit myself to some outlaw?"

"You could reform me."

"No, I wouldn't fall into that trap."

"Then why did you let me take you?"

"Does it matter?"

"Yes. Women don't just throw that type of thing away. You had to have a very good reason."

"I didn't throw it away. You know what it was like. I wanted you. All right?"

He was silent a long moment, a silence full of suspicion. "I wish I could believe you, but you're up to something. I don't know what. Maybe you're working for the railroad, or something."

"I am. Remember, I'm a Harvey Girl."

"Nothing about you fits."

"I seemed to fit you just fine earlier."

"Oh, that fits all right. The only thing about us that fits, and it fits too fine."

"Look, I don't want to discuss this anymore. I'm terribly sorry if you were surprised, but you were the one who kept pushing this. Now I just want to get to Montezuma."

"Whatever you are, Raven, whatever your crafty little plans are, there's one fact between us. I fought for you, and I won. You're mine while we're in these mountains."

"Maybe I'll just take up with one of the other outlaws, like that Arn."

"Don't try it. I won't tolerate that of you or them. You're mine and I'm keeping you."

"I'm going back to the camp. I'd rather be with the other outlaws than you."

"You're going no place until I say so. I won you and we're going to stay right here and enjoy all day long what you've just discovered."

"Don't push me, Slate. I'm getting angry."

"You think that matters? Just what do you think Hank would have done with you if he'd won.?"

She didn't respond.

"And he wouldn't have been nearly so gentle."

"I don't feel like you were very gentle."

"The first time can be painful, but it shouldn't be again."

"I'm delighted to know that," she said sarcastically, not knowing whether to cry, or run, or hit him.

"Look, I'm sorry. I shouldn't have said what I did. I wanted you bad, too. I still want you. You just caught me by surprise."

"Fine time for you to start being nice," she remarked flippantly.

"Don't be so smart. I'm not being nice. I'm trying to be honest. I don't know why things are so mixed up between us, Raven. I don't know why they can't just be straightforward. All I ever wanted to do was buy you for the night and now I find out you never were really for sale after all. Why were you all dressed up like that?"

Raven suddenly realized she was very close to losing her cover. She had to be careful. Her father and fiancé had been killed on this case. Everything pointed to the fact that Slate worked for the mastermind and Comanche Jack. She couldn't let him know the truth, or she might be the third one dead.

144

"I . . . I'm looking for my uncle."

"I thought that was just some story you told Sadie so she wouldn't question your past."

"No, I told her the truth. You were the one who insisted I was a lady of the evening."

"That's what you were dressed like."

"Well, I needed to visit the silver exchanges. I couldn't very well have gone as a real lady, could I? Who would have given me information then?"

"You've got a point, but you're not like any lady I ever knew."

"And you've known a lot of ladies?"

Slate grinned. "Ladies of the evening."

"Just what I thought."

"So, who is this uncle of yours? He must mean a lot for a well-brought-up little lady like you to come West, dress up like a madam, and give her virginity to an outlaw."

"He's my only living relative."

"And he's worth a small fortune?"

Raven made it up as she went. "Well, it seems he did do quite well in mining, but he disappeared."

"And if he's proven dead, the next of kin to take over the nice little bankroll is you."

"Well, I could use the money, Slate."

"I was right the first time. Your heart's made of gold."

"Maybe you could melt it."

"Not me. I don't care what you say, you're really a whore at heart, Raven."

"Is that an insult?" she quipped sarcastically.

"Take it any way you want. All I know is that I just never offered enough."

Ignoring his barb, she continued, "Like I said, I'm here to find my uncle."

"Dead or alive."

"Right."

"And then?"

"Well, it was rather dull in Chicago. I mean, the West is turning out to be quite exciting."

"I guess so. You probably didn't seduce too many outlaws in that fair city."

"I *didn't* seduce you, Slate."

"That's the only rational explanation for what just happened. You aren't the kind of woman I admire."

"But I'm the kind of woman you want."

"Seems like it."

"Well, I've found that to be the case with me, too. You are a despicable man, preying on others, but there's something magnetic about you. Thanks for awakening me. I think I'll be better off without my virginity in the West."

"Damn you, Raven. If you think I did that just so you can go out and seduce other men to your whims, you've got another think coming."

"Yes, and what is that?"

Slate paused, and smiled coldly. "This."

He kissed her long and hard, and eventually when her anger turned to passion she opened her mouth to him and he pushed deep inside. As their wild desire began to eclipse everything else, Raven clung to Slate and the fire of their passion forged another link in the chain that bound them together.

Chapter Eleven

Raven was a changed woman when Slate headed them toward the outlaw camp at dusk. The change was internal as well as external, and she didn't like it one bit. Slate had left his mark on her in too many ways and she didn't know how to get rid of it, didn't even know if she could.

He'd branded her. That's the way he'd put it. And it hurt. She felt like she'd lost a part of herself, or gained a part of him. She didn't know which, didn't want to know, just wanted everything to go back to the way it was. But it wouldn't just yet, and she didn't know how to deal with it.

She glanced at the tall lean man who walked beside her. Possessive. Radiating male satisfaction. And pride.

And she? A tiny quiver invaded her just at the thought of his hands on her, of his lips arousing her once more, of him thrusting deep inside her. How could she stand it? How could she keep on going, knowing what she knew now, knowing what she wanted now, and knowing only one man—a totally unacceptable man—could give it to her.

She bit her lower lip, winced at the pain, then touched her reddened, swollen lips. Slate had said she looked well loved. She supposed he was right. Her hair was a long, tassled, silvery blond mass down her back, her lips were rosy red and pouty from being kissed so often, her body felt all tingly and fiery and moulten, still ready for love.

They'd left the white apron behind, her black dress was unbuttoned, revealing just the beginning of her cleavage, for she couldn't seem to cool off. She wore no corset, no stockings, simply a pair of black leather shoes. She no longer resembled an efficient Harvey Girl, or professional Chicago private investigator. She looked and felt vulnerable, and it made her want to strike out at Slate Slayton.

For he looked carefree and relaxed, swinging his gunbelt and cotton shirt in one hand, leaving the other free to caress her now and then. Every time he touched her she burned up and down her body. She didn't know what to think, or say, or do. It was all wrong, and yet he had invaded her senses, her body, her thoughts, and she didn't know if she could ever get him out again. And yet she must.

Slate suddenly stopped and said, "We'll be there soon, Raven. I want you to know that if things were different, I could—"

"Could what? Keep me in the mountains longer?"

"I'd like to stay with you longer, yes, but—"

"Burn your brand deeper?"

"I don't know what you're mad about."

"I'm not exactly mad. I'm just—"

"You're tired and scared and you've got to go back into that camp and deal with it. I understand, but I'll be there beside you."

"You're part of that gang, Slate."

"But you're my woman now. I'll protect you. And

I'll protect Sadie because of you."

Raven remembered a time when she'd protected herself, or at least thought she had. "I can take care of myself and Sadie." And she could. She had to remember that. At least she could protect herself from most things. But how did she protect herself from Slate? And could she really believe he would help save Sadie just because of his desire for her?

"That's what you keep telling me, but you're in the West now, and there are a lot of mean hombres around."

"Such as you?"

"Not where you've concerned. Like I said, I'll take care of you. And Sadie. Don't worry. I just wish things were different for us now."

"Well, they aren't, and the only sensible thing to do is go our separate ways."

"We *aren't* going our separate ways, Raven. At least not yet. We're going back to that camp, and if you want to stay healthy you'd better act like I'm the man of your dreams. You'd better not even look at one of the other men or—"

"You'll do what?"

"I won't stand for it. Not now. I've branded you and that's that. But if you encourage them, they'll try for you, and I don't want to be forced to hurt somebody else over you. But I will."

"I'm not interested in those other men. They're outlaws! I'm not even interested in you."

"You can't expect me to believe that."

"All right. You *make* me interested in you, but I don't want to be."

"You're more stubborn than any mule I ever knew."

"Slate, would you say we've got it out of our system now?"

149

"No."

"But I thought—"

"So did I. I guess we'll have to work at it a while longer."

"No! I can't stand it." She turned on him, wanting to strike out at him, hurt him, make him feel the pain she felt, but didn't know how. "It's all wrong between us. It's just all wrong. I want to be left alone."

He pulled her to him, craddling her gently against his chest, stroking her silvery blond hair. "I know this is all new to you. I know you don't like me being an outlaw. Maybe I could change my ways for you, but not right now. I've got a job I have to finish first."

"Just let me go please."

"I can't do that, either. I'll hold on to you as long as I can. Damn, Raven! You felt it between us. We can't deny it. I *won't,* and I won't let you. Now lets get back to camp. I've got to figure a way to get you and Sadie out of there safely." He released her, took her hand, and started for the camp again.

Raven went along quietly, thinking about everything Slate had said. Slate wasn't going to give her up until he'd had his fill. When would that be? Could she continue, knowing it had to end, knowing it was wrong, and yet unable to stop the craving? It was much worse than a desire for peppermint candy.

Maybe she should look at it that way. If she could somehow separate it into a small part of her mind and life, maybe she could deal with her strange craving for Slate Slayton. She took a deep breath, and felt a little better. That was it. She had just been overcome with the overwhelming intensity of it all. That was probably normal. After all, it had been her first time and since Slate was her first lover, she probably had attributed more to her emotions than she should have.

That's right. Wanting Slate was like wanting peppermint candy. You got what you wanted, had your fill, then set it aside until you craved it again or you had time for a little treat. Now she was definitely feeling better. She ran a hand through her hair, pushing it from her face. All right. She could handle that. It didn't mean he'd branded her forever. It meant that every once in a while, they'd take each other off the counter, peel off the outer wrapping, and enjoy all the sweetness they could handle.

She smiled. Everything was going to be fine. She'd had her piece of candy, now she had to concentrate on getting some information. She still had to find her father and fiancé's murderer, and complete the railroad job. Of course, what she'd experienced with Slate had nothing to do with what she'd felt for Sam. Sam had been a forever love, Slate was just a momentary excitement.

She was feeling a lot better now. She could handle the situation, handle Slate, and handle the outlaws. She'd get Sadie free, and they'd go to the Montezuma. If ever two people needed the luxury of a fancy hotel, she and Sadie needed it now.

Slate hesitated outside the hidden arroyo, and glanced down at Raven. "Feel up to going back?"

She looked up at him. He was just a too tall Texas outlaw and he was back on the shelf with all the other candy. "Sure," she said. "I want to get to the Montezuma."

Slate looked surprised for a moment, then nodded. "Remember, I'll protect you."

"Thanks. And, Slate, it was a fine day. I never dreamed you could give me so much pleasure."

He brightened. "I knew it would be good between us, Raven. I just didn't know how good."

"Very good," she said, smiling, then stepped into the arroyo, her mind set on her next move. If she had to, she'd steal a pistol and force her way out. No two-bit outlaws were going to stop her plans.

They walked down the narrow gully and found the outlaws lying around a low campfire, occasionally prodding Sadie with a long stick. It obviously had been a quiet, boring day for them. They were glad to see Slate and Raven arrive.

"Looks like you broke her in good, Slate," Arn said. "That's the way I like to see them, soft and willing."

Raven simply raised her chin, and knelt beside Sadie. Her friend had been hogtied, and her circulation had been severely restricted. Sadie looked in considerable pain.

"Untie her at once," Raven demanded, looking at Arn. "You can't keep her bound up like this all the time. You'll hurt her."

"That's the idea," one of the outlaws replied.

"But it's been all day," Raven protested.

"She's all right," Arn said.

"She is not," Raven insisted. "At least, let her up and tie her more loosely."

"Any of you men want to do that?" Arn asked lazily.

One of the outlaws got up and sauntered over. He slowly began to untie her, careful to make sure he touched her as much as the rope.

Raven gave Slate a hard stare, but he shook his head, warning her to leave it alone. She sat down beside Sadie, and began massaging her wrists and hands while the cowboy finished untying her ankles. "How are you, Sadie?"

Sadie smiled wanly. "I'll be all right. I just keep imagining I'm in the Montezuma, relaxing in a warm, healing mineral bath."

"Does it help?"

"Not much."

"You must be hungry. Is there something to eat?" Raven asked, glancing at Arn.

He indicated some dried beef, beans, and coffee.

Raven got some for Sadie, then found that she was hungry, too. They ate in silence for a time, watching the outlaws. At least Sadie didn't seem to be hurt, other than the agony of having been tied up all day.

Slate got some food, then hunkered down beside Arn. "We've been talking about what's best to do with the Harvey Girls," Arn said.

"And?" Slate asked.

"Going to keep Miss Sadie here, and send the other one back."

Raven felt her heart sink, and Sadie dropped her cup of coffee.

"The railroad's been nosing around too much. Fact is, they sent in a couple of fancy guns to ferret us out. Also happens, those two guys wound up dead, so it's been harder to get information lately."

Raven poured Sadie more coffee, her mind whirling. Another lead. Arn had to be discussing her father's and Sam's deaths. She needed more information, but this was a good beginning and T.R. Simpson seemed to be right in the middle of it. She didn't know if Ted were protecting his position by keeping information from the outlaw gangs, or if he were truly more careful because he was innocent. In any case, someone had leaked the news about the Montezuma payroll, and Ted was a prime suspect.

"Plus, we got this Harvey Girl kidnapping hang-

153

ing over our heads. They probably think the women are dead by now."

"How're you planning to handle it?" Slate asked, taking a gulp of hot coffee.

"Going to send your Harvey Girl back alone. With a message. We want that Montezuma Special sent south through New Mexico. There's a major gold mine down there. They're getting a big shipment ready. We want the Montezuma Special to handle it real careful for them, and then we'll be kind enough to relieve the train of its burden."

"How can a Harvey Girl manage that?" Slate asked.

"Alone, she can't. But we send her back and she tells Simpson we're holding his sweetheart hostage. He either does what we say, or we kill her. Simple, right?"

"Real smart," Slate agreed.

"And she tells him to lay off us, or the Harvey Girl gets it."

"Good protection," Slate agreed again, then asked, "How're you going to make sure my Harvey Girl does what you want?"

"We got two ways, and one of those is where you come in. First, the Harvey Girls are friends. We're going to send your woman back, but if she does anything we don't like, or tells anything she shouldn't, Sadie here's going to get hurt. We might send her one of Sadie's fingers one at a time."

Horrified, Raven said, "I'll do whatever you want, just don't hurt Sadie."

Arn looked at Slate. "See, it's easy. She'll do what we say and you'll be there to make sure she does. You got a fresh face around here. Nobody'll connect you with the gang since you're just up from Texas. You'll go in separate. We'll have some men in the area. There'll be an accident on the train, and you'll be Johnny on the spot and take over. Okay?"

"Sounds good," Slate replied, nodding.

"This'll put us in good with Comanche Jack, and make us all richer."

The other outlaws all murmured in agreement.

Raven squeezed Sadie's hand, and whispered, "Don't worry, Sadie. I'll get you out of this. It'll be all right. Just be strong."

Sadie nodded, then clinched Raven's hand for a moment. "Thanks, Raven. I know I can depend on you and Ted. Tell him . . . I love him, and that I'm all right."

"I will. Don't worry. We'll get you out of here as soon as possible."

There wasn't much else to say, although Raven wished she could do or say something more. But right now they were at the mercy of the outlaws and they had to play by their rules until Raven could get free.

"I'd just as soon not ride in separately," Slate said, eyeing Raven possessively.

"We thought you might be tired of her by now," Arn replied. "We were discussing Hank taking her back to Las Vegas, or maybe to the station at Santa Fe."

Slate frowned. "I'm not tired of her. I won that fight fair, and she's still mine. I'm going to be on the train with her and I'll keep her under control."

Arn laughed, looking at Raven's subdued face. "Okay, I'll send her back with you, but several of the men will go along. Then you separate outside of town. I want her walking in alone, confused and lost. The railroad'll take over at that point."

"Sounds good," Slate agreed, but Hank scowled and muttered to himself.

"You hear that, Harvey Girl?" Arn called. "You'll walk in alone, but my men'll be all around watching. No word to anybody except Simpson." Turning to his men, Arn added, "I think you'd better ride over to Las Vegas. It's closer than Santa Fe. But be careful. I don't want any of you recognized. Okay, that's the plan."

"When do we leave?" Slate asked.

"Tomorrow at dawn. Now we might as well get a good night's sleep. I don't want anything going wrong tomorrow."

Although it was still early, night had fallen and Raven was very tired. She watched, unable to stop them, as they tied Sadie up again, but not as tightly or severely as before. When Slate came for her, indicating she should share his blanket, she went with him quietly. The main thing was to get out of the camp safely, then she could do something to help free Sadie.

They lay down together. When Slate pulled her into his warmth, she felt the quick response of her body, and his. He tossed a blanket over them.

"I could take you here and now and not give a damn," he whispered into her ear. "That's how much I want you."

Raven shook her head in denial, well aware that Hank was watching them from his bedroll not far away.

"I know Hank's watching, but I don't care. I've got a fever for you that won't quit."

"Slate, please."

"It's going to be a long time before I can make you mine again. I wish we were going to Las Vegas alone."

"Please, Hank's watching and listening."

"Let him. Nothing says we have to stay here

tonight."

"Slate, I have to ride a horse tomorrow. I don't know if I can sit one now, much less if you . . ."

Slate chuckled. "Sore?"

"Yes," she hissed, already craving the feel of him inside her, already hot for him again, already anxious to lose herself in their passion. But she couldn't allow herself that pleasure, not now. Too much else was at stake.

Slate cupped her hips with a long, strong hand, and replied, "Maybe you'd better ride with me."

"No!"

He rolled her over so he could look into her face. "You're beautiful, Raven," he whispered, then covered her lips with his.

It was a gentle kiss, restrained and yet reminding her of all the power he could suddenly unleash. When he ended it, she wanted more.

"I'm not going to hurt you, or endanger you or Sadie, but that doesn't stop me from wanting you all the time. Now get some sleep. It'll be just as dangerous tomorrow. I wouldn't put it past Hank to try and shoot me in the back on the way to Las Vegas."

Raven didn't doubt that Hank would kill Slate in a minute, but she wondered again if his motive for saving her and Sadie was based solely on the fact that he had made her his woman.

That at least was true she thought as she gently touched his face. The bruises he'd gotten from fighting were beginning to darken and discolor his face. That was one other thing she couldn't deny, too. He *had* saved her from Hank! She smiled. "Thanks."

"Wait till you're safe, and Sadie, too, to thank me."

She nodded again, then snuggled close to him, feeling safe in his arms, despite her doubts. She watched the campfire for a while, listened to Slate's rhythmic breathing, and fell asleep to the sound of coyotes howling in the distance.

Part Two
Bright Desert Days

Chapter Twelve

Standing outside the train station at Las Vegas, New Mexico, Raven felt the strain of the long day just passed. She'd said tearful good-byes with Sadie at dawn, then started for Las Vegas with Slate, Hank, and two other of Arn's best men. They'd ridden hard and fast all day, with only a few stops to rest the horses along the way.

Slate had stayed close beside her, his eyes hot with desire whenever he looked at her. But Hank had been close, too, watching her, watching Slate. She had feared for Slate's life, but Hank had done nothing with so many people around. She had also feared being along again with Slate, knowing what his touch could do to her.

But there had been no time for them to be alone. Hank had been there, and there had been the pressure of reaching Las Vegas by dusk. Raven was glad there hadn't been time for another confrontation with Slate. She'd felt much too vulnerable to make the right decision, the decision she knew must eventually win out because Slate was an outlaw and her job was to bring criminals to justice. There could never be anything between them, and yet her body continued to deny that fact.

But now was not the time to think about Slate Slayton. She had to think about Arn's plan and how she was going to reach Ted as quickly as possible. So far, everything had gone according to plan. Slate had disappeared into the dusty streets of Las Vegas and Hank and the other outlaws had joined the crowd milling around the train station. Now it was up to her.

With so many people about, it was obvious a train was due in soon and Raven was glad all the people would camouflage her entrance. She wanted as little attention as possible, for the less anyone other than Ted knew about Sadie and the situation the safer they would all be.

She started up the stairs to the wooden depot, knowing she was dusty, bedraggled, and didn't look in the least like a Harvey Girl, especially without her identifying white apron. For that matter, she didn't feel like a Harvey Girl, or even like a private investigator. She felt tired, sore, and vulnerable.

But she couldn't let any of that stop her. Sadie was depending on her. She had to keep going. Raising her chin and strengthening her courage, she walked into the Santa Fe train station. It was crowded inside, too. She glanced around, trying to decide what to do and yet knowing all she really wanted was a hot bath, a big meal, and to sleep for several days.

Maybe then she could forget Slate and what he did to her. He was bad for her, no doubt, even if he did seem to want to help her and Sadie. If she could just have walked away from him at this point, it would have been easier to forget him. But that wasn't going to be the case.

She was being forced into his company and she must deal with him. But how? She reminded herself that he was like peppermint candy, and right now he was on the shelf. She couldn't let him make her forget all her responsibilities. Sadie depended on her. Justice for her father and fiancé depended on her. And yet, Slate would be there, tempting her to forget everything but what she felt in his arms.

She had to get tough, really tough. After all, she *was* a private investigator from Chicago. It was time she started thinking like one. Tough.

She glanced at a wall with circulars advertising Atchison, Topeka and Santa Fe train schedules and Harvey House menus, then looked closer. There was a full color poster for the Montezuma, advertising Margarita, the famous singing and dancing sensation from Texas. Raven stepped nearer. Yes, the drawing of the beautiful woman was certainly the same entertainer Slate had introduced her to in Topeka.

Raven's heart seemed to contract. Margarita! So Slate was playing a double game. He and Margarita, working together, were probably planning some jewelry heists at the luxury hotel. And Slate as part of the outlaw gang was helping them rob the railroads. Well, he wasn't going to get away with it.

He'd probably seen Margarita frequently since leaving Topeka. He may have acted like he was starved for a woman when he was with her in the mountains, but Margarita's presence so near the outlaw camp was proof he hadn't been hurting at all.

Now it was she who hurt. She felt used and misled. Yet she had known about Margarita in Topeka. She'd just conveniently forgotten the other woman, for she couldn't deny there was something about Slate that made her ache for his embraces, even now when she knew he was a no-good two-timer. She bit her lower lip in frustration.

Here she'd been worrying about him being hurt by Hank. She'd be better off if Hank did shoot him in the back. No, that wasn't true. She didn't want that. She just wanted him to not be an outlaw and to be true to her.

Stupid, sentimental desires. It just wasn't like her. There was no place in her life for those types of feelings right now, especially not with a man like Slate. She had a job to do, a friend to rescue, and she had to get on with that.

But knowing Margarita had been so close to Slate all along still hurt, even when she knew it shouldn't. She tried to bring a vision of Sam's beloved face into her mind, but found she could no longer seem to remember his features very well. That was wrong. Sam had been her one true love and Slate was a passing fancy. But she could remember his face in detail while Sam's was quickly fading.

Taking a deep breath, she began making her way through the crowd. Suddenly a man bumped into her, grabbed her arm, and jerked her to one side.

She glanced at his face. It was Hank.

"Pretty Harvey Girl. Didn't think I'd forget about our personal business, did you?"

"Go away. Arn didn't want you to be seen with me."

"Nobody'll notice, and Arn would understand."

"I doubt if he would. Now leave me alone." She tried to pull out of his grip, but his hand tightened, sending pain radiating through her arm.

"I ain't never going to leave you alone, pretty woman. I stole you and you're mine."

"Ridiculous."

"Don't think you and Texas got it all to yourselves on that special train. Arn's no fool. We'll be around, watching you both. All the way."

"What do you mean?"

"What I said. Thought you'd be on that train alone with the Texan, didn't you? Well, you won't. We'll be there, too. So don't try anything smart."

"But I thought Arn said—"

"Don't matter. We'll be there. You'll never know where we are, but we'll always know where you are."

Raven shuddered.

"And when the job's over, I'm taking you back. Texas tricked me. I was all tired out from the robbery and the ride back. He was fresh. Fight wasn't fair. Everybody in the gang knows it now. That means you're still mine and when we get the gold, I get you."

"I am *not* yours and you're not taking me anywhere when this is over."

"Wrong, little lady. I'm taking you back as my woman."

"No you're not!"

"I don't like to hear you say no. Keep it up and I may have to punish you. It ain't so far across the border. Mexico has a lot of uses for pretty white women."

"You try anything like that and you'll be sorry."

"Trying to scare me?"

"No. That's fact."

"Good joke, pretty woman. Me and the men'll laugh about it while we're killing bottles at the Red Rooster."

"Go ahead and laugh, but you'd better leave me alone."

"I will for now. But soon, real soon, it's me going to make you happy, not that Texan."

He looked her up and down, squeezed her arm for emphasis, then headed for the door.

Raven stood motionless a long moment, trying to still her racing heart. She wished she had her father's .45, but it had been left on the train when she was kidnapped. Besides, it would only harm everything she was trying to do to show her hand now. But it infuriated her that a man like Hank thought he could do whatever he wanted with her and she could do nothing to stop him. Well, he had a surprise coming and she'd be glad to give it to him.

She'd simply watch out for him, and warn Slate. Hank wanted Slate dead, and wasn't above putting a bullet in Slate's back. But Slate had dealt with men like Hank before and could take care of himself. There was no need to worry about him. And yet she did, even knowing all she knew.

The important thing was the knowledge that Hank and the other two outlaws would be on the Montezuma Special. How they would get on, she didn't know. But she had faith that if Arn had ordered it, they would carry it out. She'd have to warn Slate about that, too, and Ted would need to know.

But for now she had other things to think about. She had to get to Ted Simpson as quickly and quietly as possible. Sadie's safety depended on it.

She glanced around the station. People sat on benches, clutching bags and boxes while others milled about, talking, waiting, anxious to begin their journey. Everyone was so busy with their own concerns they hardly noticed her, although a few gave her questioning looks. Those she stared down, then headed for one of the ticket windows. And stopped. There was something else she needed to do and she might not get another chance.

When the outlaws had brought her into town, she'd noticed a small telegraph office near the train station. She'd thought at the time that she should check for messages, for as R. Cunningham she had sent a telegram to both T.R. Simpson and Jeremy Luis Centrano telling them that they could communicate with her by leaving messages. She had then listed the towns she would be traveling through on her way from Kansas to Texas in search of the mastermind.

She didn't know when she would have another opportunity to be alone once she revealed her identity and she didn't want anyone to connect her with R. Cunningham. She stepped outside, then glanced around the crowd and down the street. She didn't see any of the outlaws. They were probably already on their way to the Red Rooster. Even if they saw her, they still wouldn't know exactly what she was doing.

As she started for the telegraph station, she realized she couldn't walk far. Her legs were so weak and sore that she could hardly move. She was an inexperienced rider and the long day on horseback had been rough. Fortunately the small building was not far and she soon reached it.

Stepping inside, she said, "I've been sent to collect any messages for R. Cunningham."

The clerk looked at her suspiciously, then checked the telegrams. He hesitated before handing her a slip of paper.

"Thank you," she said, taking it and noticing that he continued to watch her closely.

She turned her back, read the telegram, and smiled. Good. Her undercover role was working. Ted had sent R. Cunningham a telegram, requesting him to rescue Sadie Perkins. Perfect. Just what she would have wanted him to do.

She turned back to the counter and said, "I'd like

167

to send a telegram."

The man nodded and picked up a pencil.

Then Raven remembered she didn't have any money except the gold piece Slate had given her and she didn't want to use that. She also didn't want to send for funds from her Chicago bank. It was too risky here, what with the outlaws and her possible notoriety as the kidnapped Harvey Girl.

"Well?" the clerk finally prompted.

"It's for T.R. Simpson at the Montezuma."

"You mean *the* T.R. Simpson?"

"That's right, and he'll pay for it."

"Now wait a minute."

"He'll be very upset if he doesn't receive this message and will be glad to pay for it."

The clerk hesitated again, looked at her hard, then said, "All right, but you'll have to wait until someone on the other end agrees to accept the charge."

"Fine. Please send, 'Received your message. Am moving on new problem immediately. R. Cuningham.' "

"That's all?"

"Yes."

He began tapping it in, trying to keep an eye on her at the same time. "If they don't accept this, you'll have to pay anyway," he warned as he finished.

Raven edged toward the door.

He waited a moment, then said, "It's okay since it's from R. Cunningham."

"Thanks."

She was out the door and into the sunshine before he could say anything more. She exhaled in relief and started the slow, painful trip back to the depot. If she ever got near any hot water again, she was going to soak in it for days. Maybe then her legs would feel normal again. That is, if she could keep Slate away from her.

A tiny smile lifted the corners of her mouth as she remembered a moment of pleasure in the mountain glade. Then she pushed it away, forcing herself to remember that he was a two-timing outlaw, nothing more.

The lines were still long in the train station, and she got into place. It seemed a little ridiculous that one of the kidnapped Harvey Girls should have to wait in line. Yet it seemed the most reasonable and inconspicuous thing to do.

She didn't know how long she could stand there. Her legs were really weak and getting stiff as well as sore. If not for the urgency of telling Ted about Sadie, she might have just sat down and waited for the crowd to clear.

But Sadie was depending on her. There was no time to lose. She continued to stand until her turn came, then said, "I'm Raven West, one of the Harvey Girls who—"

"Miss West!" the young man exclaimed and immediately closed the ticket window. "I'm so sorry you had to wait. Please come into the back room. I'll notify T.R. Simpson at once. Everyone's been in an uproar about you and Sadie Perkins. Are you all right? Where's Miss Perkins? How did you escape? The sheriff'll want to know."

"I'm very tired. Please just contact Mr. Simpson."

"Certainly, but the authorities will have to know. Sit down right here and relax. Can I get you something? Coffee?"

"Yes, coffee. Thank you."

Raven eased herself onto a hard chair and accepted a steaming cup of coffee. The strong hot brew tasted good, and she watched as Santa Fe employees poked their heads in to have a look at her as word of her arrival spread from one employee to another. Soon the inbound train arrived and they were too busy to pay much attention to her for a while.

"Don't worry, Miss West," the young man returned, smiling. "I've sent a telegram to Montezuma. We'll be hearing back shortly from Mr. Simpson. In the meantime, I sent a boy over to the jail. The sheriff'll want to know all about the robbery and kidnapping and everything. We can't let outlaws get away with this type of thing. Imagine, kidnapping two Harvey Girls!"

"Thank you for your help, but I'm not talking to anyone except T.R. Simpson. This is Santa Fe business. I don't know how they'll want it handled."

"But the sheriff, ma'am?"

"He'll have to wait."

"There's a newspaper reporter, too. She works for the local—"

"Mr. Simpson and Santa Fe will want to see that I'm not disturbed by anyone until they've had a chance to review the facts. Everyone will have to wait until I've talked to T.R. Simpson."

"I don't know if I can—"

"That's all right, Bob," the station master said as he walked in, carrying a small piece of paper. "She's correct. Just got this message from Mr. Simpson. Soon as the train that just left for Montezuma unloads, he'll be back on it. Says to keep everything quiet. No law. No reporters. No noisy people around. Got it?"

"Yes, sir!"

"Miss West, Santa Fe is very sorry for this terrible situation. We will do everything in our power to

170

keep you safe now and apprehend the outlaws."

"Thank you. I just need to see T.R. Simpson as soon as possible."

"He'll be here right away. He especially asked about Miss Perkins."

Raven looked away, then back. "I'm sorry, but I returned alone."

"I see. Is there any chance—"

"That's what I need to see Mr. Simpson about, but rest assured we will get her safely back."

The station master nodded, and ran a hand through his thinning hair. "Is there anything else I can do for you, ma'am?"

"Nothing, thank you. I'll just rest here while I wait."

"We'll see you aren't disturbed."

"Thank you."

Raven knew the station master had many questions he wanted to ask her. After all, it had to be big news within the Santa Fe line, or perhaps Ted had kept the news down to this one station. She reminded herself that Ted could be the mastermind. This could all be some elaborate hoax of his to get the New Mexico gold. On the other hand, he could be doing all he could to help them by keeping news of their kidnapping as quiet as possible.

She didn't know what to believe, and was so tired it was hard to focus anymore. There had been too much strain, too much tension, too much emotion. All she wanted to do was rest and sleep and be alone.

For the first time in days, she felt relatively safe. She laid her head back against a wall and shut her eyes. Visions of Slate appeared. Nude, his hard-muscled body beckoning to her. Happy, laughing with her. Erotic, teaching her new ways of enjoying

171

her body.

Slate. So much to love and so much to hate. How would she ever deal with him?

She closed off that corner of her mind, and pushed out all the hopes and fears and struggles. She was so very tired. Finally, exhausted, she slept.

Chapter Thirteen

Raven didn't know how long she slept, but suddenly she was awakened by a hand on her shoulder.

"Wake up, Raven."

She opened her eyes. Ted was a welcome sight, and for a moment she simply couldn't believe he was the mastermind. He had obviously not slept since their abduction. His red hair was a wild mess where he'd been running his hands through it. His shirt was unbuttoned, his suit wrinkled, and he looked thinner, as if he hadn't eaten in days.

"I've got to ask you first thing. Is Sadie alive?"

"Yes. She's all right. They haven't harmed her in any way."

Ted sat down suddenly, obviously weak with relief. He pulled out a white handkerchief and wiped at his eyes. "I can't tell you what it means to me to hear you say that."

"I know you must have been very worried."

"Out of my mind with fear. I thought by now you'd both be . . ."

"Used and dead."

"Dead was what I feared the most. Even though it would have been horrible for Sadie, I could have lived with them using her body. It was her death I simply could not live with. Until the moment when I was told she'd been taken, I don't think I realized how much she meant to me. I mean, I knew I loved her. I was thinking of marriage. But when she was suddenly gone, I was overwhelmed. Nothing mattered anymore. And to think those outlaws took her. Raven, she's everything to me. How can we get her back?"

"It won't be easy, but if we're clever I think we can."

"Why did they let you go and not her?"

"Because of you. They were going to use us and kill us, but we told them about you and Sadie being friends. The leader decided Sadie would be of more use to them alive and well. They sent me to tell you how you can get her back."

"How? And do you believe they'll let her go?"

"I don't think so. We can't trust them, Ted. You know that."

"You're right, of course. But I know even more than you how ruthless these robbers can be, or outlaws like them. I suppose I shouldn't tell you this, but I've been trying to deal with a number of robberies, although this is the first kidnapping."

"What do you mean?" Raven's stomach tightened. At last maybe Ted would confide in her, then she'd prove him innocent or take him to jail, but not before she got Sadie back.

"We've kept it out of the newspapers for fear of losing passengers and cargo, but Santa Fe and the Southern Pacific have been hit with a series of robberies from Kansas to Texas. We couldn't stop the robberies and finally decided a mastermind was behind the outlaw gangs, someone with inside information, so we hired a Chicago detective agency to catch the mastermind but two of their men were killed on the case."

"That's terrible," Raven said quietly, watching for any sign of Ted's guilt.

"It's horrible, and now this. I'm thankful you're both alive. In comparison, the money doesn't matter."

"Is someone from the Chicago agency on the case now?"

"Yes. A man named R. Cunningham. I haven't met him, and I don't blame him for not introducing himself. He's being extremely cautious since two of his partners were killed. But he's somewhere in the area, watching, waiting, keeping his head down. Smart man."

"How do you communicate with him?"

"Telegram. He's on the mastermind's trail, traveling from Kansas to Texas, and I've got a list of towns along his route where I can send telegrams. He'll pick them up and send a telegram in reply. I already sent him a telegram from Montezuma, requesting that he help out on this kidnapping, and he answered that he would. If anybody can get Sadie back, he'll do it."

"Good," Raven replied, thinking so far Ted was being completely honest with her. Everything he'd just told her, she'd already set up. Of course, there was one important thing he didn't know. R. Cunningham was a woman.

"Please tell me how you think we can save Sadie?"

"I'll tell you everything, but first you must make sure the law stays out of this. The outlaws insist on it."

"I anticipated that. The sheriff is waiting for further information from me and I'll let him know that Sadie's life depends on keeping the law far away from her."

175

"There won't be a problem then?"

"No. The Santa Fe is powerful around here. Besides, the sheriff won't want to be responsible for the death of a Harvey Girl."

"That's a relief. I almost feel like I can relax." She sighed. "What I want most next to getting Sadie back is a long hot bath and a big Harvey meal. Do you think I could have both?"

Ted smiled. "Of course. What you need now is some luxurious treatment."

Raven smiled tiredly, and nodded in agreement.

"I've already reserved for you a very private suite in the Montezuma. You'll be wined and dined as you've never been before, my dear, and all at the expense of Santa Fe. The railway is very proud of your courage and commitment to the company in the face of great danger."

"Thank you, but we can't wait too long. Sadie needs us."

"We'll move as soon as you explain what we need to do."

"We need the Montezuma Special."

Ted frowned a moment. "We sent it back to Topeka for a second run."

"But we have to have it. Right away. The outlaws want you to take the Special south through New Mexico and pick up a load of gold from Shrangi-la Mines. They want that gold and you're to be told, through me, the dates, times, everything that will help them steal it off the Special. But you're to keep the robbery plans secret from everyone else."

"In other words, we'll be working as part of the gang while they hold Sadie hostage."

"Right."

"We can't let them use us, and yet we can't let them hurt Sadie."

"I've been thinking about it, and I may have a plan to save both Sadie and the gold. But it'll be dangerous, and it may not be the best idea. I don't want to take a chance on Sadie getting hurt, but I don't trust the outlaws to release her once they have the gold."

"Neither do I. What's your idea?"

"How soon will the Montezuma Special be back?"

"In a few days."

"Good, although I hate the thought of Sadie being held any longer than necessary."

"So do I, but we can't do anything unusual. The outlaws will be watching, won't they?"

Raven nodded.

"Then let the Montezuma Special run on schedule. I'll need that amount of time if I'm to schedule that gold shipment anyway."

"Does Santa Fe usually ship the Shangri-la's gold?"

"Yes, so that won't be difficult, but it'll take some time. However, I can't set plans into motion until I know exactly what we need to do."

A train whistled in the distance.

Ted glanced up, then back at Raven. "That train'll take us to Montezuma. Why don't we discuss this on the way, then you can rest while I set everything in motion."

"All right," Raven agreed, then added, "Sadie and I had been looking forward to staying at the Montezuma. Without her it won't be the same."

"Not for any of us, but we'll get her back and then she can visit the Montezuma for as long as she wants."

Raven took a long hard look at Ted. It was difficult to imagine him as the mastermind. Either he was a very good actor, or he was innocent and

177

genuinely in love with Sadie. But there was no way to tell, not yet.

When Ted escorted her to the train, Raven found she didn't feel quite the same about the luxurious transportation anymore. The possibility of being robbed and kidnapped would always lie just beneath the surface of her mind, but she decided she could deal with that. She would not be caught off guard again. She glanced around, checked to make sure everything in the car looked in order, then sat down in a plush seat. Ted joined her.

As the train pulled out of the Las Vegas station, he turned to her. "Now what can we do to save Sadie?"

"Something, I hope. I've told you basically what the outlaws want. We're to take the Montezuma Special, pick up the gold, then they'll steal it from us, presumably giving us Sadie in return."

"And you're to give me instructions and then report to one of the outlaws?"

"Yes." Raven hesitated to tell him more. Arn had warned her not to involve Slate directly. He wanted Ted to know only about her. She didn't know how much to tell Ted. If he were the mastermind, he already knew everything. If he wasn't, he'd be safer knowing less, and so would Sadie. She hoped. "They're going to have a couple of outlaws on the train."

"How do they plan to do that?"

"I suppose they'll buy tickets like regular customers, or slip on the train unnoticed."

"But we'll be watching everyone closely on that train. Surely we'd recognize outlaws."

"You probably would, but they mustn't be stopped. Or maybe they'll hide in the baggage car and only come out at night. I don't know how they'll manage it, but I've been told that's the plan."

"All right. I just hope they're inconspicuous. If we can't tell anyone about this, it's going to be difficult."

"We'll have to tell someone sometime. You'll have to judge when it's best."

"Okay. Is Sadie truly all right? Does she have enough to eat?"

"Yes. It's certainly not food fit for a Harvey House, but it'll keep her alive."

He nodded thoughtfully. "She's probably so frightened, but she'll be safe again once we finally get her to the Montezuma."

"Or just into any Harvey House."

They both lapsed into silence for a moment, thinking about Sadie, then Raven said, "We've got to get her back. The only thing I can think of is to let the outlaws think we're going along with their plans, take on the Shangri-la gold, but somehow get some soldiers on the train in secret. The engineer will have to know, and when he stops for the outlaws to board, the soldiers will surprise them."

"That's very dangerous, Raven. What if some of the outlaws get away?"

"I know. They'll go straight back to their camp and—"

"Don't say it. I can't even bear the thought of what they might do to Sadie."

"We don't have to make up our minds now about this idea, Ted. You might think of something better. Or maybe we should just go along with the outlaws and hope they'll keep their end of the bargain."

"No, I think it's a good plan. The soldiers could be dressed as civilians. And if a few army nurses would help, they would all look fairly normal as passengers. Also, if someone were hurt, we'd have skilled help available."

"That's a good idea. But you'd have to be very careful the outlaws didn't find out there were soldier's on board."

"Right. The soldiers and nurses would have to arrive in disguise and maintain that disguise at all times."

"Instead of getting on all at the same time, some could board the train at various stops along the way."

"If we do this, I want to keep civilians out of it as much as possible."

"I agree, but can you do that?"

"Possibly, but would it appear normal?"

"That's what I meant."

"Perhaps, since it's not a normally scheduled run, if things aren't quite the same the outlaws won't notice."

"That's right, and they probably wouldn't know what was exactly normal on a train schedule anyway. But the real question is whether or not this is the right thing to do."

"I don't know, but I trust your judgment. You've been there. You've been with those men. You've seen how they've treated Sadie. We have to depend on you to decide."

"And take the chance?"

"Yes, but we'll have to make very sure we get every one of those outlaws, Raven. If even one gets away, he'll take revenge on Sadie."

"That's the risk. I hope it's worth it."

"The choice is accepting their word that'll she be returned unharmed and we know we can't do that. Sadie has a better chance of coming out alive our way than waiting for the outlaws to safely return her."

Ted gripped Raven's hand, and said, "I don't know how to thank you. You've been so courageous, watching, listening, even devising a plan to save Sadie. I hope she realizes what a fine friend she has in you."

"She's been a good friend to me, too, and we'll get her out alive, Ted. You can count on that."

He nodded, then let her hand go and quickly wiped his eyes with a large white handkerchief.

Raven found it almost impossible to believe that Ted could be the mastermind. He simply cared too deeply for Sadie and was too upset by what the outlaws had done to be behind it all. Still, there was the chance he was and she couldn't mark him off her list yet.

"But to more pleasant matters," Ted said, gesturing out the window. "We approach Montezuma. It's a breathtaking sight."

Raven looked out her window. He was right. An elaborate hotel constructed entirely of wood stood on the side of a beautiful valley. Mountains loomed high in the distance, purple and white in the soft evening light. An evergreen forest framed it in deep verdant green. The structure was four stories with a massive tower of eight or nine stories connecting the balconies that ran along the front of the building.

"Majestic, isn't it?" Ted said, then added, "It's over three hundred feet long. Imagine. And wait until you see the inside. Its furnishings rival the hostelries at Saratoga Springs."

"It *is* beautiful."

"I don't know if you can see them from here, but nestled in the trees are bathhouses capable of housing five hundred health seekers each day."

"It's very impressive."

"It has two hundred seventy rooms which are

181

filled to capacity most of the time. Montezuma has quickly become a major health and pleasure resort, thanks to the first-class service and surroundings guaranteed by Fred Harvey."

"I'm looking forward to staying there. I just wish—"

"I know. But when Sadie does get here, Fred's going to pull out all the stops. Not that you won't have the best of everything. I've already been given special instructions to see to your comfort."

"I appreciate that."

"Of course, nothing will take the place of Sadie."

"But we're going to get her back."

"That's right. And soon. I'll put everything into motion as soon as we get to Montezuma, and I'll be very discreet so the outlaws will suspect nothing."

"Good. That's very important. I don't know if the outlaws will be at the Montezuma or not, but I think we'd better act like they are."

"Absolutely. It's just a matter of time now until Sadie will be with us again."

Raven was glad to see him so positive. She just hoped he wasn't the mastermind. If so, all their plans might come to naught. But would he give himself away by foiling their attempt to rescue Sadie and save the gold? No, probably not. He was too clever to do that. Protecting his position would be more important. Even if he were the mastermind, she didn't think he'd interfere with their plans. That was a relief.

"Here we are, my dear," Ted said, interrupting her thoughts. "Let's hurry. There's so much to do before getting our Sadie back."

They debarked at a small station, then hurried toward the Montezuma. The huge hotel was even more impressive at this distance. The Queen Anne style made use of several wood sidings, giving a patchwork effect. Steep gables and a massive round tower made the huge structure a superb architectural achievement. The balconies that ran the length of all four floors gave each room a beautiful view of the valley or the mountains.

They entered the Montezuma, and Raven was unprepared for the magnificence of the huge, lushly decorated lobby. The floor was parquet in a geometric inlay of imported Jarcaranda. The ceiling rose two stories with a wide staircase of dark exotic wood and gleaming brass leading upward. Crystal chandeliers hung from the ceiling, and in one corner was a massive fireplace. The furniture was of dark wood and velvets in vivid colors.

"What do you think?" Ted asked.

"It's truly opulent."

"Wait till you see your suite. Your trunk has already been sent up and unpacked for you. All you have to do is relax now. Leave the rest to us."

"Thank you. I'm very tired."

"And no wonder. Just a moment while I get the keys to your suite."

While Ted checked in for her, Raven glanced around some more, trying to take in every detail of the hotel. It was obvious that everything was of the finest quality and craftmanship, and it reminded her of the luxury of the Montezuma Special, only on a much grander scale.

She walked around a little, noticing the elegantly and expensively dressed people sitting, standing, and walking around the lobby. They were so very different from the outlaws she'd just been with. In fact, it was hard to believe she was in the wild West, deep in New Mexico. She might easily have been in Chicago or back East. The West must certainly be changing.

Maybe it wasn't so wild anymore.

Then she saw Slate. Her heart thumped. As far as he was concerned, the West was still very, very wild. But what was he doing here? She thought she might not see him again until they boarded the Special. She glanced around. Were Hank and the others already here, too? But she didn't see them.

Slate nodded at her.

She smiled slightly, then glanced to see if Ted had noticed, but his back was to her.

She looked back, but Slate was gone. Glancing around, she still couldn't see him anywhere. Had she truly seen him, or had her imagination conjured him up to plague her? No, he'd been there, a tired, dusty-looking cowboy. But he was really an outlaw, and nobody knew it but her. And Margarita. And the gang. But they wouldn't tell, and neither would she.

"Ready to go, my dear?" Ted asked, returning to her side with the keys.

"Yes. I noticed in the depot that a woman named Margarita was performing here."

"Indeed. A bit of Western excitement for our clients. Would you like to see her show?"

"Yes."

"I'll check the seating and arrange for you to see her before we leave."

"Thank you. I'd like that."

"Good, then come along. I know how anxious you are to rest."

Raven followed him up the huge staircase, but her legs began to ache halfway up. She slowed, and Ted solicitously took her arm to help her upward.

They made it to the top of the stairs and she looked down. The Montezuma was even more impressive from this angle. She glanced around again for Slate, but didn't see him. Maybe he had been a figment of her imagination after all.

She wished Sadie were with them, but promised herself that her friend would be free soon. Then they would all enjoy the pleasures of the Montezuma together.

Ted led her down the hall, and opened the door to her suite.

on the vanity, her eyes half-open, the water up to a
moment. She knelt again, scrubbing——her
dress going back, her arms white, her pinned-up
hair falling, all enjoying the pleasure, all the more
than usual.
She looked at herself and, opening the door
to let him—

Chapter Fourteen

Raven eased her sore body into the steaming, fragrant water of a footed porcelain tub painted with rose designs. She sighed. There was nothing like the convenience of indoor plumbing. With just the turn of a knob, one could quickly enjoy a full hot bath.

She sighed again and took a sip of claret from a sparkling crystal glass. She was already feeling better as the hot water drew the aches and pains from her muscles. She played with the bubbles piled high under her chin, then took another sip of wine.

This was luxury. True to his word, Ted had installed her in sumptuous splendor at the Montezuma. Her suite had all the modern conveniences, plus the beautiful decor of the Queen Anne style. The bedroom was draped and papered in shades of rose. Original oil paintings of roses in gilt frames decorated the walls. A huge, high tester bed of dark wood dominated the room, swathed in layers of ivory lace and rose-colored velvet.

The suite also had a large sitting room with a

writing desk and chair, a round table for eating meals, a formal arrangement of sofa and chairs, and even a small library. All done, of course, in the Queen Anne style.

But Raven was most impressed with the menu. Fred Harvey had outdone himself in making the Montezuma a complete luxury resort. Trains brought in fresh sea food, vegetables, and fruit from southern Texas and Mexico every week. Prime beef was readily available from Santa Fe's shipping lines. And to prepare the best in fresh quality foods, Fred Harvey had hired a chef trained in Europe.

Raven thought about the feast she had ordered from the famous Montezuma kitchen as she relaxed in the slowly cooling water. Ted had kept insisting that she try this dish or that delicacy until the order had grown huge.

She had agreed to all the food, partly because she was ravenous but also because she had realized that Ted was trying hard to make up for the ordeal of her kidnapping. The more she had ordered, the happier he had been. Also, she thought he viewed her as his closest connection to Sadie and was doing for Raven what he would have done for the woman he loved if she'd been there.

Raven sipped more claret. She was really relaxing now, feeling safe for the first time in a long, long while. She wiggled her toes, feeling the tension drain from her. It had been much too long since she'd felt so relaxed. She took another sip of the fine vintage wine.

She just wished Sadie was with her now, installed in her own suite, enjoying the luxuries of the resort and the attentions of the man she loved.

Thinking of Sadie made her feel guilty. Here she

was basking in luxury while Sadie was somewhere in the mountains in an outlaw camp, tied up and with little to eat. Or by now, Sadie might have been moved to a worse location.

She frowned, worrying about her friend. Was Sadie truly safe and alive, or had the outlaws decided to do whatever they wanted to her friend once Raven had agreed to their bargain and left to persuade the Atchison, Topeka and Santa Fe to help rob the Shangri-la Mines?

Of course, there was no answer to that question. Raven suddenly didn't feel so relaxed anymore. She was really worried about Sadie and wanted to help her now, not some time in the future. Enjoying the comforts of the Montezuma was not getting her friend set free.

But Raven reminded herself there was nothing more she could do for Sadie at the moment. Ted was setting their plans into motion. They had to wait for the Montezuma Special to return. And she would do Sadie no good if she were too exhausted to think or react clearly. She needed to rest and heal, then she could go on.

She began to relax again, running more hot water and letting the water soothe her. She started to feel drowsy, and rested her head against the back of the tub. It was so peaceful here. So safe.

As she began to drift off to sleep, a sound at the front door startled her. She tensed, then relaxed. Her food must have arrived.

"Just leave it in the sitting room," she called, loud enough to penetrate the closed door of her bathing room. She would have to end her bath now. She didn't want all that delicious food getting cold. She pulled the plug, then stepped from the tub, and was shocked when the door suddenly swung open.

She grabbed for one of the big fluffy towels nearby, but not before a male voice drawled, "You're sure a sight for sore eyes."

Raven gasped, and jerked the towel around her. Slate Slayton stood leaning against the doorjamb.

"You're not supposed to be in here," Raven protested. "I though that was someone with my dinner."

"It was your food all right. *I* brought it. Thought I'd break my back carrying it. You must have ordered enough for two. Knew I was coming, or did you plan on entertaining that Simpson fellow?"

Raven pulled the towel tighter. "Please leave. You can see I'm not dressed for visitors."

"You were friendlier in the mountains, Raven."

"If anybody saw you come in—"

"Don't worry. I just happened by and helped out the poor boy staggering under that load of food. I carried it in for him, then we both left."

"But you didn't relock the door, did you?"

"No, and I circled back."

"Of course, what else could I expect from an outlaw."

"Don't know what you've got against my profession. Takes a lot of cunning and experience to do a job well."

"I don't want to discuss it. I don't want to see you. I don't want to know you. In fact, I've forgotten all about what happened in the mountains."

"Forgotten?" Slate's body tensed.

"Yes. I was frightened, overwrought. After all, I'd just been kidnapped and my friend was tied up. Yes, I've tried to forget it all."

"But you can't."

"I'm going to rescue Sadie."

189

"You mean you aren't going along with Arn's plan?"

"Not exactly."

"Don't you think it's dangerous to be telling one of his gang your plans?"

"It could be."

"*Could?*"

"Well, I was thinking there might be a better way for us to handle the situation."

"Something I'd be interested in?"

"Maybe. But I'd rather not talk about it now."

"Why not? Now seems like a good time."

"Obviously I'm not dressed for any type of discussion."

"I can think of several discussions—"

"I'm not interested, Slate. I've got to concentrate on getting Sadie back."

"Want my help?"

"Would you be willing to help me?"

"Might be. I offered it once before."

She hesitated. She needed him. But she couldn't discuss any of this wearing nothing but a towel. She thought of the food and gestured toward the other room, saying, "I can't possibly eat all that. You might join me and we could discuss how we're going to handle this situation."

Slate grinned. "Thanks. I'm damned hungry." He walked into the other room and began removing covers from several trays. The aroma of food filled the air. "I must say you know how to order up a meal."

Suddenly reminded that she hadn't eaten in a long time, Raven joined him. "It does look good, doesn't it?"

"You as hungry as me?"

"Hungrier."

He glanced down at her warm, moist body covered only by a white towel.

She blushed and was furious that she couldn't control the telltale sign. "I'll get dressed."

"Not on my account. Anyway, the food'll be cold by the time you're done. You wouldn't want that, would you?"

He was right. It would take her forever to get fully dressed. "I'll just slip on a robe then."

Raven hurried into the bedroom, pulled a pale gray satin robe from her trunk, made sure Slate was busy with the food, then dropped the towel and slipped on the robe. She tied it around the waist, made sure the pins holding up her hair were still in place, then started across the room.

But she stopped, noticing her reflection in the full-length oval mirror. The satin clung to all her curves, her breasts thrust against the soft fabric, her waist was hugged by the belt, and her hips flared out, caressed by the robe as she moved. She blushed again but walked into the sitting room anyway. She was more hungry than modest. Slate had seen her nude anyway. What she hadn't noticed was that her skin was rosy and moist, her silvery blond hair was highlighted by the satiny gray of her robe, and her eyes were dark luminous orbs in her pale face.

Slate looked up as she entered and hesitated, caught in her enchanting spell. "I don't think I'm hungry for food anymore, Raven."

She knew what he meant for she suddenly noticed again how handsome he was. He'd been somewhere and cleaned up. Maybe he'd rented a room. He looked good, maybe leaner, meaner. He wasn't wearing a six-gun. He'd exchanged his denims for black twill trousers, a gray dress shirt, and a black and gray tapestry vest. He was clean-shaven, his hair recently trimmed, and he smelled of a man's shaving lotion.

He moved closer.

"You've been taking advantage of Montezuma's luxuries, haven't you?"

He rubbed a hand across his cheek. "Yes, and now I smell like a damn whorehouse."

Raven laughed. "Is that what they smell like?"

"You were supposed to know."

She frowned, suddenly remembering her loss of virginity and of all the games and roles she was playing. She quickly reminded herself that Slate was a dangerous outlaw, part of the gang which was holding Sadie captive. She'd have to be more cautious around him. She needed him if her plan to rescue Sadie was going to work.

"Why don't we have something to eat? I really am starved."

"All right, if you insist," he agreed, although the hunger in his eyes was obviously for her body.

He held her chair out and, when she was seated, bent to place a warm kiss on top of her head.

The small gesture made her shiver with memories, but she quelled the reaction.

He sat down across from her and began piling food on his plate. "Looks great. I haven't eaten anything decent since Topeka."

"But a tough outlaw like you wouldn't care, would he?"

"We like our luxury just as much as anybody," Slate replied, cutting into a thick juicy steak.

"I had plenty of it on the Montezuma Special."

"That's what Ted told me."

"Ted?"

"Oh, did I forget to mention he's hired me as an extra gun for the Special?"

"You forgot, indeed. You certainly work fast."

"Have to. In fact, Simpson practically fell all over me to hire my services at top dollar. I didn't complain, of course, but I was a little surprised it was so easy."

The succulent piece of lobster salad stuck in Raven's throat. Was Ted the mastermind then? Had Arn let him know that Slate was on his way and was part of the outlaws' plan? Why else would Ted have been so eager to hire Slate? Of course, Arn wouldn't have told Slate, a new man, anything about Ted. It was all getting very, very dangerous.

"Eat up, Raven. Remember what the food was like in that camp."

Raven swallowed the lobster and toyed with another salad. Ted's hiring Slate was the best proof she'd had yet that Ted was the mastermind, and it made her sick. He'd been so solicitous, so concerned, so upset about Sadie. She had almost convinced herself he was innocent because she'd wanted to believe in him. Now she couldn't dismiss him as the mastermind. She didn't have final proof, but she was very close to connecting Ted with the robberies.

"Raven, what's wrong?"

She shook her head, regretting that there were so many lies between them, but she added another. "I was thinking of Sadie. Do you think she'll be all right?"

"Yes, or I wouldn't have left her there. She did me a favor in Topeka and I owe her."

"You mean when she let you see me?"

"Yes. I made sure before we left that everybody

193

knew I had an interest in her and that I expected to come back and find her able to handle my attentions. They'll leave her alive and alone if they know what's good for them. They also need her as a hostage."

"And do they?"

"Know what's good for them? I damn well hope so. She's a spunky little lady, but there's only so much she can take."

"She has to be all right, Slate. I'd never forgive myself if—"

"Raven, I know it's hard on you, but it won't do Sadie any good for you to worry so much. Eat up. She needs you sharp and smart."

Raven took a deep breath. He was right. She couldn't let her worry for Sadie or her suspicions about Ted weaken her. She had to keep everything in perspective. She had a job to do and she was going to do it, no matter her feelings."

"You're right." She took a bite of sea bass brought all the way from Mexico. It was delicious.

"So what did you and Ted work out? I never did figure it'd go as easy as Arn planned." As he talked Slate spread fresh butter on a crusty hot roll.

"I think we'd go along with Arn's plans if we could be sure of getting Sadie back, but I don't trust those outlaws. They've killed before." She thought of her father and fiancé.

"Yes, they've killed."

"Do you think they'd give us Sadie in exchange for the gold?"

"Am I included in these questions about Arn's gang?"

"I suppose you must be, but I find it hard to think of you like the others."

"Thanks. I'm usually more of an independent, but times are hard."

"I see. Then you aren't fond of working for others?"

"Not much."

"Could you be persuaded to part company with Arn's group?"

"I might if the right person asked."

"Am I that person, Slate?"

"Could be."

Slate wasn't making it easy on her, and she'd had no experience in this type of negotiation. She supposed he'd want a great deal of money to change sides. She didn't have much and she hadn't been able to ask Ted about including Slate in their plans since Arn had warned her not to tell Ted about Slate's true identity, and she thought that was safest for everybody, too. Ted was going to have to continue thinking Slate was simply the man he'd hired to guard the train.

"I'm sure the Santa Fe line would be willing to pay a reward for the rescue of Sadie," she finally said.

"Would I have to split it?"

"No. What amount did you have in mind?"

"What do you think is fair?"

"Maybe five hundred dollars."

"Well, I could ask Ted. He'd probably be willing to put in some of his own money to get Sadie back."

"That's not quite what I had in mind, but we'll get back to that. So you're offering me at least five hundred to turn on my partners."

"Yes, I suppose that's actually what I'm doing."

"Do you realize how dangerous that could be for

me? I'd be risking my neck, my reputation, and it's not that much cash."

"We can probably get more."

"It's more than the money. I have a reputation to uphold."

"You mean with the outlaws?"

"Sure. We've got a code in the West, and it includes outlaws. My honor is involved here."

"Seven hundred fifty."

"Not enough."

"Remember, you owe Sadie."

"Not this much."

"I don't think I could possibly go more than a thousand. I'm not even sure I could get that."

"What? We're talking about rescuing a Harvey Girl."

"That's true. Fred Harvey would help on the reward too. Okay, a thousand."

"I owe Sadie and I need the money, but none of that's what will get me to help you."

"I don't understand. What do you want?"

"What only you can give me, Raven."

"Oh," She hesitated a long moment, then said, "How many times do I have to tell you I'm not for sale?"

"Maybe I'll even help you find your uncle."

"I don't think I need your help. I'm doing well enough on my own."

"Doesn't look that way to me. Besides, you just asked me to help on this railroad job."

"If you helped find my uncle you'd want a big cut of my inheritance, wouldn't you?" She didn't know how she could keep playing so many roles, inventing so many stories, and yet keep it all straight. But she had to do it. So much depended on her.

"You keep giving me what you gave me in the mountains, and I'm not going to push for more."

Raven stood up. "I don't know how many times I have to tell you, Slate. I'm not for sale. Take the thousand and let it go."

"I could make you want me."

"Is there a point?"

"You know the point."

"A thousand five hundred."

"Obviously all the money in the world won't buy you, and you're what I want." He suddenly reached out and pulled her close to him.

She could feel his heat through her satin robe. It ignited her own body's needs. She swayed into him, then caught herself and pulled back. "No."

"You want me, Raven. Okay, no bargains. Just us. Just what's between us. I'll help you. You help me. Nobody knows."

"I can't. I just can't."

He stood up, towered over her a long moment, then put a single finger under her chin. He tilted her head back and looked long and hard into her soft dark eyes. "Someday you're going to say 'no' one too many times, and I won't be there anymore."

Slate stepped around her and strode to the door. He hesitated with his back to her a moment, then looked around. She was watching him, a hand clutching his chair. "Thanks for the dinner. I'd planned to ask you out dancing. The Montezuma's got a big dance floor. But you don't want to do anything with me, do you?"

"You're an outlaw," she whispered.

"And you're just a money-grubbing little Yankee, but I'm not letting that stop me."

"It's wrong."

"So, what's right?"

He slammed the door behind him.

Raven hesitated a long moment, her mind whirling in all directions, then ran to the door and wrenched it open.

Slate was standing just outside. "What took you so long?" He lifted her in his arms, kicked the door shut, and strode into the bedroom.

Chapter Fifteen

"You're the only food I want or need," Slate said as he laid Raven down in the center of the big tester bed.

His words sent a tremor through her and she reached out for him, drawing him close. She could smell the after-shave blending with his own personal scent. He smelled almost as good as the food they'd just eaten. She nibbled his ear and felt him respond.

"It won't take much, Raven. I've been needing you since I stopped holding you back in the mountains. Seems like it's been years since we were together."

"Surely much longer," she murmured, tasting his ear with the tip of her tongue.

He shuddered, and rolled off her. "Let's do it right this time." He pulled back the covers. "We might as well enjoy the comfort while we've got it."

Raven helped him, wondering how she could so willingly respond to him, throwing aside all her decisions, beliefs, concerns whenever he was near. But there was no denying what he made her feel, no denying the passion that sparked between them. He made her feel wild and wanton. And she couldn't seem to care. All she wanted was to be in his arms.

When the soft white sheets of the bed lay exposed, Slate turned to her. "I wish it could have been like this for you the first time."

She shook her head in denial. "The mountain glade was perfect."

"But this'll be a lot more comfortable." He lay down and stretched out full-length to prove his point. "Look at that, Raven. This bed is long enough for me."

Raven laughed. "The famous Fred Harvey hospitality."

"I'm glad he doesn't have you downstairs working in the restaurant. I don't want you anywhere except in this bed and I don't want you serving anybody but me."

"Should I be serving you right now? I believe there's some food left on the trays."

"That's not what I want to eat. Come here."

Slate pulled her close and began nibbling her soft, pale flesh. She shivered at his touch, feeing her body begin to melt in his embrace.

"You taste good. Like I said, you're all I need."

"For now, maybe."

"Now's enough, too. Nothing else matters."

He parted the gray satin robe, exposing her full breasts, the tips already hard, beckoning him to fulfill her again. He didn't wait long to respond to their message. He kissed each nipple, then began toying with them, teasing them into harder peaks with the tip of his tongue.

Raven moaned, moving restlessly against him. "I don't know how you do this to me."

"Talent."

"Does it work for every woman?"

"There aren't any other women except you."

But a vision of Margarita's lovely face suddenly flashed in Raven's mind, and she winced in pain. How could she have forgotten his other lover? How could she lay with him now, knowing he would always return to Margarita, a woman of his own Texas heritage. And yet . . .

He blazed a trail of kisses from her breasts to her lips, then captured her mouth with his and plunged inside. Raven was lost once more to seething emotions as he plummeted the depths of her mouth, then drew her tongue deep into his own mouth.

She reveled in the taste, touch, smell of him, unable to get close enough, unable to sense enough, unable to accept enough. Slate. How could there be another man for her? He was everything her body craved, everything her mind wanted, everything her heart desired.

Jerking away, she said softly, "I have to think."

"Think?" Slate tried to pull her back to him, but she resisted.

"This is just a passing fancy for you, Slate. You must have many women, or perhaps one special one who—"

"That's right. I *do* have one special one."

She flinched.

"You.'"

How could he be so cruel? If she hadn't known about Margarita she might have believed him.

"I meant back in Texas."

"What does that have to do with us?"

"It's just that—"

"Damn, Raven! Do you want me or not?"

"Yes! But there's more to it than that."

"No there's not. Forget everything, everybody but us, here, now."

"I don't think I can."

He growled and jerked her close. "I'll make you."

Slate rampaged over her body, his lips, his hands creating fiery trails down her sensitive flesh. She was soon caught up in a wild frenzy of emotions and

201

feelings as he overwhelmed her senses, leaving no part of her body untouched.

She responded, just as he'd said she would. She couldn't resist what he did to her. Dragging fingers through his thick black hair, she reveled in the feel of him, then moved lower, feeling the muscles of his back tense and relax under her fingertips. He was so lean and strong and yet sensitive. She wanted him so, and nestled closer, wanting to taste him, touch him as completely as possible.

She toyed with his face, teasing him with her tongue, glorying in the scent of him. She felt the lightest of stubbles along his jawline with her tongue. Then she kissed the corners of his mouth, a feathery light touch that tickled and brought a groan from him.

But nothing was enough. She moved lower still, kissing, teasing, and tasting his throat until she reached his chest where she played in the black hair, then tormented his nipples until they were hard. She forced more groans from him as she pushed him back against the pillow, placing hard kisses from his chest to his shoulders where she lightly bit the muscles, then harder, wanting to consume him completely.

The same thought and feeling must have filled him, too, for suddenly he could wait no longer. He lifted her, toying with her breasts, then laid her back against the soft feather mattress. Kneeling before her, he parted her thighs, and asked, "Are you ever going to come to me willing, Raven?"

"What am I if not willing now, Slate?" she moaned, tossing her head back and forth.

But she knew what he meant, and felt tears sting her eyes. She knew too much. She thought too much. What she needed to do was feel, forgetting everything else. Maybe he was right. Maybe the moment was enough. After all, they would have to go their separate ways eventually. She should enjoy what she could now.

She reached for him, drawing his face close to hers. "You make me want you. Maybe there isn't a right or wrong where passion is concerned. But, for now, it's just the two of us and that's the way I want it."

He covered her lips with a fiery kiss, then plunged his manhood into her. Raven moaned, feeling her senses ignite as he pushed deeper and deeper until he was completely buried in her softness. Then he stopped and they were poised for a timeless moment on the brink of ecstasy. When he began to move again, she shivered, almost unable to bear the pleasure of the long deep strokes.

Ignited, she began to strain toward him, instinctively moving in time with him, reaching outward for fulfillment. Their bodies became fused in a boiling cauldron of passion, and their esctasy spiraled higher and higher.

"Raven, I don't know what you do to me," Slate groaned, "but it's something I can't live without."

Then he accelerated his pace, bringing her with him as their passion exploded into a bright red blossom and she cried out, digging her nails into his back as they both spun into the fiery depths of total fulfillment.

For a long time afterward Slate held her close, then he rolled to his side, still holding her, and began smoothing the damp hair back from her face.

"You're beautiful, Raven, but most beautiful when you're mine."

"And when is that?" she asked, her voice soft and contented.

"You know when. When we melt into each other. We're joined then, and you're really mine."

"Are you mine then, too?"

"Of course. I told you I can't live without you."

"Yes, but in your line of work you must have to leave people all the time."

"I might change my job for you."

"But not now?"

"No. I have something to finish, and we've got to get Sadie back."

"And then?"

"Will you wait?"

"Is this a marriage proposal?"

"No."

"Then why should I wait?"

"I thought you didn't want to marry me."

"I don't. I was just trying to get straight what you were trying to twist me into thinking."

"Just one thing. I want you like I've never wanted any other woman in my life."

She wished she could believe that, but Margarita was just downstairs.

"You believe me, don't you?"

"Does it matter? Like you said, let's leave it for now. Who knows what may happen tomorrow."

"It does matter." He sat up, looking down at her fiercely. "My word's good, Raven. Believe that."

She almost could have, but she knew too much. "I don't need to believe that. I'm in bed with you, aren't I?"

"Your body says yes but your mind still says no. I want all of you, and I won't be satisfied until I have the whole you."

"Take what you can get," she said much more casually than she felt. She couldn't possibly let him know how close he was to taking all of her, and if

204

he ever did that she didn't know how she could walk away from him, outlaw or not, and yet she knew she must.

"Damn! Sometimes I forget you're just a heartless, money-grubbing Yankee."

"And sometimes I almost forget you're an outlaw."

"Quite a pair, aren't we?"

"Yes."

"But it was good, wasn't it?"

"You know it was."

"Want to try again?"

"Can you?"

"Look."

He was ready and Raven couldn't resist reaching out to stroke his long, hard shaft. She touched lightly, hesitantly until he showed her what felt best to him, then he groaned and pulled her closer.

"You're perfect, Raven. You know just how to please me."

"Except in one thing," she replied, releasing him.

He pushed her back into the tangled covers, nibbling her nipples and stroking her thighs. "What's that?"

"Remember, you don't have my mind."

"Maybe it doesn't matter so much after all. Your body's mine to brand."

He bit down hard, and she playfully slapped at him. He kissed the offended flesh softly, soothingly, and Raven moaned, stroking the muscles of his back.

Suddenly the front door squeaked softly open. They froze, and listened as soft footsteps sounded closer and closer.

Slate reached for his Colt .45, but it wasn't there. He'd left it in his room. Cursing his stupidity, he threw the covers over Raven and slid to the floor, keeping out of sight of the open door.

"I know you're there, Texas," a rough male voice called.

Raven's heart beat faster. Hank. And she'd forgotten to warn Slate about Hank's threats at the depot.

"Get out of my suite," Raven cried.

"Did you make her hot for you, Texas?"

Slate pulled on his trousers, motioning for Raven to stay in bed.

"Did she cry out when you showed her what she's made for, Texas?"

"Get out!" Raven cried again.

"I ain't going nowhere, pretty Harvey Girl. I got your Texas lover where I want him now. I'm packing, little lady, and he's clean as a newborn babe. When I get done with Texas he ain't going to be no good to you." The voice was closer now.

"Slate's gone," Raven said as calmly as she could.

"It ain't nice for a Harvey Girl to lie. We're on the fourth floor and he ain't come out. I figure he didn't sprout wings and fly away so he's still in there with you. Show yourself, Texas. I've got a hunting knife going to cut you down to size."

Raven looked horrified, then began to slide across the bed toward Slate. He motioned her to be still and silent.

"I got a bead on your woman, Texas. Better step out. I don't need her in too good a shape to satisfy me."

Raven stilled. Hank was right. She was in his line of sight. He aimed his .45 at her.

Slate saw it, and stepped into the open.

"Good boy," Hank said, walking closer. "Now raise your hands nice for me, Texas. And don't try

206

nothing. I won't cotton to it and I might take it out on the pretty woman."

"Leave now, Hank, and I'll forget you came here," Slate bargained.

"I'm no fool. Texans don't forget."

"My word's good. Go ahead and leave and nobody'll ever know about this."

"I told you I ain't no fool. That'd get me a bullet in the back sure as shooting."

"No. My word. Leave now."

"Shut up, Texas. All your talk is making me feel mean."

"Listen to reason, Hank. I—"

"Another word and the woman gets it."

Slate closed his mouth, watching Hank for a chance to jump him.

Raven glanced around the room. While Hank was distracted with Slate, something had to be done or they would end up dead. Slate would obviously do anything Hank said if it would save her. Maybe she meant more to him than she'd realized. But she couldn't think about that now. Something had to be done.

Her reticule was lying on the dresser. Her father's .45 was in it. She hated to let either of them know she knew how to use a weapon, but their lives were more important than preserving her true identity. She had to take a chance and save them if she could. Later she would figure out a way to explain away the pistol.

Hank stepped into the room, the .45 still aimed at Raven, but he was being very cautious of Slate. "I want you to tie Texas up, little Harvey Girl."

"I don't know anything about ropes," Raven replied as she slipped on her robe under the cover and tightly belted it around her waist.

207

"You can learn. Get some of those black Harvey Girl stockings. Those'll hold him good."

"There's no need for this," Raven protested. "Do like Slate said. Leave now and we won't tell anyone."

"Too late. I'm going to take what's mine and punish the man who tried to do me out of it. So just shut up and get the stockings before I get tired of waiting and start putting holes in you."

"Fire that .45 and people will come," Slate said.

"But not soon enough for you two. It's late. People are out drinking and dancing. Everybody's busy. I bet the floor's empty."

Raven couldn't help but think he was probably right, but she didn't say so.

"Now tie him up and quick, Harvey Girl."

"Do as he says, Raven," Slate inserted. "I don't want you hurt."

"I ain't going to hurt her unless you force me, Texas. I plan to pleasure her."

Raven decided to bide her time. She'd have to seem to go along with Hank's plans, then make her move when she could. She walked over to the dresser, opened a drawer, and pulled out two black stockings, all she had left. With those in her hands, she picked up her reticule, hoping Hank wouldn't notice.

But Hank was watching her closely. "No. Put that thing back. Nothing but the stockings."

Raven bit her lower lip in frustration. She set the reticule down. What would she do now? She couldn't get close enough for physical force since he had the pistol aimed at her all the time.

"Now tie Texas up good."

She hesitated, trying to think of a way out of the situation.

"Come on, Harvey Girl. I'm in a hurry."

She would just have to go along with Hank's commands until she could think of a way to catch him off guard.

She walked over to Slate. "I'm sorry."

"Do what you have to do, but don't worry. Hank's not going to get away with this," Slate replied.

"Fool Texan. Think you're better than the rest of us? Well you're not and I'm going to prove it. Turn him around so I can watch you tie him up. No tricks, Harvey Girl. Put your hands behind your back, Texas."

Slate did as he was told, then turned so Hank could watch the process.

Raven began winding a stocking around Slate's crossed wrists. She noticed he'd clinched his fists and was holding the muscles in his arms taut. When he relaxed, the ropes would be looser, hopefully enough for him to work free. It was an old trick and a good one. Her father had taught it to her once long ago. But she was also tying the stocking as loosely as possible.

Hank moved closer, keeping the .45 on Raven, and ran a calloused hand down her satin robe. His fingers were rough, catching on the smooth fabric, and Raven shuddered, thinking of those rough hands against her own smooth skin.

"Pull it tight, Harvey Girl."

"That's what I'm doing." But she wasn't, even though she was making hand and arm movements like she was. Finally, she tied the stocking and turned toward Hank. "There."

"Good Harvey Girl. Now tie the other stocking the same way." He ran an experienced hand through her long, flowing hair. "Been giving it to you good, has he?"

Raven blushed.

"Go ahead. Finish the job. And don't worry, I'm better with women than Texas and I'll prove it soon as you get him tied up. Lucky for him, he'll get to watch me."

Slate couldn't stand any more, and said, "There's no need to involve her. This is between us."

"Don't want her to know how much more man I am, do you?"

"You can still leave, Hank," Slate insisted.

"I told you to shut up. Give me any more of your lip and I start shooting off bits of Harvey Girl here."

Slate forced himself in to silence.

Raven began winding another stocking around his wrists. This was going to make it more difficult for him to get free without help. But she was making the bonds as loose as possible, and Hank had to keep his eyes on her so he couldn't tell exactly what she was doing.

"Why don't you just let him go, Hank," Raven said, deciding to try another tactic. "We don't need him anymore. I always fancied you more."

Slate looked daggers at her.

Hank smiled and stroked back his greasy hair. "Say now, you've got good taste, pretty woman. But I got a beef with Texas. Going to show him what a real man can do."

Raven tied off the second stocking.

"Set him in that chair, tie his feet, then tie him to the chair."

"I don't have enough stockings."

"Use some of your underclothes then. I'd like to see them anyway."

Now was Raven's chance. She went back to the

dresser and began pulling out petticoats. They were big enough to conceal the reticule which she slid in with the petticoats, then walked back to Slate.

"Pull that chair close to the bed," Hank instructed. "I want him to have a good view of the show."

Raven did as he bid, taking comfort from the weight of the pistol in her reticule.

Keeping his gun pointed at Raven, Hank pushed Slate into the chair. Slate looked mutinous a moment, then stilled, obviously waiting for his chance to attack but not while Raven was in danger.

"Okay," Hank said. "Finish tying him and make it good."

Raven knelt beside Slate and made a great fuss of trying to get the petticoats in enough shape to tie him. She decided that the safest way to handle the situation was to get Slate untied and the gun in his hands. Hank had to keep his eyes on her so Slate would have the element of surprise.

In the confusion of the petticoats, Raven acted like she was trying to tie Slate to the chair, but in reality she managed to get him loose, for he quickly understood what she was doing and helped. Then she slipped the .45 out of the reticule and into Slate's hands.

She breathed a sigh of relief. During the whole process she had expected Hank to notice and shoot her or Slate. But he hadn't noticed, not yet. She held her breath as she knelt out of Slate's way and pretended to start tying his ankles.

But Hank had finally lost his patience. "Fool woman! Don't you know nothing? I can't tell a thing about what you're doing, but it sure don't look like he's tied good."

"You're right, Hank," Slate said ominously. "Remember when I said you could walk out of here and we'd forget all about this?"

"Shut up!"

"Well, I'm going to say it again. I don't want any shooting going on at the Montezuma. Sadie Perkins's life is at stake. We don't want trouble or attention. Now I want you to walk out of here real quiet like, and go back to the camp."

"For a man on the end of a short rope, you got your nerve, Texas."

"If you'll look closely, Hank, the end of a snub-nosed .45 is pointed at your gut. I'll lay you open if I have to." Slate moved the petticoats slightly so the end of the gun's barrel was in plain sight.

But Hank couldn't look, didn't dare. He had to keep his eyes trained on his target. "Don't matter what you got, Texas. My gun's on Harvey Girl here. You can shoot, but I'll get her dead to center."

"Leave now and there won't be any trouble," Slate insisted.

"You're bluffing."

"No. Take a look, Hank. I can lay you open with this .45."

"I say you're bluffing. Take off that robe, Harvey Girl, and I'll show you what a real man can do."

"Don't touch her," Slate warned.

"Shut up! You're tied and can't do nothing."

Slate slowly raised a hand, held it to one side, and shook it.

Hank was so startled he glanced in Slate's direction.

It was all Raven needed. She dived out of Hank's line of sight, and Slate raised the pistol, hooking a foot around Hank's ankles and pulling him off balance. As he fell, throwing out a hand to catch himself, Raven caught him by surprise and twisted the pistol out of his hand.

She stepped back and nodded at Slate.

He raised his brows, obviously impressed. "Good work, Raven."

"We make a pretty good team, don't we?"

"In and out of bed."

Furious, Hank got to his feet. "Okay, you win this one, Texas, but if you don't kill me now I'll be out there just waiting for my chance. You'll be a dead man and she'll be my woman."

"What do you think, Raven?" Slate asked, standing up to let his imposing height add emphasis to his threat.

"You mean, think we should kill him?"

"Yes."

"He deserves it."

"Yes, but it'd make a mess and a lot of noise."

"That's true. Maybe we'd better let him go for now."

"Think it's funny, do you?" Hank fumed. "Well, it won't be so funny when I've got you both where I want you."

"Go on, Hank. Get out of here," Slate said, disgust in his voice. "We're tired of looking at you."

"What about my six-shooter?"

"I think you're better off without it. Besides, Raven may have taken a liking to it."

Hank scowled. "I'll get it back when I come for you." Then he stalked from the room.

Slate started to follow him, but Raven suddenly remembered the telltale initials engraved on the .45 he held. She didn't want him to see the *R.C.* on her pistol, or he might at some time identify her as R. Cunningham. She pushed Hank's gun at him, then grabbed the petticoats and the snub-nosed pistol. He looked surprised.

"That'll shoot farther and straighter," she explained.

He shrugged and followed Hank to make sure the outlaw left their suite and their floor.

As soon as Slate left the room, Raven quickly found her reticule among the petticoats and pushed the pistol safely inside. She breathed a sigh of relief, then hid the reticule in a drawer and stuffed petticoats on top of it. Saved. Slate had never even looked at the gun.

She heard Slate shut the front door and lock it. She took a moment to smooth back her hair and slow her breathing. It had been a narrow escape with Hank and they'd definitely have to be more cautious in the future.

When she turned around, Slate was watching her.

"I shut and locked the door. This time I wedged a chair under the knob. But not much'll keep out a determined outlaw."

"Thanks. I was frightened."

"You'd never have known it."

"Bluff. I was terrified for us both."

"Damn cool head on your shoulders, Raven. And a nice little pistol in your pocket. You continue to surprise me. You normally tote a .45?"

"No. Of course not. It's just that I decided I might need some extra protection when I came West. As you saw, I was right. Of course I wouldn't ever want to use it."

"Nobody does, but if you're packing, chances are you'll have to use it sooner or later."

"Not unless I was forced."

"And provided you could hit anything."

"I was sure if I stood very close I couldn't miss."

"Was it loaded?"

She hesitated and tried to look confused. "I hope

so."

Slate groaned. "You could have got us both killed."

"But I didn't. I helped saved our lives."

"Yes, you did. Quick thinking. And remind me never to have you tie up our enemies. They'd be loose in no time."

"I didn't do it well?" she asked innocently.

"Well? No, you didn't, but what I don't know is if it was intentional or ineptitude. I guess it doesn't matter, but you do begin to puzzle me."

That was something she didn't want. "No puzzle, Slate. I'm just a weak woman trying to survive in the wild West."

"You're a woman all right, but you aren't weak, not by a long shot."

"What about Hank?" she asked, determined to get his mind off her. "Was it safe to let him go?"

"No, but we didn't have a choice. I didn't want to draw any attention to us on account of Sadie, and I didn't want to kill the man, either. Hopefully he'll go back to camp and stay there."

"But you don't expect him to?"

"No. We'll have to be more careful. It was stupid of me to leave my .45 in my room."

"No. You didn't know. I should have warned you earlier that I saw Hank at the train station. He grabbed me and told me he planned to get you and take me back after the gold robbery."

"Damn fool won't give up."

"Also, he told me that he and the other three outlaws are going to be on the Montezuma Special watching us."

"So Arn didn't quite trust me?"

"Maybe he doesn't trust anyone."

"Maybe not. But I bet Hank wasn't supposed to

215

tell you they'd be there."

"No, probably not. But he did."

"And now we'll be watching and waiting for them."

"Yes. We'll have to be very, very careful, Slate."

"More careful than tonight?"

"Much more careful than tonight."

"I apologize. I'm not normally caught that far off guard, but I was thinking of nothing but you and I thought we were safe here in the Montezuma. I'm not going to leave you alone again."

"No?"

"I'll have to spend my nights here to protect you."

"Will that be so bad?"

"Very bad. I'll hardly be able to make myself do it."

"Do what?"

"You know what."

She laughed, a low, sultry sound deep in her throat. "Then perhaps I could get someone else."

He pulled her against his chest. "You've just become a one-man woman, Raven. And I'm the man."

She ran a hand up his bare chest. "How much man are you?"

"Try me."

And she did.

Chapter Sixteen

Two nights later Raven finished dressing and looked at herself in the suite's full-length mirror. After two days of mineral baths and Slate's loving, her skin positively glowed. So did her eyes, but not because of the mineral baths — and she knew it. That was Slate's influence alone.

She glanced at his reflection in the mirror. He was relaxed across one corner of the bed waiting for her, but not anxious to be gone. He had wanted to spend the evening alone with her in the suite, for it was their last night at the Montezuma. The Special had come in late that afternoon and was being readied for their journey to the Shangri-la Mines.

But they weren't going to spend their evening alone. Ted had formally introduced them that afternoon and gotten them all seats for Margarita's last show of the evening. Then he had promised them the best of culinary delights in the Harvey Restaurant, including fresh turtle steak served with giant sea celery salad. Slate had rolled his eyes at that delicacy, but she had told him he must learn to live adventurously.

She didn't really want to go down tonight, either. She didn't want their brief idyll to end, even knowing it must, even knowing how much she depended on them. For once they left the contained, illusory world of the Montezuma, she knew would again be plagued with doubts and fears concerning Slate.

She didn't want to see Margarita perform now, either, didn't want to be reminded of the Texan's beauty and talent. But she had asked Ted for a seat to the show when they'd first arrived and she couldn't refuse now.

She glanced at Slate again in the mirror. He looked very fine in a simple black broadcloth suit with a gray brocade vest. She didn't know where he was getting the clothes he wore at the Montezuma, but they had to be custom-made since he was so tall.

That meant he had brought them with him and kept them somewhere when he was with the outlaws. What she didn't want to think but couldn't avoid was the fact that Margarita must have kept those clothes for him with her costumes until he needed them. He probably had various clothes to wear depending on the robbery.

She hated that idea, and wished her analytical mind wouldn't notice every little detail. Why couldn't she just have enjoyed Slate dressed like a gentleman and let it go? Why did she have to know how and why? But she'd been trained as an investigator and it was as much a part of her as breathing.

"Think you could get a job as a Harvey Girl here, Raven?"

"I don't know. Maybe. But don't get any ideas. Contrary to what you may think, this is not going to be a plush haven for stealing expensive jewelery from guests."

"I wouldn't think of it."

"I bet you wouldn't. Seriously, don't you dare

218

steal anything here."

"Do you think I'd put Sadie's life in any more danger by doing that?"

"I don't know."

"Well, I wouldn't. And thanks for the confidence."

"How do I know what you'd do? I hardly know you."

Slate got up, walked over, and put an arm around her waist. He turned her toward him, tilting her chin up so she'd have to look into his blue-gray eyes. "I don't think you could get to know a man much better than you know me, and you'd better not try."

"All I need is another man underfoot while I'm trying to rescue Sadie."

"You know your plan could get her killed."

"But you promised to help."

"I promised not to tell the outlaws what you're really planning and to give them false information."

"There's one other thing. Ted wants the soldiers to go after Sadie when the outlaws have been subdued, but I'm worried about that."

Slate nodded.

"You've already thought about it?"

"Yes, but I was waiting to mention it until closer to the time of the robbery."

"I hate to ask you for more, but I'd rather you went in after Sadie. Even if the soldiers have the directions to the outlaw camp, we don't know what they'll meet when they get there. If they make a big show of force, Sadie could be killed before they ever reach her."

"That's what I've been thinking. I want to go in after her, if Arn doesn't bring her to the train. I think we can keep hoping for that. I haven't received any message about it yet, and I don't expect to until closer to the time."

"I agree. We can keep hoping they'll bring her with them, but I don't really expect it so we have to have another plan. I just don't like the idea of the soldiers going after her. For one thing, they won't go until the outlaws are subdued, and what if one or more get away and the soldiers don't have time to notice? That really scares me."

"But Ted thinks Sadie'll be safer with more show of force."

"That's right. But I don't agree."

"I don't, either. Back home, the Texas Rangers have a motto, 'One Ranger, One Job.' In other words, no matter how big the problem, or how many outlaws, it takes only one Texas Ranger to handle it. I think that's what this situation needs. One man. I want to go in after her, and I'll do that no matter what Ted wants."

"I guess you'd know about Texas Rangers, considering your occupation."

"I've met a few."

"I agree with you in this, except for one thing."

"What's that?"

"It's going to be a one-man, one-woman job."

"What!"

"I'm going with you."

"Raven, there is no way I'm going to endanger you."

"I've thought about it, and it's the best thing to do."

"You can barely ride a horse, and Ted would never agree."

"I *can* ride. Maybe not as well as you, but I can keep up with you."

"You'll hold me back if it comes to fighting. I'll have to look out for you."

"That's not true, either. You saw me deal with Hank. I'm not completely helpless and you know it."

"I don't want you in danger."

"There's no way to stop me. I'm going with or without you. Besides, how close do you think you can get to Sadie?"

"What do you mean?"

"The last time she saw you at the camp you were part of the outlaw gang. She won't go with you willingly."

"I hadn't thought of that, but I could bring her back anyway."

"She'll have had enough fright by then, Slate. She won't need any more. I'll go, if Arn doesn't bring her to the train. Just make sure you know where they're keeping her."

"They're changing camps, moving closer to the robbery site, but I don't know where or when."

"Arn will send word."

"I hope so, but I still don't want you in on the final battle, Raven. And I sure don't want you going after Sadie, no matter if you can ride or handle a gun or anything. I just don't want you in danger."

"I don't want you in danger, either."

"It's not the same."

"Of course it is."

"You're a woman."

"And you're a man. So? Sadie still needs to be rescued, and if I go she'll stand a better chance of coming out alive. Nothing else matters and you know it."

Slate hesitated a long moment. "You sure don't lack courage, but I'd be worried out of my mind if you went."

"You won't have time to worry."

He pulled her closer and gently stroked her back. "I'd rather put you in an ivory tower so you'd always be safe, but you'd never stand for that, would you?"

"No. You know we can't always stay safe, Slate, no matter how much we might want it. There are some things that are more important."

"And Sadie's one of them."

"Right."

"Okay. I know I'm going to regret it, but we'll work together on this. But if anything happens to you, I'll never forgive myself."

"I'll be fine. It's Sadie we have to worry about."

"I know, but we'll get her back one way or another."

"Yes, we will. And those outlaws will be punished. You don't regret going against your gang, do you?"

"No. Like I told you before, I usually work alone. Besides, there's a code in the West and that gang broke it when they kidnapped two innocent women. I owe Sadie and I always pay my debts."

"Fine, now that that's settled, we should go downstairs."

"Are you sure?"

"Ted's waiting for us. You know, he seems quite taken with you."

"I'm surprised. Far as he knows, I'm just a drifting gun for hire."

"I suppose he must see some finer qualities in you that evade the rest of us."

"I thought you were well aware of all my finer qualities."

"Come on. I can see I'll never win this discussion."

"Not dressed like that."

Raven was wearing a shimmering black gown with

black glass beads woven around the décolletage and down the front of the dress to the small bustle in back. Her arms were bare and she had pulled a sheer black shawl around her shoulders. The gown emphasized her black eyes, making them glow mysteriously. Her hair glimmered silvery gold in the soft light.

"You don't like my gown?"

"I like it so much I want to tear it off."

"Not yet," she said, smiling at him.

He shook his head, put her arm through his, then led her to the door. "It's hard to believe you're just a shy little Harvey Girl."

"I thought I was a money-grubbing—"

"Only when I'm mad at you."

Raven laughed softly, and they left the suite.

As they walked down the hall, she wondered what he'd think if he knew she always wore the gold piece he'd given her in Topeka tucked in a handkerchief that was placed carefully inside her clothes above her heart. It was a silly, sentimental gesture but she still thought of the coin as a good-luck piece and planned to wear it until Sadie was safely returned to them and justice had been won for her father and fiancé.

The Montezuma was even more magnificent at night. The chandeliers blazed on women in brightly colored gowns and men in dark suits who walked and talked through the great lobby. Soft music from a small orchestra came from one end of the Montezuma while the strumming of a guitar and accompanying piano came from another. Slate and Raven followed the second sound.

They made their way to a small theater lavishly decorated in shades of burgundy and coral and were taken to Ted's table near the stage.

"Welcome," he said, standing. "I'm glad to see you two are getting along so well."

Raven smiled softly. Ted had no idea just how well.

"We do seem to have a lot in common," Slate replied, "especially since we all have the welfare of Sadie Perkins as our main concern."

"Yes, indeed," Ted responded. "I'm glad you've agreed to help. Please sit down."

When they were seated at the small table, champagne was served.

Ted held out a glass of the sparkling drink and proposed a toast. "To the quick recovery of my beloved Sadie."

They all clinked glasses, then drank.

"Fine champagne," Slate said.

"Certainly better than what I've heard they serve in the saloons in Topeka," Raven added.

Slate grinned at her. "Rotgut is simple but effective."

Ted laughed. "That's the truth. Can't stand the stuff myself, but, you're right, it's effective."

A dignified announcer in a dark suit walked onto the stage and held up his hands for silence. "Ladies and gentlemen, may I present the one and only Margarita."

A round of applause followed, but Raven privately decided she preferred the boisterous announcer at the Silver Slipper in Topeka.

Margarita made a grand entrance, looking as beautiful and fascinating as ever. her purple satin gown emphasized her diminutive form to perfection, and she moved gracefully to center stage.

Cued by the piano, she began a lilting ballad about dangerous desire, then sang a slow haunting number about lost love. Her eyes went frequently to

Slate, but also included Raven and Ted.

Raven tried not to be jealous of the Spanish beauty, so prized in San Antonio for her talent and charm. How could Slate not be in love with Margarita, especially since they had so much in common and so much to share? But Slate had spent the past two days with her, not Margarita.

Did it mean he could change? And what if he did? What if he came to her with no ties, a changed man? What then? She shivered. No. He would still be a too tall Texas outlaw. She couldn't possible think about getting involved permanently with him. She had her father's agency to run. There was no place in her life for a man like Slate.

Anyway, there was no need to worry about that now. Slate was in no danger of changing, and Margarita was right here near him, no matter where he had spent the past two days. She tried not to let that fact bother her, but it did.

Margarita's repertoire was similar to what she had performed in Topeka, but somehow Raven found herself longing for the rowdy cowboys, so outspoken in their appreciation of Margarita's talents. Maybe she was already becoming used to the wild West and perhaps the luxurious Montezuma was too tame for her now.

The idea surprised her, but maybe it was so. She suddenly realized she was ready to go, anxious to rescue Sadie and get on with finding the mastermind and her father's and fiancé's killer. She need more clues, but she'd already learned a lot. Ted was a prime suspect, no matter how much she wished he wasn't. She liked him and would try to prove him innocent, but if he turned out to be guilty, she'd have to turn him in.

Margarita danced several fast Spanish numbers,

then exited the stage. She was called back twice more before the audience finally let her go.

"I've invited her to dinner," Ted said. "I hope you don't mind."

"I'd like to meet her," Slate replied.

Raven almost choked on her champagne. He was smooth all right. If he *were* undercover, she'd never know. But could he really be undercover? Not an outlaw at all? But why? Who could he really be? Her heart beat faster.

Then she scoffed at herself. She was dreaming, wanting so much to believe that he was something other than a criminal that she would make up stories about him being undercover just like her. But that would be too much of a coincidence. She pushed the thought away.

"I'd like to meet her, too," Raven said, just as smoothly as Slate.

Slate raised a brow at her, and she smiled in reply.

When Margarita joined them, she had changed to a simple gown of pale lavender. It complemented her exotic coloring perfectly. Around her neck she wore a large, gold, heart locket on a long golden chain. Even without her shimmering stage clothes, Margarita was breathtaking, and Raven couldn't resist a glance at Slate.

He was smiling warmly in greeting, and not giving away in the least the fact that he and Margarita were old friends.

"You were as wonderful as usual," Ted said, then looked at Slate and Raven. "Miss Margarita, I'd like you to meet Raven West, a Harvey Girl, and Slate Slayton. They'll both be working on the Montezuma Special."

"How nice," Margarita murmured, "and how nice to meet you both."

Margarita gave no hint of recognizing either of them. Raven didn't know what game they were all playing, but it was probably for the best that they were pretending to have just met. It would have been hard to explain how Raven had met Margarita in a silver exchange in Topeka. It was not a place a prospective Harvey Girl would have gone.

Nevertheless, it worried her to be caught up in so much intrigue. She was reminded once more that she couldn't trust anyone, not even Slate, no matter how concerned and caring he seemed to be. She had just seen how well he could act and his interest in her could all be some type of ruse. Yet, she couldn't believe that of him. He wanted her as much as she wanted him. But they both played tangled games.

"Is everyone ready to dine?" Ted asked, smiling.

"I'm certainly hungry," Margarita replied. "After the last show, I'm always famished."

"Then you'll be especially appreciative of the Harvey Restaurant."

"I've been enjoying it all week, and if I'm not careful I'll soon be unable to wear any of my costumes."

Ted laughed. "You look in no danger of that, my dear. I'm the one who has to worry about outgrowing his clothes. But let's don't think about that now. I'm famished, too."

They were soon at the Harvey Restaurant where they were greeted warmly and given one of the best tables. The aroma of delicious food filled the air, and Harvey Girls, in their neat black and white uniforms, hurried efficiently from table to table.

Ted smiled at Raven. "How do you feel being served, instead of serving?"

"I feel like I should get up, put on my uniform, and rush to help them. You have no idea what it's like in the Harvey Houses during the lunch hours. It's amazing just how fast we can serve passengers."

"I've seen it, and it *is* amazing," Ted agreed. "Quite impressive, too."

Ted insisted they all try the fresh turtle soup. And while they ate it, he explained, "Four turtles, weighing around two hundred pounds each, are brought in over the Sonora Railway each week and kept alive in a small pool in the Rio Gallinos until they're used in the restaurant. Now you must admit that is the ultimate in fresh food."

"About as fresh as killing a rabbit, skinning it, and roasting it on the same spot," Slate replied.

Raven kicked Slate under the table, and he turned innocent eyes on her.

"You're right about there being plenty of fresh meat on the prairie, Slate," Ted agreed, "but you've got to admit there are no two-hundred-pound sea turtles just walking around waiting to be killed for dinner."

Slate laughed. "No, I have to admit I haven't seen any. None in Texas, either."

"You're sure?" Raven asked.

"Well, just because I haven't seen any in Texas doesn't mean there aren't any."

Everyone laughed, then Margarita added, "Although you might find them in the Gulf of Mexico."

"Well, anyway," Ted defended his position. "You won't find this type of culinary delight out in the prairie."

"That's for sure," Margarita agreed. "The soup *is* delicious, Ted. I can hardly wait for the rest of the meal."

Raven smiled, but didn't say anything. She was feeling rather bad about the turtles. They must be very old to be that size, and then to end their life in a stewpot. It didn't seem quite right. But on the other hand, perhaps something else would have eaten them in the sea.

Ted insisted they all try turtle steak for dinner, but he was the only one who ended up ordering it. Slate was satisfied with a very large, very rare piece of steak. Margarita took broiled fish, and Raven decided on quail. But that was just a small part of the seven-course meal they were served.

When Raven thought she couldn't eat another bite, they finally stopped bringing food. She leaned back in her chair to relax over a cup of coffee, but Ted wasn't done yet.

"Now it's time to dance," he said.

Everyone groaned.

"It's important to work off such a huge meal," he insisted.

Slate laughed. "All right, maybe we better if we're all going to work tomorrow."

They went to the ballroom which was another Montezuma luxury, with a dance floor of beautiful, dark Jacaranda wood which gleamed in the soft light of huge ornate chandeliers. Many guests were waltzing to the music of a small orchestra.

Slate didn't hesitate, but took Raven's hand and led her to the dance floor. Taking her in his arms, he began to glide smoothly around the floor. For a moment the sheer pleasure of dancing with him overrode all thought, then she realized that a Texas outlaw was dancing very well, and a waltz at that.

She had learned to dance in a Chicago girl's school, but had never used the skill very much. Now she was glad she could easily follow Slate as he led her, dipping and swaying to the rhythm of the music. Suddenly she didn't care where he'd learned to dance or how or why. She just gave herself up the pleasure of the moment.

Slate pulled her closer, and her heart beat faster. "You dance with me very well, Raven. It seems we're suited to each other."

"It seems so, but I can't help wondering where and why an outlaw learned to dance."

"I wasn't always an outlaw, and my mother hoped I'd be a gentleman."

"I see. Is she very disappointed in you?"

He hesitated, and for the second time at the mention of his mother Raven saw the pain in his eyes, then he shut it away, and replied, "Only that I never married."

"And she wants that?"

"I believe I could quote her accurately by saying that the love of a good woman will cure anything."

"Even a cold?"

"Most certainly that. A good woman will have a remedy for everything."

Raven laughed. "Then you may have to look a long time for that good a woman."

"Not so long," he said, his eyes a deep blue.

Raven blushed. "I don't have any remedies, Slate."

"And I don't have any ailments, so we're fine, aren't we?"

"Yes."

They smiled at each other, and he whirled her around the room, their bodies moving in perfect unison until the music stopped. Then they joined Ted and Margarita at a small table.

"You two certainly dance well together," Margarita said, smiling at Raven.

"Meaning I didn't step on her toes more than a dozen times?" Slate asked.

"Right," Ted agreed, but now it's my turn to prove I'm lighter on my feet than I look."

And he was. Ted and Margarita made a fascinating couple, for they were both obviously dancers at heart. As they whirled around the dance floor, the crowd soon parted to watch Ted and Margarita smoothly execute fancy steps and swirls and dips. They were magnificent, and when they stopped, laughing and breathless, the crowd clapped their approval. Margarita curtsied, and they returned to Slate and Raven.

"That was wonderful," Raven said, really impressed. "I had no idea you were such a dancer, Ted."

"A love of mine, although I'm nothing compared to a professional like Margarita."

"Don't believe him," Margarita chided. "He's very good. I think we should get him a tour, what do you think, Slate?"

"Sounds good to me."

"Thanks," Ted replied. "That'd be fun, but I'm afraid I also love the railroads and Santa Fe's got my heart first."

"Too bad," Raven said. "The stage missed a great performer."

"You are all so very kind," Ted responded, then glanced away, a sudden sorrow and worry in his eyes. "But I'm afraid I must leave you now. The Montezuma Special leaves at dawn and I've got to make sure that all the last details are in place." He looked at Raven.

She nodded, understanding his silent communication. He wanted to check everything again to make sure nothing had been overlooked when they left to rescue Sadie.

Satisfied, he put a hand on Slate's shoulder. "See you first thing in the morning, and glad to have you aboard."

"Thanks. I'll be there."

"And, Miss Margarita, it has been a rare pleasure to know you."

"Perhaps we'll meet again. I'll be performing in other New Mexico towns after my engagement at the Montezuma is over."

"I'll look forward to seeing you again then." Ted turned to them all and nodded. "Thank you for a delightful evening."

As he walked away, Margarita said, "For such a nice man, he's very sad."

Raven held her breath a moment. Had Slate told Margarita about Sadie and what they were going to do? It would mean a lot if he hadn't.

"Perhaps he lost a great love," Slate said.

Margarita glanced at him, and suddenly her eyes filled with tears. "Perhaps. It happens more frequently than one would think." Then she stood up. "Good night. I must rest now." She hurried from the table.

"Did we do something to upset her?" Raven asked, surprised at Margarita's sudden departure. Maybe she realized she had lost Slate. Or had she lost another love?

"She's an entertainer. Temperamental. She'll be all right," Slate said, but his eyes showed concern.

"Perhaps you should go to her." Raven hated to say that, but she just couldn't seem to dislike Margarita. She admired the woman's talent and determination to tour through the West all alone. Of course, she was with Slate part of the time, and then there was the robbery business. But she had trouble thinking of Margarita as a criminal. And that had been genuine sorrow in the singer's eyes. Or had it just been an act by an accomplished actor?

Raven didn't know what to think and was tired of questioning everything. Why couldn't life just be simple?

"She doesn't need me. She's an old friend and a strong woman. She'll make it on her own."

Raven should have been thrilled to hear those words, but instead she wondered if Slate were being cavalier, throwing away one woman for another, when one obviously needed comfort. Then, again, it might all have been an act.

"Dance with me again, Raven, then let's go upstairs and finish the dance in bed."

"Are you sure Margarita doesn't need us?"

"There's nothing we can do for her. Take my word for it. Now it's just the two of us and I want to feel you close to me again."

He took her hand, and led her to the dance floor.

Chapter Seventeen

The Montezuma Special traveled west from Las Vegas, crossing the Pecos River and the Sangre de Cristo Mountain Range. It stopped briefly at Lamy to pick up passengers from Santa Fe, which was connected by a branch line. It continued on to the Rio Grande River, and turned south at Santo Domingo Pueblo. From there Santa Fe tracks paralleled the Rio Grande down New Mexico to El Paso, Texas, where the Southern Pacific took over with a railway to San Antonio.

At Albuquerque the Montezuma Special stopped again. A few more passengers boarded. Telegrams were sent and received. Fresh food was stocked. But the train did not go on. The passengers became restless and were given a few hours to explore the Indian markets.

Raven changed clothes, pinned her watch to her bodice, then slipped off the Special. She made sure no one was following her, then struck out for the main part of town. If possible, she needed to get more information about Comanche Jack. She hoped he was working closely with the outlaws on the gold robbery and that they could catch him when the outlaws attacked.

Since she'd had good luck with a dry goods store in Topeka, she decided to try asking questions at that same type of store in Albuquerque. Outlaws had to have supplies the same as anybody else, and would probably prefer to buy them in a larger town to be less conspicuous.

Wearing her simple gray dress, she began asking questions in the dry goods stores. The proprietors wouldn't admit to knowing Comanche Jack or having seen a one-handed man, and by the time she reached the fifth and last store, she was in a disreputable part of town and very discouraged.

But not daunted. She entered the store. It was dim and dusty. How it stayed in business she didn't know. She glanced about. Most of the merchandise was covered with dust from long neglect. The proprietor was an unhealthy looking man of indeterminate age.

"What can I do for you, ma'am?" he asked, eyeing her intently.

"Bullets."

"Got some pretty ribbon here somewhere."

"I've got a Colt .45. I need bullets for it."

He hesitated, looked at her more closely, then said, "All right. You got a man wants them but don't want to come in. I understand. Here they are." He set a box of bullets on the counter.

Raven noticed the box wasn't dusty and the proprietor had had no trouble finding it. That and his comment made her think he might do business with outlaws frequently. Perfect.

"I also need some information."

"What kind? Ain't healthy to ask too many questions in Albuquerque."

"I need to see a man who's reported to be in the area. He has a hook in place of a left hand. Seen him?"

"Who wants to know?"

"My name's Raven. I've got a little job for Comanche Jack, but he's on the move."

The proprietor nodded. "I might have seen him, seeing as it's business."

Raven placed double the money for the bullets on the counter. "Keep the change."

"A woman who speaks my language. He was in a few days ago. Bought quite a bit."

"Guns? Bullets?"

"Right. And food, too."

"Probably planning a big job."

"Maybe, or just a little hunting trip."

"Could be. I'm not interested either way. But if he comes back sometime soon, would you tell him a woman named Raven is looking for him? I've got a job I think he'd be interested in handling."

"Sure, but I don't see much of Comanche Jack. And nobody sees him if he don't want to be seen. Comanche training, you know."

"Yes, I know. But you'll give him my message if you can?"

"Sure, lady."

"Thanks." Raven stuffed the bullets in her reticule, then stepped outside. It was a dry, dusty, and cool day. She hurried down the boardwalk, very pleased with her discovery and that her story had worked again and headed for the Santa Fe depot.

She checked the time on her watch. She wasn't late, and there was time to get back before anyone became suspicious of her whereabouts. But there was one other thing she wanted to do in Albuquerque before the Special left.

She walked back to the main part of town. There was a small confection shop near a large hotel. A young boy was sitting on the boardwalk outside, tossing a stick.

She nodded to him as she walked inside, bought six peppermint sticks, came back out, and knelt beside him.

"You can have two of these peppermint sticks if you'll do me a favor."

He glanced at the candy and nodded eagerly.

"I'd like for you to go to the telegraph office and send a telegram for me."

"Ma'am?"

"It'll be simple and I'll give you the money."

He kept his eyes on the candy and nodded again.

"The message I want sent is 'Don't worry. I'm closing in. R. Cunningham.' Do you think you can remember that?"

He scratched his head, still eyeing the candy. Raven handed him a peppermint stick. He grabbed it and began licking and chewing, his hands and face getting stickier and stickier.

"If you deliver the message exactly, there will be two more peppermint sticks for you when you return."

He nodded, finishing off the last of the candy, as Raven repeated the message. "It needs to be sent to T.R. Simpson. Can you remember that?" Then she spelled Cunningham for him.

"Don't worry. I'm closing in. R. Cunningham. Send to T.R. Simpson," he repeated, his eyes screwed shut.

"Exactly. Now, here's the money. I'll be watching."

He nodded once, took another look at the candy, then ran down the street and into the telegraph office.

Raven waited. Would he get the message right? Would he deliver it at all, or simply take off with

237

the money? She didn't know, but she had to take the chance. She didn't want to be seen twice sending messages from R. Cunningham at telegraph offices so close together.

After a short time, the door to the telegraph office banged open, and the boy rushed back to her, a proud grin on his face. "I did it. I remembered every word. It's going right now."

"Thank you. You did a good job."

She handed him all five of the peppermint sticks and he gasped in awe. "That's too much, ma'am. We only agreed on two more."

"I know. But you were very fast, and perhaps you have a young sister at home who might enjoy one."

"Hannah! But just one!" He ran away and was soon lost down a side street.

Raven smiled at his youthful enthusiasm. She had once felt young and happy, but not for a long time, not since her father and fiancé had been killed. She sighed, then walked back into the confection shop and bought six more peppermint sticks. If she needed it, she wanted an excuse for having gone into town. The candy was a perfect cover. Besides, she like peppermint.

She checked her watch, made sure there was time to walk leisurely back to the train, and took out a peppermint stick. Sucking the sweet candy, she started toward the Special.

She hadn't walked far down the boardwalk when she had the distinct feeling she was being watched. She stopped in front of a store with a large window and looked at the reflection of the street across from her. She couldn't see anything suspicious. She looked back down the boardwalk. Nothing there, either.

She decided she was probably just getting jumpy

since it would soon be time to rescue Sadie. She started walking again, a little faster. Again the feeling came. She hesitated, then kept on walking. The feeling became very distinct, and she whirled around. A man ducked into a store out of sight, but not before she'd recognized him. Hank!

Her breath caught in her throat. Had he been following her long? Had he seen her go into the dry goods store where Comanche Jack had shopped? If he had, would he know Jack had been there and get suspicious about Sadie?

She turned back and began to walk faster. Hank couldn't do anything in broad daylight. He was probably just in town for a few drinks and had happened to see her. She'd been careful when she left the Special to make sure no one had seen her or was following her. Of course, she might have missed Hank if he'd been extremely cautious.

Well, there was nothing she could do about it now, and there was no point in worrying. She looked back again, but didn't see him. What she saw instead was Slate going into the telegraph office. She was surprised. Why hadn't Slate used the one at the train station? Ted would have been glad for him to have used it in an official capacity. Why had he come into town to use one in secret, like she had?

Perhaps it wasn't in secret. There was no need to think there was something ominous about Slate sending or receiving a telegram. But it *was* suspicious, and she especially hated to have witnessed it when they were so close to rescuing Sadie.

It was just one more thing she didn't understand and couldn't control. This was a terribly complicated case. No wonder her father and fiancé had had so much trouble solving it. And it was very dangerous, too. She had to remember that. She didn't know how many people had already been killed at the mastermind's command. But she was going to stop him, somehow, someway.

She decided to see what Slate did next so she turned the next corner, stopped, and caught her breath. Using the side of the building as cover, she glanced around the corner.

Hank crossed the street to join Slate outside the telegraph office. Then Arn arrived. They talked intently for several minutes. Hank pointed in Raven's direction. She ducked out of sight, sure they hadn't seen her but also sure they'd been discussing her. When she looked again, they'd separated and Slate was walking toward the train station.

She berathed a sigh of relief, and hurried after Slate. Now she knew why he'd gone to the telegraph office, and why Hank had been in the area. Arn had arranged to meet them there. Maybe now Slate had the last of their instructions and they could start the final run to Sadie.

When she caught up with Slate, she said, "Well, fancy meeting you here, cowboy."

Startled, he spun around, going for his gun.

She threw up her hands in mock surrender.

He frowned, then relaxed. "Damn, Raven, don't sneak up on a man like that. You could get yourself shot."

"I didn't sneak. Your mind must have been elsewhere."

"It probably was," he responded, drawing her hand through the crook of his arm.

As usual, she thrilled to the touch of him, and noticed that he shortened his long stride so she could easily walk with him. "Want a peppermint stick?" she asked.

"So that's why you're in town." He took one and began eating it. "Reminds me of Topeka. You sure ran me a merry chase there."

"Not at all. You just decided to make me your business." She made a point of stroking the long piece of candy with her tongue, and noticed how his eyes turned an intense blue as he watched the motion.

"You *are* my business. Do that long enough, and I'm going to take you back to the Special and see how well a Pullman berth handles two."

"Whatever do you mean, sir?"

"You know exactly what I mean."

"Want a bite of my candy?"

"I'm going to take a bite out of you here and now if you don't stop that."

"Why, Mr. Slayton, where are your manners?"

"In bed. Want to go find them?"

Raven laughed, finished her stick of peppermint, and squeezed Slate's hard arm. "I think we'd better find Sadie first."

"A wise woman." Slate crunched the last of his candy and added, "I've got the news we've been waiting for."

"Oh, Slate. Is it soon?"

"Yes. But let's not discuss it now. We'll meet alone with Ted as soon as we get back to the Special."

"Good. Poor Sadie. I just hope she's still all right."

"Far as I know she is, but Hank's going to be a problem. He's more alert than the others, watching too much, seeing too much, too suspicious."

"Should we stop him?"

"We can't afford to make Arn any more suspicious than Hank already has. No, we've got to go

241

on like we have, but he's the man we'll have to watch when it all happens."

"I won't let him out of my sight."

"Good. Now let's get to Ted's car."

Ted's private coach was coupled to the end of the Montezuma Special, and Raven and Slate walked directly there. Slate helped Raven up the several steps to the platform, and knocked on the door.

Ted jerked it open. "Come in. Any news?"

"Yes," Slate replied.

"Sit down and I'll get you a drink. Whiskey?"

"Yes, thanks."

Raven and Slate sat down on a deeply cushioned velvet couch. Ted handed Slate a whiskey, a brandy to Raven, then sat down across from them, a glass of port in his hand and a rapt expression on his face.

"I just met with Arn," Slate began.

Raven glanced around the compact parlor and marveled that, if anything, the room was more ornate and opulent than the Montezuma Special. Heavy velvets and rich brocades, dark, delicately carved woods, and gleaming brass filled the room. Heavy lead crystal decanters displayed a wide assortment of liquors, and delicate crystal glasses set gleaming on a massive mahogany bar.

"Where are we supposed to stop to let them rob the Special?" Ted asked.

"I don't know," Slate replied.

"What?"

"Hank's been trying to convince Arn that Raven's made me change sides. It was all I could do to make Arn believe the robbery should go ahead and take place on schedule."

"But Arn wouldn't tell you where?"

"A precaution on his part so we couldn't have the

242

law waiting there for him."

"And he doesn't suspect that the passengers on this train are soldiers and army nurses?"

"No. At least I hope not."

"Then what's going to happen?" Raven asked.

"We're to pick up the gold, then continue on toward El Paso like we were taking the gold there as usual."

"Good. Just as we'd planned," Ted said. "In fact, to make everything look as normal as possible, I've already wired ahead that we're coming to El Paso. I've invited Southern Pacific's special representative to meet us there."

"Why?" Raven asked, as casually as she could. If they actually could meet Jeremy Luis Centrano there, she would be able to observe her other prime suspect without his being the least wary of her. This was excellent news.

"Santa Fe wants to run all the way to the West Coast. The Southern Pacific already has a railway in that area and we're negotiating to use it. I want Centrano, that's their special representative, to see the Montezuma Special, even ride on it, to get an idea of what we can do with a special train running nonstop from the coast clear to Chicago."

"That's an impressive ambition," Slate said.

"Yes, and we'll do it, too. Problem is, Southern Pacific hasn't been very anxious to work with us before. We're hoping if we can solve this robbery problem together and they can get an idea of the scope of our Montezuma Special dream, they'll be willing to work with us."

"Or maybe they'll see you as too much competition," Slate suggested.

"That's been the problem so far. But none of this has anything to do with rescuing Sadie. I'm just explaining that for Santa Fe's records, as well as the Southern Pacific's, there's a reason for using the Montezuma Special to pick up this gold shipment and take it to El Paso."

"Good thinking," Slate replied approvingly. "You've done a good job of setting it all up."

"I've tried to think of everything," Ted said, "and anticipate any problems."

"Wasn't it hard to keep the soldiers and nurses a secret?"

Ted smiled. "Not really. A commander I know owed me a favor. Only he and I and the people on this train know exactly where those men and women were sent."

"And after it's all over?" Raven asked.

"When Sadie's safely back and the robbery ring is caught, then we'll all be happy to announce our success. Until then, only a few of us will really know what is going on."

Raven was surprised to realize that Ted must have told Slate about the robberies plaguing the Santa Fe and the Southern Pacific. That must mean he'd also told Slate about the Cunningham Agency and her father and fiancé. That was putting a lot of trust in a relative stranger, and she couldn't help but wonder why. It also made her very suspicious of Ted. He could so easily be the mastermind. Everything pointed to it.

"I think we can all relax until tomorrow when we pick up the gold," Slate said. "After that, they could strike at any time and we'll have to be ready."

Ted finished his port, "I'll be ready, and those outlaws had better not have hurt my Sadie."

"Arn says they're bringing Sadie with them. If all goes smoothly, he'll turn her over to you then," Slate added.

244

"Do you believe him?" Ted asked.

"I'd like to, but Hank has poisoned his mind so much that I don't think we can."

"But we'll have to wait and see if they bring her, won't we?" Raven asked.

"Yes," Slate agreed. "When the robbery is taking place, someone is going to have to slip off the train and check the outlaws horses."

"And see if Sadie's with them?" Raven asked.

"But they might have hidden her nearby," Ted added. "We can't take a chance. How can we attack when gunfire might be the death of her?"

"That's a good question," Slate said. "Hank has complicated things."

"But we've got to know," Raven insisted.

"I agree, but how?" Ted asked.

"I'll do it," Raven said.

"What can you do?" Slate questioned.

"I'll find Hank and ask him."

"That's too dangerous," Slate replied.

"Of course it's dangerous, but Sadie's position is even worse. Hank will know and I can goad him into telling me."

"But you don't know where he is," Ted said.

"He's on this train, and if I make myself available he'll come to me."

"It's too dangerous," Slate objected again. "I can force him to tell me."

"And give yourself away?" Raven asked. "No. That won't do at all."

"We could let them rob the train as planned and I could go with them," Slate suggested.

"You'd never get Sadie out alone, Slate," Raven insisted.

"We could send the soldiers after him," Ted added.

"You know what their last hideout was like, Slate," Raven continued. "No one could sneak up on them. "They'd kill Sadie at the first sign of a soldier. No, I'll have to get the information from Hank and that's that."

Neither of the men protested again, but they both looked worried.

"Look," Raven said. "You can be nearby, Slate, and I can call for help if I need it."

"No. I'll be nearby, but I'll give you just so long before I come and get you."

"Okay," Raven agreed.

"Let me know as soon as you learn something," Ted said.

"All right," Raven replied, "but for now I'm going to relax a little. Tonight I'll stalk Hank."

"And I'll be right with you," Slate added, standing up.

"Thanks for the brandy," Raven said, then left Ted's coach.

Not long after, the Montezuma Special pulled out of Albuquerque for the Shangri-la Mines.

Chapter Eighteen

That night Raven went to the library car. It was late, very late. Past midnight. The passengers were all tucked in their Pullman berths, sleeping or supposedly so. Some were on watch, of course.

Raven pretended she couldn't sleep and was in search of a book. Slate was hiding behind the curtain separating the library from the barber shop. The light was low, and shadows lurked around the big, comfortable chairs. She unlocked a cabinet, thumbed through several books. And waited.

Nothing. She selected one, relocked the cabinet, and sat down. She pretended to read, but couldn't. What if Hank hadn't been watching her and hadn't seen her go into the library car?

She waited. Time passed. She checked her watch. Past one now. Where was he? She put the book up and selected another. Slate was so still she'd never have known he was there.

Then suddenly there was a slight sound.

She whirled around.

"Miss me, Harvey Girl?" Hank asked.

Raven gasped, not having to feign her surprise.

"Sneak out on Texas, did you? Not enough man to keep you busy all night?"

"I enjoy reading."

"Sure you do. Need some company? I remember what you said back at Montezuma. You liked me best. You meant it, didn't you?"

"No more than you mean to take me when Arn comes for the gold."

"Oh, you're going with me all right. You and me and the other Harvey Girl are going to have a good time with the gold in Mexico."

"But Arn's bringing Sadie to the train, isn't he? That's the bargain, right?"

Hank laughed. "Damn stupid railroad people. We're going to get the Harvey Girls *and* the gold. They're going to get nothing."

"But Slate wouldn't let you take me."

"I wouldn't worry about that if I were you. Texas is going home the easy way."

"What do you mean?"

"In a pine box."

"You're going to kill him?"

"Sure. I already told you that, pretty woman, so you'd better start being nice to me so I'll be nice to you later. Now give me a kiss. I've been thinking about how soft and willing you looked in that big bed at Montezuma. I wanted you bad then. I still do."

"Slate's around somewhere, checking things. You don't want to ruin Arn's plans, do you?"

"Right now I don't care about nothing but getting my hands all over you."

"Aren't you afraid I'll scream and bring somebody running?"

"No, you're not going to scream. You're not going to tell anybody what you know. And you're going with me real nice and polite like when Arn comes for the gold."

248

"Why is that?"

"Because they've got your friend back at camp and they're going to keep her there. If you do anything I don't like, she'll get it when we get there. Now you know why you're going to let me put my hands all over you."

Raven frowned at him. "Stay away from me."

"Fiery, aren't you? I like my women that way, but it don't last long, not with me."

"You stay away from me," Raven warned, backing up.

He stepped close, his breath hot and sour on her face, and put a hard calloused hand on her arm. "I'm going to get a lot closer, little lady."

"No you're not," Raven countered as Slate stepped from behind the curtain and hit Hank on the head with the barrel of his gun.

Hank slumped unconscious to the carpet.

"You'd better put your book back, Raven. Let's get out of here before he wakes up and sees me and I have to deal with him more permanently."

Raven replaced her library book, and quickly followed Slate from the car.

Out on the platform, he said, "I'm going to tell the captain what you just learned. You'd better tell Ted. It changes our plans."

"All right. And, Slate, thanks for being there."

He pulled her against him. "I'd never have let you face him alone. You're *my* woman." Then he planted a hard kiss on her lips, sending waves of longing through her. When he reluctantly raised his head, he groaned. "You'd better go before I forget all our responsibilities."

Raven went one way and Slate the other. She hurried through the baggage car, feeling uneasy at all the dark shapes and shadows that filled the dimly lighted coach. Anything or anyone could be hiding and lurking there. But she had to get to Ted with her information. She continued on until she reached Ted's private coach.

She knocked on the door, feeling the cool night air surround her as the train sped toward Shangri-la Mines.

Ted jerked the door open. "Raven, come in. What have you learned?"

"Sit down, Ted. It isn't good. They're not bringing Sadie, and I don't think the soldiers should go after her."

"Why not? What better chance will she have?"

"We've discussed it before, but now I'm really sure that Slate and I should ride in after her while the soldiers are subduing the outlaws."

"But, Raven, *you* can't go. Something could happen to you, too!"

"Ted, by now Sadie's not going to trust any man she sees, and certainly not Slate. The last time she saw him he was one of the outlaws in the gang that kidnapped her. She's been terribly frightened. I'm the only person she's going to trust, other than you, and you can't go in there. You've got to stay and take care of the gold, the outlaws, and the soldiers. Who's left but me?"

"Raven, I can't let you go to that outlaw camp."

"You can't stop me. Sadie's my friend. Arn's not going to have left very many men back at the camp. Just enough to keep Sadie hostage. Maybe two or three. Slate and I can handle them if he goes in as part of the gang. Don't you see, if anyone they don't know gets close to that camp they probably have orders to kill Sadie immediately. We just can't chance that."

Ted ran a hand through his hair. He looked scared

for Sadie. "This is all almost too much for me. I don't want to endanger you. I feel very guilty, but maybe you're right. Does Slate agree?"

"Yes. He's like you, worried about me, but what choice do we have? And, Ted, we can't let any of the outlaws escape and get back there before us."

"No. I understand that. I wish I could go, too. I feel so helpless and I'm not used to the feeling."

"I understand, but Slate and I will be there. We'll get Sadie back. Don't worry."

"All right. I guess that's the way it'll have to be, but you aren't the only one I'm relying on."

"No?"

"Look at this." He handed her a small sheet of paper. "Read that."

Raven took it from him and recognized the telegram she'd had the boy in Albuquerque send him. She read it, then handed the piece of paper back. "Is this from that private investigator?"

"Yes. He's on the job, and I think I know who he is."

Raven's eyes widened and her heart sank. "Who?"

"Slate Slayton. He fits every single requirement. Listen, he was in Topeka, at the outlaws' camp, rescued you, and is now helping to find Sadie by taking a job on the Special. He's obviously a master of disguise. Have you ever heard such a perfect copy of a Texas accent? Imagine! The man's from Chicago, but I'd swear he was from Texas."

"So would I," Raven said with a sinking heart. How could Ted possibly believe Slate was R. Cunningham? No wonder he'd seemed so taken with Slate and had gone out of his way to help him. He thought Slate was her! What a crazy mess. But, on the other hand, what if this were all a clever ploy by the mastermind to throw her off the scent and make

251

him look innocent? Well, if Ted were the mastermind he was an incredible actor.

"See what I mean?" Ted continued enthusiastically. "Slate Slayton. Even the name he chose for his undercover persona sounds Texan. I tell you we must have hired the best. As long as you're going to be with Slate, I won't be so worried. R. Cunningham can take care of you if anyone can."

"Well, I believe that," Raven fervently agreed.

"But don't let on you know. Cunningham is determined to keep his true identity secret. Two others from his agency were killed on this job and he's being cautious. But what a man! Things began to break loose the minute he got on the case."

"I'm impressed," Raven said, silently fuming to hear Slate get all the praise she deserved. Slate Slayton was just a no-good, two-timing outlaw and Ted was somehow convinced that he was a Chicago detective. Or that's what Ted wanted her to believe. Either way, her true identity was safe and that's what counted, but it still rankled.

"I'm impressed, but don't tell him," Ted added.

"Oh, I won't. Anyway, he may not be this Cunningham from Chicago."

"I really think he is, and I can't wait to tell Sadie. Just get her back to me soon, all right?"

"We will. Don't worry. But right now, I'm going to get some sleep."

"Good idea. I will, too. After we pick up the gold tomorrow morning, we won't be able to rest until it's all over."

"I'll see you tomorrow then."

Raven left the private coach and made her way back to one of the Pullman sleeping cars which she shared with the nurses. They were all fast asleep and she wearily climbed into bed. She pulled the covers

252

up around her chin, but couldn't sleep. She was too tense.

She hadn't bothered to get undressed, in case something suddenly happened, so she finally got up and walked out quietly. Outside, she sat down on the platform and let the wind whip through her hair. The air was dry and dusty and the smell was very different from the grassy plains of Kansas. Here they were running near the Rio Grande and the scent of trees and flowers and bushes along the riverbank filled the air.

The rattle of the train as it ran along the tracks was a constant noise, and in the distance she heard the faint lonely whistle of another locomotive.

She felt very alone in this vast, sprawling country and so far from everything she had known and loved. Even though Slate had come along and turned her senses upside down, she still felt lonely, for he was a dangerous, unknown quantity. Sadie was her only friend here and she would find some way to save Sadie as she'd been unable to save her father and fiancé.

Suddenly the door opened. She jumped and started to get up.

"Just me, Raven," Slate said, sitting down beside her. "You all right?"

"Couldn't sleep."

"Me neither. You got it worked out with Ted?"

"Yes. We're going in after Sadie."

"Good. That's the best way to handle it." He took her hand, and rubbed a thumb across her knuckles. "Raven, sometimes these things don't go according to plan."

"It'll be all right."

"We'll do our best, but you never know. Those are tough, determined men, especially Hank. What I'm trying to say is that I may have been too rough and ready with you before. After all, you were a virgin. What I want to know is that no matter what happens, I wanted you more than any woman I've ever known."

"You've already told me that."

"I know it, but I'm getting to the new part. If things were different, if I didn't have a job to do, well, I might have asked you to marry me."

There was a long silence, and the wind howled around the platform.

"If I had asked you and if I weren't an outlaw, what would you have said?"

Once more the wind howled and Raven remained silent. Finally she said, "What about Margarita?"

"Margarita? I don't know. What has she got to do with this?"

"Well, I thought—"

"I told you we were friends. But what does it have to do with us?"

"How can you ask that?"

"You don't make any sense, Raven. Forget Margarita. Would you have said yes if I'd asked you?"

"How do I know? You *didn't* ask me, and you *are* an outlaw."

"Okay. I'm asking you."

"What!"

"Will you marry me?"

Raven stumbled to her feet, clutching the railing for support. "How can you say that? We're going into danger tomorrow. Who knows what will happen?"

Slate stood up, too, towering over her. "That's my point."

"But I thought you didn't want to marry me."

"Maybe I changed my mind."

"Maybe?"

"You've got to admit we can't be beat in bed, Raven."

"So what? I believe marriage is supposed to be more than that."

"All right. I'm committing to you. What more do you want?"

"Well, of all the crazy marriage proposals."

"Crazy? What do you mean? Do I need an expensive ring? I'll get one next stop. Do I have to get down on my knee? All right, I'm there. What more do you want?"

"You'd probably steal the ring!"

"Damn it. That's it. I told you I'd go straight."

"You did?"

"Sure."

"Now?"

"No, not now. When this job is over."

"And then it'd be the next job and the next. I'd hardly ever see you. You'd stop by for a quick kiss, then have to be on your way because a posse was after you. Or I'd suddenly get a telegram telling me you were to be hung at noon somewhere and would I like to come? Slate, I couldn't live that way!"

"You have a very vivid imagination. Does it mean you care?"

"Care? You're great in bed, Slate. Why don't we leave it at that?"

"I'm afraid you'll get away."

"Where would I go?"

"Once you get your uncle's legacy, you'll probably be off to Europe or someplace."

"Oh, so that's it. You have some misguided idea that if you marry me now, then help me get proof of my uncle's death, that you'll eventually be wed to a wealthy woman."

"No, that's not at all what I meant. I don't want your damn money, if you ever get it. I've got plenty of my own."

"You mean, you can steal plenty of your own."

"Raven, I don't know why we're having this argument. I just wanted to know if you wanted to marry me. I guess it's pretty damn obvious you don't."

"It's just that—"

"Don't bother. I think you already explained yourself damn well. When you get your uncle's money, you want to run high, wide, and free."

"You don't understand, I—"

"Sure I do, and now I'm going to get some sleep. It'll be a long day tomorrow. Anyway, asking you to marry me was damn hard. I'm plumb tuckered out. Good night."

"Slate, I—"

He opened the door, then turned back and brushed Raven's lips with his. "You're the damnedest woman I ever met, Raven. Everything you do and say makes me want you that much more. But next time you're going to have to ask *me* to marry you."

Then he was gone, and Raven collapsed back against the coach. The cool night air felt good against her hot skin. Why had she argued with him? Why hadn't she just answered him?

But she knew why and it scared her. She'd wanted to say yes, and let the chips fall where they may. But she hadn't been raised that way. She had a job to do. Justice to be won. An agency to run.

And Slate Slayton was an outlaw, no matter what Ted Simpson might think. An outlaw and the sexiest man she'd ever met. If she hadn't known better, she might even have thought she was just the least little bit in love with him. But she knew better. She knew

256

all about love. What she had felt for Sam had been love. Slate was like wildfire, constantly threatening to overwhelm her with passion.

Imagine, marriage. The problem was, she could and it kept her awake all night.

She was still sitting there, her body stiff, when the sun began to rise the next morning. It was a beautiful sunrise and she would have liked to have shared it with Slate.

There were a lot of things she'd like to share with him, too many things, and all they seemed to share was danger and desire. It was a heady combination, and one she knew she couldn't succumb to, no matter how sweet Slate's words.

By the time the Montezuma Special rolled into the small Shangri-la train station, Raven had showered, dressed, and tied her father's Colt .45 to her right thigh. It was a little bulky and uncomfortable, but not noticeable when she sat or walked. She couldn't have chanced leaving it in her reticule and she wasn't going up against Arn's gang unarmed.

She met Slate in the diner and he gave her a cool, assessing stare before saying, "Looks like you didn't sleep too well, Raven. I didn't say anything to keep you awake, did I?"

"Certainly not. I was worried about Sadie. But it doesn't look like you got much sleep, either."

"I was also worrying about Sadie. Join me for breakfast?"

"I'm sure it would be most delightful, but if you'll recall, I'm the only Harvey Girl this trip and I'm serving."

"Too bad. Take my order then?"

She rolled her eyes, but took his order and that of the other passengers while watching out the window as the gold was wheeled out to the train and loaded in a special car. Ted was on hand to supervise the entire proceeding and the Shangri-la managers seemed pleased with his personal attention.

Raven smiled grimly to herself. If they only knew what was really being planned for their gold, they wouldn't be nearly so delighted to see it boarded on the Montezuma Special.

When the job was completed, Ted led the managers back to his private car. Raven knew he was serving them breakfast there and then the Special would be on its way.

Any time after that the outlaws could strike. She shivered, then narrowed her eyes. With any luck at all, Comanche Jack would be riding with the outlaws and she'd have her man at last.

Chapter Nineteen

The Montezuma Special ran swift and smooth near the Rio Grande toward El Paso. All was quiet on the train, the passengers relaxing in the library car or the observation coach. Ted reclined in his private car, nursing a glass of sherry. Raven busied herself in the diner while Slate went forward to speak with the engineer.

One hour passed, then another. Soon it was time for lunch. Raven served the meal, while glancing at her watch and feeling the tension grow. Where were the outlaws?

Maybe the robbery wouldn't happen today, maybe they would strike at dawn, or during the night. She finally set down to her own lunch about two. The passengers had gone back to other pastimes. Everyone tried to act normally, knowing they were being watched, but it grew more difficult by the moment.

Raven glanced at her watch again. Little time had passed. She tried to eat. The food was delicious, but she didn't feel very hungry. Then she thought of Sadie with probably barely enough food to survive. She ate, swallowing quickly, then washed the food down with water.

Now she felt too full and uncomfortable. She

drummed her fingers on the table. Would the waiting never end?

Suddenly the train began to slow. She sat upright. Her heart began to beat faster, but she calmly picked up her dishes and set them in the kitchen. She and the chef exchanged encouraging looks, then she walked outside to the platform.

She knelt down, making herself as inconspicuous as possible. She wished Slate was with her, but his role was to subdue the engineer and the fireman when the outlaws attacked. To Arn, that probably meant killing them. She shivered. What if Slate were shot? Killed? Unable to move? She wouldn't know. She couldn't help him. But she'd have to go on after Sadie alone. Slate had given her the directions to the hideout, but it wouldn't be easy to find and she wouldn't even consider the fact that they might not have given Slate the right directions.

But she forced all those thoughts from her mind. Slate *would* be fine. He'd join her and they'd go after Sadie.

She glanced around. The train was slowing rapidly now. They were in a wooded area. Low hills covered with thick brush and trees grew close to the tracks on one side. On the other were the trees and vegetation that grew along the Rio Grande River. How they were going to find their way through all that dense brush she didn't know, but they would.

The train came to a complete stop. It was suddenly very quiet. No birds singing. No wheels rattling over tracks. Just the soft sound of wind in the trees. Raven shivered, pressing herself flat to the bottom of the platform. She couldn't help anybody if she were seen and taken. But where was everyone? When would it all begin?

Suddenly everything seemed to break loose at

once. A loud voice of command broke the stillness, punctuated by several rapid gunshots. She recognized Arn's voice. She carefully raised her head, trying to see what was going on, but they were at the front of the train where the gold was stored. Several more shots were fired, then came the sound of doors being pulled open.

It was going just like the outlaws had planned, but where were the soldiers?

Then other sounds came from behind her. She dropped her head, but kept watching over the side of the platform. Hank walked by, jerking Ted along, holding a gun to this head. Raven stopped herself from gasping. She'd thought Ted would be left out of the danger. Surely they wouldn't hurt him. He was too important a man. Or maybe he was the mastermind, and this was just for effect.

But she couldn't count on that. Ted was her friend, and until she knew for certain he was the mastermind she would treat him like one. She didn't know what Hank planned to do with Ted, but it couldn't be anything good.

She had to do something before it was too late. She leaped down, holding her long skirt out of the way. Quietly she followed them, keeping hidden by the trees and bushes.

Hank might foil all their plans if he still had a gun on Ted when the soldiers went into action.

She could see Ted trying to get free, but Hank jerked him roughly around, keeping the nose of the Colt .45 pressed against Ted's temple.

Hank was headed for the front of the train where Arn and the other outlaws must be, or at least most of them. A few of the outlaws would have gone into the train to subdue the passengers. Hopefully the soldiers had already taken care of them, and were now outside the train surrounding the outlaws. But she couldn't be sure of that and tried to keep out of sight.

Hank was moving faster now and Raven could see the outlaws tossing the gold bars off the train. Several stood guard while others stuffed the gold into saddlebags on nervous horses. Where were the soldiers? Where was Slate?

She had to do something about Ted now before Hank gave him to Arn and she couldn't get to him.

Her pistol would be too noisy. She glanced around, saw a long, stout branch, and quietly picked it up. She began to catch up with Hank, but just as she brought the limb up to hit him over the head, she stepped on a twig. Hank heard her and whirled around, letting go of Ted and turning his pistol on her. When he recognized her, a look of stunned disbelief twisted his features. He hesitated just long enough for her to bring the limb down on his head.

He crumpled to the ground, blood running from the open wound. She grabbed his gun and hissed, "Run, Ted. Hide."

"No. I'll help."

"No! We need you alive and well. Hide!"

But Ted wouldn't go. He wrenched Hank's pistol from her and started toward the outlaws. She went after him, trying to keep out of sight.

Suddenly the tense silence was broken.

"Lay down your weapons!" the captain shouted. "You are surrounded by the United States Army."

The outlaws didn't hesitate. They dove for cover and started shooting.

At last the soldiers had struck, and Raven was careful to get under cover, too. What she had to do now was watch the horses closely. She couldn't let one single outlaw get a mount and escape, for he would ride straight back to camp with the news. That would be the end of Sadie and she knew it.

She took a position by a big tree and behind a thick shrub. The horses were snorting and shifting, obviously wanting to leave, but their reins were on the ground and they were well trained enough to wait, even though bullets were whizzing all around them.

Ted joined her. He aimed Hank's gun toward the area where the outlaws were hiding and shooting. "I'm not going to fire unless I have to, Raven. We've got five bullets and that's it."

"Good idea." She carefully counted the horses and kept recounting them. But she didn't mention the .45 strapped to her right thigh.

"I was a damn fool."

"No you weren't."

"Hank caught me off guard. I should have guessed I'd be part of their plans."

"Maybe you weren't. It was probably all Hank's idea."

"You think so?"

"Yes. I think Slate would call him a maverick on this job."

"That makes me feel a little better."

"The main thing is not to get caught or hurt, Ted. Sadie's going to need you."

All of a sudden Ted made a strange sound and slumped forward.

Shocked, Raven looked down, and automatically reached for the fallen gun. But a booted foot stepped on her hand, grinding it into the ground while a calloused hand picked up the Colt .45. Grimacing in pain, Raven glanced up.

"You gave me a nasty headache, Harvey Girl, and

now I'm mad." He ground the sole of his boot into her hand, then lifted his foot. The gun was now trained on her.

She raised her hand, carefully moved each finger, but nothing seemed broken, only badly bruised.

"Going to be a lot worse before it gets better, pretty woman. You and me are riding out of here."

"You can't get to the horses."

"Don't need to. Arn promised to leave mounts for me and the other two outlaws on the train down by the Rio Grande. Just in case. That's where we're going."

He grabbed her arm and pulled her up. "Now it's just the two of us."

"What about the gold?"

"Who cares? I already got a couple of bars stowed in my saddlebags. Come on." He started away from the fighting, but she dug in her heels.

"I'm not going anywhere with you."

"Too bad." He lifted his .45 to hit her across the head, but a shot rang out. He grimaced and grabbed his shoulder, dropping her hand. She dove out of sight, and Hank whirled around, shooting.

There was a grunt of pain and Slate came rushing out of the brush, firing two pistols at once.

Hank dodged for cover, red running from one leg, then was lost to sight.

Raven hurried to Slate. "Are you all right?"

"Yes. Just a shoulder wound."

"But you're bleeding."

"I'll be all right. They've got the outlaws pinned down. They'll take them in either dead or alive. Hank can't get far without a horse."

"Wrong. We've got to stop him. He said Arn had left horses by the Rio Grande for him and the other outlaws on the train."

"Damn! Come on."

Slate started after Hank, and Raven was right behind him. They arrived at the riverbank just in time to seek Hank downriver. Three horses were waiting. Slate and Raven started running toward him. Slate tossed Raven a .45 and she fired, her shots going wild, as Slate reloaded.

Hank tossed his saddlebags across the back of a horse, grabbed the reins of two of the horses, then threw himself into the saddle of the third. Furiously kicking the sides of his mount, he was soon into the wide river, causing a flurry of splashing water as he pulled two horses behind him.

On the other side, Hank slapped the rumps of the two extra horses, sending them running wild, then headed into dense brush.

Slate shot after him, but Hank was out of range, then out of sight.

"He's gone," Raven said unbelievingly. "Of all of them, he was the worst and he got away."

"Not yet," Slate said, his voice hard and determined. "Come on. He's not the only one with extra horses. Two of our so-called passengers brought mounts. They're in the baggage car."

"But Hank's got a head start."

"Yes, but our mounts will be fresher."

They ran back, dodging brush and trees and stumps, until they were back at the train. Raven quickly looked to see if Ted was still lying where they had left him. With great relief, she saw him standing against one of the baggage cars, rubbing his head. Knowing he was all right, she turned her attention back to the battle still raging around them, but the outlaws had to run out of ammunition soon. The soldiers had enough to keep on all day.

The horses were saddled and ready to go. Slate led them off the coach, helped Raven to mount, then threw himself into a saddle, and they took off for the Rio Grande.

Once across, they both rode hard, saying nothing for a long time as they conserved their energy. Slate was intent on finding the narrow trail that wound through the foothills to the camp. Raven was looking for any sign that Hank had been hurt badly enough to be unable to continue, but it was obvious he was riding fast ahead of them.

Finally, Slate broke the silence between them. "Hank knows I betrayed the gang, Raven. If he gets there ahead of us, we don't stand a chance of getting Sadie."

"He'll let me in."

"You're not going in alone, no matter what."

"But, Sadie—"

"I don't want to hear any more about it. Here's the cutoff. It'll be single file here on in. And, Raven, be as quiet and as careful as you can. It'll be dangerous, and Hank may be lying in wait somewhere up ahead. The brush'll be so dense we won't be able to see him until he's on us."

"I don't think he'll wait. He knows we're coming after him. He'll go to his lair. Once he has Sadie as hostage again, he'll feel safe."

"You're probably right. Okay, let's go."

Slate was correct. The trail was narrow and dangerous. She had to constantly be alert to low branches and thorny bushes. It was not long before her stockings were snagged and her dress ripped. She vowed that the next thing she bought was going to be a riding habit. She couldn't keep making long horseback rides in a Harvey Girl uniform.

They rode on all afternoon. Raven kept hoping

they'd find Hank unconscious in his saddle, but they didn't see him. They came to a small stream. Slate got down and let his horse drink. He helped Raven down, letting her body brush the length of his.

While the horses drank, she leaned against him for strength and support. "I keep hoping we'll find him."

"I hit him more than once. He has to be losing blood."

"But so are you." In all the confusion she'd put his wound from her mind. "Slate, you're really hurt."

"It's just a scratch."

"No it's not. Let me bandage it."

"There isn't time. It'll be dark soon. We've got to overtake him."

Raven began ripping a strip of cloth off the bottom of her white petticoat. "Sit down. This won't take long. If you lose too much blood you won't be any good to me or Sadie."

Reluctantly, Slate sat down.

She tore the sleeve of his shirt open and gasped. "There's a big hole."

Slate looked down. "Check the other side of my arm. If we're lucky, the bullet went on through. You should see a hole on the other side, too."

Raven had seen her father shot a couple of times, but he'd had a professional dress the wound. She was very much afraid of infection. But there was a hole. The bullet had gone completely through. She breathed a sigh of relief. "You're right. It's a clean wound."

"Get that flask of whiskey out of my saddlebag. Better wash out the wound, then bind it up. I'll be good as new then."

"You will not, but it'll help."

She got the flask, poured the whiskey right through the wound and watched the liquid turn red as it fell to the ground. Slate didn't make a sound but he turned pale. She hated hurting him, but she'd hate even more to see him lose his arm. She bound the wound as tightly as she dared to stop the blood flow. Then she sat down abruptly, feeling lightheaded. It had just occurred to her that if the bullet had been a few inches to the left Slate would now be dead.

Slate handed her the flask. "Take a swig."

"No. I hate the stuff."

"Raven, you're white as a sheet. Take a drink."

She was too weak to argue, and swallowed the nasty-tasing brew. It had its usual effect of hitting her stomach with a hot burst then spreading outward, but for once it did make her feel better. She handed the flask back. Slate took a long drink, then gave her a hard stare.

"You look a little better, but you also look like a horse just dragged you through a briar patch."

"I'm going to buy a riding habit, Slate. These Harvey Girl uniforms are simply not made for riding through the woods."

He laughed. "That's the truth." Then he dropped the flask in horror as a bullet came zinging out of the woods straight at Raven hitting her in the left breast, cutting through the fabric of her dress. She collapsed.

Slate snarled, snapped out his .45 and began shooting toward the area where the shot had come from. At the same time he began pulling Raven's limp body to safety behind a fallen tree. Bullets followed him, hitting the dead tree as he pushed Raven over, then scrambled to safety.

Cursing his own stupidity, he began reloading, glad his gunbelt was full of bullets since he'd prepared it the night before. He was the worst damn fool in the world. He should have checked the water hole for Hank, but he'd been sure the outlaw had gone on. He'd planned to catch up with him, but Hank had caught up with them first.

Now Raven was dead, and there was only one thought in his mind. Revenge. Later, he'd feel something else, but not now. There wasn't time for it.

"Come on out, Hank," he called "Fight like a man."

"Got your Harvey Girl, didn't I, Texas?"

"Yes. And now I'm going to get you."

"But I've got another Harvey Girl at the camp. She's mine and one's as good as another, right?"

"I'm willing to draw on you, Hank. Fair. Come on out. Show me how much man you are. I've been hearing how fast you are. Why don't you prove it."

"I don't have to, Texas."

"Nobody's faster than me, Hank. I was taught by Texas Rangers. I'm real fast. I've got a reputation down in Texas, Hank. Beat me and you'll be the man who was faster than Slate Slayton. That means something in Texas. You're going there with the gold and the woman, aren't you?"

"Yes, I'm going down to Texas and Mexico. I'm fast, Texas. All right, you come on out. If you've got the nerve to face me, I'll take you on. No Texan's got nothing on me."

Slate looked down at Raven. What did anything matter now anyway? With her gone he'd lost everything that had mattered to him. He might as well take a chance that Hank would keep his word.

He stood up slowly, expecting Hank to shoot him any moment, but the outlaw held off. It had worked. Slate had guessed that Hank, like a lot of outlaws, wanted a reputation, and the fastest way to get it was by gunning down a bigger name. He'd taken the bait.

Slate walked to one end of the clearing. He'd have to be fast and steady, his sight and aim true. But he didn't feel steady. He felt weak, his vision was flickering in and out of focus. Yet he had to avenge Raven. That was the only thing he could do for her now.

Hank joined him in the clearing. He was hurt, but steady on his feet. "I always knew it was coming to this, Texas. Some men you hate on sight."

"I'm not real fond of you, either. Ready when you are."

"They're going to know me as Fast Hank from now on," Hank said, flexing the fingers of his right hand near his holstered gun.

Slate waited. Hank came in and out of focus. He blinked hard and tried to concentrate, but there was a ringing in his ears.

Hank moved. Fast.

But Slate was faster.

And there was a small neat hole on the left side of Hank's chest when he slowly crumpled to the ground.

Slate walked over to him, and kicked the outlaw's gun away. "The best you can hope for, Hank, is that somebody'll put *Fast Hank* on your tombstone."

Then Slate turned and started back toward Raven. As he got closer he saw her hand move slightly against the rough bark of the fallen tree. His heart beat fast and he ran the few feet to her side.

"Raven?" he said, kneeling and pulling her to a sitting position so she could lean against his chest.

"What happened?" she asked hesitantly, then

270

rubbed her left breast. "My chest hurts."

"I'll be damned if I know. It's a miracle."

"A miracle? There's something hard there."

Slate pulled the fabric torn by the bullet aside and probed underneath. He found the bullet, then a handkerchief with something hard in it. He pulled it all out. Curiously he opened the handkerchief. Inside was a gold piece deeply indented with the shape of a bullet.

He turned to Raven, held out the dented gold piece and the bullet. "This coin saved your life, Raven."

"Oh." She blushed. "That's my good-luck gold piece."

"It certainly brought you luck. Where'd you get it?"

She blushed again. "You."

He looked at her in confusion for a long moment, then understanding turned his eyes a deep blue. "Do you mean to say that's the coin I gave you in Topeka?"

She nodded her head, then quickly said, "Not that it meant anything except luck. I just decided that if I wore it, I'd be safe in the West."

Slate grinned. "I have never been more glad in my life that I payed a whole gold piece to see a woman take off her dress. It seemed expensive at the time but now I see it was cheap at twice the price."

Raven smiled back. "I heard a shot. That's what brought me around. I think I must have fainted or something."

"No wonder. He was pretty close when he hit you."

"Hank?"

"Yes."

"Did you—"

"He's dead. I'll take him into the camp tomorrow."

"Won't that be dangerous?"

"No. We'll get in and take over first. I don't want to leave him out here, no matter what kind of man he was."

"I agree. And, Slate, thanks. You saved us both."

"I don't deserve your thanks. It was my poor thinking that got us in trouble in the first place."

"You'd lost a lot of blood. I'm surprised you were thinking at all, and you still look bad."

Slate nodded. He was hardly able to keep her in focus. He must have lost more blood than he'd realized. But Raven was safe, alive, and still his. That's what counted. He squeezed the bullet and gold coin in his fist, then pushed them into the pocket of his jeans.

"You don't need that gold piece now, Raven. You've got me for a good-luck charm."

She smiled. "I guess I do, but you aren't going to be worth much if you don't rest tonight. Now lay down. I'll get the saddle blankets."

"There's food in the saddlebags. I had it all packed just in case."

"Okay. I'll take care of things now. You just lay back."

"No. I've got one more thing to do."

"Slate, please. You're too weak."

"Got to do it, Raven. I'm going to wrap Hank in his blanket and put him on his horse. He died with his boots on and he'll go into camp on his horse."

Raven understood, and didn't protest again. While Slate went to take care of Hank, she tied their horses to a tree and got out what looked like a fancy picnic lunch prepared by the Montezuma Special's chef. Quite a contrast to the dried beef and hard bread she'd expected.

She laid their blankets together under a tree and sat down to wait for Slate. As she leaned back against the rough bark, she thought about Hank. She was sorry he'd had to end the way he did, but he'd been a dangerous man, he'd hurt a lot of people, and sooner or later someone was going to stop him.

At the end, it was either him or them, and they'd chosen to live. She supposed that's the way it was in the West, maybe back home, too. Backed into a corner, you either fought back or allowed somebody to ruin or end your life. Her father had raised her to be a fighter, and she'd struggled to survive no matter what. She guessed Slate had been raised the same.

A little later Slate came back. He rinsed his face and hands in the stream, then came to her and sat down. He took her hands in his. "Raven, seeing you lying there thinking you were dead aged me twenty years. I don't think I could stand it if anything ever happened to you."

"But we're alive, Slate, and that's what counts. Tomorrow we'll go after Sadie and take her home."

"And they'd better not give us any trouble. I'm not in the mood for it."

"Me neither."

She started to hand him a piece of cold fried chicken, but he'd leaned back against the tree and fallen asleep. A feeling she'd never felt for him before caught at her heart. Tenderness. She touched his face gently and felt tears sting her eyes. He could be vulnerable, too, and tired and hurt and afraid.

He might be a too tall Texas outlaw, but right now he was just a tired, wounded man who needed her.

She'd keep watch tonight while he slept. She pulled a blanket up over his shoulders, noticing how much of him was still exposed. When she stopped and thought about it, the problem was not that he was too tall, but that the blanket was too short. She put his .45 in her lap, then bit into a piece of crusty chicken, savoring the delicious flavor.

The lonely howl of a coyote eched through the woods, and she smoothed the blanket more firmly around Slate's shoulders. Let a coyote come, or a bobcat, or even a bear. It didn't matter. Nothing was getting to Slate Slayton this night. She'd make sure of that.

Chapter Twenty

The next morning dawned bright and clear. Raven awoke to discover herself wrapped in Slate's arms. They were snuggled together under the blanket, and it felt good, as if they'd been sleeping together this way for years. She moved slightly, wanting to see his face.

"Morning, Raven," Slate said.

She turned on to her back and put a hand against his brow. He was cool. Relieved, she smiled. "Good morning. How do you feel?"

"The arm's a little stiff, but I'll be fine."

"Good. I'm sorry. I was going to keep watch last night while you slept. I did for a while, then I guess I fell asleep."

"No wonder. You were exhausted. Sorry I went to sleep on you first."

"I guess we made it through the night just fine anyway."

Slate glanced around the small clearing. "Everything seems to be okay. The horses are still here. Got any of that food left? I'm starved."

The chef's picnic lunch was a little squashed and dry, but it was delicious. They both ate quickly and silently for a while, smiling at each other, enjoying the peaceful morning alone together. They carefully avoided mentioning Hank. That was over and done with.

275

"I can't eat anymore," Raven finally said, "and I want to save some food for Sadie and the return trip."

"There's plenty. We haven't even started on your saddlebags. I told the chef to pack a lot."

"I'm glad you did. I think I'll go down to the stream, wash my face, and get ready to go."

"Go ahead. I'll pack things up and get the horses ready."

Raven knew she must look a mess, but it didn't matter. Not today. Sadie was waiting for them, and they couldn't relax until her friend was safely with them again. She just hoped Sadie was all right.

Raven quickly washed her face, hands, then arranged her hair in a long thick plait down her back. She took off her stained and ripped white apron, and brushed off her black dress. That was the best she could do. After a trip behind a thick bush, she rejoined Slate.

He smiled, took her hand, and gently kissed the palm. His face was scratchy with black stubble. "I want to apologize for saying I'd have to watch out for you if you came with me. It wasn't true. You've pulled your weight all the way."

"You pulled your weight, too. You took care of Hank. If you hadn't done that, we might not be going after Sadie now."

"I've no doubt you'd have found a way to get him on your own. You're my kind of woman, Raven."

"And you're my kind of man, other than—"

"Like I said, I'm planning to change my ways."

She smiled softly, wishing she could believe that, then lightly brushed her fingers across his lips. "Let's go get Sadie."

"All right. Let me make a trip to the stream, then we can go."

Not long after, they were back on the trail, Slate leading Hank's horse behind him. The farther they got from the Rio Grande the drier the land became. Soon, they rode out of the trees into desert. Cacti dotted the landscape, along with stunted, windswept piñon trees. The sun rose high in the sky and beat down on Raven's head. She knew her skin must be burning so she took out her white apron and tied it over her head and under her chin to protect her face. She knew she must look ridiculous, but it was better than a painful sunburn.

And still they rode on. She urged her horse up beside Slate's mount. He glanced over at her and grinned. "You want my hat?"

"No. This seems to be working. How much farther?"

"I'm not sure. I've already had to backtrack a couple of times, but I think we're on the right trail."

"I certainly hope so."

"Even more important, I hope they gave me the right directions. Hank was beginning to turn Arn against me, so I can't be sure."

Raven shivered, even in the heat of the sun. The directions had to be right. She couldn't allow herself to think anything else. She glanced back at Hank's horse. Insects were beginning to buzz around the body. She shivered again. That could so easily have been her or Slate.

"We could stop, rest the horses, and eat something, Raven, but I think we're getting close. It's taken us longer than it should have, longer than it would have taken the outlaws, but look at that bluff ahead. If my directions are correct, there should be a gully near there that leads into a hidden canyon."

"Let's don't stop now. I can wait. Maybe Sadie can't."

Slate took a swig of water from his canteen, then passed it to her. "Don't drink much. It'll make your thirst worse."

She took a small sip, felt it slide coolly down her throat, then handed the water back to him. She'd been drinking too much of her own water and he knew it. But as the sun had gotten hotter, she had gotten drier. She hoped they got there soon.

The bluff was farther away than it looked. Another hour had passed before they were close, and the horses were growing weary. Raven's legs ached and were getting raw where the saddle rubbed, but she said nothing about that. Sadie was more important.

When they'd ridden into the shadow of the cliff, Slate suddenly said, "Look!" He pointed to a small dry gully almost hidden by cacti and piñon trees that ran along one side of the bluff. "Let's follow that."

They maneuvered their horses single file into the gully, then began following it beside the high wall of the stone bluff. It was shady here and cool. Also very quiet. It would be easy to hear anyone coming in. Raven shivered. Were they being watched right now? Or was this even the right place?

But they kept going, the tension mounting. Finally, the gully narrowed into what looked like a cow trail around the side of the cliff. Piñon grew taller here, and as Slate started down the narrow trail, the evergreen's branches caught at him, pulling at his clothes, then at Raven behind him. The trail abruptly dead-ended at the mouth of a canyon which was empty except for a lean-to constructed out of a buffalo hide and thick branches. It stood against one wall near the far corner of the canyon.

There were no horses, no smoke from a campfire,

no sound at all. The place looked completely deserted, except for the lean-to. Raven's heart sank. They'd moved Sadie, or this was the wrong place. She glanced at Slate, tears misting her eyes. He shook his head, put a finger to his lips, then motioned for her to get quietly off her horse.

Raven sighed softly in relief. Slate must think there was still a chance Sadie was in the area. He helped Raven down, then tied their horses to a nearby piñon tree. He handed her one of his pistols. With a .45 in one hand, he took her free hand and led her into the canyon, carefully avoiding disturbing any of the loose rock. They walked quietly but quickly toward the lean-to. Raven's heart beat faster and faster. Maybe Sadie was in the lean-to, an outlaw's gun at her heart.

When they were within a few feet of the lean-to, they glanced cautiously around for any outlaws hiding in the area, but saw and heard nothing.

Slate indicated for Raven to cover the front flaps of the lean-to with her gun, then, standing to one side, jerked open a flap. It was dark in there, but no sound, no movement. He opened the other flap the same way. Still nothing.

Raven bit her lip, trying to stop the tears that were burning her eyes. Sadie wasn't there. How would they find her now? With all hope gone, she watched Slate kneel down and move into the lean-to. There was a long moment of silence, then Slate glanced back out.

"You'd better come in here, Raven."

Raven's heart jumped. Had her friend been killed and left here? Furious, she rushed inside.

Sadie lay on her side, hogtied, a dirty bandanna in her mouth. She was either asleep or dead. Raven dropped the .45 and collapsed to her knees by her friend.

"Slate, is she—"

"Alive."

"You're sure?" Raven felt happiness surge through her. "Is she hurt?"

"I don't think so."

The voices aroused Sadie, and she opened her eyes, blinking in confusion at the unaccustomed light streaming into the lean-to and at the people so close to her. Without thinking, she flinched back.

"It's all right, Sadie. It's us," Raven exclaimed, pulling the bandanna gently from Sadie's mouth. "Raven and Slate. You're safe now."

"Raven?" Sadie asked, almost unable to speak her mouth was so dry.

"Here. Feel me." Raven put a strong hand against Sadie's brow. Her friend was warm, but not feverish. "Slate, please untie her."

Slate pulled a slim knife from his boot, and quickly cut the ropes that bound Sadie. "I'm going to get some food and water in here," he said, then left.

Raven began massaging Sadie's wrists and ankles, furious with the way her friend had been treated. There was red burns and scratches where Sadie had struggled hard to get free, but she had been too tightly tied to make much progress.

When Sadie felt a little better, she sat up, leaning against Raven. "How did you find me?" Her voice was weak and halting.

"It's a long story, but Slate did it," Raven replied.

"I had a lot of help," Slate added as he returned, bending in half to get into the lean-to. He handed Raven a canteen and a package of food. She opened the canteen and held it up to Sadie's lips. Sadie began greedily drinking.

"Don't let her drink too much," Slate said.

Raven took the water away. "You'll have to take just a little at a time otherwise you'll get sick."

Sadie nodded. "I'm so thirsty."

"They didn't leave you anything?" Slate asked, a sharp edge to his voice.

Sadie shook her head and shuddered.

"She could have starved to death," Raven said in dismay.

Slate nodded.

"They said they'd be back in a couple of days," Sadie inserted. "But that's a long time."

"Yes it is," Raven agreed. "But you've got food now. Here's some bread and cheese. Think you can eat something?"

Sadie nodded and began eating.

Raven looked at Slate, communicating her horror at what had happened to Sadie.

He nodded in understanding, then said, "I'm going out there and bury what we brought with us. We'll need the extra horse going back. Get Sadie as strong as you can, then we'd better start back. I don't know who else knows about this place, but we don't want to get caught here. It would be a death trap."

"Go ahead," Raven said, then turned back to Sadie.

Sadie looked up and smiled warmly at her. "I knew you'd come for me, Raven. I knew I could depend on you and Ted. But what is Slate doing with you? I thought he was part of the gang. Can we trust him?"

"Yes. You don't have to worry about those men anymore, Sadie. We set a trap for them. Ted and some soldiers captured them yesterday afternoon. I'm sorry we didn't get here sooner, but Hank got

281

away. We caught up with him last night. Slate shot him dead."

"He's burying Hank now?"

"Yes, then we'll start back."

Sadie nodded, continuing to slowly eat. "I'm glad Hank's dead. And the others?"

"In custody or dead. I don't know which."

Sadie finally relaxed. Tears filled her eyes. But she didn't cry. "Could I have some more water, Raven?"

Raven gave her the canteen. Sadie was strong. She'd had to have been to have survived her ordeal. She was thin now, too thin. She hardly looked like herself. There were dark circles under her eyes, her hair was a dark dirty mess down her back, and her fingers were bloody and raw where she'd struggled so hard to get free. But her friend had survived, and she was very proud of her.

"Did they hurt you, Sadie?"

"If you mean, did they rape me? No. They were cruel, trying to break me mentally and emotionally, but I just tried to shut them out, thinking of Ted, of you, and of the Montezuma Special, even the Montezuma itself. Sometimes I could almost smell the delicious food we used to serve, or feel clean cool linens under me. But they didn't touch me, Raven, not in any way. Not like they wanted to."

"I'm proud of you. I'm sorry we couldn't get to you sooner, but—"

"It's all right. You came. I can't tell you how much it meant to know I had friends out there who were desperately trying to free me." Suddenly tears filled Sadie's eyes and spilled down her cheeks. "I wasn't alone, not like I used to be. You were out there. Ted was out there. I knew if I could just hold on, keep strong, my friends would come for me."

Tears were suddenly streaming down Raven's face,

too. She put her arms around her friend and pulled her close. They clung to each other, crying tears of happiness and relief. After awhile, they parted and looked deep into each other's eyes and smiled.

"I guess we'll always be friends, won't we?" Sadie said.

"Yes," Raven replied. "We're like sisters."

Sadie smiled in reply, then took another drink of water. "I don't think I'll ever get enough water again."

"You keep the canteen, but—"

"I know. I'll drink it slowly."

Slate looked in at them. "You two ready?"

Sadie and Raven glanced at each other, and the knowledge that they'd just shared something special that would always remain with them passed in that look.

"Yes, we're ready," Raven replied, and helped Sadie to her feet.

Sadie was unsteady, her legs not yet prepared to take the weight of her body, so Slate carried her to Hank's horse. Raven carefully tied her apron around Sadie's head so she wouldn't get sunburned, and Slate put his much-too-large hat on Raven's head.

When they were all in their saddles, Slate looked at Sadie. "You get too tired, let me know and we'll stop, but hang on as long as you can. I want to get us far away from this hideout by nightfall."

"I understand," Sadie said. "Believe me, I want to be far away from here even more than you do."

They started back down the trail single file, Slate first, Sadie in the middle, and Raven bringing up the rear. She had kept Slate's Colt .45. If any outlaws appeared, she wanted to be ready. She still wore her own pistol, but she didn't want anybody to know about it unless absolutely necessary.

Soon they were riding through the gully, then back by the cliff. The sun was farther down the western horizon now. Raven took a deep breath, and glanced at Sadie. Her friend smiled, obviously thrilled to be free again. Slate checked the horizon for any horses approaching, but didn't see anything. They started back toward the Rio Grande, riding three abreast.

As they rode, Raven began to think about the robbery again. She'd hoped to catch Comanche Jack, and he might have been there. But she hadn't seen him, and somehow she just didn't think he could be caught that easily. He'd let someone else take the chance of actually stealing the gold, if he'd ever been part of any of this at all. She glanced over at Sadie. Her friend might have precious information.

"Sadie, were you guarded all the time?"

"Yes, until this last time."

"Was it the same men?"

Sadie's face clouded. She obviously didn't want to think or talk about it anymore. "Yes. Except for one time. One night this man slipped into the camp. I'd never have known he was there except I couldn't sleep because the ropes were so tight."

"What do you mean you wouldn't have known?"

"He was so quiet. I've never heard or seen anybody move like that."

"Was he part Indian?"

"I don't think so. He didn't look like it, but he had a hook in place of a left hand."

"What!" Slate interrupted their conversation.

Raven glanced over at him. His eyes were gleaming. There was a deep excitement in him that he was just barely suppressing. In fact, he looked the way she felt. Could he be on the trail of Comanche

Jack, too? That would mean he was undercover like her. Or, and her feelings plummeted, did he work for Comanche Jack? Was that why he was in the camp in the first place? And was that why he was so concerned that Sadie had seen the one-handed man?

"Yes, this man had a hook," Sadie continued. "He looked mean. I was glad he only stopped by that one time. He was gone the next morning."

"I wonder who he was?" Raven asked, trying to keep her voice from sounding interested.

"Maybe just a lone outlaw who'd stopped by for some food," Slate suggested.

Raven glanced at him suspiciously. She hated to think he might work for Comanche Jack, but things were beginning to point to it. Still, she just couldn't quite accept it, maybe because she didn't want to, just like she didn't want to believe Ted was the mastermind.

"Maybe so," Sadie agreed, then added, "But I don't care who he was. I just want to forget the whole thing and go back to being a Harvey Girl. However, I think I might rather work at one of the Harvey Houses than on the Special."

"You'll get over that, Sadie. You know how much you love railroading."

"Yes, I do, and I suppose you're right."

They lapsed into silence, all eager to see the Rio Grande again. Raven had learned what she needed to know. She just wished Slate hadn't been so interested. But she pushed those thoughts from her mind. They still had a long hard ride ahead of them, and danger lurked all around. She'd have to concentrate on reaching safety, rather than thinking about Comanche Jack.

As the sun began to set, bringing on the chill of the evening, in the distance they finally saw the Rio

285

Grande sparkling in the last of the sun's brilliant rays. They cheered, knowing they were close to the Montezuma Special. There would be clean soft beds to sleep on tonight.

Raven reached over and squeezed Sadie's hand, then noticed the look of horror on her friend's face. She glanced back at the river. Coming toward them fast was a lone rider. She looked at Slate. He'd drawn his Colt. 45, but didn't seem overly concerned.

"It's all right, Sadie," Raven said, trying to calm her friend. "One rider couldn't be too much trouble."

Then suddenly Sadie cried out with joy and jerked the apron off her head, throwing it aside. She kicked her mount forward, and was off toward the rider.

"Slate?" Raven asked.

"Let her go. If I'm not mistaken—"

"Ted!" Raven interrupted, finally recognizing the lone rider.

Sadie and Ted reached each other, jerked their horses to a quick stop, then Ted was down and pulling Sadie into his arms. There was a long, quiet moment as their lips met, then an even longer embrace.

Raven smiled at Slate and he took her hand.

"Sometimes the good guys win," he said.

"Then you'd better change sides."

"What's my reward if I do?"

Raven nodded at Ted and Sadie. "That's a pretty good reward, isn't it?"

"I had a little something more personal in mind. I know this real nice hotel in El Paso and I wouldn't mind holing up there for several days with the right woman."

286

"Just several days?"

"For as long as she wants. Maybe if she likes it well enough, she'll even ask me to marry her."

"Could be. Of course, you'd have to find the right woman."

"Oh, I found her all right." And he squeezed Raven's hand. "I've just got to get her to admit it."

"Shouldn't be hard, should it?"

"Wouldn't think so, but I can't get my brand to stick."

"Maybe you should try *her* brand."

"Maybe so. In that case, I'll make sure there's plenty of fire for her in Texas."

Then he pulled his hat off her head, stuck it back on his own, slapped the rump of her horse, and raced, howling a Rebel yell all the way to the Rio Grande.

Part Three
Wild Texas Plains

Chapter Twenty-one

"Raven West, I'd like you to meet Jeremy Luis Centrano, special representative for the Southern Pacific," Ted said, indicating a slim man of medium height, around forty.

"How nice to meet you," Raven replied, smiling politely while controlling the sudden burst of excitement at meeting the other man who could so easily be the mastermind.

"It is all my pleasure, I assure you, *Señorita* West," Centrano said, bending low over her hand and placing a light kiss on it.

"Please call me Raven."

"Thank you, Raven. I would be honored if you'd use my first name, too."

"Jeremy," she responded, removing her hand from his lingering grasp and letting her eyes roam over the drawing room of the El Paso mansion. "You have a lovely home."

But she wasn't really interested in Jeremy's home. She was thinking about him. He was impeccably and expensively dressed in all black with a frilly

291

white shirt. Large emerald and gold studs were at his wrist and throat. He had thick black hair with just a touch of silver at the temples, dark olive skin, and narrow black eyes that seemed to miss nothing. He had an aristocratic nose, and sensual rosy lips.

She concluded that while Jeremy was an attractive and alluring man, obviously rich, he could also easily be the mastermind. Just because he seemed to be wealthy, like Ted, didn't mean he was innocent of the robberies. Her father had thought Simpson and Centrano were the prime suspects, and she still agreed. They'd had time, opportunity, and motive.

Now that she had them together she wanted to keep them that way until she could prove one of them guilty or both of them innocent. And at the same time finally capture the elusive Comanche Jack. It was a big job, but justice depended on her accomplishing it.

How she could keep these two men together for any length of time she didn't know. Perhaps Sadie could be of some help.

She glanced at her friend, looking very pretty but still a little thin and pale. She was standing close to Ted, a glow of happiness lighting her eyes. That glow had been there ever since Ted had asked her to marry him the moment he took her in his arms by the Rio Grande River. They had been inseparable ever since. Ted's total attention and concern for Sadie had gone a long way toward returning her to her former self.

While Sadie was now happy, fortunately Raven couldn't say that for the robbers and kidnappers. The soldiers had captured them, killing only two. Arn and his outlaws were looking at a long time behind bars, and she was glad that justice had finally been done. The gold had been saved and the two bars in Hank's saddlebags had been returned to the Shangri-la shipment.

"Ted, you've been very remiss," Jeremy said, interrupting Raven's thoughts.

"About what?"

"These lovely Harvey Girls. If all the Harvey Girls working on the Santa Fe line are this irresistible, you must have to replace them frequently."

Ted chuckled. "As a matter of fact it is a slight problem, but it's also making the Harvey Houses world famous."

"I don't doubt it," Jeremy agreed. "It also helps to make me very interested in Santa Fe's concept for the Montezuma Special. I'm most anxious to ride on this paragon of luxury you've told me about."

"That's why we brought the Special to Southern Pacific tracks. We want you to see how well it could work out between Sante Fe and Southern Pacific."

"I've been giving it some thought. How about a run all the way to San Antonio? There's a shipment I need taken there and it would give us plenty of time to discuss Santa Fe using Southern Pacific tracks to California."

"Fine. We're available. We can take a few passengers, too, so they can get an idea of what a true luxury train is like."

"The Southern Pacific trains are of first quality, Ted," Jeremy said firmly.

"Of course they are, but the Montezuma Special is most unusual. Wait until you ride on it."

"I'm looking forward to it. Then we've agreed to take the Special to San Antonio?" Jeremy asked.

"Absolutely," Ted agreed.

"Good. But excuse us, ladies. We should not be

discussing business at a party, and at your engagement party in particular, Sadie."

"That's all right," Sadie replied. "I'm glad we're going to San Antonio. I've never been there. I've never been in Texas before for that matter."

"Then we'll try to make sure you see more of El Paso before you go."

"I'd enjoy that a lot."

"Good. We'll make plans for that later. And, Raven, you're certainly welcome in all our plans."

"Thank you, although I wouldn't want to intrude."

"It would be our pleasure to include you."

"Thank you." Raven was relieved she was being made part of the plans, for it would give her the perfect opportunity to watch her suspects. She could hardly believe her good luck. As a Harvey Girl, she'd go with the Montezuma Special, and that meant being near Ted and Jeremy all the way to San Antonio. If she couldn't prove them innocent or guilty in that length of time, she might as well hang up her spurs and go home.

Pleased with the way things were going, she glanced around the drawing room. It was quite different in design and furnishings from the Montezuma Hotel's Queen Anne style, but just as luxurious.

Jeremy noticed her interest in his house and said, "This is not my family home, although it has become home to me. My family has a rancho in California. Long ago, my ancestors received a large Spanish grant of land there and still live on it. Fortunately I have an older brother so I was free to follow my own interests, which is railroading, as you might have guessed."

"It's very beautiful here."

"Thank you. I was lucky. A family from Mexico City moved here, built and furnished this house, then decided to return. I was able to buy it from them with most of the furnishings intact. That was especially fortuitous for me, since I have yet to marry, and to have had the burden of completely furnishing a home would not have been my pleasure."

"You were indeed lucky."

"Yes, I was. Of course over the years I have added my own touches, brought in my own works of art, and made it my own home."

"I can see you have."

Raven had seen much of the house that afternoon when Sadie, Ted, and she had arrived with their trunks. They were each given a suite since they were to dress and spend the night in the Centrano mansion because the party would continue until very late.

She couldn't help wishing Slate had been invited, but he had gone his own way when they'd reached El Paso, saying he had business to handle but that he'd be in touch. She wondered if maybe he had gone off alone to contact Comanche Jack and if she'd ever see him again. Had everything he'd said and everything they'd shared just been for the moment? She had no answer to that and would not allow herself to dwell on the subject. After all, he was an outlaw and she had a job to do, a job that didn't include him . . . not any longer.

She turned her mind back to her surroundings. The Centrano mansion was magnificent, and she couldn't help wondering how the railroad man could afford it. But now that she knew he came from a wealthy family, it made more sense. Still, she had also begun to wonder just how much railroad special representatives were paid and concluded that they must be paid very well, for although the outside of the mansion was simply designed, the interior was extremely luxurious. The first floor center of the house contained a large courtyard, complete with a stone and tile fountain, stone benches, and luxurious plants.

The household furniture was obviously imported from Spain or made in Mexico, and was of heavy dark wood, with rich velvets and brocades. Flocked wallpaper, imported carpet, and gleaming crystal completed the luxurious interior.

"I do not spend as much time as I would like in my home," Jeremy continued, "since I travel so much, but eventually I will retire and be at home to enjoy all my beautiful art."

"That would be nice," Raven agreed, remembering the large oil paintings in heavy gold frames on many walls of the house. She had even recognized a few of the famous painters names, such as Velazquez and El Greco. The Centrano family had obviously done very well for itself.

"But you're a long way from retirement," Ted said. "You know the Southern Pacific couldn't do without your expertise."

"Thank you," Jeremy responded. "But there are always younger men sniffing at one's heels."

"Kick them out of your way," Ted responded, laughing.

Jeremy joined his laughter, then stilled as his first guests were announced. "If you will all be in my receiving line, I would be most grateful. I've invited railroad people and those people from El Paso I

296

thought would interest you."

"Thank you," Ted replied, "we'd be glad to receive with you."

Jeremy held out his arm for Raven, and she placed a hand there, noticing how warm and muscular he was. For some reason it surprised her. Until that moment he had seemed a cold and brittle man.

Jeremy led Raven from the room, with Ted and Sadie following. As they neared the early guests, he whispered, "You are as magnificent as my most treasured piece of art, *señorita*, and, in fact, put many of them to shame."

"Thank you, Jeremy, but I'm afraid I can't possibly compare to an El Greco."

"If only he'd had you to paint, then perhaps his work could compare with your natural beauty."

"You do know how to flatter a woman."

"Not flattery at all, but the truth. And not for any woman, but for you alone."

Before Raven could reply, they had reached the guests. As they began greeting them, Sadie and Ted joined them. Raven quickly realized they were being presented to the wealthy and elite of El Paso and that she was being singled out for a great deal of attention since she was with Jeremy. No doubt the families in the area had long tried to make arrangements for their daughters to marry the handsome, wealthy railroad man and they were probably wondering if she had suddenly snatched the prize from them.

They would have been truly amazed to learn she was simply a Harvey Girl, included in the event because it was her best friend's engagement party. But no one had mentioned that fact, and the scrutiny became progressively more intense.

But she would not be daunted. She would do her utmost to see that Sadie had a perfect party and that Jeremy trusted her as a simple Harvey Girl, thrilled to be in such luxurious surroundings. She was glad she had worn the black silk gown she'd worn with Slate at the Montezuma so that she easily fit in with what Jeremy's guests were wearing. Sadie looked lovely in a pale pink gown of layers of diaphanous silk.

Raven smiled until her jaws ached and the last of the guests had arrived. Then Jeremy whisked her away to dance, and she gratefully followed him through the gliding steps of a waltz. He had hired a small but excellent orchestra and the music was exquisite. They moved around the other dancers in their silk and satin and brocade. It was a delightful evening, but something was missing.

And she would not admit that it was Slate. Instead, she smiled into Jeremy's dark, smoldering eyes and thought that he was a most attractive gentleman. It was a shame he was a suspect, or he might have helped her forget Slate.

"You were named most appropriately, Raven, for your eyes are the shade of a raven's wing."

"Thank you. Do you write poetry?"

"Alas, I am not a creative man, but I do appreciate art in its many varieties."

"So do I."

"I thought you must. You are such a vision of art yourself."

Then he whirled her around the floor again, and she smiled at the sight of Ted and Sadie clinging together in an intimate waltz. She was glad to see them so happy, but she was also afraid for her friend, afraid that Ted was the mastermind. So much pointed to his involvement in the outlaw gangs, but she hadn't mentioned that to Sadie. Her friend had been through too much already to upset her with such news. Besides, revealing what she suspected about Ted would have given away her own secret identity and she couldn't put Sadie in that kind of jeopardy.

"I am glad you're going to be on the Montezuma Special," Jeremy said. "It will give us time to get to know each other better."

"I'll be working."

"It will be an easy trip, not so many passengers. There will be time for us, if that pleases you."

"I don't know. I hardly know you."

"That is what I mean. You have inspired me as no other woman has done in a very long time. I want to get to know you very well, Señorita Raven West."

Raven blushed. She felt almost bad about thinking he was the mastermind. He was obviously such a gentle, intelligent man, far from his family. He was probably very lonely in his private coach and his huge mansion and he gave such beautiful compliments.

"You are such an innocent," he said, drawing her closer. "It is not often I see a woman blush."

She rewarded him by blushing again. "It's embarrassing really."

"Not at all. Innocence should never be an embarrassment. I understand you Harvey Girls live in dormitories under very strict supervision."

"Yes, that's true."

"It is a good thing, too, because the West is a very cruel place for innocent young women."

"Yes, I know what you mean." However, she

wasn't nearly the innocent she once was, and at the moment she didn't know how she could possibly have given herself to Slate. It had been madness. Wrong, all wrong. And, yet, somehow she had. Jeremy would be very shocked if he knew, but of course it was none of his business.

"But you've had Ted to protect you on the Montezuma Special, haven't you?"

"Yes."

"That is good, for he is obviously a very proper gentleman."

"Yes, he is," she agreed, beginning to wonder why he was going on so about Harvey Girl morality.

"Of course, a Spanish lady would never work outside the home so she could never be subjected to the harshness that you must see in your work."

"I wouldn't know about Spanish ladies." She was beginning to get a little irritated. She had the feeling he was insulting her work.

"No, of course you wouldn't, but that's where Harvey was very smart. He made sure his waitresses were respectable young ladies and made it possible for them to stay that way."

"Yes, I guess he did."

"But I am boring you, aren't I? You already know all this, otherwise you would never have consented to being a Harvey Girl."

"That's right." She was beginning to feel very stifled. He would certainly be surprised if he knew the truth, and she almost wanted to tell him just to see the look on his face. Proper. Innocent. Respectable. Well, she'd never been a proper lady and she wasn't starting now. It was far too late, and there was too much to do to suddenly sit down and start serving tea.

He whirled her around the dance floor again. "You fit perfectly into my arms. I can hardly wait to spend more time with you on the Special, but first I want to show you my paintings."

Raven stiffened. Maybe he wasn't so interested in her respectability after all. "I would enjoy that, and so would Sadie and Ted, I'm sure."

"Of course we will include them in everything. You must be properly chaperoned at all times."

"Yes, of course." If she'd had to be properly chaperoned at all times, she'd never have made it out of Chicago. She couldn't imagine this very proper gentleman as the mastermind, and she certainly couldn't imagine him taking the place of Slate.

As if thoughts of Slate had suddenly made him materialize, Raven saw him. How had he gotten inside? But then she remembered he was an experienced thief. He was leaning against a wall with a drink in one hand. He was dressed much as he had been at Montezuma, only he looked very dangerous now, his eyes burning into Jeremy's back.

Was he jealous? The thought delighted Raven, and she deliberately smiled warmly at Jeremy who smiled back in pleasure.

But it was too much for Slate. He stalked through the dancers, tapped Jeremy on the shoulder, then whirled Raven away. Jeremy stood in shock for a moment, then started after Raven. But Jeremy didn't have a chance to continue, for the El Paso mothers had simply been waiting the chance to have their daughters dance with him. Soon he was doing his duties as host, and Slate had whisked Raven deep into the crowd of dancers.

"What were you doing in that man's arms?" Slate

asked savagely as he pulled Raven hard against him.

"You're holding me too closely, and I was dancing." She tried to push him away but he ignored her efforts.

"How long did you dance with him?"

"I don't know. He's the host."

"He's trying to get you in his bed."

"Slate, really!"

"That's the truth. I saw the way he was looking at you, holding you, wanting you. My woman, too! Well, he'd damned well better stay away from you. I won't have it, you hear?"

"He's the Southern Pacific special representative, Slate. He's going to be traveling on the Special."

"So?"

"I'm a Harvey Girl. I'll be serving him like I do all the passengers. He can't stay away from me."

"I don't like it."

"It doesn't matter. You're going your way now, and I'm going mine. We knew it would be this way from the first."

"Stop thinking, just feel me against you."

That was exactly what she was trying not to do. For the moment he'd taken her into his arms, she'd begun to want him, craving what only he could give her. "I don't want to feel, Slate. This is difficult enough."

"Where's the Special going?"

"To San Antonio."

Slate hesitated, then asked, "Whose idea?"

"Jeremy Luis Centrano has a shipment he wants taken there."

"I see. Hold on a second." He whirled Raven near a chair, made sure she sat down, then stalked off toward Ted.

Shocked, Raven simply sat and watched him.

Slate pulled Ted and Sadie aside, talked intently to them several moments, then nodded in satisfaction and walked back to Raven. Before she quite realized what had happened, she was back in his arms on the dance floor.

"What are you doing?" she demanded.

"I'm going with you to San Antonio."

"What?"

"That's right." He grinned, drew her closer so that his breath was warm on her face. "You think I'd let you go that far with Centrano sniffing after you? Not likely."

"You're going to be a passenger?"

"No. Same job as before. Ted just hired me again."

"Oh." She suddenly remembered that Ted still thought Slate was R. Cunningham and of course would hire him and be glad of it, even expect it. But the worst of it was that it made Slate and Ted look even more suspicious. If Ted were the mastermind and Slate was working for him, could Comanche Jack be far behind?

"We'll have plenty of time now to try out those Pullman berths. They're highly advertised as the softest beds on wheels. Want to find out?"

"I already know."

"What!"

"I mean I've been sleeping on the Special since Topeka."

"Yes, but you've been sleeping alone. I mean to change that. Just took once to convince me that waking up in your arms is the best place to be."

"Slate, I'll be sleeping in a car with Sadie."

"I doubt it. Ted won't let her out of his sight."

"For propriety's sake, he will."

"None of that matters. We're going to try out those Pullman berths and that's that."

"You think we're just going to take up where we left off?"

"No doubt about it, Raven, starting tonight."

"I'm sleeping here tonight."

"Think I'd let you sleep under the same roof with Centrano? Not on your life."

"I don't like you telling me what to do."

"All right. Make up your own mind." He twirled her into the courtyard and away from the lights and people. In a dark corner he pressed hot lips to hers, then slipped urgent hands down her back then up under her breasts.

She moaned, feeling her body begin to melt against him, wanting him again, knowing that as long as he was near she could not say no, could do nothing but seek out his warmth and merge with him.

"You make up your mind yet, Raven?"

"It's not fair, I "

"*Señorita* Raven," Jeremy called, stepping into the courtyard.

"Oh, I've got to go."

"Not until you say you'll meet me out here later."

"But Slate—"

"*Señorita* Raven," Jeremy called again.

"Promise."

"All right. But much later."

"I'll be waiting," he said, pressed fiery lips to hers once more, then slipped into the darkness.

Feeling light-headed, Raven hurried toward Jeremy.

"My dear, I became concerned. Who was that

ruffian who dared to take you outside?"

"He works for Ted."

"Well, I'll have a word with Ted about his employees. That type of thing simply can't be allowed. I understand it wasn't your fault. The man simply overpowered you, but, have no fear, I will look out for you now. No ruffian will ever be allowed near you again."

Raven didn't say anything. She was still trembling inside from Slate's touch and trying not to be overjoyed at the news that he would be with them all the way to San Antonio. What she felt for him was wrong, so wrong, and yet he made her feel so right.

Chapter Twenty-two

"What took you so long?" Slate asked, pulling Raven close.

"I had to wait until everyone left. I shouldn't be here now. I think I'm being watched."

"Centrano. Don't worry about him. I'll take care of him if he gets any closer to you."

"Slate, leave him alone. He was just being a good host."

"You don't really expect me to believe that, do you? But I don't want to talk about him now, not with the scent of jasmine in your hair and your body next to mine. Let's go back to my hotel room. It's not far, and it's a beautiful night."

"I can't just go. What if someone noticed?"

"They'll all sleep late tomorrow. We'll have you back before then."

He stepped away, tugging at her hand but she pulled back. He stopped, looked down at her, then grinned, picking her up in his arms.

"Slate!" she hissed. "Put me down. This is kidnapping."

"Call it whatever you like, but it'll get you into my bed all the same."

She pushed at his shoulders, and felt the muscles contract. He was so hard, so strong, and his body heat was beginning to wash over her. She felt the traitorous response in her body, and the fire that would soon ignite inside her. She had to get away from him before that happened or she'd lose all control. She struggled harder against him.

"Be still. You're going to wake the whole house before I can get us out of here."

"I could scream."

"You don't want that, do you? You know what you want. Stop being stubborn."

"I think I *will* scream."

Slate covered her mouth with his, kissing her with a force that took her breath away. She felt the tremble that shook his body as his tongue pushed into the soft warm depths of her mouth. She clung closer, reveling in the kiss, her own tongue seeking out his, following it into his own dark depths. His scent washed over her, she could taste him, feel him, and suddenly nothing else mattered. She wanted him, no matter what.

Slate tore his mouth away, breathing hard. He took long strides through the courtyard and slipped out a door he had left unlocked. The Centrano mansion was soon far behind them.

"You can put me down now," Raven said quietly. "I'll go with you. It seems I'll go anywhere with you once you touch me."

"It's the same for me. I can't get you out of my

blood, and I've tried."

"Want to be rid of me so soon?"

"No, not now. At first I thought that's all we needed, but I know better now. We belong together."

Raven tried to restrain the thrill that rushed through her at his words, but couldn't stop the rapid beat of her heart. Outlaw or not, he made her senses reel and she couldn't seem to stop wanting him.

"You can put me down now. I'll go quietly."

"I don't want to put you down. I could walk all night with you in my arms, you make me feel so strong."

She nestled closer. She liked his strength, liked the feel of him carrying her, liked responding to his power. As for the future, she once more pushed it from her mind. This might be their last night together. Once on the train there wouldn't be much opportunity since there would be so many other people around and she'd be working. It would be impossible for him to hold her close, or kiss her, or take her in his arms, or share a Pullman berth with her. Yes, this might be their last time together.

The night was still young in El Paso. The bars and dance halls and gambling houses were in full swing. Slate set her down when they reached these, and she remembered asking questions about Comanche Jack in establishments just like them in Topeka. That's the way she'd met Slate. And she'd need to ask questions in these bars before she left San Antonio. She had to know if Comanche Jack were still trailing them.

She looked up at Slate, so tall, really too tall, and yet she'd come to like that height despite herself.

Slate looked down at her and grinned, put an arm around her waist and pulled her close. "This is the way it ought to be all the time, Raven. I don't like having to sneak you out of mansions and sneak into your bedroom in hotels. Why don't you ask me to marry you?"

She smiled, suddenly feeling tender inside. "Outlaws shouldn't get married. It's not fair."

"But I'm going to change my ways."

"That's what you say. I just hope you don't plan to change *all* your ways."

He laughed, bent to place a warm kiss on her face, then replied, "No, not all my ways."

He quickly led her to the Rio Grande Hotel, one of the better hotels in town, and slipped her upstairs away from prying eyes.

When he turned on the light in his bedroom, he said, "I'm tired of all this sneaking around, Raven. It was easier when I thought you were a lady of the evening. But now that you're a Harvey Girl, we have to think of your reputation."

"And when we think of that, we know I shouldn't be here."

"If you'd ask me to marry you, I could make an honest woman of you."

"Oh, Slate," she suddenly exclaimed, sitting down on the bed, "what are we going to do?"

"Make love."

"I don't mean that. I mean—"

"I know what you mean, but if we make love we won't worry about it. Trust me, everything's going to be all right. Just give it a little more time."

"Until you finish this job?"

"Yes. I'm working for Ted and I have to complete

what I'm doing. You understand that."

"Yes, I suppose I do, but you're still an outlaw."

"Not at heart."

He sat down beside her, gently took her hand, and began rubbing a hard thumb across her soft palm. "You have beautiful hands. Everything about you is just right."

"Even my height?"

"Well, maybe you're too short, but I can learn to live with it."

"Too short!" She jerked her hand away and punched him in the stomach. Not very hard, but he reacted as if she'd given him a death blow, falling back against the bed. "You're the one who's too tall!" She threw herself on top of him for emphasis. "Too tall!" She grabbed his wrists and pushed his hands up over his head. "My height is perfect. You're too tall. Now, admit it!'

"Not fair, Raven. You've got me pinned down. You can do whatever you want with me. I'd have to agree and it wouldn't be fair."

"Fair! You called me too short, when you know perfectly well that you're too tall. Now, admit it."

"Make me."

"Oh!" She hesitated, then added, "All right, I will."

She carefully wrapped her legs around his so he couldn't move and increased the pressure on his wrists.

"How are you going to make me admit I'm too tall?"

"Like this," she said, then began to nibble gently along his lower lip.

"Ouch! That tickles."

"Really? But that wouldn't bother a big, strong, too tall Texan like you, would it?"

He mumbled something in reply, but she couldn't understand him because she was teasing his upper lip with her tongue, feeling the slightly abrasive stubble of his beard. Then she moved upward, planting soft kisses on his cheekbones and closing his eyes with her lips before returning to his mouth.

With her lips to his, she whispered, "You're so beautiful, Slate. I adore the constantly changing color of your eyes. I never know if they'll be blue or gray or both. And I can hardly keep my hands out of your thick ebony hair. I'd even like to see you with a mustache and beard just out of curiosity. I want to know everything about you. Touch all of you."

"Since you've got me helpless, I suppose you can do whatever you want," Slate said, his voice humours but his eyes a deep searing blue.

"Yes, you *are* helpless, and you're going to admit finally that you're too tall."

"Think you can make me?"

"Yes. Oh, yes.'"

She teased his ears, nibbling the soft flesh, then darting her tongue inside. She felt him tremble, and smiled in triumph. He was not immune to her touch, not at all, no matter how hard he tried. She tormented his other ear, then returned to his face. She smiled.

"Why don't you kiss me?"

"Oh, no. You're trying to lure me into satisfying you and that won't get you to admit you're too tall."

"I'm about ready to admit anything as long as you'll kiss me."

"No. You're just trying to take advantage of my weakness."

"I think you're the stronger of the two of us right now."

"We'll see."

She unbuttoned a few buttons of his shirt, then placed hot kisses against the dark hair there, feeling his heart increase in tempo. She finished the rest of the buttons, then jerked the shirt free. His chest was bare to his trousers, and this time it was she who trembled.

His arms were still stretched up beside his head, and it caused the muscles of his chest to expand, pushing hard against his smooth bronzed flesh. Dark hair rippled down his chest, then thinned around his navel before it thickened again to disappear into his trousers. She ran her fingers through the dark hair on his chest, then stopped to toy with each nipple until it was hard.

"What are you trying to do, Raven?" he gasped, his breath suddenly ragged.

"Make you willing to admit you're too tall, of course."

"I'm not ready to admit it yet."

"Think you can hold out longer?"

"Try me."

She undid his trousers. They both stopped breathing for a moment, then she opened them to expose the heart of his desire. He was ready for her, so very ready. She touched him, gently at first, marveling at the size and length of him, the power that could so easily bring her to such joyous heights. How could she not want him? She stroked his long length, and Slate groaned.

"You don't know what you're doing to me."

"Then teach me what to do."

He covered her hand with his and soon she was oving in an increasing rhythm, creating a pressure at made his body seem more feverish than before. hen she no longer needed his instruction, he opped his hand and she glanced up. Sweat beaded s forehead.

She smiled, slowing her movements. "Now, are u or are you not too tall?"

Slate laughed and grabbed her, pulling her against e length of him, and, twisting, turning them over she lay beneath him. "Now, who's too tall or too ort?"

"That's not fair!"

"Isn't it?"

"I wasn't done."

"No, but I had to feel you, Raven. I had to get y hands all over you. You were driving me crazy. ow much do you think I can take?"

"All you had to do was admit you're too tall."

"But I'm not too tall, nor too young, nor too old, d I'll prove it."

"How old are you?"

"Old enough for you."

"Tell me."

"You first."

"Oh, Slate, don't you ever give anything away? n twenty-five. Too old for you?"

"Perfect for my twenty-eight, and now I'll prove "

He stripped completely, and she couldn't help oticing how enticing his long, lean body was to her nses. He pulled her to her feet, and began gently

313

peeling off one layer after another until she w
down to her corset and stockings. He stopped ar
looked her up and down. "Maybe I'll just sto
there. You look totally appealing."

"Oh, Slate," she whispered, pulling his long, ha
length to her. "You make me feel all weak and sil
and wanton. I can't think straight around you. Ar
it doesn't seem to get any better."

"Sure it does."

He tilted her head back and covered her lips wi
his in a gentle, tender movement, then presse
inside, his tongue delving deep, seeking out all h
warm hidden depths. She moaned, pushing again
him, and felt his long shaft slide between her leg
She groaned, wanting him, feeling the heat rise
her, knowing she couldn't do without him.

"Still think I'm too tall?"

"No. Nor too long, either."

He laughed softly against her mouth. "You arer
too short. You're perfect to me. I don't want ar
other woman. Only you. Always you."

He picked her up and laid her on the bed.

She felt tears sting her eyes, then blinked the
away. Ridiculous to feel so strongly about him. H
was just a too tall Texas outlaw who . . . no, he wa
the man she wanted, right or wrong. And for th
moment he was hers. She lifted her arms to him ar
pulled him to her. She felt his long body caress th
length of her, then she pulled him even closer.

"Give what only you can give me, Slate, and let
forget everything except the happiness we can gi
each other."

He kissed her hard, possessively, then lifted her
one arm while he turned back the covers.

This time it was Raven who had her hands pulled ~~gh~~ over her head, and imprisoned by one large, ~~rong~~ hand. Then Slate slowly unhooked her cor-~~t~~, taking his time, letting his fingers linger until ~~ie~~ was hot and damp all over. When her breasts ~~ere~~ exposed to him, he lowered his head, took one ~~sy~~ nipple into his mouth, and sucked until she was ~~rithing~~ beneath him. Then he teased the other ~~ntil~~ it, too, was taut with desire.

Finally, he jerked the corset free and spread her ~~gs~~, running a hand up and down her silk-encased ~~gs~~. Then he leaned forward and lightly touched his ~~outh~~ to her hot, pulsing center.

"Slate," she moaned.

"Still think I'm too tall?"

"No. Oh, no, please . . ."

His long tongue delved deeply into her moist ~~ftness~~, delighting in her taste, her scent, the feel ~~her~~ hidden passions as a strong hand kept her ~~rists~~ pinned above her head and the other fondled ~~r~~ breasts.

Raven writhed upward, her tension and desire ~~ounting~~ as he created more and more havoc within ~~r~~.

"Still convinced?" Slate persisted, a fine sheen of ~~eat~~ covering his body as his own passion ~~ounted~~.

"Yes, Slate. You're perfect, not too tall at all."

"Good."

He let her arms go as he rose to kneel between ~~r~~ legs, then raised her hips with strong fingers ~~gging~~ into her pale, firm flesh. He touched the tip ~~his~~ manhood to her pulsing softness, and hesi-~~ted~~.

315

She moaned, and tried to force him deep into her

"No, wait. Raven, look at me."

She turned dark turbulent eyes on him, her hair a wild silver-blond mass around her head and shoulders.

"I want to watch your eyes when I enter you."

"Slate, please . . ."

"You're always beautiful, but never more beautiful than when you're responding to me."

And he pushed inside her. She shuddered, taking him in deep, feeling him sheathe himself completely She watched his eyes darken and she felt as if his gaze had pierced her, too. She shivered, and he began to move, long, hard, slow strokes that made her twine her legs about him and begin to move in rhythm with him.

He moved in and out, harder and harder, until she grasped the bars of the brass bed to hold herself in place. The pressure increased. Their bodies were slick with sweat, sliding against each other. The passion intensified until Raven clinched the brass bed, not knowing if it were pleasure or pain that made her body writhe up against his in such desperate bid to reach the pinnacle of their desire

She heard him groan, his movements increased in tempo, and still their eyes were locked, as their bodies were locked in the struggle to find their way to ecstasy. Then suddenly she felt it coming, knew he felt it, too, and arched upward, flinging herself on him, feeling his deep thrusts fill her completely and then they both spun away into total ecstasy baring their souls to each other, merging their bodies and their spirits before they separated and returned to lie panting, their bodies hot and wet upon the soft sheets of the bed.

"Raven," Slate groaned. "You can't deny you're mine now. Not after that."

"You're mine," she whispered in response. "You wild Texan you."

"You make me wild. You make me lose all control. Only you can make me feel this way."

"And only you, Slate—"

"It'd better stay that way, too," he growled, rolling off her and pulling her to his side. "No other man is ever going to see you or touch you the way I do, and if that damn Centrano thinks he has any right to touch you—"

"He has nothing to do with us."

"He's going to be on the Montezuma Special and you're going to be serving him."

"But only meals."

"That's all you'd better serve him."

"There won't be many passengers, so maybe Sadie can serve him."

"I like the sound of that. Or maybe you can recruit Margarita."

Raven sat up in bed. "Margarita?"

"Sure. She's in town. Didn't you know? I caught her in between acts while I was waiting for you. She's homesick for San Antonio. I told her about the Montezuma Special and she couldn't think of a better way to go home."

Raven couldn't believe her ears. "Margarita? On the Montezuma Special?"

"Yes. Good idea, isn't it? Maybe she'll even perform for us."

"Good idea?" Raven scrambled away from him, pulling the sheet up to her chin. "How can you say

317

that after what we just shared?"

"What are you talking about?"

"You must have thought it was going to be nice and cozy having *both* your women on the luxurious Montezuma Special, but I have a surprise for you, Mr. Slate Slayton, and—"

"Wait a minute." Slate sat up in bed. "Do you mean you think Margarita and I are—"

"Lovers!"

He laughed.

Raven looked wilder.

"Now don't get mad, but it's funny. I mean, Margarita would laugh, too."

"I'm sure she would. Now, if you'll excuse me I'll get dressed and leave."

He grabbed her arm. "Not so fast. Margarita and I are friends, I've told you that. We're not lovers. That's a fact. You can ask her."

"You're both outlaws. Why should I believe either one of you?"

"What makes you think Margarita's an outlaw?"

"She's with you, isn't she? She's kept your clothes, hasn't she?"

Slate frowned and looked at her a long time. "You've got the damnedest mind, Raven. Seems to work a lot like mine. You noticed all that, then put it together. Well, I can see your point, but you've got the story wrong. You know, sometimes I wonder just who the hell you really are. I get to thinking you're a Harvey Girl and forget you're nothing but a money-grubbing little Yankee looking for her uncle. I don't know why I let you get under my skin like I do."

"Well, if you don't, I certainly do. You're still

hoping I'll marry you, get proof of my uncle's death, and then be rich the easy way. And then you'd probably kill me off and share it all with Margarita."

"You're starting to insult me, Raven, and I don't like it."

"Insult you? You've got your nerve. I think inviting Margarita on the Montezuma Special insults me!"

"I told you she's just my friend."

"Right. Just the way Jeremy Centrano is going to be my friend. Now let me go!"

"I will not, not until we've straightened this out."

"There's nothing to straighten out. You're trying to use me." She felt tears sting her eyes.

"No, I'm not. Just have some faith in me." He saw the tears and pulled her against his chest. "I promise. Margarita is just my friend. How many times do I have to tell you that? But let's make a deal, you stay away from Centrano and I'll stay away from Margarita. All right?"

"We can't. We'll all be thrown together on the Montezuma Special."

"I mean away from their beds."

"You mean it? Not that I ever had any intention of getting near Jeremy's bed."

"Yes, I mean it, but I'm sure he's got plans for you."

"I'm going to stay away from your bed, too."

"No you're not. You can't."

"Yes, I can. At least, I can try. I can be very strong if I put my mind to it, Slate."

"I don't want you to be strong. I want you to melt into my arms and forget everything and everybody

319

outside the two of us."

"It's just wrong. You're nothing but a—"

She didn't finish her words for Slate covered her lips with his and began a kiss that made her shiver all over. But she was determined to be strong where he was concerned, and pulled away from him.

"I hate what you do to me, and you *are* too tall."

"You don't hate what I do to you and I'm *not* too tall. Before you leave this room, I'm going to prove it to you once and for all."

And prove it he did.

Chapter Twenty-three

Raven had decided it was becoming more and more difficult to think of Slate Slayton as a piece of peppermint candy to be taken off the shelf and enjoyed for a little while then put away until she wanted him again. For one thing, he had a mind of his own, which a piece of candy didn't have, and for another it was hard not to want him all the time when he was around.

The situation was getting dangerous, almost as dangerous as the case she was working on, and she didn't know quite what to do about it. Everything she'd tried didn't seem to work where Slate was concerned. He overwhelmed her senses, her beliefs, her values, and put her in jeopardy.

But what could she do? He was going to be on the Montezuma Special all the way to San Antonio. And it was during this time that she needed to finally crack the identity of the mastermind and catch Comanche Jack. But Slate would be there, a constant distraction, and, worse yet, possibly working for the mastermind and Comanche Jack.

It was a terrible situation, one she could not possibly have imagined getting into back in Chicago when she had made all her plans. After the death of her father and fiancé, she had thought her senses dead, too. It had taken a Texas outlaw to awaken them again and she wished he hadn't. She had to figure out someway to control herself when she was around him. But she hadn't been able to do that yet, and it was time to turn her mind back to business.

She was wearing a pale mauve dress of cool cotton, and over it she had thrown a brightly colored shawl she had bought in the Mexican market earlier where she had also bought one for Sadie. The shawl was intended to camouflage her identity and help her pass as a lady of the evening, and it seemed to be working. She had been in and out of bars and silver exchanges for several hours asking questions, but had learned nothing new about Comanche Jack.

She had finally worked her way down to a seedy part of town, and decided she probably should have started there first, for it was the type of area in Topeka and Albuquerque where she'd gotten her best information. But she would rather avoid the section because it seemed so much more dangerous. Still, she had her father's Colt .45 in her reticule and would defend herself if necessary.

But so far everything had gone smoothly, or at least she hadn't had too much trouble with men trying to buy her for the afternoon. Most of them accepted no and went back to their gambling or drinking. But it was getting later now. The sun would soon set, and she knew the men would get more persistent. She didn't want that. Besides, she had to be back at the Montezuma Special by six.

Everyone had slept late after Jeremy's party the night before, and true to his word, Slate had slipped her safely back to her room and no one had been the wiser. But *she* had known and afterward worried about her actions. How could she continue to succumb to Slate's embraces?

But she didn't want to think about Slate now. There was no answer to her involvement with him, and she had other things to accomplish. The Montezuma Special was being loaded this afternoon. Her trunk had already been put aboard, and Sadie was there now.

Raven had gotten away from the Special by using the excuse of wanting to do some shopping before leaving El Paso. Sadie had considered going with her, but had decided against it since she was still insecure after her kidnapping. She didn't like to be too far from Ted.

Which, in this case, was fortunate for Raven. She couldn't have done all she needed to do this afternoon if her friend had been with her. She really needed to know if Comanche Jack was still near them. If she could get confirmation of that, she would feel comfortable about continuing on the Montezuma Special, for she would be fairly certain then that Comanche Jack would continue to stalk them. But she hadn't found anyone yet who remembered seeing him or would admit to having seen him, and she wanted that information if at all possible.

She glanced around the street. A few men sat in

wooden chairs leaned back against store fronts. They smoked and talked and watched her. She returned a few stares, then took a deep breath and stepped into the next gambling hall. It smelled of cheap whiskey, and little light entered the long, dark hall of a room. She stopped at the bar, and put a coin on the counter.

"Whiskey?" the bartender asked.

She nodded.

When he'd served it, she put a larger coin on the bar. "I'm looking for a man," she said, beginning her cover story, once again.

He took the coin. "Pretty thing like you shouldn't have trouble finding a man."

"If just any man would do, you'd be right, but this man is special. I need to find him. He has a hook in place of a left hand."

The bartender glanced around them, then back at her. "Lady, you ought to be careful asking about that man."

"Then you know him?"

"Wouldn't say if I did."

She put another coin on the bar. "I just need to know if you saw him around town recently."

He hesitated, then picked up the coin. "We get a lot of customers in here. I don't remember their faces and I sure don't remember their names, but something like a hook might stick in my mind."

"Yes?"

"Now, mind you, I don't know who you're talking about, but it seems like there might have been a man in here last night with a hook."

Raven felt relief flood her. "Thank you."

"If anybody asks, I never said that, I never saw

you, I never saw a man with a hook. Understand?"

"Yes. Perfectly. I won't mention this to anybody."

"That's real smart, lady. If I was you, I'd forget I ever heard of that man. Whatever he's done, you ought to forget."

"Thank you for your advice, but some things can't be forgotten."

She put a final coin on the bar, ignored the drink, then left.

Outside the air seemed clearer, the sun warmer, and she glanced up at the mountains ringing El Paso. The town was truly a pass through the mountains and had become an important center for transporting people and goods. They might have spent more time in the city, but Ted and Jeremy had been anxious to get started today. Whatever Jeremy wanted transported seemed to have made them both a little uneasy and they wanted to get on their way.

She'd find out what had been loaded on the Special later, but for now she'd completed her first task and knew Comanche Jack was still following them, which made her fairly certain the mastermind had to be nearby, too. Simpson or Centrano? Or perhaps neither. But she didn't believe that. Her father had been too good a detective to have been investigating the wrong men, and everything she'd learned so far pointed to them, too.

She started back toward the central part of town. It was getting late. She checked the watch on her bodice. After five now. She'd have to hurry to be back at the Special in time for it to leave at six.

There was a telegraph office in town and she headed for that. But as she neared it, she saw Slate come out. Startled, she hid behind a cheese barrel in

325

front of a dry goods store, then peeked out from behind it. Slate glanced around, then started walking quickly toward the train station.

What was he doing? Sending messages to the mastermind? Or to Comanche Jack? Maybe he was the in-between man for the mastermind and Comanche Jack. She had wondered about that when he had taken off alone in El Paso. If so, the mastermind was clever enough to have no direct contact with his gangs.

She shivered. Now the day didn't seem quite so sunny and warm. But what else could she believe of Slate? That he *was* simply a small-time outlaw trying to change his ways by working for Ted? No, she just couldn't accept that. There were too many coincidences. Nothing added up correctly. And there was Margarita, who would be on the train.

Well, if she had ever wanted all her suspects together, now she had them where she wanted them. She just wished she didn't feel so alone or so inexperienced or so vulnerable. If only her father and fiancé were here to help her, but they weren't. It was all up to her.

She squared her shoulders, and walked to the telegraph office. It didn't take her long to send a short message to Ted, telling him that R. Cunningham had helped rescue Sadie Perkins and was now back on the railroad case. Of course, Ted would think the telegram was from Slate and that the Chicago detective was on the train with him, or at least that's what Ted would tell her if he were the mastermind.

It was all so confusing she could hardly keep any of it straight anymore, and it only seemed to get worse. Feeling slightly overwhelmed, she stopped and bought six pieces of peppermint candy and started for the Montezuma Special. Maybe the candy would make her feel better.

She hoped she could get the case solved soon, for she was so tired of not knowing whom to trust. For Sadie's sake she hoped she could prove Ted innocent, but that would mean Jeremy was the mastermind and she found that hard to believe. Maybe the wily Comanche Jack was really the mastermind, too, and was manipulating Ted or Jeremy. Actually, she liked that idea best, and decided to cling to it for a while.

Passengers were boarding the Montezuma Special when she got there, and Slate was standing near a Pullman coach. When he saw her, he nodded and started toward her. At the sight of him, her heart began to beat faster and she remembered vividly their passion of the night before. But she stopped those thoughts and she warned herself to stay in control. She couldn't let Slate affect her so strongly, not anymore.

When he reached her, he handed her a paper twist of peppermint sticks, then laughed when he saw the ones she'd bought. "Do I take mine back, or do you need them all to get you to San Antonio?"

She carefully pushed them all together in one hand, laughing with him. "It's a long way to San Antonio. I think I'd better have them all. I might even have to share some."

"That's true. I almost ate them while I waited."

"Thanks, Slate, but you didn't have to buy them for me."

"I wanted to. I find myself wanting to buy you all

327

kinds of things I see in the stores. I almost bought you a beautiful silk and lace nightgown, but I thought you'd—"

"Rather have the candy."

"Right. If you'd ask me to marry you, I could buy you anything I wanted."

"But I'd worry about it begin bought with stolen money."

"I'm working a straight job right now, and you know it."

"I know, but for how long?"

"We're headed for San Antonio. If you want, we can discuss it again after that."

"What I want is for things to be different."

"Oh, I got you something else. I probably should wait, but I can't. Come over here."

He led her to the side of the depot where they could be alone. As Slate dug in his vest pocket, Raven watched the Special being readied for departure. Jeremy's private coach had been coupled to the end of Ted's car and was now the last coach on the Montezuma Special. From El Paso to San Antonio. That was the run. And somewhere along that route she was going to catch the mastermind and Comanche Jack.

"Shut your eyes, Raven."

"Oh, Slate, really, I'm not in the mood for games."

"What are you in the mood for? We haven't tried those Pullman berths yet."

"And we're not going to, either."

"Wait and see. In the meantime, shut your eyes."

"I don't want you to give me anything else."

"You'll want this. Now shut your eyes."

"Oh, all right." She shut her eyes.

"Now hold out your hands."

"That's silly. What if someone sees us?"

"Who cares? Now hold out your hands."

"This had better be good." She held out her nds, cupping them, and felt a heavy warm object de into her palms.

"You can open your eyes now, Raven."

She did, and discovered she was holding a long, avy gold chain. On it was the dented gold coin at had saved her life when Hank had shot her. ate had had a ring punched through the coin, then ing on a chain. She was deeply touched. Tears ing her eyes, and she flung her arms around ate's neck.

"Thank you," she said, then stepped back and ld the necklace up to examine it in the sunlight. "I ought you said I didn't need my lucky coin any-ore."

"That's why I'm giving it to you. I think you do ed it, now more than ever."

She glanced up at him. His eyes were a stormy ay. He looked worried.

"Has something happened?"

"Let me put it around your neck." He carefully did the clasp, then gently put it around her neck aking sure the clasp was tightly secured. Finally, : straightened the chain, letting his hands linger ainst her warmth. The gold coin hung just be-een her breasts. "The length's perfect, but maybe ou should put it inside your dress like it was fore."

She unbuttoned several buttons, then slipped it side. It was cool against her skin, then warmed to

her flesh. When she glanced back at Slate, his ey
had turned more blue than gray. She could feel t
passion that still lingered between them from t
night before.

"I can't help wanting you every time I see yo
Raven, and I keep remembering what we shared la
night. I want you right now, this minute."

Raven knew what he was feeling, but hung
tightly to her determination to keep her distan
from him. "Thank you, Slate. This is very though
ful, but I really shouldn't accept gifts from you

"It was already yours. Remember, it bought me
glimpse of your underclothes and a little more
you."

"Yes, I remember, but the chain is expensive.

"I just wanted to make sure you didn't lose yo
lucky coin. A solid chain is a lot more secure than
handkerchief."

"You're right, but it's still an expensive gift."

"Just wear it for good luck like you were doin
and maybe think of me sometimes when it slid
across your skin."

"I told you it was strictly a good-luck charm

"That's what you told me, but I can always ho
for more, can't I?"

She smiled. "Yes, I suppose you can, and thar
you."

"My pleasure. It's already brought you luc
Saved your life, in fact. And that's why I wante
you to have it again now. I think we're both going
need a lot of luck this trip."

"What's wrong?"

"Nothing, far as I know. But I've got a feeling
don't like. Also, I found out Centrano's shipment

330

ver."

Raven's eyes widened. "Silver!"

"Yes. Nobody's supposed to know but the rail-
ad men and some of the crew, but Ted told me,
n't imagine why except that I'm suppose to be
arding you and Sadie."

Raven knew why, but didn't say so because if
ate were working for the mastermind he might or
ght not know about the story that he was sup-
sed to be the Chicago detective. She felt frus-
ted because she knew so little of the truth, but
e knew for sure she couldn't trust Slate, no matter
w concerned he seemed to be about her.

"Ted obviously trusts you," Raven finally said.
o you think we'll be attacked again because of the
ver?"

"If any outlaws find out we're carrying it, I've got
doubts we'll be attacked."

"Will you notify any of your friends?"

"You mean my outlaw friends?"

"Yes."

"You sure don't trust anybody, do you?"

"I don't think I can afford to."

"You've got a point, but you *can* trust me, Raven.
never hurt you, and I'll do everything in my
wer to protect you."

"And Sadie."

"Sadie, too."

"Because Ted's paying you."

"No. Because life wouldn't be worth much with-
t you. But you won't believe that and I'm not
ing to push the point now. It's about time to
ve. Let's get back to the Special."

He tucked her hand in the crook of his arm and

331

started for the train.

Raven didn't object, and let the conversati
lapse as they walked back. He was right. As mu
as she wanted to believe him, she couldn't let he
self. She had to be the tough private detective fro
Chicago if she were going to see the mastermi
and Comanche Jack captured.

Perhaps Slate wouldn't contact any of his outl
friends about the silver, but if the mastermind kne
about it, which he surely must, then the Montezur
Special would be attacked. After all, the mast
mind had already lost the gold he'd planned
getting in New Mexico so he was bound to go aft
the silver. And she'd be there to catch him.

Slate walked her to one of the Pullman sleepe
squeezed her hand, then headed for the front of t
train. Raven watched him walk away, noticing I
long muscular legs. Too tall, or just right. S
shook her head. She couldn't think about Slat
body, not now. She'd promised herself to be stro
and keep her mind on business, and she must.

She opened the door to the coach, and stepp
inside.

"Buenos tardes," Margarita said.

"Raven, come on in and join us," Sadie adde
looking happy and pretty in a pale yellow gow

Raven felt her heart tighten at the sight of Marg
rita, but smiled anyway and sat down beside Sac
on one of the plush Pullman seats. Margarita w
across from them, looking lovely in a cool cott
rose-colored gown.

"You've got a new shawl, haven't you, Raven
Sadie asked. "It's so unusual. Now I wish I'd go
shopping with you. And peppermint sticks!"

332

"Don't worry," Raven replied, smiling. "You didn't miss very much. Look what I brought you." She pulled out the shawl she'd bought for Sadie. "This one's for you."

"Oh! It's beautiful, Raven. You are a dear." Sadie kissed her lightly on the cheek before standing up and throwing the shawl about her shoulders. "Well, now do I look?"

"Lovely," Raven said, delighted to see Sadie so happy. Her friend needed as much happiness as possible.

"Quite beautiful," Margarita agreed.

"I'm sorry I didn't bring you one, too, Margarita, but you're welcome to the other one," Raven quickly added.

"Thank you, but no. Keep it for yourself. I have a similar one at home which my grandmother made for me."

"Really?" Sadie said, sitting down next to Raven again.

"Yes. She did wonderful work on the loom. Although my people have long lived in Texas, they originally came from Spain like so many in Mexico and intermarried with the local Indians."

"It's beautiful work," Sadie said. "I'm from back East so I've never seen such unusual designs before."

"They're been handed down to us from the Maya and other native nations. We're very proud of our combined heritage and inherited skills."

"I know what you mean," Sadie agreed. "I'm very proud of my Harvey Girl skills."

"So am I," Raven agreed. "But you haven't seen Margarita perform, Sadie. She's very talented."

"Thank you," Margarita responded quietly.

"Again, I simply use skills handed down throug[h] my family for generations."

"That must be wonderful," Sadie said wistfully. "[I] have no idea what my family might have done o[r] what skills they might have had."

"Why is that?" Margarita asked, concern in he[r] voice.

"Sadie grew up in an orphanage," Raven re[sponded].

"I see," Margarita said. "But that is not so sad after all. You will have the opportunity to buil[d] your own family, start your own dynasty. Now tha[t] is truly exciting."

Sadie smiled. "I'd never thought of it that way. When I first came West, the Harvey Girls were m[y] family and Raven my best friend, practically m[y] sister. Then I met Ted, and suddenly I not only ha[d] family and friends but a future husband. Comin[g] West was the most wonderful thing that ever hap[pened to me except —"

"Now she has to choose between being a Harvey Girl or Ted's wife," Raven quickly inserted, realizing that Sadie was about to mention her kidnapping. No one but Santa Fe and the people actually in[volved were supposed to know about it.

"No, that's not quite true, Raven," Sadie re[sponded. "Ted and I discussed it. As long as h[e] travels with the Montezuma Special, I can still be [a] Harvey Girl, and I want to be. They've been very good to me and I like the work. Also, I'm used t[o] being busy and while Ted works so can I."

"You really like the railways, don't you?" Marga[rita asked.

"Yes," Sadie replied. "That's why marrying Te[d]

334

ill be so fine. Even when we have children, we'll
ill travel across the country in his private coach."

"I can see you love the life," Margarita replied,
ut for me I always miss my San Antonio, my
xas when I travel. I am a woman very attached to
er roots. What about you, Raven?"

"Me? I guess I like a little of both."

"She's from Chicago," Sadie confided, "but you'd
ink she was born in the West, wouldn't you?"

Margarita laughed softly. "Perhaps to you, but
ot so much to a native. We are a special breed,
ose of us born and raised in the West, but we are
ver ready to accept newcomers. That has always
een the way here."

The Montezuma Special's whistle sounded three
mes, then the train began to roll forward, picking
p speed rapidly. All three women turned their
ttention to the windows.

"I'm looking forward to getting home," Margarita
aid, then glanced around the coach. "And it should
ertainly be a comfortable trip."

"Yes, it should," Sadie quickly agreed, for there
ould be only the three of them in the Pullman
oach. The other passengers were riding in another
ar, and the men working the train had another to
emselves. Ted and Jeremy would be living in their
rivate coaches.

As they left El Paso and the dusty plains outside
f town came into view, Raven relaxed against the
eat. It was a long way to San Antonio. She had
nough time to be very careful, plot her moves, and
et the information she needed.

But she'd also have to be careful of Margarita.
he woman was probably on board to watch her

335

when Slate couldn't. Perhaps they even suspecte
she was R. Cunningham. After all, Sadie had ju
told Margarita she was from Chicago and somebod
might put that information together with the loca
tion of the detective agency Ted had hired.

Still, she wouldn't worry about that now. The
were on their way and it was time to get som
answers, especially about one too tall Texas outlaw

Chapter Twenty-four

The Montezuma Special followed the Rio Grande River along the Texas-Mexican border southeast. The land was dry, dusty, stark, with purple mountains rising in the distance. The Special sped through several small border towns, then turned away from the Rio Grande, passed through the Quitman Mountain Range, then headed south toward Marfa.

As the Special sped through open plains, the days grew hotter and the passengers were soon bored with the flat land filled with grass and cacti and windswept mountains. Lone coyotes howled in the distance and an occasional rattlesnake slithered near the railroad track. For the most part it was wild country stretching endlessly into the distance, a vast land that made many a traveler feel small, alone, and wary.

The Montezuma Special protected its passengers from the harsh country, but it could not protect them from the growing feeling that if anything

337

happened to the train they would suddenly be alone and vulnerable in the vast Texas plains. Even the Texans aboard were not immune to the awesome land, for they knew better than most that death could come quickly in many ways.

After the brief stop in Marfa, tempers grew short and tension built. The observation coach was abandoned for the library car where there were not nearly enough seats. Soon the passengers took books and retired to their Pullman coach, waiting the next meal. That put more pressure on the chef and the Harvey Girls aboard, for the most exciting event on the Special had become the food.

More than anyone, Raven and Sadie had the responsibility of keeping the passengers happy, and they felt the growing tension acutely. They were still a long way from San Antonio, and, in fact, far from any town. Raven finally decided to seek help and went to Margarita.

The entertainer was reading in the Pullman sleeper she shared with Raven and Sadie, obviously enjoying the trip since she was so happy to be going home.

"Margarita," Raven said, sitting down across from the entertainer. "Excuse me, but could I have a moment of your time?"

"Certainly. How may I help you?"

"I don't know if you've noticed, but the other passengers are getting more and more restless. Sadie and I are doing the best we can to keep them entertained with books and meals, but we wondered if you might help us by entertaining this evening?"

"I hadn't realized the trip would be boring for some. I'm enjoying the rest and relaxation of the

338

rip. But certainly I'd be glad to help you. I don't think there's room to dance, but I could play and sing. How would that be?"

"That would be wonderful. I'm sure Santa Fe would pay you."

"That's not necessary. I'd enjoy it."

"Thank you. Sadie and I will announce it at dinner, then everyone who wants to come can meet in the observation car after the dinner hour."

"Excellent. I'll look forward to it."

"So will I. Well, I'd better get back to the library."

"You're staying busy there?"

"I've never seen anything like it, but this land has a strange, powerful, almost mystic quality to it. I think it makes us all feel uneasy."

Margarita nodded. "You're right. It affects everyone strongly, even us natives. You can see why I hate to leave Texas."

"Yes, but I'm not sure I like the feeling."

"Some people never feel the call of Texas, but those who do, come to think of it as home, no matter how far they roam. I think in time you may come to love Texas as I do, Raven."

"I don't know. It's so big, so empty. I think I'll feel more comfortable in a city. That's why I can't wait to see San Antonio. Well, like I said I'd better get back to the library car now."

"Raven I don't mean to pry, but I think you've grown rather close to Slate."

"We've been working together since Ted hired him for the Special," Raven replied cautiously.

"No, I mean more than that. A personal closeness."

Raven stood up. She didn't want to discuss Slate

with anyone, and especially not with Margarita.

"I just wanted you to know that I think you're good for him." Margarita persisted. "He's needed a strong woman like you for a long time, a woman who can deal and raise with the best of them."

"Deal and raise?"

"A poker term. Anyway, you can hold your own with him, and I've never seen any woman do that before." She laughed softly. "I don't think he knows if he's coming or going with you, and I couldn't be more pleased."

"Pleased?"

"Yes, of course. Slate and I are old friends. Perhaps there might have been something more than friendship between us once, but that time has long passed. We remain friends because we are bound by old loyalties, but those have nothing to do with you. I thought you might want to know."

Raven edged toward the door. She didn't want to hear what Margarita had to say. The entertainer was so smooth, so sure of herself. Perhaps it was because she was five or so years older than Raven, but perhaps it was because she knew Slate was really hers and that Raven was just for the moment. Either way, Raven felt very uneasy. Margarita was acting much too confident.

"I've obviously surprised you by speaking so personally. Believe me, I have no intention of embarrassing you or Slate, but I know him and I've seen how he watches you. He is a strong, powerful man, but gentle and loving to the right woman. He needs what you can give him, Raven. He needs it very much. He needs a friend, as we all do." Her voice suddenly broke, revealing pain and loneliness.

Shocked, Raven was suddenly overwhelmed by compassion. She sat down beside Margarita and took one of her small hands. "I don't understand what you're trying to tell me."

"I just want you to know that I consider you a friend of mine as well as Slate's, and if you ever need my help just let me know."

Raven took a deep breath. "Thank you. I still don't understand, but it's true that Slate and I have become friends. I think we can all call on each other if we need anything."

Margarita looked relieved, them smiled. "That's true, but I'm keeping you from your work. I wish more than anything for it all to be done and be back home in San Antonio."

"What done?"

"Why, the trip of course."

"Yes, I look forward to seeing San Antonio. But I must go now. I'll see you this evening."

Raven quickly left, her mind seething with unanswered questions as she made her way toward the library car. What had Margarita been talking about? What did she know? Raven was suddenly terrified that the entertainer knew her true identity as R. Cunningham. But surely that couldn't be true. No one would believe a Chicago detective was a woman, unless it was another woman.

She shivered. Was Margarita giving her blessing to Raven's relationship with Slate? But why would she do that unless it was a very clever ploy to throw her off the scent of the mastermind and Comanche Jack? Or maybe she and Slate were planning to heist the silver themselves and just wanted there to be no suspicions.

The plot thickened every moment, and she didn't have nearly enough answers. She hurried into the library car seeking refuge. How could she possibly apprehend the criminals when there seemed to be so many and she was all alone?

But her thoughts were suddenly cut short as she glanced around in surprise. The car was empty. Where was everyone?

"Sadie lured them all to the observation car with a snack," Slate said, stepping from behind the curtain that led to the barber shop and shower. "And it's empty in there, too."

"Oh! You startled me, Slate." Her heart beat faster at the sight of him, but she was determined to keep her emotions under control.

"Didn't mean to. Jumpy?"

"Everybody is. I think it's this land. Just look out there. Is there no end to it? Are there no towns?"

"We'll be stopping in Marathon tomorrow before heading back down toward the Rio Grande and the Mexican border."

"At last, civilization."

"Maybe not exactly, but the trip hasn't been that bad, has it?"

"No, except that Sadie and I have really been kept busy."

"I know. I've been busy, too. I think I know where they've hidden the silver."

Raven's heart jumped. Maybe she was right. Maybe Slate was after the silver for himself. "Are there any soldiers guarding it?"

"Not as far as I can tell. Centrano probably thought the unexpectedness of transferring Southern Pacific cargo to a Santa Fe train, and one like the

342

Special, would throw off any outlaws in the area."

"I suppose it should. But you don't think it will?"

"I don't know, but we're in Texas now and the Texas Rangers will have something to say about anything stolen here."

"I suppose you *would* know how good they are."

Slate grinned. "I just might at that."

"Well, I hope you've changed your ways because you wouldn't want a Ranger coming after you, would you?"

"No, ma'am."

"Should I feel safer now that I'm in Texas?"

"You should feel safer now that I'm around."

Raven struggled to keep her emotions under control, but his nearness made her want to melt into his arms. "Your job's to make me feel safer."

"That's what Ted hired me for, and I'll do everything in my power to see we reach San Antonio safely."

"I know you will." She hesitated, then added, "I just spoke with Margarita."

"How is she?"

"Lonely."

"I know, but there's nothing anybody can do about it."

"I hope it's not because of me. I mean, you'd think a beautiful woman like that would have married by now, or be engaged or something."

"Her loneliness has nothing to do with you or me. Anyway, maybe she was engaged once. Texas is rough country. Maybe her fiancé was killed."

"Do you really think so?"

"I'm not saying she was engaged or her fiancé was killed. I'm just saying there are lots of reasons to be

343

lonely in Texas."

"I see. Well, I can't help but like her even though I know you two are close."

"You're the only woman in my life, Raven. The only woman I want. Do you want me to prove it again?" He stepped close to her.

She could feel his body heat, and wanted him to hold her, kiss her, make her forget everything but their passion. Instead, she moved away from him and said, "Anyone could come in."

"They're all busy eating."

"Don't even think about touching me."

"I think about it all the time. But I don't believe you think about it enough."

"That's not true! I mean . . ."

Slate's eyes turned a dark blue. "Since we settled the fact that I'm just the right height, maybe we should start working on the idea that I'm a one-woman man and you're my woman."

"Oh, Slate, I wish I could believe you."

"That's another thing we need to work on."

"What?"

"You trusting me."

"I believe Margarita just said something like that, and it makes me very suspicious."

Slate laughed. "You're the damnedest woman I know. I should be the suspicious one with that Centrano sniffing after you. But you're the one always questioning me. I want more than just your body, and I'd walk through fire to earn your trust."

"I don't believe that will be necessary."

"Maybe not, but I'm ready."

"Ready for what?"

"For you."

And he began stalking her around the library. "Slate, no!"

But he didn't listen and she couldn't keep out of the reach of his arms for long. Yet she had to retain her distance, emotionally and physically. She headed for the curtains that led outside and bumped into someone on the other side.

"Oh, excuse me," she said, stepping back.

"Not at all," Jeremy replied, walking into the library. "You look as lovely as ever, Raven." Then he saw Slate and added, "Oh, does the ruffian read?"

Slate scowled.

Raven slapped a book in Slate's hands. "He was just leaving. He came by for a book on . . ."

"Birds," Slate completed, glancing at the book Raven had picked at random. "Had some of the passengers asking about the vultures they saw waiting near the railroad track. Seem to be more around than usual.'

"Really?" Jeremy said. "And that is part of your job?"

"My job's whatever I make it," Slate responded. "But my primary concern is to see that everything on this train gets to San Antonio."

"Excellent."

"I'm glad you agree," Slate replied, "because a riled Texan isn't something you want to argue with."

"A gentleman never argues, Señor Slayton."

"I guess it's a good thing I'm not a gentleman then," Slate said, and left the car.

"A very rude man," Jeremy added when Slate had gone. "I'm surprised a gentleman like Ted would hire him."

"I suppose he thought a ruffian would do a better

345

job of guarding the train than a gentleman."

"I suppose so, but I'm also sure we don't need the extra protection."

"I certainly hope not, but this seems like a wild and lonely country."

"My dear girl, are you frightened? You have no need to be. I will be at hand. A gentleman is always more dependable than a ruffian. Trust me to protect you. See?" He pulled a two-shot derringer from his inside vest pocket. "I always wear this. As a last resort it is undefeatable."

"You're very clever." Raven was glad he'd shown her the concealed weapon. She just might need that information vitally some time later. "Could I help you find a book?"

"Why yes. Is there much left of interest?"

While he looked through the books, Raven glanced around the library, thinking about the conversations she'd just had. Everyone was showing the strain of the trip, and she was surprised because she hadn't noticed any similar tension from Topeka to Las Vegas, New Mexico. It was as if everyone could feel the building tension she felt as she waited for the mastermind and Comanche Jack to make their move.

Too, Raven had not been sleeping well, every little sound woke her because she expected the outlaws to strike at any time and she had to be ready. She'd started wearing her father's snub-nosed Colt .45 strapped to her right thigh. Maybe it wasn't necessary, but she felt that something was going to happen soon and she wanted to be prepared.

"Raven," Jeremy said, interrupting her thoughts. "I was hoping you could dine in my private car this evening, but the passengers are keeping you very busy. Do you think we could make it a late dinner and invite Ted and Sadie?" He took out a black silk handkerchief and dusted off the cover of a book he'd selected.

"I'm sure that would be delightful, but I've invited Margarita to perform in the observation coach for everyone tonight. I couldn't very well not attend, and I'm sure you'd enjoy her music. She's very good.'

"I'm sure I would, too. Perhaps we could make it tomorrow night then."

"I'd like that."

"Good. I'll make plans with Ted and Sadie."

"I'll look forward to it." Raven wanted to get a look in his private car and this would be the perfect opportunity. She'd already searched Ted's coach and found nothing incriminating. Not that it meant he wasn't guilty, but it was a point in his favor.

"Then I'll see you this evening." He took her hand and pressed warm lips to her soft skin. "You smell delectable. If I had you, I don't think I would be hungry for food again."

"If you continue flattering me so, you'll turn my head."

"As long as you look in my direction, that will be fine."

Raven smiled, and pulled her hand free.

"Till this evening." He left, looking very pleased.

There was no doubt in her mind that Jeremy was a very attractive, attentive man. She should be flattered, but instead she was suspicious. There was something about him she didn't quite trust, like him concealing a derringer. That seemed out of character

347

for a railroad representative, but perhaps Ted carried one, too. She'd have to find out, and Sadie would know.

She pushed a few stray hairs back into the neat chignon at her nape. She was tired. The stress and strain of the trip were beginning to affect her. And worse than that was the fact that she'd turned up no real clues. She was no closer to learning the identity of the mastermind than she had been. It was discouraging. What would her father and fiancé have done now? How would they have broken open the case? Or would they have waited just like she was doing?

Rubbing her hand over the back of a velvet chair, she sat down. She really did feel tired, and there was still the dinner meal to serve and Margarita's performance afterward. But Slate had said that tomorrow they'd stop in Marathon. Maybe she could get some clues there. At least she could find out if Comanche Jack had been seen in town. Although how he could keep up with the train on horseback she didn't know. But that wasn't her worry. She'd bet the gold piece around her neck that he'd be there, somehow, someway.

She drifted into a light sleep and the next thing she knew Sadie was shaking her awake.

"All right, I'm awake," she groaned, stretching.

"I'm sorry to wake you, but you cried out in your sleep," Sadie said. "I think you're worried about something. Can I help?"

Raven smiled. Her friend was looking more confident every day and she would do nothing to disrupt Sadie's recovery and newfound happiness. "I think it's just a delayed reaction to that robbery and

348

kidnapping business. We were all terribly worried about you."

"I understand. Sometimes I wake up from dreams and I'm still a prisoner. But Ted says they'll go away in time if I have nothing but love and happiness around me from now on."

"He's right. That's what we all need."

"And Slate? He seems a changed man. Do you think now that you know he's not really an outlaw you two might get together permanently?"

"You mean marriage?"

"Yes. I can't tell you how happy I am to be engaged to Ted."

"I'm glad for you, Sadie, but Slate's a different matter. I know Ted thinks he's a private detective from Chicago, but until we know for sure I can't quite trust him."

"But Slate doesn't seem like an outlaw. I bet once his case is solved he'll be free for you, and that shouldn't be long now, should it?"

"I hope not," Raven agreed, wishing she could confide completely in her friend, but she couldn't upset Sadie or put her in any more danger with the truth.

"Don't you worry, Raven. Slate's in love with you if ever a man loved a woman. He can't keep his eyes off you, and I remember how he was in Topeka. One day soon, he'll probably ask you to mary him."

"I'm not sure if I should marry him."

"Just wait. He'll ask, then we'll both be engaged."

"We'll see." Raven would like to have told Sadie that Slate had already asked her to mary him in a peculiar sort of way. And, in fact, he was now waiting for her to ask *him* for a marriage ring.

Sadie wouldn't have understood. She wasn't sure she did herself. But then Slate wasn't the usual sort of man a woman thought about marrying. For that matter, she wasn't exactly considered prime marriage material either. Maybe they suited each other. She chuckled to herself.

"What's so funny, Raven?"

"I was just thinking how differently things have gone than what we'd planned in Topeka."

Sadie smiled. "You're right, but I'd have gone through anything to get my darling Ted."

"You're lucky. He's perfect for you."

"And such a gentleman."

"Oh, yes. Sadie, does Ted carry a derringer in his coat or vest in the line of business?"

"What?" Sadie was obviously shocked.

"I just thought it might be normal for a railroad representative to be armed."

"I don't know how you could think that of Ted. He's such a gentle person."

"I know. I just thought it might be a common practice."

"I don't know how common it is, but Ted definitely does not carry a weapon. And I'd know."

Raven nodded, thinking about Jeremy and his gun. Just precaution or something more? She didn't know, but she wanted to search his coach soon. Then she said, teasingly, "Just how would you know Ted doesn't carry a gun?"

Sadie blushed. "On occasion I have been known to throw myself wantonly into his arms. And he just as wantonly presses me close. I'd know if he wore a gun, Raven."

"I guess you would at that."

"And you'd know if Slate wore one?"

"We all know he does, and we don't even have to throw ourselves into his arms to find out."

"But you like to be in his arms, don't you?"

"Yes, I'm afraid I do. I've tried not to want him, but there's something about him, Sadie."

"I know how it is. Don't worry, it'll all work out perfectly in the end. Now, come on to the dining car. It's time to serve the hungry hordes."

"That's a good way to put it," Raven said as she followed Sadie from the library coach.

Chapter Twenty-five

Late the next afternoon the Montezuma Special pulled into the Southern Pacific depot at Marathon. Even though it was a small dusty town with just one main street, the passengers piled off, eager to stretch their legs and look around.

Raven threw her brightly colored shawl over her Harvey Girl uniform and slipped away by herself. There wouldn't be many places in town where she could get information about Comanche Jack, but she would do her best. She nodded at a few passengers as she passed them, then went inside one of the town's two dry goods stores.

It didn't take her long to buy peppermint candy and find out they hadn't seen a one-handed man with a hook. She wasn't surprised. She hadn't expected Comanche Jack to be conspicuous in a town this size. She tried the other dry goods store, bought more peppermint sticks, but learned nothing else.

Back on the boardwalk, she nodded to a few more passengers, then headed for the three bars in town. She hesitated outside the first one, realizing a Harvey Girl would have no excuse for being inside a bar. She'd seen several of the male passengers head toward the bars as soon as the train had stopped, so she left. It simply wasn't worth the chance of ruining her cover as a Harvey Girl by entering. She walked around for a while, looking in store windows. She didn't know what to do next.

The train would be leaving soon. She glanced back down the main street and noticed Slate looking around, then entering the telegraph station. Who was he communicating with? Comanche Jack? The mastermind? She wished she could trust him, but he made it more impossible all the time, even though her body cried out for her to believe in him.

She turned a corner, not wanting Slate to see her looking around the town. He was already suspicious of her, and she didn't want to make it worse. She was near a blacksmith's shop, and a horse was being shod. She decided to talk to the blacksmith. If Comanche Jack were on horseback, he might have come here, but most likely he'd have taken a Southern Pacific train to keep up with them.

As she approached the blacksmith shop, there was movement in the shadows of the building, then a short, heavily muscled man with a wide-brimmed hat stepped into the bright sunlight. He was smoking a cheroot, but stopped to drop it in the dirt and grind it with the heel of a black lizard cowboy boot. Then he looked straight in her direction.

She couldn't tell if he were looking at her, for his face was cast in shadow by the wide brim of his hat. But as far as she knew there was no one else in the street behind her. After a brief pause, he raised his left hand, tipped his hat, then turned away and headed down an alley.

She almost gasped out loud. In place of a left hand he'd had a hook. Comanche Jack! She hurried after him, opening her reticule and grasping the Colt .45. She followed him into the alley, but it was empty. Glancing around, she saw nothing, no one. She tried several doors but they were all locked. He couldn't have just disappeared. She retraced her steps, but still could find no clue that he'd ever been there or that she'd seen him at all.

She gave up. She was running out of time. The man had lived with the Comanche and had obviously learned their stealth and cunning. She walked back to the blacksmith's shop, and stopped.

"Excuse me, but could you tell me about that man who was just here?"

"What man?"

"The man with a hook in place of a left hand."

"Never saw such a man."

"What? But I just saw him. He disappeared down a street."

"Heat getting to you, lady?"

"No. I just wanted to ask him about the hook. My . . . my brother recently lost his hand and I wanted to find out what type of hook that man was wearing and if he liked it," she fabricated her story quickly.

The blacksmith raised his head, looked at her hard, then said, "Lady, I wasn't born yesterday. Now go on back to your fancy train."

Raven blushed. She supposed it was a pretty lame excuse, but she wasn't giving up. "Actually, I kind of liked his looks. I wanted to talk to him."

"I don't know nothing about no man, but if I did I'd say a man likes to do his own chasing. If he wants you, he'll come for you."

"I see. Well, I think Comanche Jack will be a little disappointed if he missed me. I've got a message for him."

The blacksmith looked at her again, this time with more interest. "Jack's particular about the way he gets messages. He saw you, and if he wants to talk to you he'll find you."

Raven's breath caught in her throat. Her story had worked very well this time, more than she could have even hoped. She suddenly had confirmation that the man with the hook had actually been Comanche Jack. Now she had a body to go with the name. "Yes, he saw me. If he stops back by, would you give him a message that Raven wants to talk to him about a job."

"If I see him again I will, but he's always on the move."

"I understand. Thanks."

She walked away as quickly as she could, trying to conceal her growing excitement. Comanche Jack! She'd actually seen him. The most she'd expected on this stop was to get news that someone had seen him. But *she* had seen him, and he looked very dangerous, very strong, very cold. She'd have to be extremely careful when she came up against him again.

She bit off the end of a peppermint stick, relaxing her tight grip on the hot sticky candy as she walked down the main street of town. She smiled happily at several customers, then saw Sadie and Ted. They waved and she started their way. But before she reached them, Jeremy stepped out of a dry goods store and said, "Raven, I have been looking for you."

"Oh, hello, Jeremy. How are you?"

"Fine, now that I'm with you. I had thought we could see the sights of Marathon together, but you've already done that, haven't you?" He glanced curiously at the candy she was holding.

"Yes. I've already looked around. Want a peppermint stick?"

"No thank you. They look rather sticky."

"Well, it's hot and I've been holding them, but they still taste good."

"I'm sure they do. Could I get you something else?"

"No thanks. I'm fine, but let's join Ted and Sadie."

"Certainly."

As they walked together, Raven glanced inside a bar and saw Slate. He was talking to the bartender, but when he saw her with Jeremy he hurried toward the door. She glanced back and he was watching her, a scowl on his face, but he didn't follow them and she was glad. She didn't want Slate making anyone suspicious.

"Raven, I see you bought more peppermint," Sadie exclaimed, drawing Raven close. "But look what I have."

Sadie had a bag of roasted peanuts which Ted was patiently shelling. She popped several in her mouth, then offered some to Raven and Jeremy.

"No thanks," Raven replied. "They look good, but my peppermint is enough. Want some of it?"

Sadie shook her head and they started walking toward the Montezuma Special.

"We're looking forward to dining with you tonight, Jeremy," Sadie said. "Ted tells me your private coach is even more sumptuous than his."

"It's simply a comfortable home away from home, but I think you'll like it."

"I'm sure we all will," Sadie responded. "And after serving dinner tonight, I'll really appreciate sitting back and being served myself."

"I thought you both might enjoy that," Jeremy replied. "And I'm looking forward to having all of you as my guests."

"Thank you," Raven said, "but I'm afraid it's about time to get to the dining car and set everything up for the dinner hour, isn't it, Sadie?"

"Yes, it's that time again."

"We'll be leaving in about fifteen minutes," Ted added, "and the passengers will be hungry after their stroll in town."

"They're *always* hungry," Sadie laughed.

"And no wonder," Jeremy added, "with two such beautiful ladies to serve him."

"Doesn't he know just how to flatter a woman?" Raven asked.

"He certainly does," Sadie agreed.

They parted company at the train, and as Sadie and Raven entered the dining car, Raven glanced back. Slate was walking toward the train, watching her closely. She waved, then slipped inside.

By the time Raven and Sadie had finished serving dinner, the sun had set and they were both tired and hungry. After they'd changed out of their Harvey Girl uniforms, Ted escorted them to the last coach on the train, Jeremy's private car. Although they were accustomed to the luxury of the Montezuma Special and Ted's private coach, they were still unprepared for Jeremy's palatial railway car.

Fabulous collections of art, crystal, sculpture, plus luxurious furnishings filled every nook and cranny of the railway car. Dressed in black silk, Jeremy looked very handsome and very much the gentleman amongst his wonderful collection of art.

"Buenos noches," Jeremy said, drawing them inside. "My man, Tomas, has prepared a very special dinner for us tonight. I hope you will enjoy it."

"I'm sure we will," Raven responded.

"Since the Montezuma Special is equipped with a diner and stewards, I didn't have a man travel in my private coach this trip," Ted remarked.

"Certainly understandable, but Tomas has been with me so long I don't know what I'd do without him. He serves as my chef, steward, and waiter, but doesn't speak English so please don't be offended if I use Spanish with him."

"That's perfectly all right," Sadie said, glancing around in wonder. "I hardly know where to look first you have so many treasures here."

"Thank you. Next to the railroad, my art is my life. But, Ted, wouldn't you say our lovely ladies are perfect examples of fine art, too?"

Ted chuckled. "I agree, but I don't think they'd allow anyone to hide them away in a treasure trove."

"Perhaps not, but on the other hand perhaps that is the best place for a truly beautiful woman. That way she would be protected, loved, but not subject to all the ugliness of the world outside her . . ."

"Gilded cage," Raven finished for him.

Jeremy smiled at her. "You misunderstand me, my dear. A man would never want to hide you away forever, merely protect you, spoil you, as is only right."

"I don't mind being spoiled," Sadie agreed, "but I don't want a gilded cage, either."

"No one could ever cage you, Sadie," Ted replied,

"but I'm going to get a ring on your finger as quickly as I can before you get away."

"That shouldn't be hard to do since I'm not running."

Everyone chuckled, and Jeremy led them into dinner. The furniture was Queen Anne, very delicate, and obviously very expensive. It even looked like it might have been imported from Europe, but that seemed a little much for a railroad car and Raven decided she must be mistaken. Nevertheless, it was all beautiful. Jeremy had excellent taste.

Which proved to be true again as Tomas served course after sumptuous course. Jeremy explained they were eating a combination of Spanish and Mexican dishes which had been handed down in his family for generations. Everything was delicious and compared equally to the sumptuous food served at the Montezuma Hotel.

Jeremy was a generous and entertaining host, and once more Raven could not imagine him as the mastermind. But then neither could she believe Sadie's beloved Ted was the mastermind, either. Perhaps she had been right earlier in thinking that Comanche Jack was in control of one or both of the railroad men.

But she still didn't have the information she needed to prove the mastermind's identity, and when the meal was over she excused herself to powder her nose in Jeremy's bathing room. Fortunately, to get there she had to go into his bedroom. And, even more fortunate, Sadie stayed behind with Ted and Jeremy.

She shut the door behind her and was in a small sitting room with a large desk and chair. Jeremy must do his work here, she decided. She quickly sat

359

down at the desk and began quietly pulling out drawers. She flipped through papers, trying to find something that might indicate his involvement as the mastermind. But it all seemed to be railroad charts, times, dates, places, nothing that obviously linked him to the robbers. Unless he used all that information to plot the trains to be robbed. Of course, that information could just as easily be used in his work, and it probably was. Then she noticed he also had information on Atchison, Topeka and Santa Fe schedules. If he were the mastermind, he'd need that, wouldn't he? Of course, since he was working out a deal with Santa Fe he'd need it, too. She sighed and stood up. She'd try the bedroom.

Walking into that room, she was momentarily stunned. She'd had no idea Jeremy Luis Centrano would be such a sensual man. A huge round bed dominated the area and was covered in layers of shiny black satin. Exotic animal skins hung on the walls and covered the floor. Several animal heads, including a buffalo, hung on one wall.

She'd had no idea Jeremy liked to hunt, as well as collect art. But in this room there was not one single piece of art. That surprised her, too. Jeremy was a very interesting man, but how he decorated his private coach wasn't her concern. She was here to find evidence.

Jerking open his dresser drawer, she'd started to go through his clothing when she heard the door to the sitting room open and close. She froze, then hurried to his bathing room. She slipped in there and began quickly dabbing powder on her face, leaving the door ajar.

"My dear," Jeremy said, "how lovely of you to find an excuse to visit my bedroom."

Raven glanced up in alarm. She'd expected Sadie.

Jeremy leaned against the doorjamb, watching her. "And do you like what you've seen?"

"It's most unusual."

"Unusual? I'd have thought you'd have more to say about it than that."

"I didn't know you hunted."

"Oh, yes. It is much like collecting art. Something exotic is always a trophy worth collecting. Wouldn't you agree?"

"I'm not a collector," she responded quickly, putting her powder away and feeling for her pistol. Its weight reassured her. For some reason, Jeremy was making her feel very uneasy.

"That is why you must be collected, my dear."

"Collected? I don't think so."

"Come here." He extended a hand to her, and she took it. He led her toward the bed. "You are a very sensual woman, Raven. I sensed it immediately about you. You need only the right man to awaken your slumbering fires."

"I'm a Harvey Girl."

"Of course, and wonderfully innocent, but I can change that. Would you like me to touch you?"

"That wouldn't be proper."

"Just a light touch." Sensitive fingers traced her collarbone exposed by the décolletage of her gown.

She shivered.

"See. You respond to my slightest touch. Would you like to come live with me in splendor, Raven?"

"I don't think you're asking me to marry you." She had to get out of here, but she couldn't antagonize him. She still needed to get information from him.

"Perhaps we could discuss marriage later. For

now, I would educate you to the most exquisite wonders of the world. We would travel in our tiny palace and experience all the pleasures you dream about in your young girl fantasies." His hand roamed lower, brushing the top of her breasts.

She caught her breath, but didn't move. What would her father and fiancé have done? But they'd never have been in this situation.

"Say you'll come live with me, Raven." He raised her chin and touched soft, searching lips to hers.

She shivered and wanted to run, but forced herself to stand still. There was too much at stake. And, after all, he was a handsome man, exciting, alluring, and he wanted her.

"You're so quiet. Have I taken you by surprise? I don't think so. You must have had other men want you, but you've saved yourself."

"For marriage."

"I was afraid you might hold out for that." He kissed her again, letting his lips linger possessively this time. "For you, I might even consider that."

She took a deep breath. "I'd better go back. Sadie will be worried."

"Not just yet. I told them I had some trophies I wanted to show you. Of course, what I want you to appreciate most is my own personal trophy." He grabbed her hand and thrust it against the front of his trousers.

He was hot and hard, and Raven was shocked.

"Feel me. Think what we could do together."

She tried to jerk her hand away, but he was strong, much stronger than he looked, and soon he'd put his arm around her shoulders and was drawing her closer.

"Please," Raven said. "I must go."

"I love that innocent look in your eyes. You're shocked. Tell me you are."

"Yes, I'm shocked. You shouldn't be doing this."

"Marry me."

She gasped again.

"See how you affect me. I've been in a fever for you since I first saw you. I'll lay the world at your feet if you'll marry me and give me all of your sweet, beautiful body."

"Please, let me go. I have to think about this. It's all so sudden."

"All right. I understand. You are so innocent, and so shocked. I will let you be for now."

When he let her go, Raven stepped back.

"You will let me know your answer soon."

"Yes, of course."

"How beautiful you are, and you will soon be all mine."

When Raven said nothing more, he smiled. "Perhaps we should rejoin our guests."

Raven knew her color was high when they walked out of the bedroom. She also knew that Jeremy looked very smug and satisfied. Ted and Sadie glanced at them in surprise, then Sadie was very quick to get Raven out of there.

Their good-byes were brief and once they were in Ted's private coach, Sadie exclaimed, "Raven, what happened? What did he do? Did he try something?"

Raven sat down in the nearest chair. "I need a drink."

"Whiskey?" a deep male voice asked out of the shadows.

Raven jumped, but relaxed again when she saw Slate step into the light. "Slate, you frightened me."

"You startled us all," Sadie agreed, pouring Raven

a brandy and handing it to her.

"How did you get in here?" Ted asked.

"Wasn't hard," Slate replied, pouring himself a whiskey and throwing it back in one swallow. His eyes never left Raven's face. "Why don't you answer Sadie's question?"

Raven took a sip of brandy, felt a little stronger, and replied, "As a matter of fact, Jeremy Luis Centrano just asked me to marry him."

"What?" Sadie exclaimed.

Slate's eyes narrowed. "Did he?"

"What did you say?" Sadie persisted.

"He's waiting for an answer."

"I had no idea Jeremy was so enthralled with you," Ted said, confusion in his voice. "For as long as I've known him, he's been a confirmed bachelor."

"Well, I guess Raven's make him change his mind," Sadie replied, glancing at Slate.

"Or he's up to something," Slate said.

"I'm not enough for a man to ask me to marry him?" Raven asked.

"Of course you are, Raven," Sadie replied. "Slate's just suspicious because it's his job."

"It must be another case of true love," Ted said. "Look what happened to Sadie and me."

"I don't know what it is," Raven said, "but I'm going to my berth. It'll be another long day tomorrow, and I'm exhausted."

"But what are you going to do?" Sadie asked.

"Sleep."

"I mean about Jeremy."

"I don't know. I'll think about it tomorrow." Raven stood up and glanced at Sadie. "Coming?"

Sadie looked wistfully at Ted. He put an arm around her waist. "No. I'll be along later."

"Slate, make sure Raven gets safely to her coach, will you?" Ted asked.

"Just what I planned to do," Slate responded, and took Raven's arm. "See you tomorrow."

Outside, Slate wasn't quite so gentle. "What the hell's going on? I don't like you going behind my back and getting marriage proposals."

"I was as surprised as anybody, Slate. But you have to admit he's an attractive man."

"No, he's not, and he's not man enough for you."

"Maybe he is."

"It doesn't matter now. Come on."

"Where're we going?"

"Where do you think we're going?"

"Well, I'm going to my coach."

"So am I. It's about time we tried out one of those Pullman berths."

"Slate! Margarita sleeps there, too."

"Not right now. She's in the observation deck entertaining the passengers. They're crazy about her, so don't expect to see her soon."

"She could be back anytime."

"But not before I've had my fill of you."

"Slate, this isn't right."

He stopped on the platform to her sleeping car, and pulled her close. "If this isn't right, you tell me what is." He pressed warm lips to hers, kissing her slowly at first, then more intensely until she was clinging to him, wondering how she ever thought she could stay away from him.

Then she thought how very different Slate's kisses were from Jeremy's possessive kiss. For that matter, Sam's kisses could not in any way compare to what Slate made her feel. When had her fiancé become a distant memory and Slate an overwhelming present?

She wasn't quite sure when or how it had happened, but Slate now overshadowed anything that had come before, no matter how tender and sweet a love she and Sam had shared.

"Coming?" Slate asked against her lips.

"Yes," she replied, lost to him again.

Chapter Twenty-six

"Raven," Slate said as he began to undress her in the soft light of the Pullman coach, "I've never met a woman before who touched every part of my life so completely."

"I think it's more that you've touched *me* completely."

Slate stroked her face gently, then let down her ash-blond hair, running his hands through its silken length. "Yes, I've touched you, held you, loved you, but it's never been enough. At first I thought having you physically would put an end to the fever that's burned in me since I first met you. But it hasn't."

Raven didn't want to hear his words. She only wanted his touch. She began undressing him, needing to be close to him, joined with him, sharing with him all she could.

"It confused me," he continued, "haunted me until I realized we share more than a physical desire for each other. I want you in so many ways."

"Kiss me, Slate."

He pressed warm lips to hers, a sweet, gentle, loving kiss that went all the way to Raven's heart.

Suddenly she sagged against him.

"What's wrong?"

"Nothing. Please hold me tight." But there *was* something wrong, for in that one kiss she'd experienced the gentle, tender love she'd shared with Sam. *Love.* She shivered, and Slate held her tighter, pressing kisses in her hair. But that couldn't be. She and Slate shared only desire, and eventually that would burn out. She had shared love with Sam, love she'd thought would last a lifetime. But there had been no passion with it, not like she'd known with Slate, and she felt confused.

Could it be that love and passion weren't complete without each other? Could it be that she had to have both to be totally happy? But she couldn't love Slate Slayton—or could she?

She didn't want to think about it, didn't want to know if it were true. "Love me, Slate. I want to forget everything except the happiness you make me feel."

"Yes, I'll love you, but I want more than that from you. I need you. I want you with me all the time, sharing, doing, accomplishing like we've done on the Montezuma Special. Can you give me that much of you?"

"I don't care about that now. Please, let me feel you close, let me think of nothing but our pleasure."

"That's what I mean. I want more than that from you. I want you to marry me so we can share our lives, our complete lives, not just moments stolen here and there."

"But you told me in Topeka you wanted to buy me for the night, and that once we'd shared our passion we'd go our separate ways."

"I was a fool. We can never go our separate ways. You've felt it, Raven. It's more than passion."

"No. I won't believe that. When this job is over, you'll go back to your old work."

"I told you I'd give up everything for you, and I meant it. When are you going to believe me?"

"How can I?"

"Trust me. Ask me to marry you."

She pushed away and turned her back to him. "I didn't want you, Slate. I'd never felt much passion until you awakened it in me. You've swept into my life and tried to take it over. But I won't let you. You're just a too tall Texas outlaw and I won't, I can't, succumb to you."

Slate turned her gently toward him. "We settled the fact that I'm not too tall, and now we're going to have to settle something else."

Raven trembled, afraid of him, afraid of what he could make her feel and know about herself. But she couldn't deny how the kisses he began softly pressing to her face made her feel. He was gentle, so very gentle. She shivered, and melted against his strong muscular body.

He finished undressing her and helped her into the lower berth of the Pullman car. Then he quickly stripped off the rest of his clothes and joined her. He was very tender when he began tracing fiery paths down her body with his lips. So gentle, so caring, so . . . loving.

Raven moaned softly, feeling desire rise in her. She wanted the wild feelings he could cause in her to burn out all her thoughts. She didn't want to think. She only wanted to feel. But Slate wasn't letting her. He was being so slow, so gentle, arousing her like a lover. *Love.* Did Slate love her? Could that be possible? Is that why he was willing to change his life for her?

She shivered, and parted her legs, wanting to draw him into her, make her forget everything except their passion, but he wouldn't let her. He held back, toying with her, making her ache for him. Sweat beaded her body. She writhed under him, feeling his lips, his hands, his body caress her.

"Slate, please. I can't wait. I want you."

"I want you, too, but you must realize how much I feel for you, how you feel about me."

She twisted under him, twining her arms and legs around him, trying to force him to complete their union.

"It won't work, Raven. I have your body. Now I want your trust."

"Oh, how can I trust you?"

He lowered himself to her, letting their bodies touch completely, except that his manhood slid between her legs, not inside her.

She groaned, digging her fingers into his hair. "Don't do this to me. I need you so."

"And I need you. I'll give up everything in my life for your trust. Do you believe me?"

Suddenly her mind began to clear. She still wanted him desperately, but his words were finally reaching her. She hesitated, then asked, "Slate, do you love me?"

"Do you trust me?"

"I shouldn't. Everything I've ever been taught or believed in tells me I shouldn't, but you've been there for me, for Sadie, and I've always been able to trust you since I met you. Yes, I guess I've been trusting you for a long time but didn't realize it."

"And I've been loving you for a long time."

"Do you really?" She carefully didn't mention her fictitious uncle. She was tired of all the lies between

370

them. Whatever Slate thought or believed about her besides his love suddenly didn't matter. She *did* trust him.

"Can you doubt I love you?"

"And you won't go back to your outlaw ways?"

"Not with you by my side."

"Oh, Slate!" She felt as if a great burden had been lifted from her. Tears stung her eyes. She smiled, her lips trembling. "I . . . I think I might love you, too."

"Think?"

"Well, I'm not sure."

"Then I'll make you sure."

He entered her in one savage movement that took her breath away. She held him close as he began moving inside her. This time when their passion rose it carried them to new heights of awareness and new feelings flooded them until, rocking together, they cried out in union, feeling total ecstasy blaze through them as they became one.

Later, when Raven's bliss had passed, she found that this time she continued to feel close to Slate, as if they were still merged, although he rolled to one side and pulled her near. They were bound now by some invisible cord. Perhaps it was love, perhaps it was simply her new awareness of their feelings for each other. Their passion had been as wonderful as before, maybe more so, only this time they had shared it, really shared each other.

For the first time she thought about Slate and children. She could imagine a tiny duplicate of him. A little girl or boy. It didn't matter. And then she thought of love. Her heart seemed to expand, as if large enough to encompass the entire universe, but all she really wanted to enclose was Slate and their children.

She loved him. It was so obvious now. She must have loved him from the first, but denied it because she'd felt unfaithful to Sam. Sam had been a wonderful man and she could have been happy with him, but he could never have made her feel what Slate did, and now that she knew what true love was she could never mistake it again.

Slate stroked her damp hair back from her face. "I love you, Raven. I want to share the rest of my life with you, but I won't push you."

"I love you, too."

He sat up, and looked deeply into her eyes. "Do you mean that?"

"Yes."

"Then I'm waiting."

"Waiting?"

"There's a question I told you I'd wait for you to ask."

Marriage. Oh, how she wanted to marry him and spend the rest of her life with him. But it wouldn't be fair to ask him now. She didn't even know if she'd come out alive when she confronted the mastermind and Comanche Jack. She had business from the past she had to complete before she was free to merge her life with Slate's.

And then there was the Cunningham National Detective Agency. Her father had worked a lifetime to build it. She couldn't just let it die. On the other hand, if Slate stopped being an outlaw he would be out of work, and who better than an outlaw to ferret out other outlaws?

She smiled and pulled him closer. "I love you, Slate Slayton, you too tall Texas outlaw, but I'm not going to ask you to marry me."

"What?"

"You have to finish your job for Ted, and I have an obligation to the Harvey Girls."

"And your uncle?"

"That's not so important now. If you can wait until we get to San Antonio, we can make plans then."

"It won't make any difference. No matter what happens between here and San Antonio, I'll still want to marry you. And I'll still walk through fire to do it."

"But you'll wait?"

"Do you love me?"

"Yes."

"That'll do for now, but I'm not a patient man."

"And I'm not a patient woman."

She pulled him back into her arms, and kissed him again. Before they knew it, their hidden passions were blazing again and they clung together as their desire spiraled higher and higher, drawing them closer and closer until they were merged in the fires of love.

Later, Slate stirred, kissed Raven softly on her forehead, and said, "I've got to leave."

"No," she murmured sleepily. "I want you to spend the night with me. I don't want you to ever go."

"I can't tell you how much I long to sleep with you in my arms again, like we did that night on the trail. But Sadie and Margarita will be coming back soon."

Margarita. Raven's mind cleared. "You're sure you don't love Margarita?"

Slate kissed her gently again. "I love Margarita like a sister, and believe me that is nothing like what

I feel for you."

She hesitated.

"Trust me, Raven. You said you would."

She smiled. "Yes. I trust you."

"And love me?"

"Yes." She pulled his face close, kissed him urgently on the lips, then pushed him away. "You'd better go before I decide to prove just how much I love you again."

Slate chuckled. "Maybe I'd better stay. A man can hardly pass up an offer like that."

Raven laughed softly. "I do love you so much."

"I love you, too." He stood up, bent down to place another kiss on her lips, then walked to the door. "I'll see you in the morning."

Raven could hardly sleep after he left, and when she heard Sadie and Margarita come in later she pretended to be asleep, hugging the knowledge of the love she and Slate shared to her breast. She felt too vulnerable to share their news with anyone else just yet.

When she did finally fall asleep she dreamed of Slate, wild, exciting dreams that made her love him all the more, but after a time into her dreams came the sound of someone calling her name. She tried to resist the insistent noise, preferring her dreams, but finally she sleepily opened her eyes, expecting to see Slate.

It was morning, and a strange man was bending over her. He had a completely unremarkable face, except for a thin white scar running across his left cheekbone. He had a shock of dark hair, a deeply tanned face, and he smelled like he had not been close to bath water in some time.

Raven resisted the impulse to scream and fling

374

herself out of the Pullman berth. Instead, she calmly said, "I believe you have the wrong coach."

He grinned, showing teeth stained by tobacco.

That brought back a memory. Who had she seen smoking recently? But the vision eluded her. Then she noticed something shiny near her head where he stroked her long hair. She glanced that way and saw a hook. She almost screamed again. Comanche Jack!

He noticed the recognition in her eyes. "That's right. I'm the man with the hook in place of a left hand. And you must be Raven."

She nodded, unable to speak. Where was her gun when she needed it? Unfortunately, it was in her reticule on the next berth.

"I hear you've been asking for me."

"Yes," she whispered, then cleared her throat.

"What kind of job would a Harvey Girl have for Comanche Jack?"

She hadn't thought this far. Never in her wildest imagination could she have dreamed of being in this position, that Comanche Jack would ever find her, much less come to her. Not only was her pistol in the next berth, but her clothes were, too. How could she possibly capture Comanche Jack totally defenseless? The only thing she had was her wits, and she'd have to get them in order fast or all was lost.

"There's a silver shipment on board," she finally said. "I want to steal it."

"A Harvey Girl wants to steal silver?"

"Yes."

"I don't believe it. Fact is, you've been dogging my tracks since Topeka. I want the truth, lady, and I want it now."

Raven didn't say anything. What would he believe?

"Do I have to get tough?" He rubbed the cold steel of his hook against her left cheek.

She shivered, but was determined to conceal her fear. "You don't frighten me. I'm not alone. In fact, the other Harvey Girl will be back any minute."

Raven actually didn't have any idea where Sadie and Margarita were. She didn't even know what time it was, but it was obviously morning and she should be in the dining car serving breakfast. What was going on? And how had Comanche Jack gotten on the train?

"I'm not worried about a Harvey Girl, or anybody else. What I want is the truth. Who hired you to spy on me?"

He wasn't going to believe anything she said. The situation called for drastic measures. Taking a deep breath, she threw the covers over his head. While he struggled to get free, she hit him hard on the back of the neck with her hands clenched as one fist. He collapsed to the floor. She quickly slipped on her robe, grabbed her reticule, and jerked out the snubnosed .45 just as he threw off the covers.

They faced each other. His hand went to the Colt .45 worn low on his right hip. She had no doubt he was very fast, but her gun was already drawn. She cocked her pistol.

"You wouldn't shoot me, would you, Harvey Girl?"

"She might not, but I will," Slate said from the open door of the coach, his .45 pointed at Comanche Jack's back.

Raven gasped in surprise, and her gun wavered.

The one-handed man took advantage of her distraction and leaped for the window. Slate couldn't shoot for fear of hitting Raven. The outlaw levered himself out the window just as Raven got her gun trained on him, but by then Slate was after the outlaw and in her line of fire. Slate grabbed Comanche Jack's foot just as the outlaw pulled himself out the window toward the roof of the moving train.

Slate jerked him back into the Pullman coach and they fought, struggling up and down the aisle. Raven tried to get a clear shot at Comanche Jack, but the men kept moving, rolling, struggling, hitting. The two were obviously equally matched, although Slate was much taller. They kept crashing into berths, and Raven bit her lower lip in frustration. She had to do something soon.

Comanche Jack came into range and she hit him on the back of his head with the barrel of the .45. He struggled a moment longer, then collapsed unconscious.

Slate staggered up. "Thanks. You handled that like a professional." He wiped blood off his lip with the back of his hand. "You've been handling yourself like that all along. It makes me wonder. Who the hell are you anyway?"

"I'm wondering the same thing about you. It was pretty obvious you didn't shoot Comanche Jack when you had the chance."

"I was afraid of hitting you."

"An outlaw should be a good enough shot that it wouldn't matter. He almost got away, thanks to you. I had him completely under control until you showed up."

"He wasn't under control, and I wouldn't have risked your life by shooting. But you're used to handling a pistol, aren't you?"

"It doesn't matter."

"I think it does. You're not just a woman looking for her uncle. Who are you?"

"And who are you? A friend of Comanche Jack's?"

Slate's brows drew together. "You know who he is?"

"Yes, and obviously so do you." She turned the .45 on Slate.

"What do you think you're doing?" he asked in surprise, automatically letting his right hand move toward the pistol on his hip.

"You asked me to trust you last night, Slate. I did, but that was then. Today you look like you're working with Comanche Jack."

"What? How can you say that? I just saved you from him."

"I didn't need saving. That little fight was obviously a convenient way to free Comanche Jack, throw me off guard, make me trust you even more, then get information from me. Well, it didn't work."

"That's crazy. Who are you?"

"That doesn't matter. Now tie up your partner, and don't doubt that I can be very tough if I have to be."

"My partner? I thought he was *your* partner."

"What! That's ridiculous."

But Slate's remark gave him the advantage he needed, for she hesitated, suddenly unsure. He moved fast and jerked the pistol from her hand. Raven tried to get it back, but he held her off with one long arm. Finally, she gave up and stepped back, glaring at him.

Watching her through narrowed eyes, Slate weighed the snub-nosed .45 in his hand a moment, then absently rubbed his thumb across the handle.

Suddenly he frowned, and glanced down. He studied the butt a moment, then looked back at Raven, a smile on his lips.

"You were a hard puzzle to solve, but I've finally done it," he said, satisfaction in his voice.

"Really? I guess that means you'll kill me now. I'm the only one who knows the truth about you, aren't I? Well, you've taken everything else from me so I suppose you might as well take my life."

"Trust me. I want you very much alive, Raven, or should I say *Miss* Cunningham."

"What do you mean?"

"You know what I mean, and your game's up."

"I have no idea what you're talking about."

"R. Cunningham. You're Ted's private investigator from Chicago, aren't you?"

"Of course not. I'm Raven West."

"You're Raven Cunningham. Ted's going to be surprised."

"You have no proof."

"This little gun of yours has *R.C.* engraved on the handle. Raven Cunningham."

"When I bought that gun for protection those initials were already on it."

"Not good enough, Raven. You're R. Cunningham all right, and it explains everything. Who'd ever have thought Ted's detective was a woman? Clever. Really clever. And it's worked, too."

"This is total fantasy, Slate."

"No. I'm right. You were with Ted all the way, and nobody ever suspected you. I had to deal with Ted watching me, waiting for me to bring his suspects to justice. And you just tripped by serving meals and digging out clues. It also explains why you were dressed as a lady of the evening in Topeka.

379

Damn good job. Best I've seen in some time."

"I suppose you'd know, being an outlaw."

"I know all right, but not because I'm an outlaw."

"No? Let's see, I'm a private investigator from Chicago, and you . . . you're a Texas Ranger."

"Right. You're quick, no doubt about it."

"Please stop the games, Slate. I've got a meal to serve."

"That's why I'm here. Sadie was worried about you. She and Margarita let you sleep late, but when you hadn't showed up she became worried."

"And you arrived just in time. Clever, but you don't really expect me to believe your story, do you?"

"This also explains your suspicious nature. I couldn't be more pleased."

"Look, we've meant a lot to each other. I won't take you in if you'll just get off the train at the next stop and leave Comanche Jack to me."

"I'm not getting off, Raven. I'm going all the way to San Antonio. You don't know how long I've waited to get my hands on Comanche Jack." He nudged the outlaw with the toe of his boot, but Comanche Jack didn't move.

"You expect me to believe that?"

"You said you trusted me last night, and I'm going to hold you to that now, no matter what you're thinking."

She folded her arms across her chest and looked at him skeptically.

"I *am* a Texas Ranger, or I was before I went after Comanche Jack several months ago."

"I can believe you're a Texan, but where's your Ranger badge?"

"I turned it in before I left Texas. It was a dead

giveaway, but also I was leaving the state and I didn't know when I'd be back."

"That's an easy explanation."

"Yes, and true. What I'd like to do now is string Comanche Jack up and watch him die. I'd be there to make sure it was a long, slow, painful death. I know some Comanche tricks of my own. I'm sure Jack would recognize them."

For the first time Raven started to consider Slate's words seriously because there was such a depth of emotion when he spoke of Comanche Jack. "Why?"

"He killed my father, my mother, and my brother, then burned down our ranch house."

Raven looked shocked, then suddenly remembered the pain in his voice whenever he'd spoken of his mother before. Could he be telling the truth? Could Slate actually be a Texas Ranger, fighting on the same side of the law as she? Had Comanche Jack taken Slate's family from him just as he'd taken hers?

"Why would Comanche Jack have killed your family?" she finally asked.

"My older brother Tom was a Texas Ranger, too. He brought in Comanche Jack, left him in jail, then went to visit my parents. I was in San Antonio at the time. But Comanche Jack escaped. By the time I got to the ranch, it was all over. Jack had killed them all, but not before he'd cut off the left hand of every one of them."

Raven gasped. "But why?"

"Tom caught Comanche Jack all right, but in the process Jack's left hand got pinched off by a rope."

"That's all horrible."

"Yes, and it's true. Now you've heard my story. What's yours?"

"All right, I'm going to continue to trust you. I *am* R. Cunningham. The gun belonged to my father, Robert Cunningham. He ran the Cunningham National Detective Agency where I grew up helping out, then ran the office for several years. I was engaged to his one employee besides me, Sam Fairfield."

"You were engaged?"

"Yes."

"Did you love him?"

"Yes."

"I see."

"No you don't. What I felt for Sam was love, but it was vastly different from what I've known with you. But that's not part of my story."

"I think it is."

Raven ignored his words, and continued. "The Atchison, Topeka and Santa Fe, as well as the Southern Pacific, hired the Cunningham Agency to solve a series of railroad robberies from Kansas to Texas. It was a great opportunity to expand out of Chicago. Sam went out West first. He was killed. The report came back that a one-handed man was seen at the scene of the crime. But no arrests. My father was furious. He went out there, but he was killed, too. No arrests again, but a one-handed man was seen in town that day."

"So you came looking for a one-handed man and justice."

"That's right."

"And found me," Comanche Jack said, sitting up, his Colt .45 aimed at Raven. "I learned from the Comanche that a quiet man learns a lot more than a loud man."

"Put down your gun," Slate commanded. "You

can't get away from a moving train."

"You're the two that won't get away. You're already dead, just like the others, so I'll admit what I did. I killed them all and they deserved it. Slayton cost me my hand. Nobody does that to Comanche Jack and gets away with it. Then Cunningham and his boy were trying to do me out of the sweetest job I ever had. Nobody does that to me, either."

"Give yourself up," Raven said, disgusted that she and Slate had been so intent on each other that they hadn't watched Comanche Jack.

"I don't mind getting rid of Slayton here," Comanche Jack continued, "since I'm just finishing up what I started in the hill country. But you're a looker, Harvey Girl, and it's a shame that I'll have to throw you out a window."

"Please," Raven pleaded, trying to keep his total attention on her. If she could do that, maybe Slate would have the chance to try something.

"Begging won't help. I'm going to—"

Slate threw himself, rolling, against Comanche Jack's legs. The outlaw went down, cursing, scrambling, trying to come up with his gun on Raven. But Slate was desperate and just a little faster. Comanche Jack came up, but Slate had the outlaw's pistol.

"Raven," Slate said, tossing back her Colt .45. "Cover Comanche Jack. I'm going to tie him up and find out what's planned for the silver."

"Forget it," Comanche Jack blustered.

"You'll tell us," Raven said, training her gun on the one-handed man as Slate tied him up with bed linens. "We'd both rather see you dead than alive so don't expect any mercy. We want to know who's masterminding the train robberies from Kansas to Texas, and we want to know when they're planning

Chapter Twenty-seven

The Montezuma Special started slowing down, blowing its whistle to alert the next depot. Raven and Slate glanced at each other in alarm.

"Dryden station," Slate said.

"Anybody could come in here," Raven replied. "Sadie and Margarita will probably be here any minute since I haven't been to the dining car yet. We've got to get Comanche Jack out of here, but how?"

"Now's the best time we're ever going to have. The train will be empty with everybody in Dryden. I can take him through to the baggage car and stow him there."

"That's a good idea. I'll help."

"Okay. I'll need you to open the doors and make sure nobody's looking, but before we do anything else I'm going to gag him." Slate pulled the bandanna Comanche Jack wore around his throat up over his mouth, then tied it tightly.

"But I'm not dressed yet," Raven exclaimed,

glancing down at herself.

"Throw something on. I'll make sure Jack doesn' watch you, but don't take time for all those unde clothes."

"I won't." Raven slipped on a chemise, then hu riedly put on her Harvey Girl dress, but left off th apron. "I'm ready," she said, then opened the doo of the coach.

Slate picked up the struggling Comanche Jack tossed him over a shoulder, and followed Raven t the door. They waited for the train to stop, watche the passengers step down, then started their journe toward the baggage car at the front of the trair

It was dangerous, especially each time the crossed the platforms from one car to the next, fo they didn't want anyone to see them. They sti didn't know who Comanche Jack was working fo or if he had accomplices on the train so they didn want to alert anyone.

They paused in the library car, and Raven glance out the windows to see if anyone was coming towar the train. She saw Jeremy start toward them, an motioned for Slate to hide. He slipped past th curtain into the barber shop area where the couldn't be seen.

Raven watched Jeremy go into a store, then sig naled to Slate that it was safe to continue. Onc more they started down the train and finally arrive at the baggage car. Safely inside, Slate droppe Comanche Jack to the floor, then hid him behind large crate.

"Raven, you'd better get out there so people ca see you. They're bound to be looking for you b now. I'll take care of Jack."

"We've got to find out about that silver ship

ient."

"I'll question him, but not till the train leaves the depot."

"All right. I'll be back as soon as I can."

Raven hated to leave Comanche Jack now that he'd finally caught up with him, and she was just a little uneasy about leaving him in Slate's custody. She was placing a lot of trust in Slate because she had no proof whatsoever that he was a Texas Ranger. But she had promised to trust him and she was going to, up to a point.

She left Slate and Comanche Jack and started back down the train. She didn't go to the dining car. She knew it must be well past time for serving breakfast and that Sadie would probably be with Ed in town. Instead, she went to the Pullman sleeper, put her .45 in her reticule, and slipped her brightly colored shawl around her shoulders.

Then she headed into Dryden. It was another small, dusty Texas town, but it had a telegraph office and that was what she needed. Her father's connections as head of the Cunningham Agency gave her the power to find out if Slate's story were true. She had put her trust in him for now, but there was too much at stake and too many other people involved for her to complete the case without knowing for sure that Slate was a Texas Ranger.

The telegraph office was empty and it didn't take her long to send a telegram inquiring about Slate Clayton's identity. The message carried the proper code, and she requested a reply be sent to R. Cunningham at Del Rio. Now there was nothing more she could do but keep on trusting Slate.

She stepped outside, and glanced around. A voice hailed her from across the street. She looked up and

saw Jeremy hurrying toward her, carrying somethi
in his left hand. Then she remembered his propos
of the night before. That seemed a long time ag
and hardly real, but Jeremy's rapt expression to
her it was true.

When he reached her, Jeremy handed her a pape
containing a dozen peppermint sticks. "For you," h
said. "I remembered you were fond of them."

"Thank you, but you shouldn't have."

"My pleasure. I missed you at breakfast."

"I'm sorry to say I overslept, and Sadie let me

"That was good of her. She probably realized ho
excited you were from the night before."

"Perhaps, although I haven't mentioned what w
discussed."

He took her hand and placed it in the crook c
his arm. "I understand your reticence, but it's only
matter of time until the whole world knows, m
dear. It will be such a pleasure to introduce you a
my wife."

"But I haven't accepted yet."

"I understand you need to get used to the idea
but don't keep me waiting long."

"I won't."

"Good. There are Ted and Sadie. Why don't w
join them?"

"All right."

Sadie saw them and exclaimed, "Raven, I've neve
known you to sleep so long. Are you all right?"

"Yes. I guess all the excitement of the trip i
catching up with me, but you should have awakene
me. I'm sorry I didn't help you at breakfast."

"That's all right. I decided you needed your sleep
but I'll be glad of your help at lunch."

"I'll be there."

Unfortunately, by the time Raven had gotten rid of Jeremy, it was time to begin serving lunch and she hadn't gotten back to Slate and Comanche Jack. But the train had left Dryden and she hoped that at any time Slate would come to her with the information they so desperately needed from the one-handed man.

The passengers were hungry at lunch as they discussed the rest of their trip across Texas. The Special was headed down toward the Mexican border now and would soon pass through Judge Roy Bean's Langtry near where the Pecos River joined the Rio Grande. After that, they'd travel on to the much bigger town of Del Rio on the border, then head east across Texas to San Antonio.

Raven was distracted as she served the passengers, and finally Sadie remarked, "Raven, what's wrong with you? I've never seen you so absentminded."

"I can't quite seem to get awake today," she lied, wishing she could tell Sadie the truth. Serving the passengers just didn't seem very important when Slate was questioning Comanche Jack. But shouldn't Slate be done by now? Or wouldn't Comanche Jack talk?

"It's all right. Everyone's getting served. I'm just a little concerned about you. It's Jeremy, isn't it?"

"I don't know what to do about him."

"That's simple. He's not the man you're interested in and you know it, no matter if he's handsome and fabulously wealthy."

"I just wish I knew more about Slate."

"You will in time, and Ted trusts him."

"I know." But who could trust Ted?

Raven determinedly kept her mind on business while she finished serving because the last thing she wanted was to call attention to herself.

Just as the last diner left, Margarita entered and took a seat. Sadie took her order, then Margarita motioned Raven over to her side.

"You were a heavy sleeper last night, Raven," Margarita said.

"Yes, it seems so."

"I straightened your bed for you."

"I'm sorry I left the place in such a mess, but I was in a hurry when I finally got up."

"I understand, but some of the linens seemed to be missing.

Raven blanched. "I imagine the steward took them."

"Perhaps." Margarita gave her a long look. "If you need my help, you have only to ask. You know, after Del Rio the train turns east and leaves the border behind."

"Yes, that's what I've been told."

"I'm glad Slate is guarding the train because that would be the last safe place for outlaws to strike us."

"Why?"

"With the border so close, they could be safely across in no time. Later they would be deep into Texas and easy prey for Texas Rangers."

"I see. But like you said, fortunately Slate is guarding us all. Besides, the Special should be safe since it's not on the regular Southern Pacific run."

"I'm glad you think so. But here's my lunch. Thank you, Raven."

"Enjoy your meal," Raven said, then hurried away, already distracted again. What Margarita had said made sense, and the native Texan would know the area well. That meant the outlaws would probably hit somewhere before or just after Del Rio. She had to talk to Slate. Maybe they didn't need Comanche Jack's information after all. They already had his confession about the murders, and the word of a Texas Ranger and a private detective would surely be enough to convict him.

"Raven," Sadie laughed. "You're gone again. Why don't you go on. Margarita's the last customer, and I can handle her."

"Thanks. I'm sorry, but there's just so much on my mind."

"I understand, but, remember, love's the only thing that matters."

"I'll remember that. See you later."

Raven headed straight for the baggage car. She hadn't seen Slate since she'd left him with Comanche Jack and she was beginning to be worried that perhaps something had gone wrong. What if Comanche Jack had somehow gotten loose and overpowered Slate? Maybe killed him?

She was shocked at that thought, and walked faster, but she simply would not believe that anything could have happened to Slate. He had Comanche Jack completely under control.

Many of the passengers had settled into the observation car, looking forward to seeing the Rio Grande and the border again. Others were reading in the library car, and doing fine without an attendant. She and Sadie had given up trying to entertain the passengers at all times and simply left the books unlocked. It was easier for everyone that way.

Outside the baggage car, she hesitated, made sure no one was watching, and slipped inside. It was dim and quiet. She took out her pistol. "Slate?"

"Over here."

Relieved, she stepped behind the crate where'd she left Slate and Comanche Jack at Dryden. The outlaw was slumped against a wall, his head hung down and his chin bobbed against his chest with the motion of the train. He looked unconscious.

"What's wrong with him?"

Slate looked grim. "Fainted from the pain."

"Pain?"

"Damn it, Raven, I'm trying to get some information out of him."

"You're torturing him?"

"How did you expect me to get the information out of him? Pretty please won't get Comanche Jack to talk."

"No, of course not. I just didn't expect . . . I don't see any marks on him."

"Comanche tricks."

"Has he told you anything?"

"Not a damned thing. He's tough. I never thought he wouldn't be."

"No, I guess not, but I've had an idea. Perhaps we'd better discuss it out on the platform. I don't want him waking up and hearing us."

"He'll be out for a while unless I force him awake, but I agree we shouldn't take any more chances."

Outside, the wind whipped against them. It was hot, dry, and dusty. Raven leaned against the coach, watching Slate. He looked tired and discouraged. She hated to see him that way.

"You've got the man you were looking for, Slate. It's my job from here on out. You don't have to help me anymore."

"What?"

"It's true. You were after Comanche Jack. I was

ter him, too, but as Ted has told you he hired the unningham Agency to find the mastermind behind series of train robberies. I owe it to my father and ancé to finish what they started. Besides, my gency needs the fee."

"Are you running the Cunningham Agency alone ow?"

She nodded. "I'm the only one left alive, and I'm etermined to see that my father and fiancé didn't ie in vain."

"You must have loved them a lot."

"I did." She felt her chest tighten, and tears stung er eyes. She would always miss them.

"I know how you feel. Nobody can ever replace 1ose you love, can they?"

"No. I know how much you must miss your imily, but you've caught their killer now. You've ot what you came for and you can arrest Coman- 1e Jack right now."

"Yes, I got what I came for, but much more than 1at, too. I was only after revenge until I met you, 1en my life took on new meaning. And when Ted arted talking about railroad heists, a private detec- ve from Chicago, and Sadie was kidnapped, I got 1volved a lot more. There's no way I'd step out ow. I'm in it with you to the end. Besides, you eed me."

"Do I?"

"Yes. I don't know how you thought you could andle this case all on your own."

"If I'd known in Chicago what I know now I 1ight have done things differently, but I'd never een out on a case like this before. I'd primarily orked in the office, and that's a whole lot differ- 1t."

"You've done a good job for a beginner."

"Thanks, but I haven't caught the mastermind yet."

"Who do you think it is?"

Raven hesitated. How much should she trust Slate? She didn't know for sure if he were really a Texas Ranger or working for the mastermind. He hadn't gotten any information out of Comanche Jack. That made him look suspicious.

"I don't know," she finally replied, "but I think we can find out if outlaws strike the Special for the silver. There are only a limited number of people who have the information that silver is being carried on this train."

"You're right, and the prime suspects are Ted and Jeremy, aren't they?"

Raven hesitated again. Slate was very sharp, or perhaps part of the mastermind's gang. But she had decided to trust him, and her heart told her he could never work for the mastermind. "Yes, those are the two men I came after. They're the ones my father and fiancé suspected. As far as I know, Comanche Jack works for the mastermind and that's why I wanted whatever information he could give us."

"I don't know if he'll talk. He's stubborn, and I don't want to kill him. I want him brought to justice, and he'll make an excellent witness against the mastermind."

"Slate, I've been thinking. Perhaps we don't have to have his information right now."

"No?"

"You probably already know this, being from Texas, but at lunch Margarita suggested that after Del Rio the train turns east and heads into Texas.

ward San Antonio. She said smart outlaws ouldn't hit later than the Del Rio area because it ould be safer near the Mexican border."

Slate smiled. "Margarita's smart, and my brother ught her a lot about Ranger business. She's right. d already been thinking the same thing."

"What's this about your brother and Margarita?"

"They were engaged. Their wedding was planned r this summer. They'd been sweethearts for a long me, and finally they were both ready to settle own and have a family."

"Oh, Slate, I'm so sorry. That explains why she's sad."

"And why she followed me in the hunt for Co-anche Jack. When she caught up with me in opeka she insisted she could go places and learn ings I couldn't, and she was right. Plus, I couldn't nd her home. She was determined to see justice one, too. She'd loved my parents just like her wn."

"Have you told her about Comanche Jack yet?"

"No, and I'm not going to until it's all settled. he'll want to see him, confront him, and it's not e right time. We don't know who's loose on this ain. Jack may have outlaws already on the Special, r he may be working alone. We don't have enough formation yet and I don't want to jeopardize Margarita's life."

"She may already have guessed. I think she knows lot more about what's going on than we realize. hat's why she told me about Del Rio."

"You're probably right, but let's leave her out of until we need her help."

"Okay. Then what's next?"

"It's safe to assume that if the mastermind's men

are going to attack it'll be someplace between he
and Del Rio or shortly thereafter."

"I agree."

"There's no time to get Rangers on the train i
time."

"What about the sheriff in Del Rio?"

"What kind of proof do we have?"

"None. And, besides, the railways stipulated tha
this had to be handled with no publicity."

"Then we're on our own."

"With maybe Margarita and Sadie as backups.

"Yes. I'm going to talk to the engineer, and mak
sure he's got a loaded Winchester and extra ammu
nition. You make sure you've got your .45 with yo
at all times and carry extra bullets. I know Margar
ta's got a derringer that she carries all the time.

"Surely there's more we can do."

"I'll continue to try and get some information ou
of Comanche Jack. You can watch the passengers
See if anyone looks or acts suspicious, or gives an
signals. That's about all we can do to prepare fo
the heist. If and when they strike, we'll have to ac
fast. In the end, it usually comes down to a faste
mind, and a fast gun helps."

"I'm beginning to see that. Okay, I'd better star
watching the passengers."

"Raven," he said softly, and pulled her to hi
chest. "One thing. Don't endanger yourself. I don'
think I could stand to lose you, too."

"The same goes for you. We'll get them one wa
or another, but I want you alive when we get to Sa
Antonio."

"There's no way I'd miss that appointment."

He brushed a warm kiss across her lips, the
stepped quietly back into the baggage car.

For a long moment Raven stood on the platform, a fingertip to the place he'd kissed on her lips, thinking about how much they'd shared and how close they were to losing each other. Trust. That's what it all came down to. She had to trust in him, and he had to trust in her. There was no one else they could depend on, not now when it was really rough. She squared her shoulders, then headed for the observation coach.

Absolutely nothing unusual happened all afternoon, and as the time dragged by Raven became more and more tense. Finally she decided that perhaps they were all wrong. Maybe the mastermind's gang wasn't going to hit the Montezuma Special. Maybe the mastermind was just toying with them all. But she didn't want to believe that. She'd worked too hard, and been at it too long. She was ready for the confrontation. She was ready to get the mastermind once and for all.

The days were long now, and as the sun began its descent in the west, it was time to serve dinner. Raven wanted to be anywhere else than the dining car and could hardly keep her mind on her job. She made small mistakes and soon Sadie became concerned about her again. Ted and Jeremy watched her closely, and she found it difficult to be polite. She wanted desperately to be with Slate, but could do nothing to arouse suspicions and so continued to serve the passengers.

Finally, the Montezuma Special pulled into the depot at Del Rio and Raven breathed a sigh of relief. The dinner hour was over. She was off duty. Now she could devote herself to her real job. She changed clothes, putting on the simple gray gown that had served her so well on the trip. She made

sure her pistol was in her reticule, along with extr
bullets, then stepped off the train.

There was one last important thing to do befor
being ready for whatever the mastermind planne
after Del Rio. She walked into the telegraph office
It was empty.

"Is there a telegram for R. Cunningham?" sh
asked.

The telegraph operator leafed through several tele
grams, then handed one to her.

"Thank you." Her hand shook as she took th
thin piece of paper.

She stepped outside. She dreaded seeing almost a
much as she *wanted* to see what was written on th
paper. If Slate weren't a Texas Ranger she didn'
know if she could stand the betrayal. But she had t
trust him, and that trust began with reading th
telegram. She opened it, and read.

*Slate Slayton is a Texas Ranger. On leave o
absence. Appreciate notification of whereabouts.*

Tears stung Raven's eyes. Slate hadn't lied. He
was a lawman. No wonder they'd been drawn t
each other. They had so much in common. Trust
He'd asked her to trust him and she had becaus
she'd followed her heart, and now she was so ver
glad.

She started to put the telegram in her reticule
then stopped. Keeping it could be dangerous fo
Slate, even fatal. She tore the telegram into tiny
pieces, then let the wind scatter it across the dusty
plains. Now he was safe, and so was she, safe in th
knowledge that they could trust each other come
what may.

She wanted to rush straight to Slate and throw
herself into his arms and ask him to marry her. She

ouldn't wait to see his face when she told him how much she loved him, how much they could share, and how much she trusted him.

But she couldn't do any of that yet. They had the mastermind to catch. The Special would leave soon, and if the outlaws were going to strike it would probably be a few miles out of town. She had better get back aboard and make sure Margarita and Sadie were in a safe place.

She started toward the train, but suddenly noticed movement by the last car, Jeremy's private coach. A hand was holding a black handkerchief out the window, then snapped it three times before disappearing back inside. How strange. Could it have been some type of signal?

Suddenly the train started forward and was obviously going to pick up speed fast. She glanced around. Not all the passengers were aboard. Even Tomas, the man who worked for Jeremy, was carrying packages toward the Special. What was going on? Maybe the engineer had looked at his watch wrong. She didn't know what had happened, but she couldn't be left behind.

Fortunately, the telegraph office wasn't far from the tracks. She began to run. The locomotive was already past the depot. She ran faster. If she didn't hurry, she was going to miss the Special.

The train was picking up speed fast now, and she leaped for the steps of the first car she came to, grabbing the railing and swinging herself toward safety. But her skirt tripped her. She fell, and barely caught the platform. As the Special sped out of Del Rio she lay still, clinging to the railing as her heart raced and her breath came fast.

Then she noticed she was clinging to the baggage

car. She wasn't far from Slate and safety. She slowl[y] stood up, made sure she hadn't twisted an ankle o[r] wrist, and started to open the door. But it suddenl[y] crashed open, and a hand jerked her inside, slam[-]ming her up against the wall of the coach.

It was dim inside. She couldn't see who ha[d] grabbed her. "Slate?" she asked hesitantly.

In reply, a cold metal hook dug into the soft fles[h] of her throat.

Chapter Twenty-eight

"You give me a good reason not to rip out your throat right now," Comanche Jack said.

"It would be messy," Raven whispered, hardly breathing she was holding herself so still.

"Got to say one thing for you, Harvey Girl, you wouldn't know yellow if you saw it."

"I'm very scared right now."

"You ought to be. If I had time I'd teach you all about fear, but I don't. And to kill a woman like you would be an insult to the Great Spirit, unless I had time to eat your heart, which I don't. So you live.

"Tie her up, men," he said, then threw her into a group of masked outlaws.

They quickly, efficiently gagged her, then bound her with rope. Even though she kept her muscles tense while the outlaws tied her, the ropes were still tight when she relaxed. Her father's trick must have worked better for men with bigger muscles, for it hadn't helped her much. Her bonds were still very tight.

She was pushed down in a dim corner of the baggage car, and Comanche Jack walked over. He towered above her. As he looked at her, she looked back. He and his outlaws wore a six-shooter on each hip, ammunition belts crossed their chests, and bandannas covered the lower half of their faces. They looked deadly and professional.

Comanche Jack nudged her with the toe of his cowboy boot, "We're going to take the silver. You stay here real quiet and you get to live. If you find a way to get loose and come after us, it'll be the death of you and whoever's with you." He pulled his bandanna up over his nose, then turned away.

He motioned for the outlaws to follow him, and they quickly filed out of the baggage car. With them gone, it was suddenly quiet in the coach and Raven noticed the sound of the train's wheels clattering over the railroad tracks. It was a lulling, monotonous sound, and she could so easily just let herself drift off to sleep.

Why not let Comanche Jack and the mastermind have the silver as long as she was safe? She had so much to live for now.

Suddenly she thought of Slate. Where could he be? Was he with Comanche Jack when the outlaws freed Jack? If he were, was he dead now? No, she wouldn't believe that. Slate had probably left Comanche Jack alone for a while. He had plenty to do besides question the outlaw. Yes, she was sure that's what had happened. He was safe somewhere on the Special.

With Slate safe and so much to live for it would

be a shame to endanger herself now that she'd found so much happiness. All she had to do was lie here and be quiet. But *was* Slate safe, and what about all the others on the Special?

She couldn't chance them being hurt. Comanche Jack was a dangerous, ruthless man. If she could get free she had to do it because she couldn't live with herself if she didn't try to help. Her father and fiancé had to have justice, as did Slate's family, and the only way to get it was by capturing Comanche Jack and the mastermind. There was no easy way to do that. She must put her life on the line, but she'd been doing that since she'd left Chicago. Only then she hadn't had so much to lose.

Nevertheless, Slate would understand. He was a Texas Ranger and he knew the risks. That's why their lives had meshed so perfectly. Neither of them shrank from danger when there was a job to be done.

But right now she felt like a stupid fool. How could she have allowed herself to be captured by Comanche Jack? How had those outlaws known where Comanche Jack was and how had they gotten on the Special? Nothing made sense. She'd tried to be so careful, so prepared, and now she was tied up and Slate had disappeared.

She tried her bonds, but no matter how she pulled and strained they remained tight. She could hardly breathe because of the bandanna that tasted of stale sweat. This must have been how Sadie had felt when she had been held hostage. There must be someway to get free, but she remembered Sadie's bloody, rope-burned wrists and ankles. Her friend had tried desperately to get free, but hadn't succeeded.

But she wasn't giving up. There were people who needed her. As she twisted against the ropes, she felt the gold piece Slate had given her slide against her skin. *Good luck*. She hadn't lost her lucky gold piece so there still had to be hope of escape.

Suddenly she heard a weak groan not far from her. Shocked, she listened more closely. It came again.

Someone was in there with her. Slate? Was he wounded? She started to call out, but realized she was gagged. Instead she moaned as loudly as she could through the gag, then tried to move toward the sound. But she was hogtied.

The groan came again, louder this time.

That scared her. Perhaps the person was dying. Maybe it was Slate. She had to get to him. She was on her side, her hands tied behind her and bound to her tied ankles by a single rope. Although it was almost impossible to move, she began to worm her way across the floor toward the sound. It was a very slow process and she had to work around boxes and trunks. Soon she was panting and beaded with sweat. She paused to rest.

This time the groan sounded nearer.

She inched forward again, bumped into a crate and stopped. It would take her forever to get around it. She jerked at the ropes, desperate to get free. What was happening in the rest of the train? Where was everyone?

Suddenly a hand grasped her shoulder and she gasped.

"Raven?" The gag was wrenched from her mouth.

"Slate!"

"What happened?"

"Comanche Jack and his gang caught me, tied me up, left me here. They're robbing the train!"

"I know. Just a minute . . . and I'll untie you." His voice was slurred, his hands unsteady where they touched her.

"What's wrong?"

"They left me for dead."

"Slate, are you shot?"

"No. Busted my damn head open, but it's harder than they thought. Can't get my eyes to focus yet."

"Don't push yourself. You might be badly hurt."

"Doesn't matter. We've got to stop them."

"Did they surprise you?"

"Yes. Jack's gang must have gotten on at Del Rio. First thing I knew they came busting in here, overpowered me, freed him, then gave me what they thought was a killing blow. It was all nice and quiet since they didn't want to alert anybody."

"I was in town and the train started to move. I couldn't believe it, but I wasn't going to be left behind. I caught the first car I saw, but it happened to be this one, and you know the rest."

"I'm feeling stronger now, although my head still aches. Turn around so I can start on your ropes."

As he worked on her bonds, she lay as still as possible. "We've got to do something fast."

"I know. There. Your wrists are free, and I'm feeling stronger every minute."

"Good." Raven massaged her wrists as he worked on her ankles. "Slate," she said, then hesitated before continuing. "I got confirmation in Del Rio that you're a Texas Ranger, but they want to know where you are."

405

"I bet they do." He paused. "I thought you trusted me."

"I did. I do. But a lot of people are involved in this and I had to know for sure."

"Now that you do, does it make a difference?"

"Yes. And as soon as we get all this settled, we're going to have a long talk about us."

Suddenly the door to the baggage car banged open and Sadie and Margarita rushed inside.

"Slate?" Margarita called.

"Over here."

"Are you all right?"

"Yes. We had a run-in with Comanche Jack." Slate finished untying Raven and began massaging her ankles.

"What?" Margarita gasped. "You found him at last?"

"Yes," Slate replied. "We didn't tell you before, but we captured him this morning."

"Didn't tell me? But, Slate, you know how much I've wanted to see him brought to justice."

"I know, but there's more going on than that."

"I've guessed as much."

"What are you talking about?" Sadie asked. "The train's being robbed!"

"We know," Slate replied quietly. "There isn't time to go into it all now, but Comanche Jack is caught up in it and we're trying to use him to catch a bigger criminal."

"Who's Comanche Jack?" Sadie asked.

"He's robbing the Special," Raven explained, "and he's the man with a hook for a left hand you saw at the outlaw camp."

"Then we have to stop him," Sadie insisted.

406

"That's exactly what we're going to do," Slate said grimly. "Margarita, I'm sorry I was caught off guard and Comanche Jack's gang set him free."

"As long as you came out of it alive I don't care."

Suddenly the Montezuma Special began to slow down.

"Now's our time," Slate said. "They'll have reinforcements riding up with horses. We've got to scatter those outlaws and horses so the robbers on the train won't be able to get away."

"I'll do that," Raven replied. "I just wish I knew where the silver was."

"I think you'll find it in one of the private cars," Margarita said quietly.

When everyone looked at her in surprise, she added, "I've been watching everything very closely since Slate told me about the silver shipment, and that's where the silver must be."

"I thought it was in the baggage car," Slate said.

"A trick," Margarita replied. "If it were here, the outlaws would be here, too."

"You're right," Slate agreed.

"I'm worried about the passengers," Raven said. "I think we should separate the silver from the train. Slate, could you get to Ted's car and uncouple it? While you're doing that, I'll go forward, free the engineer, and scatter the outlaw's horses."

"Sadie and I will go with you, Raven," Margarita added.

"No, it's much too dangerous," Raven replied.

Margarita pulled out a derringer to show her determination. "Sadie and I both have a lot at stake here. We're going to help."

"That's right," Sadie agreed. "You saved my life

in New Mexico. Now it's my turn to help you and Ted."

"All right," Raven said. "There's no doubt I need your help. Slate, we'll try to meet you at Ted's car if we can get away. Otherwise . . ."

"I'm going over the top. Take care of the outlaws on your way through, will you?" Then he grinned.

"Sure. That's no problem. Is it, Margarita, Sadie?"

They smiled grimly.

"Good luck," Slate said, then added, "You'll need this, Sadie." He handed her one of his pistols. "Comanche Jack was so sure I was dead he left both my six-shooters, and I'll only need one."

Sadie hesitated, then took the weapon. "I've never used one before, but nobody's going to get away with hurting us or Ted."

"Just point, aim, and pull the trigger," Slate said, then glanced at Raven. He pulled her close, placed a gentle kiss on her lips, then headed for the platform outside.

Raven turned to Sadie and Margarita. "I don't want to endanger either of you, but the engineer will probably be held at gunpoint and I don't know how many outlaws there'll be."

"I'll go first," Margarita said, starting for the door that led to the fuel car. "I'm so small and I'll act so scared and helpless that I'll be able to catch them off guard and distract them."

"Are you sure?" Raven asked.

"Yes. Catching Comanche Jack is all that's kept me going for a long time," Margarita replied, then slipped out the door.

"Why is she after Comanche Jack?" Sadie whispered as she and Raven went after Margarita.

"He killed Margarita's fiancé."

"Oh! Then we have even more reason to get him."

They all knelt on the platform facing the fuel car, its wood load lowered by the long trip across Texas. The train continued to slow, then began grinding to a stop, its brakes hissing.

"Now!" Margarita said, and leaped to the fuel car, hurried across it, with Raven and Sadie behind her.

While Margarita went on to the locomotive, Raven and Sadie hid in the fuel car. Just like Slate had said, several outlaws leading horses were headed toward the Special. Those men had to be stopped, but her snub-nosed pistol would do her no good at this distance.

Raven and Sadie hesitated a moment longer, giving Margarita enough time to have taken the outlaws by surprise or be in trouble herself, then they leaped onto the locomotive and slipped quietly to the control area, the sound of their movement masked by the noise of the brakes.

The engineer stood at the controls, the fireman was unconscious on the floor, and Margarita had maneuvered the two outlaws so that their backs were to Raven and Sadie. The two men were obviously totally distracted by the diminutive beauty.

As the train came to a complete stop, Raven nodded to Sadie and they crept forward. Swiveling her snub-nosed .45 around, Raven used its butt to hit one of the outlaws on the back of his head. Sadie simultaneously did the same, coldcocking the other one with the barrel of her pistol. Margarita draw her derringer just in case the blows weren't

409

enough, but they were, and the outlaws crumpled to the floor of the locomotive.

"Good work," Margarita said.

"You're the one who did good," Raven replied.

"I can't believe I hit that man," Sadie said, looking in disbelief at the two fallen outlaws. "We didn't kill them, did we? I put every bit of strength I had behind that blow."

Margarita put a hand to the pulse in the temple of each man's head. "No, they're alive, although they probably don't deserve to be.'

"I'm relieved," Sadie said. "I wouldn't want to kill anyone, but I'd do anything to protect Ted and my friends."

"We wouldn't have had to hit them," Raven replied, "if I'd thought we could convince them that three women were actually going to take their guns or shoot them."

"That's the problem in dealing with men," Margarita said, picking up the outlaws' pistols where they had fallen, "they take women seriously only after it's much too late." She tossed one of the guns to the engineer, who pointed the pistol at the subdued outlaws, and kept the other for herself, tucking her derringer into her dress.

Sadie noticed the fireman was recovering from his blow, and helped him to his feet.

"Slate sent us," Raven said to the engineer. "He said there was a Winchester up here."

"Sorry. He warned us, but they caught us off guard anyway. The rifle's over there."

"Thanks. They caught us all off guard, too, but we'll get them."

Raven pulled out the Winchester and aimed it at

the outlaws who were riding in close with the extra horses. She started shooting at the horses' feet, driving them wild. They began to buck and rear and prance in fear and confusion. The outlaws could barely keep them under control.

Raven reloaded several times, firing until the horses finally broke free and ran wildly away. The outlaws who had been holding the animals scattered with them, seeking cover before they were shot.

"All right," Raven said, turning back. "I don't think they'll be back, but just in case I'll leave the Winchester here."

"Don't worry," the engineer said. "We won't be caught off guard again and we won't let these two get away, either."

"Thank you," Raven replied. "But we need something else from you."

"Anything. Nobody should try robbing the Montezuma Special."

"We agree," Raven said. "And these outlaws aren't going to get away with it, but we need your help to stop them. We're going back in the train, and we want you to give us two minutes before moving the train forward until there's a safe distance between the Special and the two private cars."

"Slate's already gone back to uncouple the private coaches," Margarita explained.

"You can count on us," the engineer replied. "Go ahead. Save the Special, ladies, and you'll have our undying gratitude."

The three women hurried back the way they'd come, not knowing what they'd find once they reached the passengers. Now that the train was stopped, it was very quiet. They listened for gunfire, but heard nothing. They grew more tense and suspicious as they continued down the Special.

In the library car, most of the books had been throw on the floor, then trampled as the outlaws went through. But there were still no passengers. They were getting very worried so they stopped on the platform of the observation car, took deep breaths, then plunged inside.

Here, at last, were the passengers, at least the ones who hadn't been left in Del Rio. The outlaws had obviously crowded them into this one car. Most of them sat in chairs, but where there wasn't room, people sat on the floor. It was cramped, but very quiet. No one spoke. And there was a noticeable lack of jewelry on all the passengers. Also missing were any outlaws.

"Are you all right?" Raven asked.

Recognizing the Harvey Girls as authority, the passengers all started talking at once. It was impossible to understand what they were saying, but they didn't seem to have been hurt. Relieved the passengers were all right, Raven, Sadie, and Margarita hurried through their midst, trying to be reassuring as they went by.

At the other end of the car, Raven shouted, "If you will all remain calm, we will have this matter under control as soon as possible." She sounded a lot more calm and assured than she felt, but she hoped she had reassured the passengers.

Suddenly Raven felt the coach move. She glanced at Sadie and Margarita. The two minutes must be up. They instantly left the car, jumping from one platform to the next. They ran through a Pullman sleeper, then another until they reached the last one.

412

They jerked open the door, stepped inside, then abruptly stopped.

Slate was pinned down on the platform at the other end by two outlaws shooting at him from inside the Pullman. Their backs were toward the three women. The train lurched, making a lot of noise, and began creeping forward.

There was no time to lose. The three women advanced down the aisle, their guns aimed at the two outlaws' backs.

Margarita took a deep breath and said, "Throw down your guns, gentlemen. You are covered." And she fired one shot between them to prove her point.

They jerked in surprise, but kept their pistols trained on Slate.

"I'll be only too happy to shoot you two if you don't throw down your guns immediately," Raven added.

"And I," Sadie concluded.

The outlaws hesitated. They were caught between guns in front and back. But the guns in back were women. One of the outlaws swiveled, firing in the direction of the voices.

Margarita shot him. He grabbed his right shoulder, his fingers lifeless, and his gun fell to the floor. The other outlaw didn't hesitate, but threw down his gun and raised his hands.

"Very sensible," Margarita remarked.

The train suddenly picked up speed.

"Quick!" Slate yelled, jumping from the back of the Pullman onto the platform of Ted's private car.

"Go ahead," Margarita said. "I'll handle these two. Slate needs you. Just make sure you get Comanche Jack."

413

Raven and Sadie raced down the aisle, then jumped across the ever-widening gap between the two platforms. Slate caught one in each arm, then hugged them both close.

"You ready?" he asked.

"They've got my Ted, don't they?" Sadie said.

"He has to be in one of the cars," Slate replied.

"Then I'm ready," Sadie responded. "I'll fight to the death for him."

"Okay, let's go."

Chapter Twenty-nine

They burst into Ted's private car, but the sitting room was empty. They carefully worked their way from room to room, making sure no outlaw was hiding to catch them by surprise or from behind.

They heard the Special pull away and knew they were completely alone with the outlaws on the two private coaches in the middle of the Texas plains. Either the three of them would win, or the outlaws would kill them all and take the silver. It would be done here and now, and there was no back-up support.

Finding Ted's car empty, they went out to the platform. It was quiet, much too quiet. They crossed over to Jeremy's car and burst inside, their guns ready. Again it was too quiet, and they saw no one. They went from room to room until they came to the bedroom. Once more they rushed inside.

Comanche Jack had a Colt .45 on Ted and Jeremy. An expensive oriental rug had been thrown back, and three outlaws were pulling silver bars out from under the floor and tossing them to the platform outside.

"Drop your guns," Comanche Jack ordered, "or I'll plug holes in these railroad men."

Raven and Slate hesitated, but Sadie threw her pistol to the floor.

"All the six-shooters," Comanche Jack insisted.

Raven and Slate reluctantly threw their guns down, too.

"Now come here," Comanche Jack commanded, nodding at Sadie.

"No," Raven said. "Take me instead."

He ignored Raven, continuing to look at Sadie. "Come here or you know what I'll do to these men."

Sadie stepped close to Comanche Jack, obviously determined to do anything to save Ted.

He grabbed her and put his gun to her temple. "Now I have the best possible hostage."

"Let her go," Ted begged. "I'll remain your hostage, but leave her alone."

Comanche Jack ignored him.

"Please let Sadie go," Ted insisted. "She can't take any more of this. She's already been through so much."

"I agree," Jeremy added. "I will be your hostage. Let Sadie go."

For the first time Raven really began to believe Ted was innocent. She didn't see how he could fake the depth of emotion he was showing for Sadie. Jeremy had offered, too, but not first and not as convincingly. Of course, he also wasn't in love with Sadie.

"You railroad men shut up," Comanche Jack ordered. "I've got the hostage I want and I'm keeping her."

Raven's mind was racing wildly. Could she have been correct? Could Comanche Jack actually be the mastermind? Both Ted and Jeremy seemed to be in his power, but could it all be a ploy to protect the identity of the mastermind? She had to find out now, no matter what it cost.

She looked hard at Ted, then at Jeremy. Jeremy had a black silk handkerchief in the pocket of his coat. She remembered him using it once before with her, and then she remembered seeing the black handkerchief snap three times from the window of Jeremy's private coach just before the Special left del Rio early. Could Jeremy be the mastermind? She stared intently at him.

He noticed. "I am so sorry, Raven. This ugly business will surely be over soon. You ladies should never have been involved."

"I tried to keep her out of it," Comanche Jack said. "I left her tied up in the baggage car, but she's determined woman."

"I know," Jeremy replied, "but you must not hurt her."

"I'll hurt who I please," Comanche Jack blustered.

Jeremy did not reply.

Raven didn't see how Jeremy could be the mastermind. Someone else could have snapped a handkerchief from his coach's window. And yet . . . Ted was so sincere, so concerned about Sadie.

Suddenly she noticed there was a cut across the back of Sadie's right hand. It was bleeding. Glancing at Ted, she said, "Ted, please give Sadie your handkerchief. She's bleeding."

Shocked, Ted pulled out a white handkerchief and started to hand it to Sadie.

417

"Get back," Comanche Jack commanded. "I[t]'s nothing but a scratch."

"She's hurt," Ted insisted.

"Leave her be, or I'll hurt her worse," Comanch[e] Jack replied, twisting Sadie's arm.

Ted put his handkerchief back, but Raven ha[d] seen what she needed to see. Ted had a whi[te] handkerchief. Jeremy's was black. Still, that wasn[']t enough proof. She was going to have to push th[e] situation further before the outlaws finished takin[g] out the silver and rode away with it, leaving her n[o] wiser about the mastermind.

She had to get Ted or Jeremy to confess, or she['d] have to decide once and for all that Comanche Jac[k] was really behind it all.

"I think you outlaws should know there's a Texa[s] Ranger present," Raven said.

Ted and Jeremy looked shocked. The outla[w] lifting out the silver hesitated a moment, but Co[-] manche Jack frowned at them and they continue[d.]

"What're you trying to do, Harvey Girl, sca[re] us?" Comanche Jack asked.

"I just thought you should all know that Sla[te] Slayton is a Texas Ranger. He suspected what wa[s] going to happen and had me send a telegram at D[el] Rio. Reinforcements should be arriving any m[o]ment."

Comanche Jack laughed. "One man, one job. N[o] reinforcements. Your scare didn't work."

"But I thought Slate was from Chicago," Ted sai[d] in confusion. "Then who . . ."

Jeremy looked confused, too, and concerned.

"No, I'm not from Chicago," Slate replied. "I'[ve] been on Comanche Jack's trail for some time. H[e] killed my parents and brother."

418

"They deserved it, too," Comanche Jack bragged. "Tom Slayton took my hand."

"I thought the Rangers were always prepared," Jeremy said, looking coldly at Slate. "You're supposed to be saving us."

"No, that's Raven's department."

"What?" Ted and Jeremy asked in unison.

"She's your Chicago detective," Slate replied, "And she's the one who sent the telegram asking for back-up force."

"Raven!" Ted exclaimed. "But I thought . . . I mean . . . she's a woman!"

"Raven is a Harvey Girl," Jeremy said. "If this is some ruse to confuse Comanche Jack, I don't think will work. You are going to have to do better than that to save us."

"It's true all right," Slate continued. "And when the Cunningham National Detective Agency sends for a back-up force, they get it."

For the first time Comanche Jack looked worried. He twisted Sadie's arm, and kicked at one of the outlaws. "Hurry it up. We may have Rangers and I don't know what-all bearing down on us. None of us can afford to get captured. It'll be the noose this time."

"That's right," Raven agreed. "Comanche Jack killed two of my firm's employees. I have a score to settle."

"Raven?" Sadie asked hesitantly. "You're a private detective?"

"Yes."

"You're not looking for a lost uncle?"

"No. I'm sorry I lied to you, but it was a dangerous case and I wanted you to be as safe as possible."

"I can hardly believe it."

419

"You've been a big help to me, Sadie. I do[n't] think I'd have gotten this far without you."

"Just imagine, I've been helping solve an impo[r]tant case."

"Shut up," Comanche Jack commanded. "You[r'e] all making me sick. Get that damn silver on t[he] platform."

"It'll go easier for you, Comanche Jack," Rav[en] said, "if you'll tell us the name of your boss. [We] want the mastermind who's behind all these robb[er]ies."

"Mastermind!" Comanche Jack scoffed. "I do[n't] need anybody telling me my business."

"You had to have someone on the inside getti[ng] the information for you, and I want his name[,]" Raven insisted. "Give it to me now before my peop[le] arrive and we'll try to keep you alive. Otherwis[e] you'll hang and you know it."

Comanche Jack started sweating. "We've g[ot] enough silver. I'm not waiting."

"Your horses aren't out there," Raven said. "[We] ran them off and the engineer is keeping them off[.]"

Comanche Jack started looking wild.

Suddenly Jeremy jerked a derringer from an i[n]side vest pocket and turned it on Ted. "Comanc[he] Jack, you are an idiot. Glance outside like I ju[st] did. Two of the men are coming back with horses[.]"

Raven's elation at having discovered the maste[r]mind was short-lived. She eyed her gun on the flo[or] where she'd dropped it. She felt sure Slate was doi[ng] the same, both of them watching and waiting wit[h] hair-trigger tension for even the slightest chance [to] dive for the pistols.

Comanche Jack pulled Sadie toward the doo[r,] checked outside, saw two men riding up wit[h]

rses. "You're right." The wild look in his eyes
lmed somewhat.

"You fell for Raven's clever words," Jeremy said.
he is a professional, no doubt about it. She even
d me fooled. But none of that matters now."

"Jeremy," Ted said, "how could you have been
rt of the robberies we've been trying to stop? It's
believable—"

"You are unbelievably naive, Ted. Why do you
ink those two Cunningham detectives had to be
lled? They had narrowed the mastermind down to
e two of us."

"Us!" Ted exclaimed.

"You suspected Ted?" Sadie asked.

"Yes, I'm afraid I did," Raven responded.

"But you never told me," Sadie said.

"I didn't want to endanger you, and I was hoping
could prove Ted innocent."

"If you'd asked, I could have told you he wasn't
e mastermind," Sadie replied.

"I know that's what you would have said, but I
ad to have proof. It was the only way to catch the
al mastermind and make it possible for you and
ed to have a happy life together."

"I understand," Sadie said, "and I appreciate all
ou've done for us. I just wish I'd known so I could
ave helped more."

"You did help, more than you realize. But the
ain thing is that we now know Ted is innocent and
ou two can be together."

Jeremy laughed. "They will be together all right,
or as long as they live, which won't be much
nger."

"What do you mean?" Raven asked, playing for
me, again eyeing her pistol.

421

"Too bad Cunningham didn't send another ma[n]," Jeremy replied. "We would have gotten him, to[o,] and Ted would eventually have been convicted wh[en] I planted some evidence in his private coach. As [it] is, I was as taken in as everyone else by Rave[n's] clever Harvey Girl trick. I hate to admit it, but y[ou] are quite good."

"Thanks for the compliment. If you give yours[elf] up, it'll probably go easier on you."

"Not a chance," he laughed again. "We are taki[ng] the silver and riding for the border. And yo[u,] Señorita Raven, are going with us. I'll come ba[ck] later and say I escaped from the outlaws who to[ok] me hostage. None of the rest of you will be alive [to] say differently. But you won't be coming bac[k,] Raven. You will be my pampered prisoner on [my] isolated Mexican estate. And you will stay alive on[ly] as long as you amuse me sufficiently."

"I won't come with you, unless you promise to [let] the others live."

"You are in no position to make deals. I hold [all] the cards. And I am not yet ready to see you dea[d.] As for your Texas Ranger, I will enjoy killing hi[m.] He helped catch me, and that makes me angry. [I] think Comanche Jack would like to see him dea[d] too."

"Yes," Comanche Jack agreed. "And all of the[m.] They tricked me."

"So, I will start the killing with Sadie," Jere[my] said. He jerked her from Comanche Jack's gra[sp] and put the derringer to her head.

Horrified, Ted threw himself at Jeremy. The g[un] went off and Ted slumped to the floor, blo[od] running from his side.

"Ted!" Sadie cried, and jerked from Jeremy's gr[asp]

fling herself at Ted.

It was all the opportunity Raven and Slate
eded. They dove for their guns, and shots went
'f all around them as the outlaws decided to escape
the confusion. Slate and Raven came up shoot-
g, trying to protect Ted and Sadie, but Jeremy and
omanche Jack were already at the door and the
tlaws were laying down a cover of bullets.

Raven and Slate fired back. One of the outlaws
ent down, clutching his stomach. Jeremy and Co-
anche Jack ducked out the door and the other two
tlaws followed, still shooting.

Slate and Raven went after them, dodging bullets
l the way to the door. A bullet tugged at her skirt
. it tore through the fabric, missing her flesh. She
nored it.

When they reached the door, they paused, quickly
loaded with bullets from Slate's gunbelt, then
epped into the open doorway, their pistols raised
fore them.

One of the outlaws was struggling to mount. Slate
icked him off with a clean shot, and the outlaw fell
the ground, his horse racing off to safety. The
thers were already mounted, and Raven caught
nother outlaw with a bullet in the side just as he
heeled his horse to follow Jeremy, Comanche
ack, and the other two outlaws.

"Make your shots count," Slate said through grit-
d teeth.

"I am," Raven replied grimly and took aim.

Slate's first bullet caught Comanche Jack, but it
idn't stop him. The outlaw fired back, clipping
late's shoulder. Slate shot again and Comanche
ack pitched to the side of his saddle, tried to stop
imself from falling, but his hook caught under the

cinch as he toppled out of the saddle. But he was free.

The hook slipped down to the underbelly of t horse, still caught under the cinch. The anim galloped away, dragging Comanche Jack across t rough ground, hooves pounding his body as t outlaw screamed in pain.

"He'll never live through that," Slate said cold "and I couldn't think of a more fitting death."

But Raven didn't hear him. She was aiming Jeremy, the man who had ordered the deaths of h father and fiancé. If she couldn't bring him in, s could at least stop him from more murders. S aimed, slowly squeezed the trigger, trying to rema perfectly calm, perfectly still. Jeremy fired fir missed, then jerked in his saddle as her bullet home. He fell free of the saddle and lay still on t ground.

"The others are getting out of range," Rav exclaimed.

"That's why I've got this," Ted said through gr ted teeth as he stepped out on the platform su ported by Sadie. His face was deathly pale from lo of blood, but he was on his feet and carryi Jeremy's hunting gun. "Stand back. I'll get tho last two."

The outlaws fired back, but their pistols were o of range. Ted shot until the rifle was empty and t two outlaws lay on the ground. Then he collaps against Sadie.

"Oh, no!" Sadie exclaimed as she pulled hi closer.

Slate looked at Ted in concern, then checked t railroad man's wound. "He'll be all right. It's clean wound. The bullet went right through his sid

But you've got to stop the bleeding, Sadie. Can you bind him with your petticoat?"

"Yes. Are you sure he's okay?" she asked as she began tearing strips off her petticoat.

"We'll get him to a doctor later, but he's a strong man. He'll live."

Tears sprang to Sadie's eyes.

"Don't cry," Slate replied. "Just get that blood stopped."

"I will," Sadie said, wiping her eyes and turning her full attention to Ted.

"We'd better check on the outlaws, Slate," Raven said quietly. "If they aren't dead, we better bring them in.

He nodded, glanced at Ted, then stepped down from the platform with Raven.

They reloaded as they walked toward the outlaws. One near the train would live. The other was dead. There was no sign of Comanche Jack. They kept walking and came to Jeremy. He lay still on the hard earth. Slate turned him over with his boot.

Jeremy's eyes flickered toward Raven. "You were to be my . . . most prized piece of art," he rasped, blood trickling from the corner of his mouth.

"Slate, he's alive."

"Not for long."

"Come closer," Jeremy hissed.

Slate hunkered down beside him. "Any last confessions?"

"Yes," Jeremy said, his dark eyes glittering. "This." He pulled out a knife and plunged it toward Slate's heart.

Raven gasped, and shot Jeremy before the knife could reach Slate. The sound echoed in her ears for a long moment and she shivered, realizing she'd killed a man, the man who'd had her father and fiancé murdered. She felt dizzy, and all the strength seemed to flow out of her. She'd killed. She hated that fact. But she couldn't have let Slate die.

Slate pulled her close, and she buried her face against his chest. "It's okay. I know you didn't want to kill him, but there was no other way."

Suddenly they heard the sound of hoofbeats rapidly approaching. Slate glanced up as a horse came near, Comanche Jack's horse returning. "Don't look, Raven. It's what's left of Comanche Jack, and it isn't pretty."

"I don't want to see. He was a terrible man."

"And he got what he deserved." Slate paused a moment, then said, "Are you sure you want to check on the other outlaws? I can go alone."

"No. I'll go with you. I have to see it to the end. They all helped in destroying my father and fiancé."

The other two outlaws were dead. Ted's rifle had finished them both. Raven and Slate walked back toward the train.

"I'll call in the Rangers to clean up this mess," Slate said. "I imagine most of these men have a price on their heads, and they'll have to be identified."

"I'll be glad to turn it over to the authorities," Raven answered, with relief in her voice.

When they got back to the coach, they joined Ted and Sadie on the platform. Ted looked a little better and Sadie looked less worried since she'd gotten the blood flow under control.

"What did you find?" Ted asked.

"They're all dead, except for one near the train," Raven replied.

"And he'll need to see a doctor," Slate added.

"You have my official thanks for stopping the robbery ring, Raven," Ted said. "And you, too, Slate. But if you think this is the end of your work, you're wrong."

"What do you mean?" Raven asked.

"I'm sure Santa Fe will want to put the Cunningham National Detective Agency on retainer. We're going all the way to California and we need somebody with your expertise."

"I'm glad you're happy with the service, but before I can make any decisions I have to talk with Slate."

"Raven," Sadie said. "Ted and I are getting married at Montezuma and we want you and Slate to stand up with us. Will you?"

"Of course I will."

"Me too," Slate agreed.

"It's a wonderful place for a honeymoon," Sadie added, glancing from Raven to Slate. "Anybody's honeymoon."

Raven smiled fondly at her matchmaking friend, then pulled Slate to one side of the platform.

"This may not be the best time to mention it, Slate, but before you get yourself into any more danger you'd better marry me. That way I can make sure you live a good long life."

"Me get into danger? It's you who needs to be protected."

"I have to admit you've been helpful. In fact, I've learned to like having you around so why don't you marry me?"

"At last, the lady asks. Yes, on one condition."

"Condition?"

"Let's let Ted hire the Cunningham and Slayton National Detective Agency."

Now you can get more of **HEARTFIRE**
right at home and $ave.

Preview
Four Brand New
ZEBRA
Heartfire
Romance Novels...

FREE for 10 days.

No Obligation
and No Strings Attached!

*Enjoy all of the passion and fiery romance as
you soar back through history, right in the
comfort of your own home.*

**Now that you have read a Zebra HEARTFIRE
Romance novel, we're sure you'll agree that
HEARTFIRE sets new standards of excellence
for historical romantic fiction. Each Zebra
HEARTFIRE novel is the ultimate blend of intimate romance and grand adventure and each
takes place in the kinds of historical settings you
want most...the American Revolution, the Old
West, Civil War and more.**

FREE Preview Each Month and $ave

ebra has made arrangements for you to preview 4 rand new HEARTFIRE novels each month...FREE for 0 days. You'll get them as soon as they are published. If ou are not delighted with any of them, just return them vith no questions asked. But if you decide these are verything we said they are, you'll pay just $3.25 each— total of $13.00 (a $15.00 value). **That's a $2.00 saving ach month off the regular price.** Plus there is NO hipping or handling charge. These are delivered right o your door absolutely free! There is no obligation and here is no minimum number of books to buy.

TO GET YOUR FIRST MONTH'S PREVIEW... Mail the Coupon Below!

SWEET MEDICINE'S PROPHECY
by Karen A. Bale

#1: SUNDANCER'S PASSION (1778, $3.

Stalking Horse was the strongest and most desirable of the tri
and Sun Dancer surrounded him with her spell-binding radian
But the innocence of their love gave way to passion — and passi
to betrayal. Would their relationship ever survive the ultimate si

#2: LITTLE FLOWER'S DESIRE (1779, $3.

Taken captive by savage Crows, Little Flower fell in love with
enemy, handsome brave Young Eagle. Though their hearts spe
what they could not say, they could only dream of what co
never be. . . .

#4: SAVAGE FURY (1768, $3.

Aeneva's rage knew no bounds when her handsome mate Tr
commanded her to tend their tepee as he rode into danger. I
under cover of night, she stole away to be with Trent and sh
whatever perils fate dealt them.

#5: SUN DANCER'S LEGACY (1878, $3.

Aeneva's and Trenton's adopted daughter Anna becomes the li
of their lives. As she grows into womanhood, she falls in le
with blond Steven Randall. Together they discover the secrets
their passion, the bitterness of betrayal — and fight to fulfill
prophecy that is Anna's birthright.